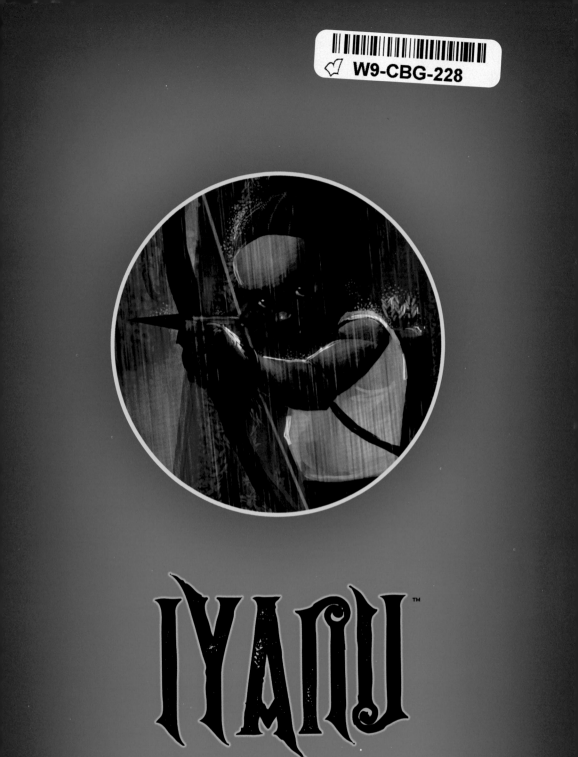

IYANU™

CHILD OF WONDER

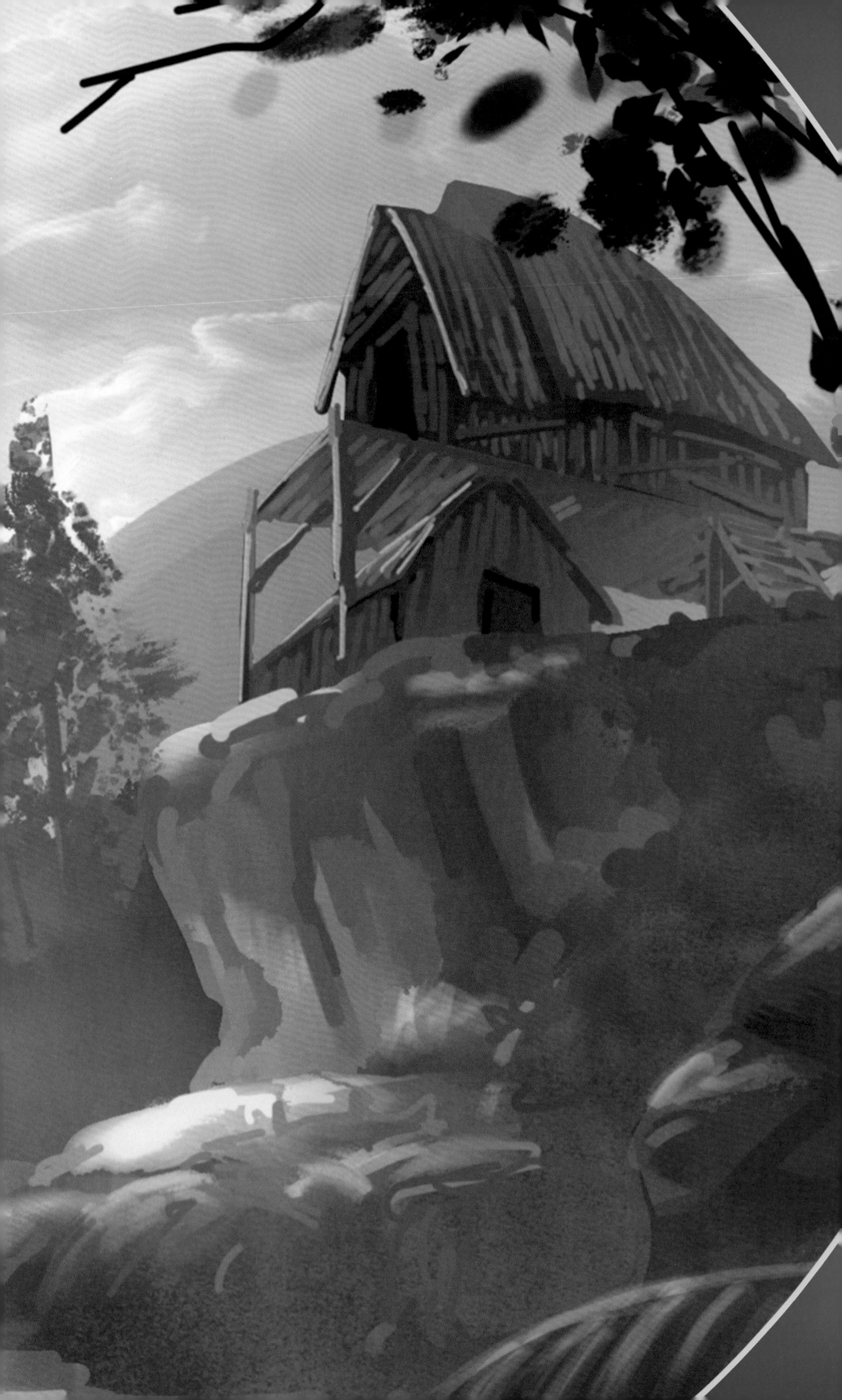

IYANU™

CHILD OF WONDER

VOLUME ONE

Creator and Writer
ROYE OKUPE

Cover and Interior Art
GODWIN AKPAN

Letters
SPOOF ANIMATION

YOUNEEK
STUDIOS

DARK HORSE BOOKS

Publisher
MIKE RICHARDSON

Associate Editor
JUDY KHUU

Designer
KATHLEEN BARNETT

Senior Editor
PHILIP R. SIMON

Assistant Editor
ROSE WEITZ

Digital Art Technician
ADAM PRUETT

IYANU: CHILD OF WONDER

Published by Dark Horse Books | A division of Dark Horse Comics LLC
10956 SE Main Street, Milwaukie, OR 97222
DarkHorse.com

To find a comics shop in your area, visit comicshoplocator.com

Library of Congress Cataloging-in-Publication Data

Names: Okupe, Roye, writer. | Akpan, Godwin, artist, colourist. | Spoof Animation, letterer.
Title: Iyanu : child of wonder / writer, Roye Okupe ; artist, Godwin Akpan ; colors, Godwin Akpan ; letters, Spoof Animation.
Description: Milwaukie, OR : Dark Horse Books, 2021. | Series: Iyanu ; volume 1 | Audience: Ages 10+ | Audience: Grades 7-9 | Summary: "A teenage orphan with no recollection of her past, suddenly discovers that she has abilities that rival the ancient deities told in the folklore of her people."-- Provided by publisher.
Identifiers: LCCN 2021009242 | ISBN 9781506723044 (trade paperback)
Subjects: LCSH: Graphic novels. | CYAC: Graphic novels. | Folklore, Africa--Fiction. | Fantasy--Fiction. | Orphans--Fiction. | Ability--Fiction. | Adventure and adventurers--Fiction.
Classification: LCC PZ7.7.O424 I93 2021 | DDC 741.5/973--dc23
LC record available at https://lccn.loc.gov/2021009242

First edition: September 2021
ISBN: 978-1-50672-304-4
Ebook ISBN: 978-1-50672-314-3

1 3 5 7 9 10 8 6 4 2

Printed in China

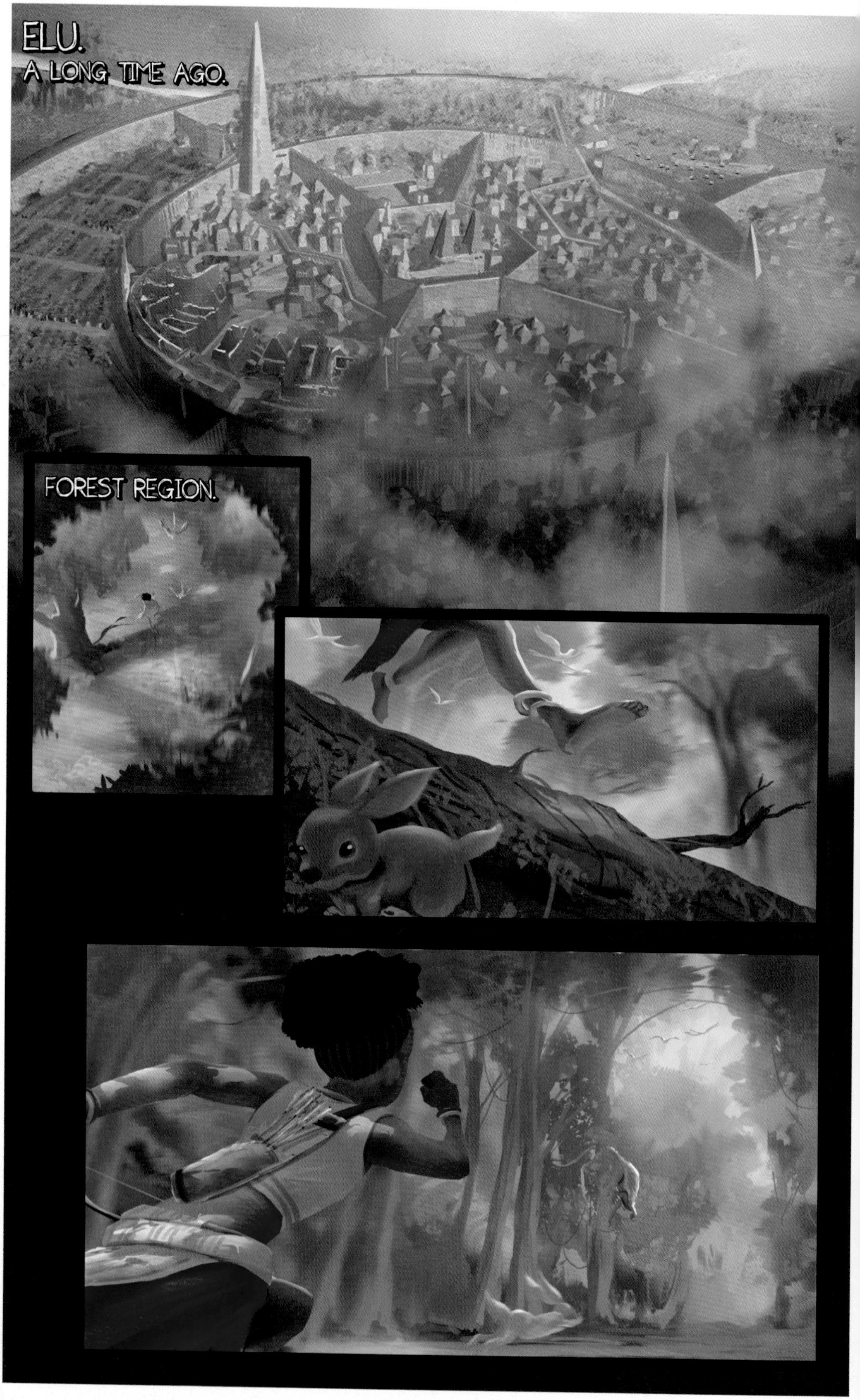

ELU.
A LONG TIME AGO.
FOREST REGION.

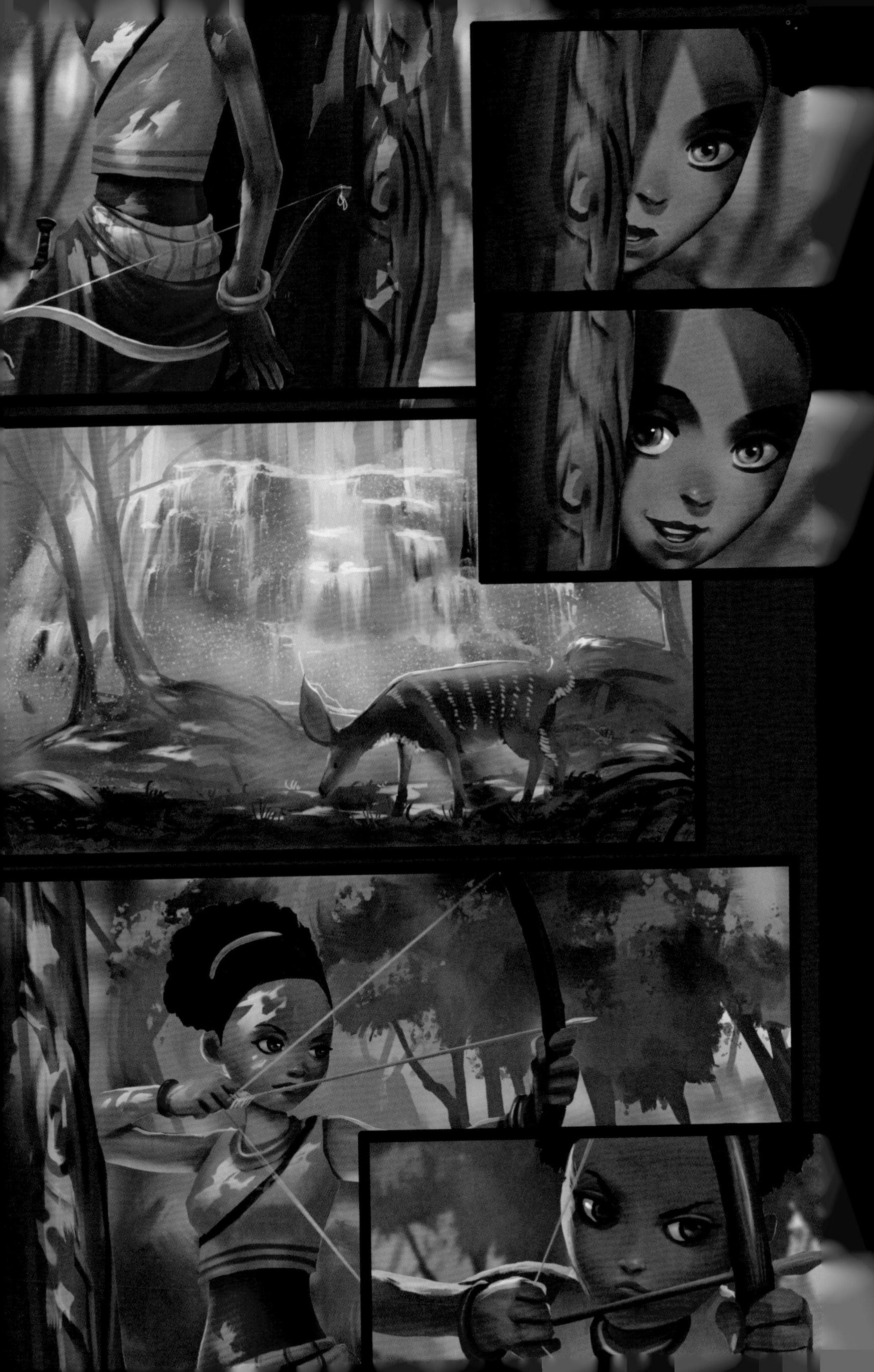

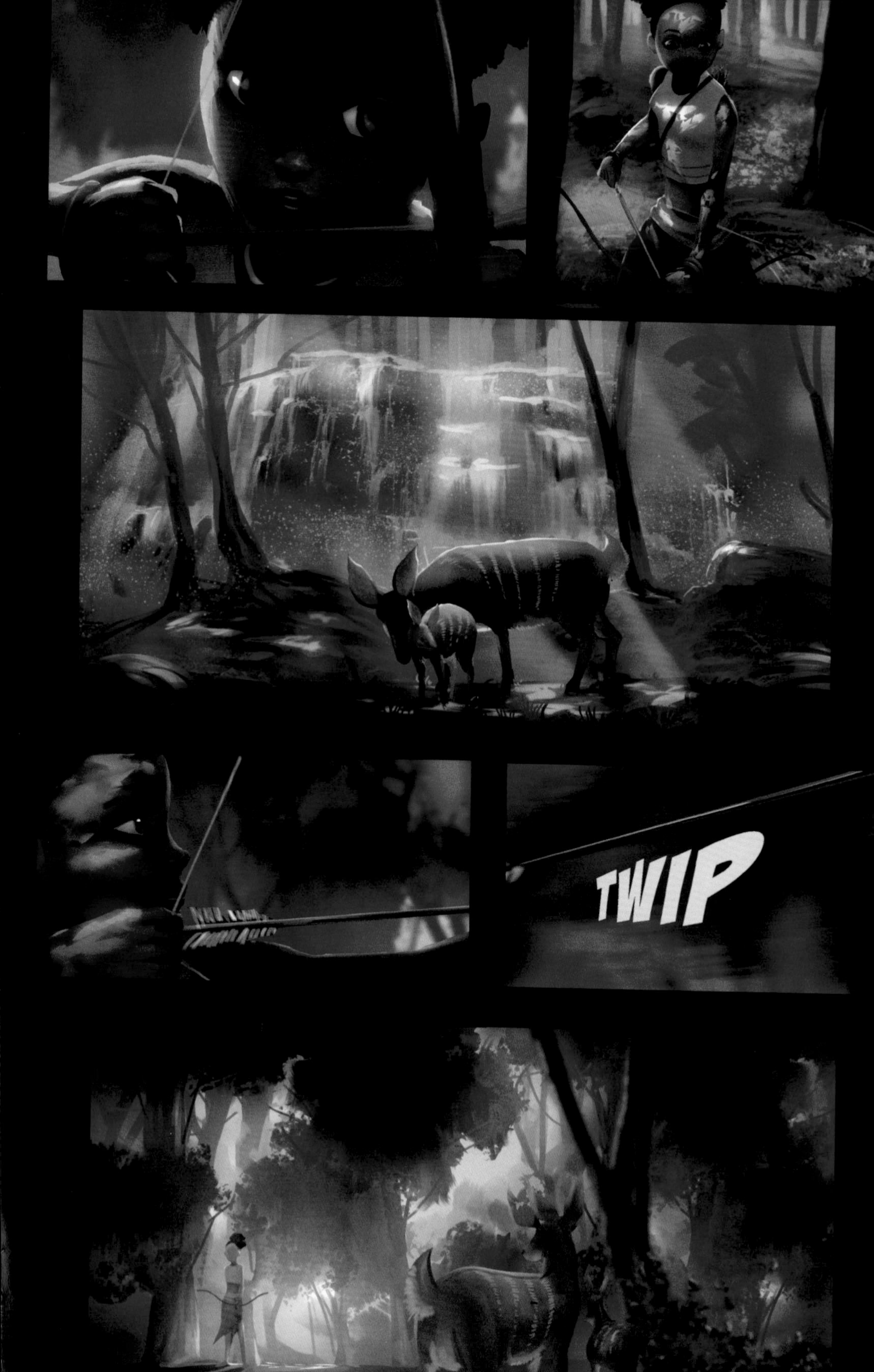
TWIP

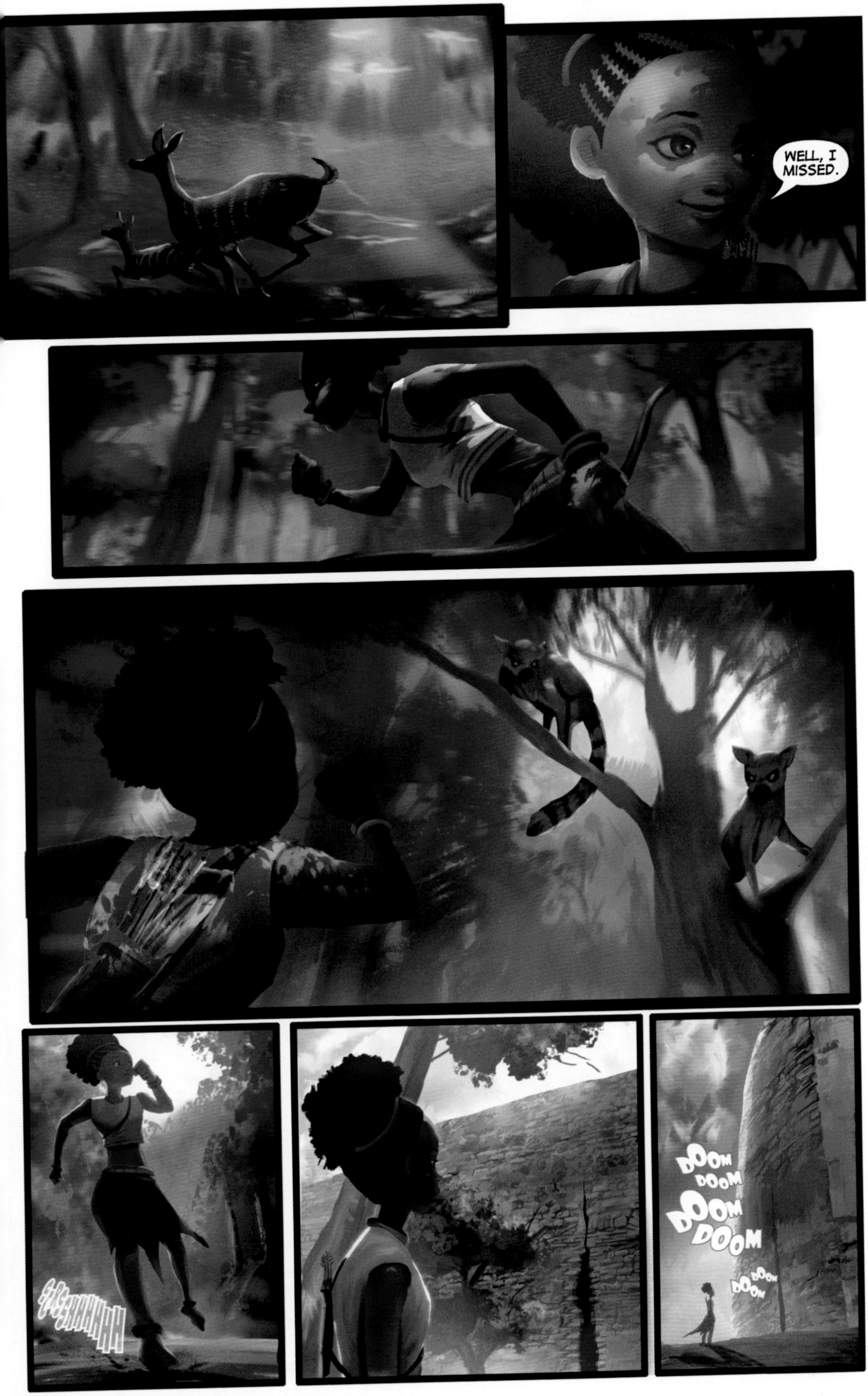
WELL, I MISSED.
SSSHHHHHHHH
DOOM
DOOM
DOOM
DOOM
DOOM
DOOM

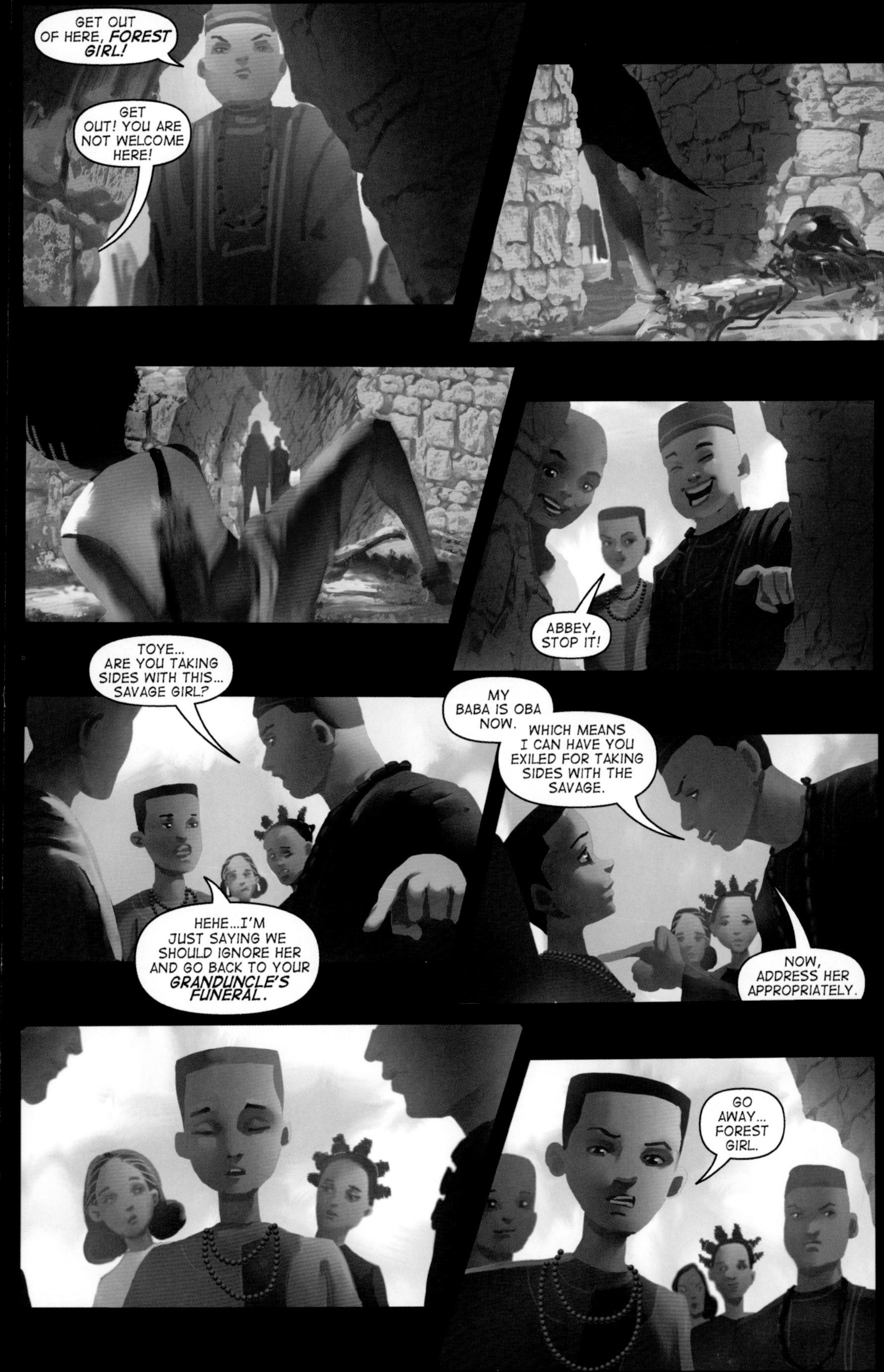
GET OUT OF HERE, FOREST GIRL!
GET OUT! YOU ARE NOT WELCOME HERE!
ABBEY, STOP IT!
TOYE... ARE YOU TAKING SIDES WITH THIS... SAVAGE GIRL?
HEHE...I'M JUST SAYING WE SHOULD IGNORE HER AND GO BACK TO YOUR GRANDUNCLE'S FUNERAL.
MY BABA IS OBA NOW.
WHICH MEANS I CAN HAVE YOU EXILED FOR TAKING SIDES WITH THE SAVAGE.
NOW, ADDRESS HER APPROPRIATELY.
GO AWAY... FOREST GIRL.

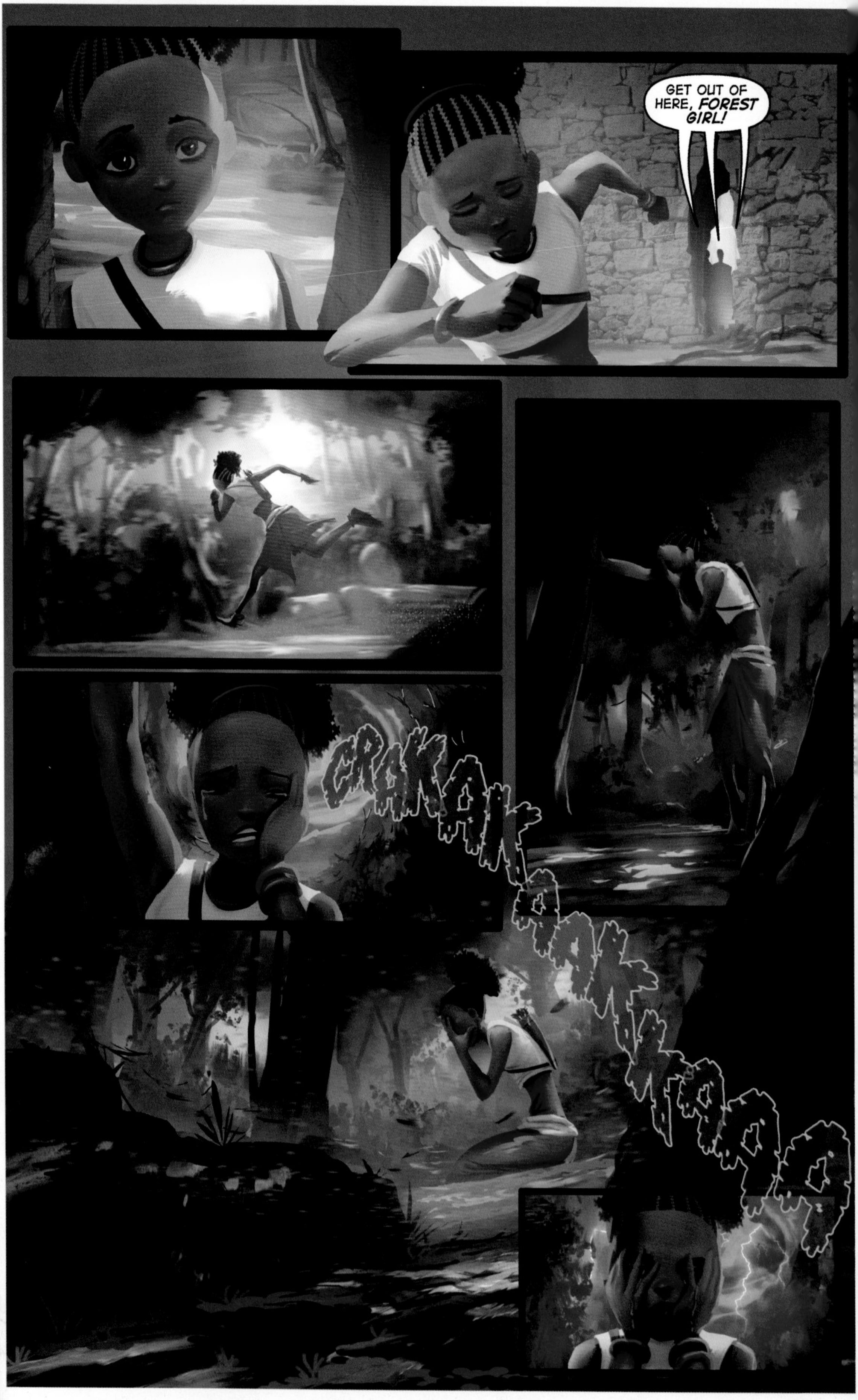
GET OUT OF HERE, FOREST GIRL!

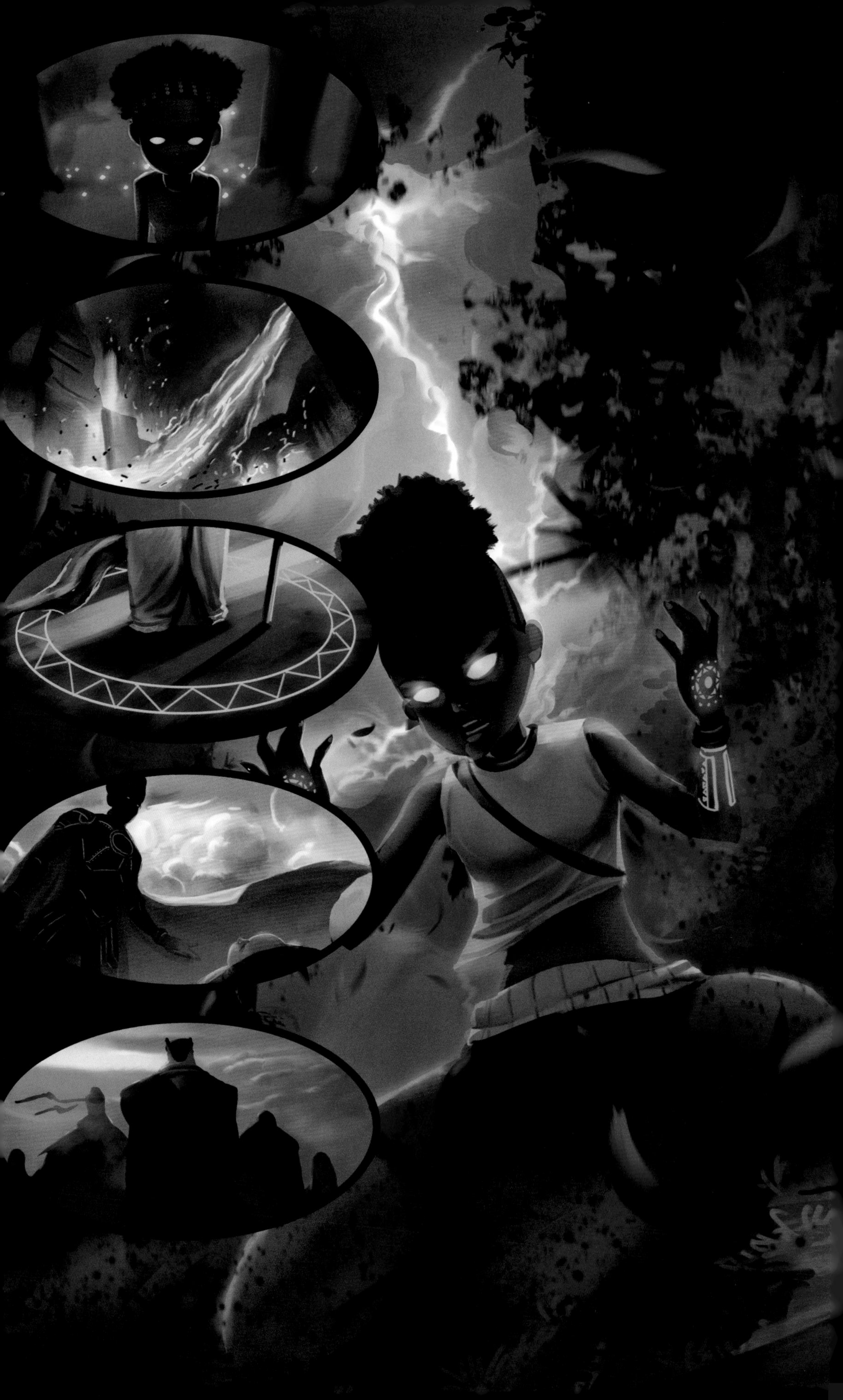

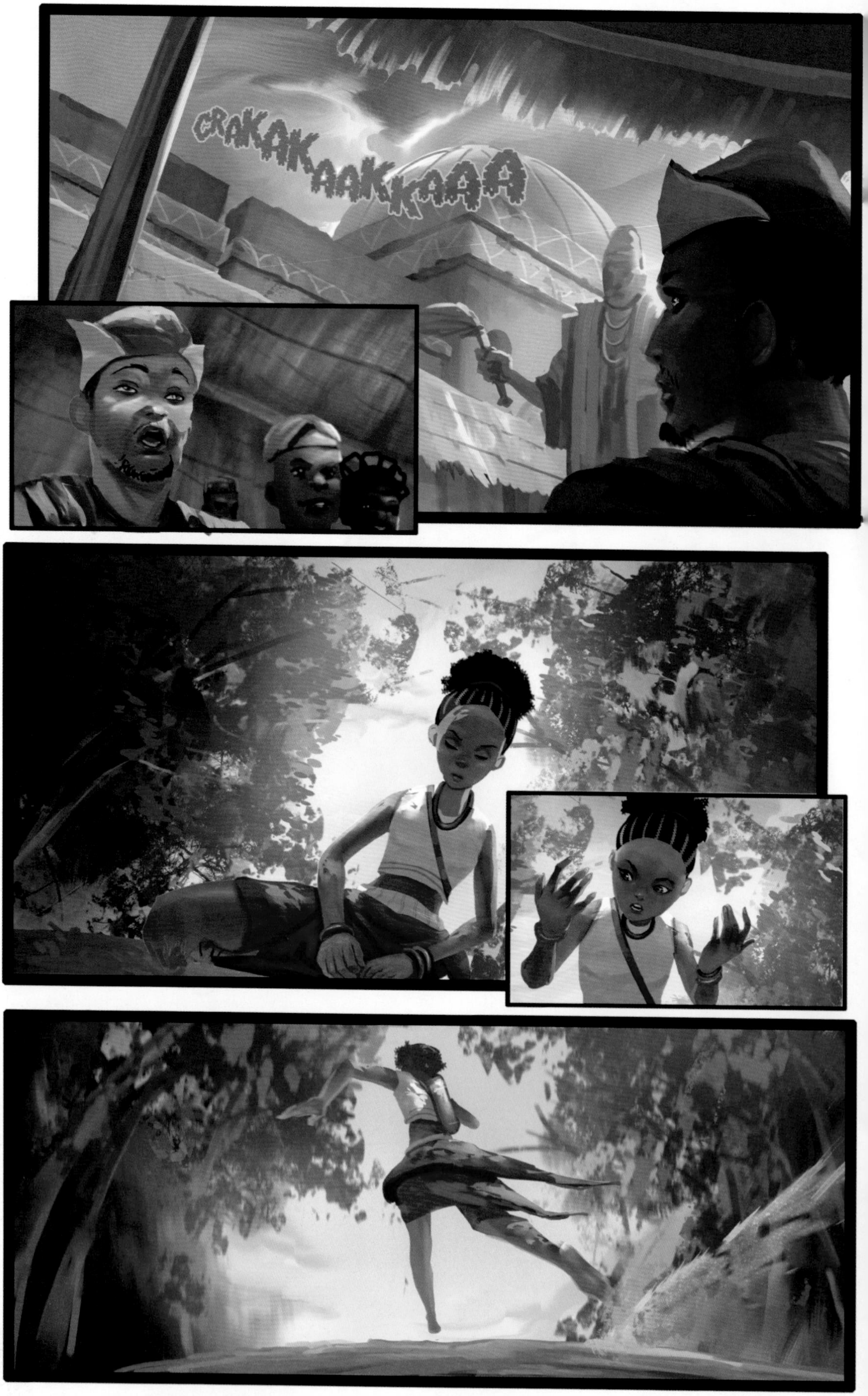
CRAKAKAAKKAAA

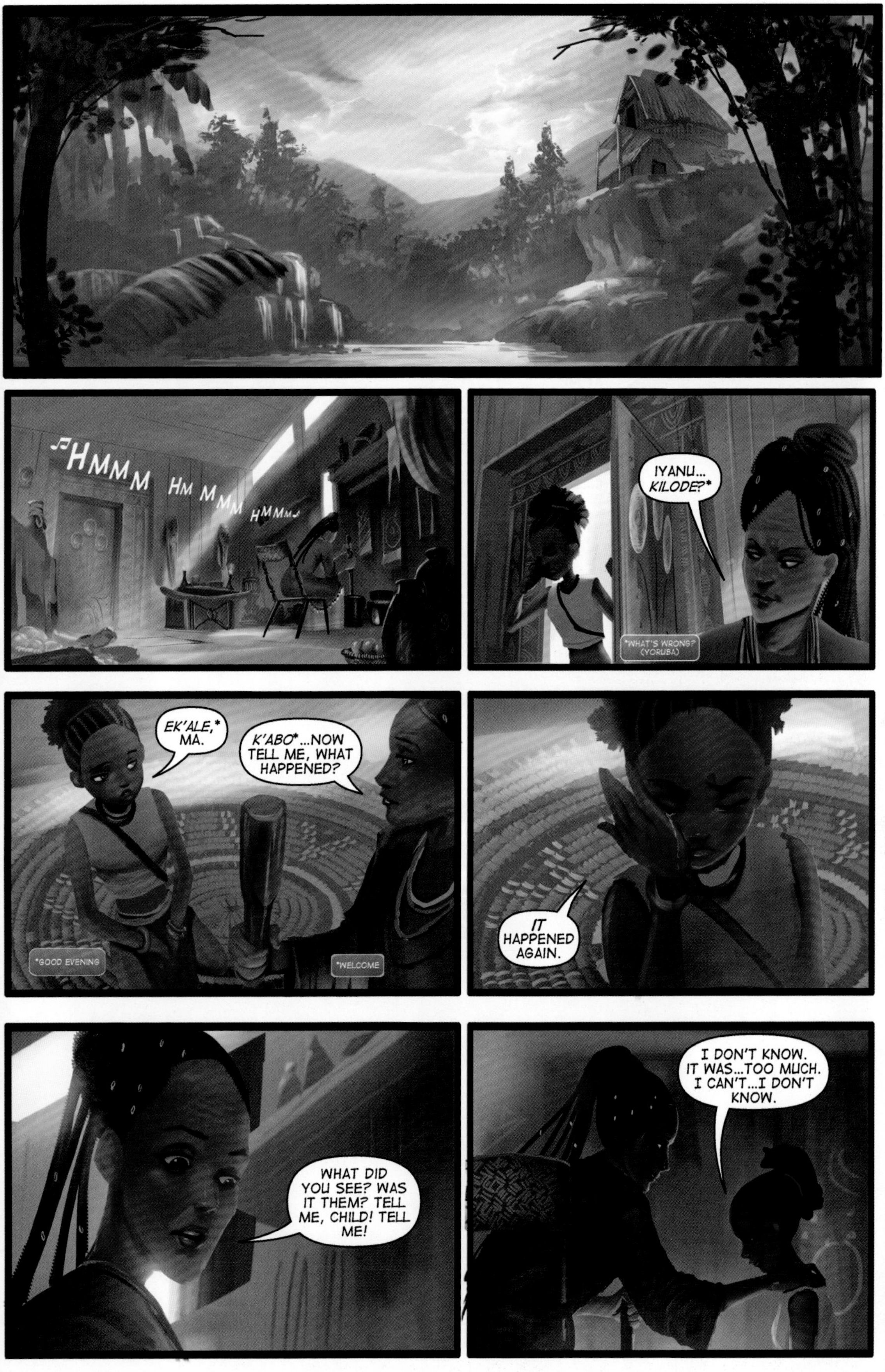

HMMM HM MMM HMMM
IYANU... KILODE?*
*WHAT'S WRONG? (YORUBA)
EK'ALE,* MA.
K'ABO*...NOW TELL ME, WHAT HAPPENED?
*GOOD EVENING
*WELCOME
IT HAPPENED AGAIN.
WHAT DID YOU SEE? WAS IT THEM? TELL ME, CHILD! TELL ME!
I DON'T KNOW. IT WAS...TOO MUCH. I CAN'T...I DON'T KNOW.

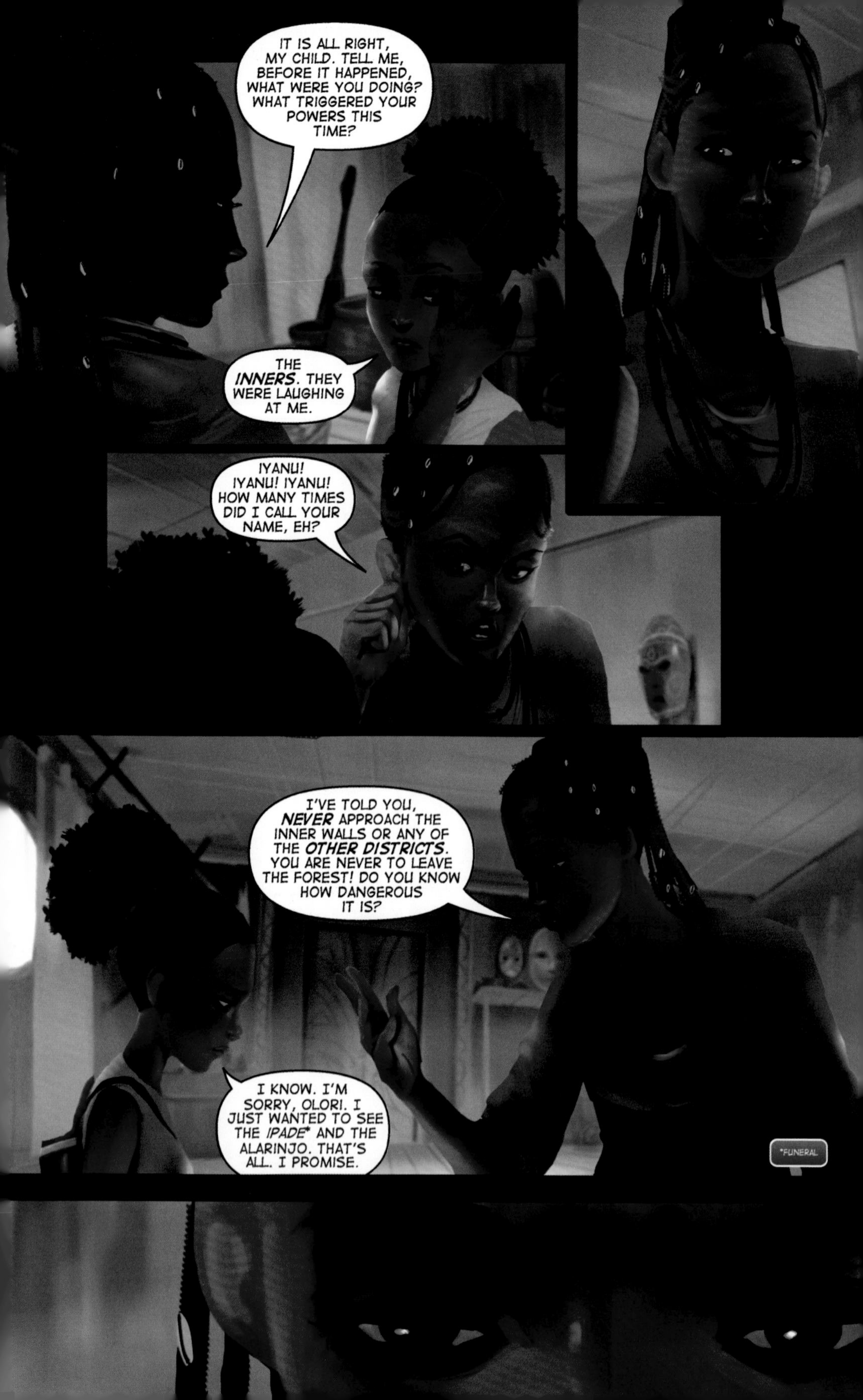
IT IS ALL RIGHT, MY CHILD. TELL ME, BEFORE IT HAPPENED, WHAT WERE YOU DOING? WHAT TRIGGERED YOUR POWERS THIS TIME?
THE *INNERS*. THEY WERE LAUGHING AT ME.
IYANU! IYANU! IYANU! HOW MANY TIMES DID I CALL YOUR NAME, EH?
I'VE TOLD YOU, ***NEVER*** APPROACH THE INNER WALLS OR ANY OF THE ***OTHER DISTRICTS***. YOU ARE NEVER TO LEAVE THE FOREST! DO YOU KNOW HOW DANGEROUS IT IS?
I KNOW. I'M SORRY, OLORI. I JUST WANTED TO SEE THE *IPADE** AND THE ALARINJO. THAT'S ALL. I PROMISE.
*FUNERAL

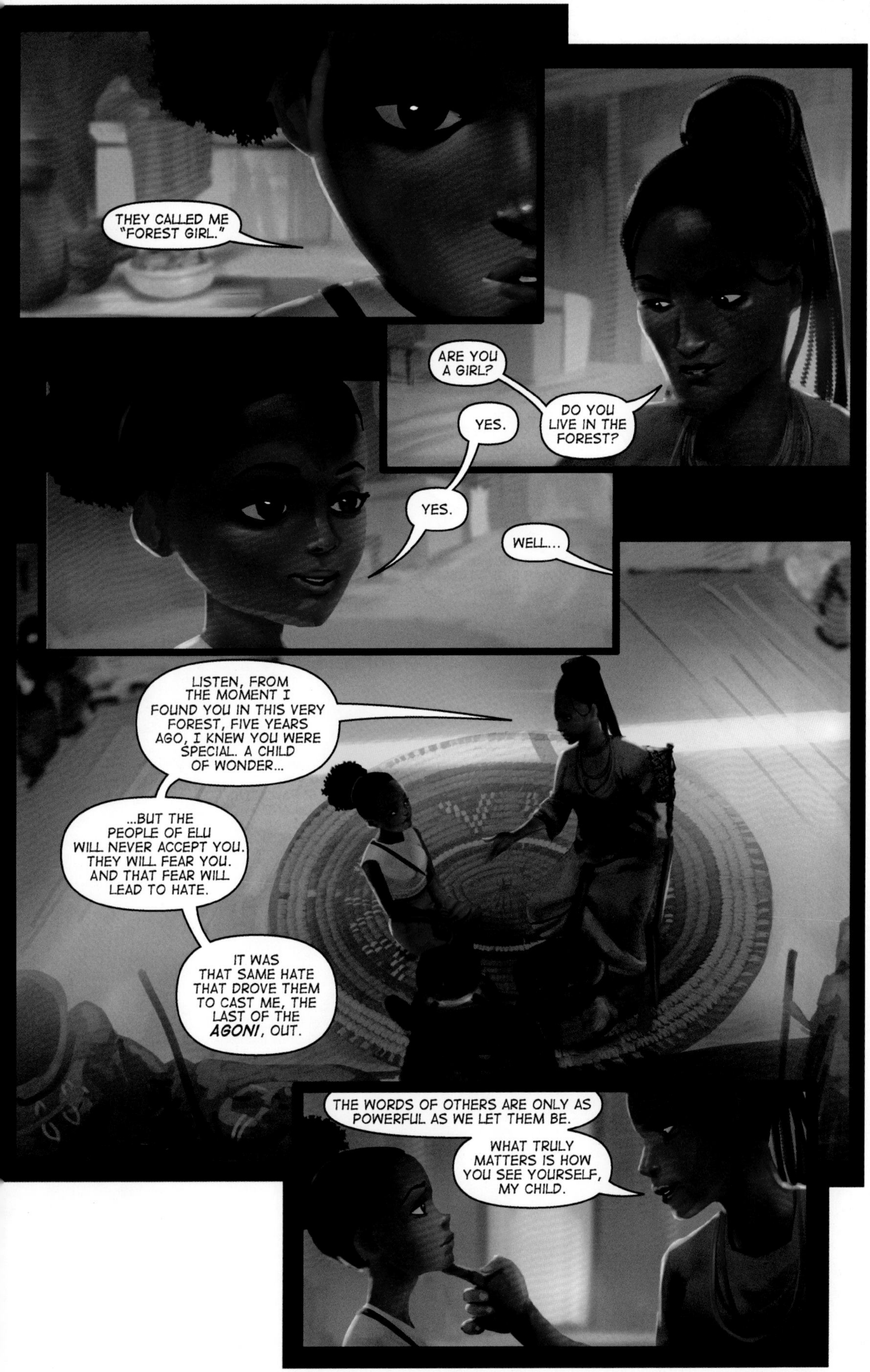
THEY CALLED ME "FOREST GIRL."
ARE YOU A GIRL?
YES.
DO YOU LIVE IN THE FOREST?
YES.
WELL...
LISTEN, FROM THE MOMENT I FOUND YOU IN THIS VERY FOREST, FIVE YEARS AGO, I KNEW YOU WERE SPECIAL. A CHILD OF WONDER...
...BUT THE PEOPLE OF ELU WILL NEVER ACCEPT YOU. THEY WILL FEAR YOU. AND THAT FEAR WILL LEAD TO HATE.
IT WAS THAT SAME HATE THAT DROVE THEM TO CAST ME, THE LAST OF THE AGONI, OUT.
THE WORDS OF OTHERS ARE ONLY AS POWERFUL AS WE LET THEM BE.
WHAT TRULY MATTERS IS HOW YOU SEE YOURSELF, MY CHILD.

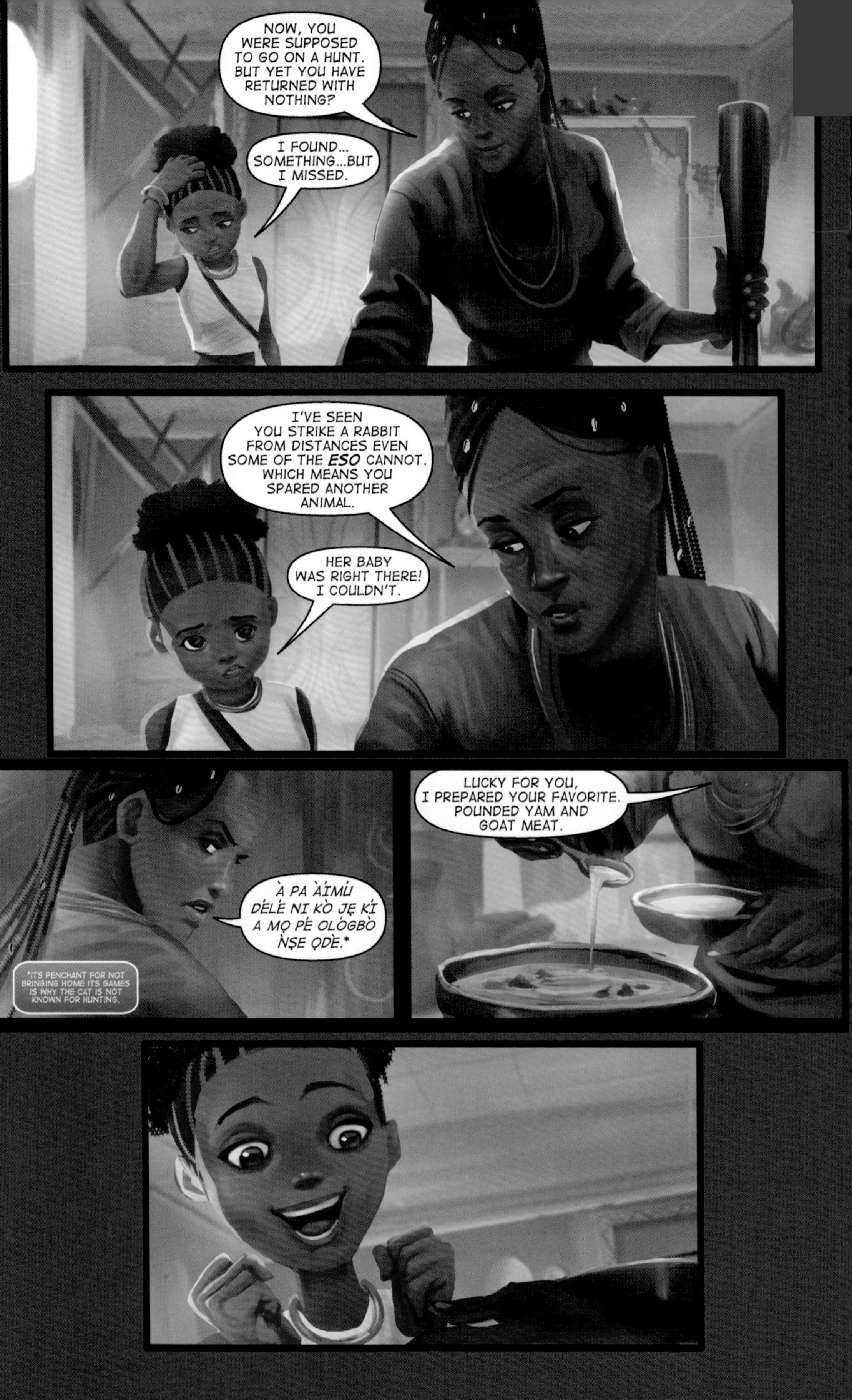
NOW, YOU WERE SUPPOSED TO GO ON A HUNT. BUT YET YOU HAVE RETURNED WITH NOTHING?
I FOUND... SOMETHING...BUT I MISSED.
I'VE SEEN YOU STRIKE A RABBIT FROM DISTANCES EVEN SOME OF THE ***ESO*** CANNOT. WHICH MEANS YOU SPARED ANOTHER ANIMAL.
HER BABY WAS RIGHT THERE! I COULDN'T.
À PA ÀÍMÚ DÉLÉ NI KÒ JẸ KÍ A MỌ PÉ OLÓGBÒ ǸṢE ỌDÈ.*
*ITS PENCHANT FOR NOT BRINGING HOME ITS GAMES IS WHY THE CAT IS NOT KNOWN FOR HUNTING.
LUCKY FOR YOU, I PREPARED YOUR FAVORITE. POUNDED YAM AND GOAT MEAT.

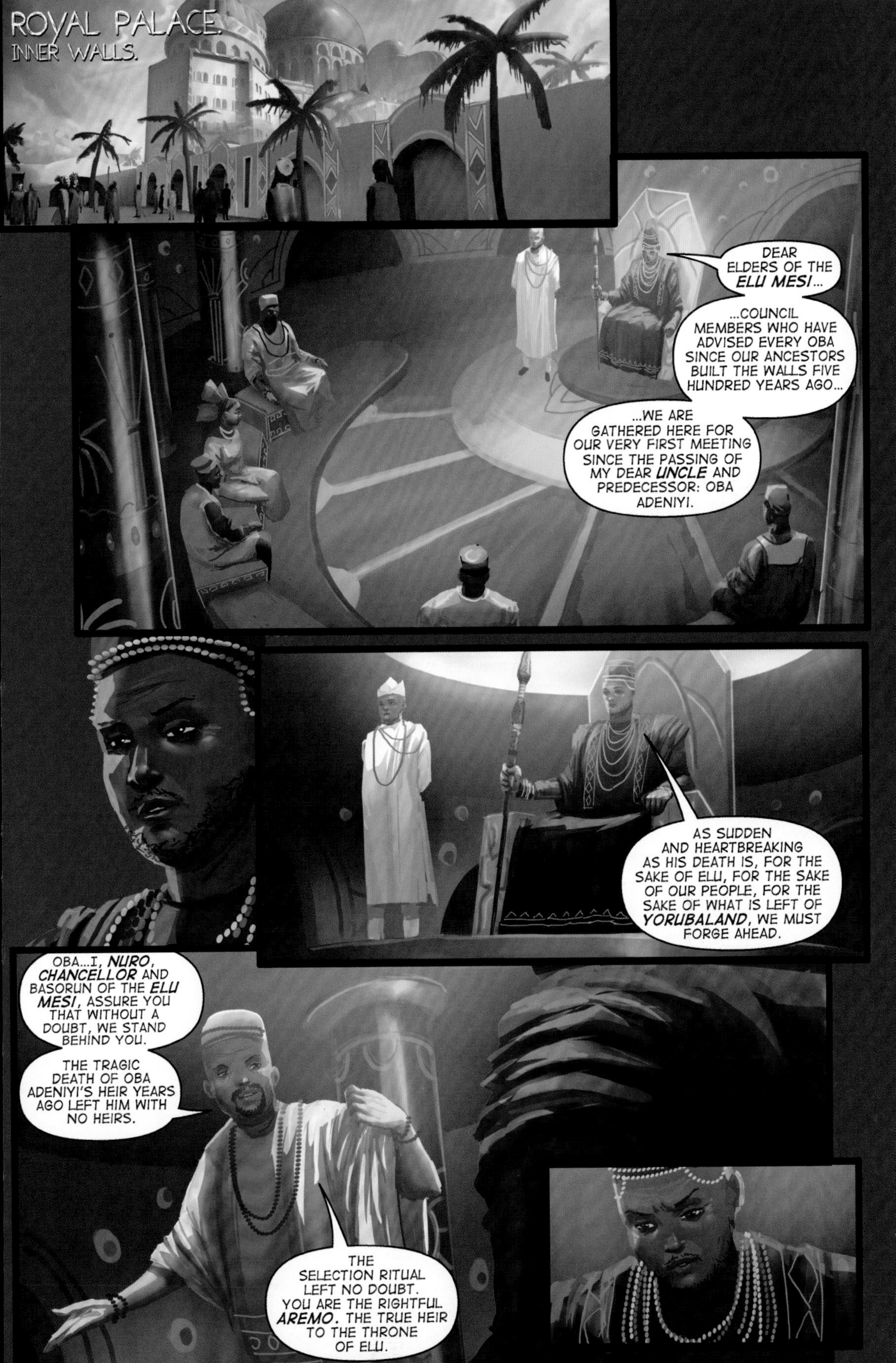
ROYAL PALACE.
INNER WALLS.
DEAR ELDERS OF THE ELU MESI...
...COUNCIL MEMBERS WHO HAVE ADVISED EVERY OBA SINCE OUR ANCESTORS BUILT THE WALLS FIVE HUNDRED YEARS AGO...
...WE ARE GATHERED HERE FOR OUR VERY FIRST MEETING SINCE THE PASSING OF MY DEAR UNCLE AND PREDECESSOR: OBA ADENIYI.
AS SUDDEN AND HEARTBREAKING AS HIS DEATH IS, FOR THE SAKE OF ELU, FOR THE SAKE OF OUR PEOPLE, FOR THE SAKE OF WHAT IS LEFT OF YORUBALAND, WE MUST FORGE AHEAD.
OBA...I, NURO, CHANCELLOR AND BASORUN OF THE ELU MESI, ASSURE YOU THAT WITHOUT A DOUBT, WE STAND BEHIND YOU.
THE TRAGIC DEATH OF OBA ADENIYI'S HEIR YEARS AGO LEFT HIM WITH NO HEIRS.
THE SELECTION RITUAL LEFT NO DOUBT. YOU ARE THE RIGHTFUL AREMO. THE TRUE HEIR TO THE THRONE OF ELU.

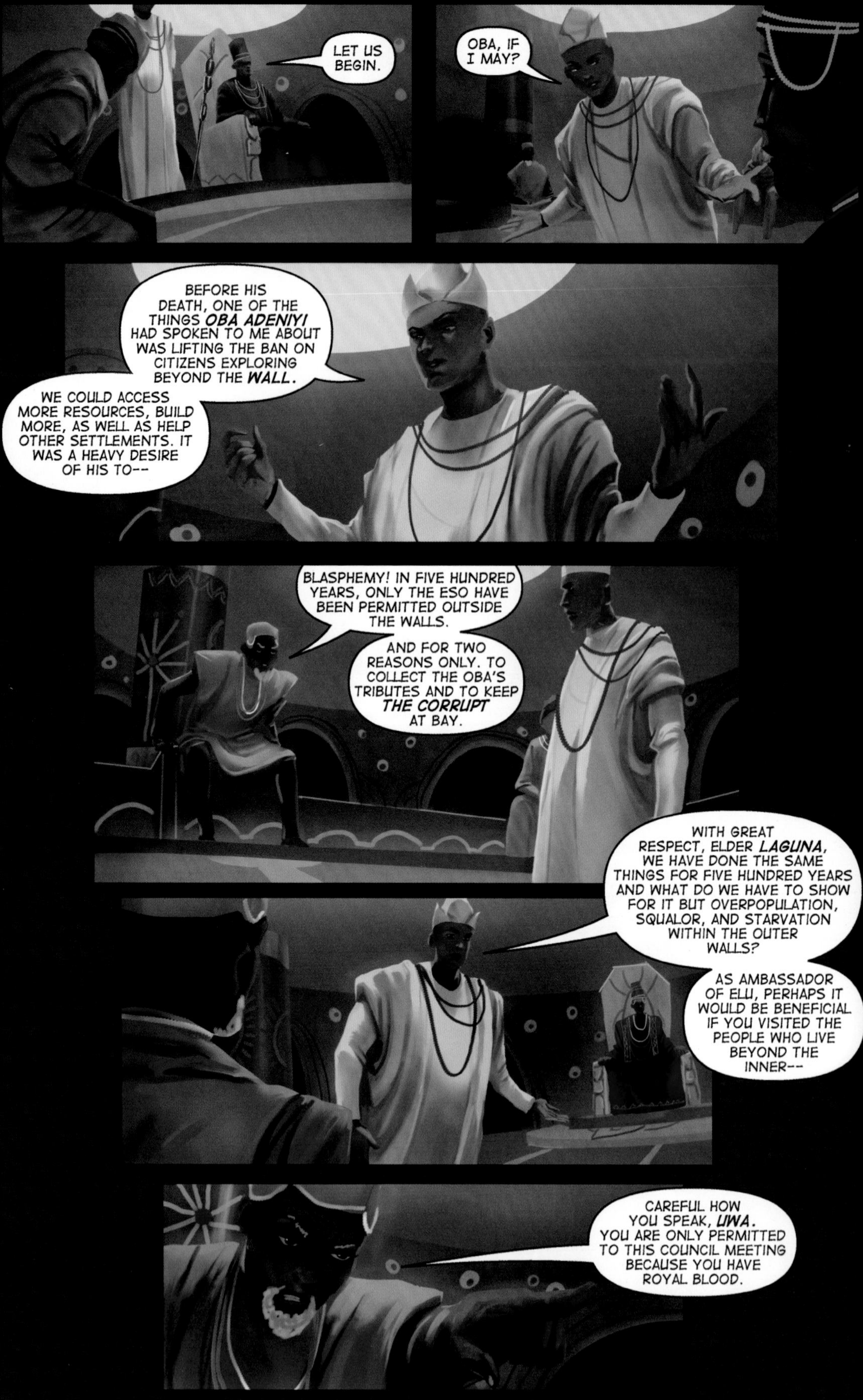
LET US BEGIN.
OBA, IF I MAY?
BEFORE HIS DEATH, ONE OF THE THINGS OBA ADENIYI HAD SPOKEN TO ME ABOUT WAS LIFTING THE BAN ON CITIZENS EXPLORING BEYOND THE WALL.
WE COULD ACCESS MORE RESOURCES, BUILD MORE, AS WELL AS HELP OTHER SETTLEMENTS. IT WAS A HEAVY DESIRE OF HIS TO--
BLASPHEMY! IN FIVE HUNDRED YEARS, ONLY THE ESO HAVE BEEN PERMITTED OUTSIDE THE WALLS.
AND FOR TWO REASONS ONLY. TO COLLECT THE OBA'S TRIBUTES AND TO KEEP THE CORRUPT AT BAY.
WITH GREAT RESPECT, ELDER LAGUNA, WE HAVE DONE THE SAME THINGS FOR FIVE HUNDRED YEARS AND WHAT DO WE HAVE TO SHOW FOR IT BUT OVERPOPULATION, SQUALOR, AND STARVATION WITHIN THE OUTER WALLS?
AS AMBASSADOR OF ELU, PERHAPS IT WOULD BE BENEFICIAL IF YOU VISITED THE PEOPLE WHO LIVE BEYOND THE INNER--
CAREFUL HOW YOU SPEAK, UWA. YOU ARE ONLY PERMITTED TO THIS COUNCIL MEETING BECAUSE YOU HAVE ROYAL BLOOD.

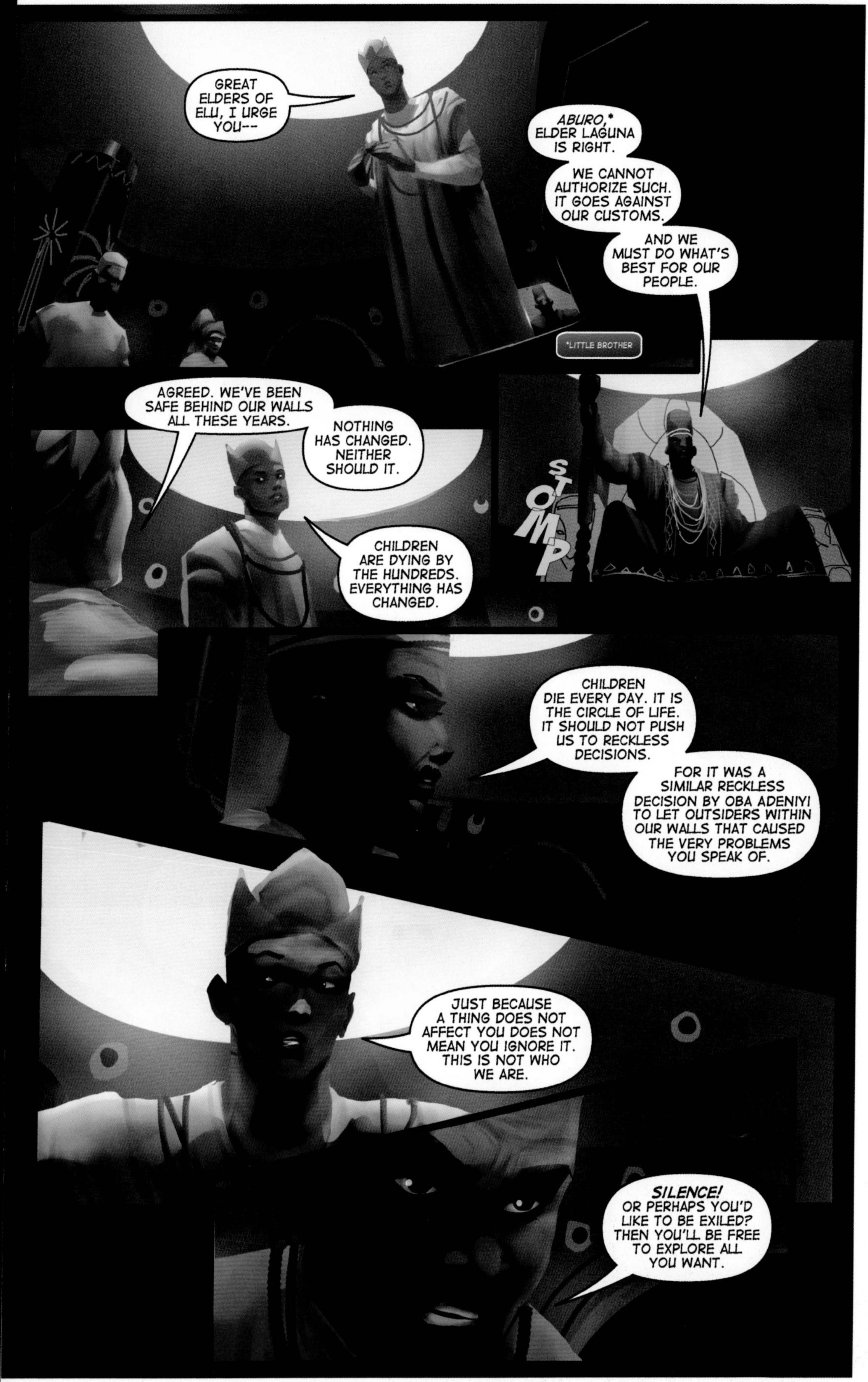

GREAT ELDERS OF ELU, I URGE YOU--
ABURO,* ELDER LAGUNA IS RIGHT.
WE CANNOT AUTHORIZE SUCH. IT GOES AGAINST OUR CUSTOMS.
AND WE MUST DO WHAT'S BEST FOR OUR PEOPLE.
*LITTLE BROTHER
AGREED. WE'VE BEEN SAFE BEHIND OUR WALLS ALL THESE YEARS.
NOTHING HAS CHANGED. NEITHER SHOULD IT.
CHILDREN ARE DYING BY THE HUNDREDS. EVERYTHING HAS CHANGED.
STOMP
CHILDREN DIE EVERY DAY. IT IS THE CIRCLE OF LIFE. IT SHOULD NOT PUSH US TO RECKLESS DECISIONS.
FOR IT WAS A SIMILAR RECKLESS DECISION BY OBA ADENIYI TO LET OUTSIDERS WITHIN OUR WALLS THAT CAUSED THE VERY PROBLEMS YOU SPEAK OF.
JUST BECAUSE A THING DOES NOT AFFECT YOU DOES NOT MEAN YOU IGNORE IT. THIS IS NOT WHO WE ARE.
SILENCE! OR PERHAPS YOU'D LIKE TO BE EXILED? THEN YOU'LL BE FREE TO EXPLORE ALL YOU WANT.

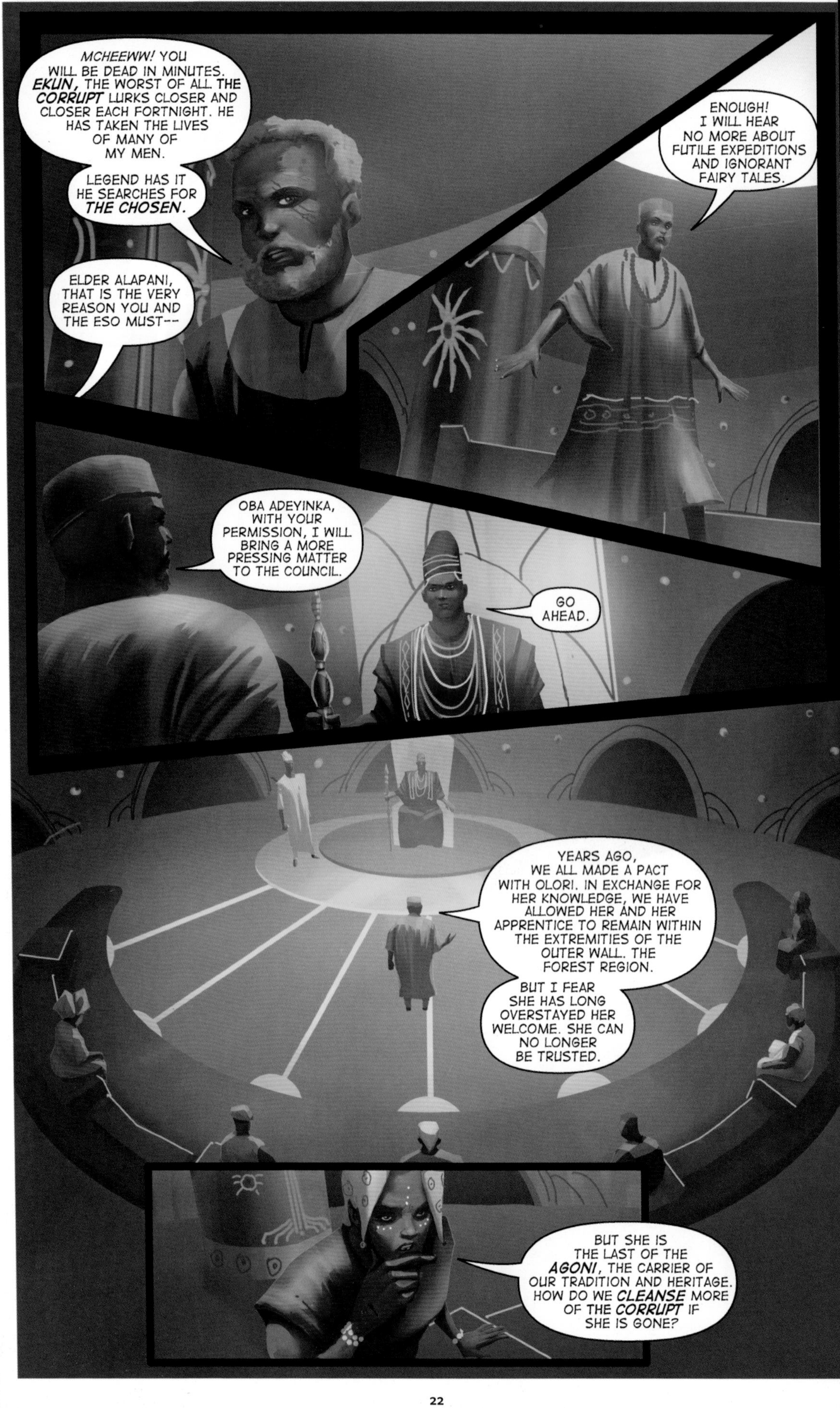
MCHEEWW! YOU WILL BE DEAD IN MINUTES. EKUN, THE WORST OF ALL THE CORRUPT LURKS CLOSER AND CLOSER EACH FORTNIGHT. HE HAS TAKEN THE LIVES OF MANY OF MY MEN.
LEGEND HAS IT HE SEARCHES FOR THE CHOSEN.
ELDER ALAPANI, THAT IS THE VERY REASON YOU AND THE ESO MUST--
ENOUGH! I WILL HEAR NO MORE ABOUT FUTILE EXPEDITIONS AND IGNORANT FAIRY TALES.
OBA ADEYINKA, WITH YOUR PERMISSION, I WILL BRING A MORE PRESSING MATTER TO THE COUNCIL.
GO AHEAD.
YEARS AGO, WE ALL MADE A PACT WITH OLORI. IN EXCHANGE FOR HER KNOWLEDGE, WE HAVE ALLOWED HER AND HER APPRENTICE TO REMAIN WITHIN THE EXTREMITIES OF THE OUTER WALL. THE FOREST REGION.
BUT I FEAR SHE HAS LONG OVERSTAYED HER WELCOME. SHE CAN NO LONGER BE TRUSTED.
BUT SHE IS THE LAST OF THE AGONI, THE CARRIER OF OUR TRADITION AND HERITAGE. HOW DO WE CLEANSE MORE OF THE CORRUPT IF SHE IS GONE?

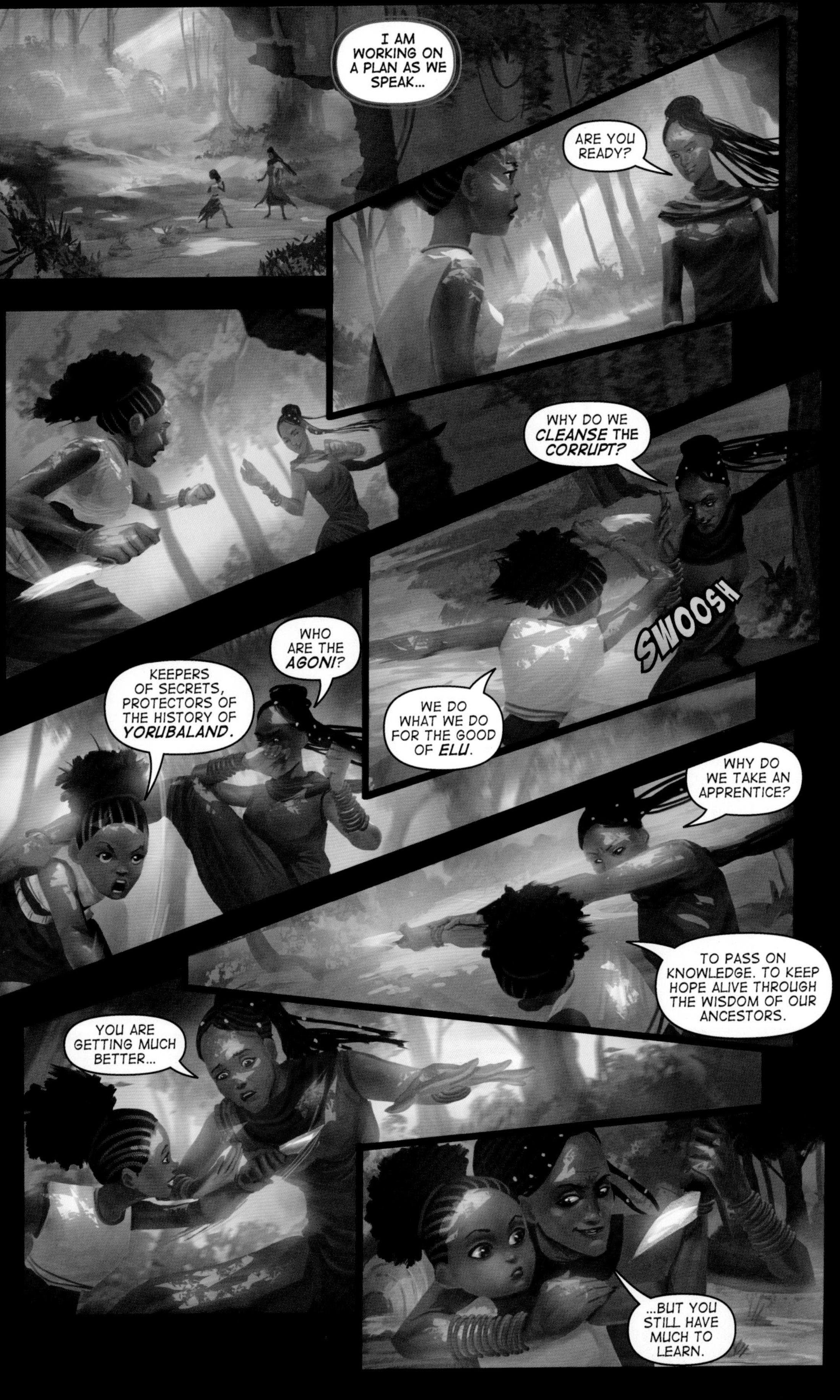

I AM WORKING ON A PLAN AS WE SPEAK...
ARE YOU READY?
WHY DO WE CLEANSE THE CORRUPT?
SWOOSH
WE DO WHAT WE DO FOR THE GOOD OF ELU.
WHO ARE THE AGONI?
KEEPERS OF SECRETS, PROTECTORS OF THE HISTORY OF YORUBALAND.
WHY DO WE TAKE AN APPRENTICE?
TO PASS ON KNOWLEDGE. TO KEEP HOPE ALIVE THROUGH THE WISDOM OF OUR ANCESTORS.
YOU ARE GETTING MUCH BETTER...
...BUT YOU STILL HAVE MUCH TO LEARN.

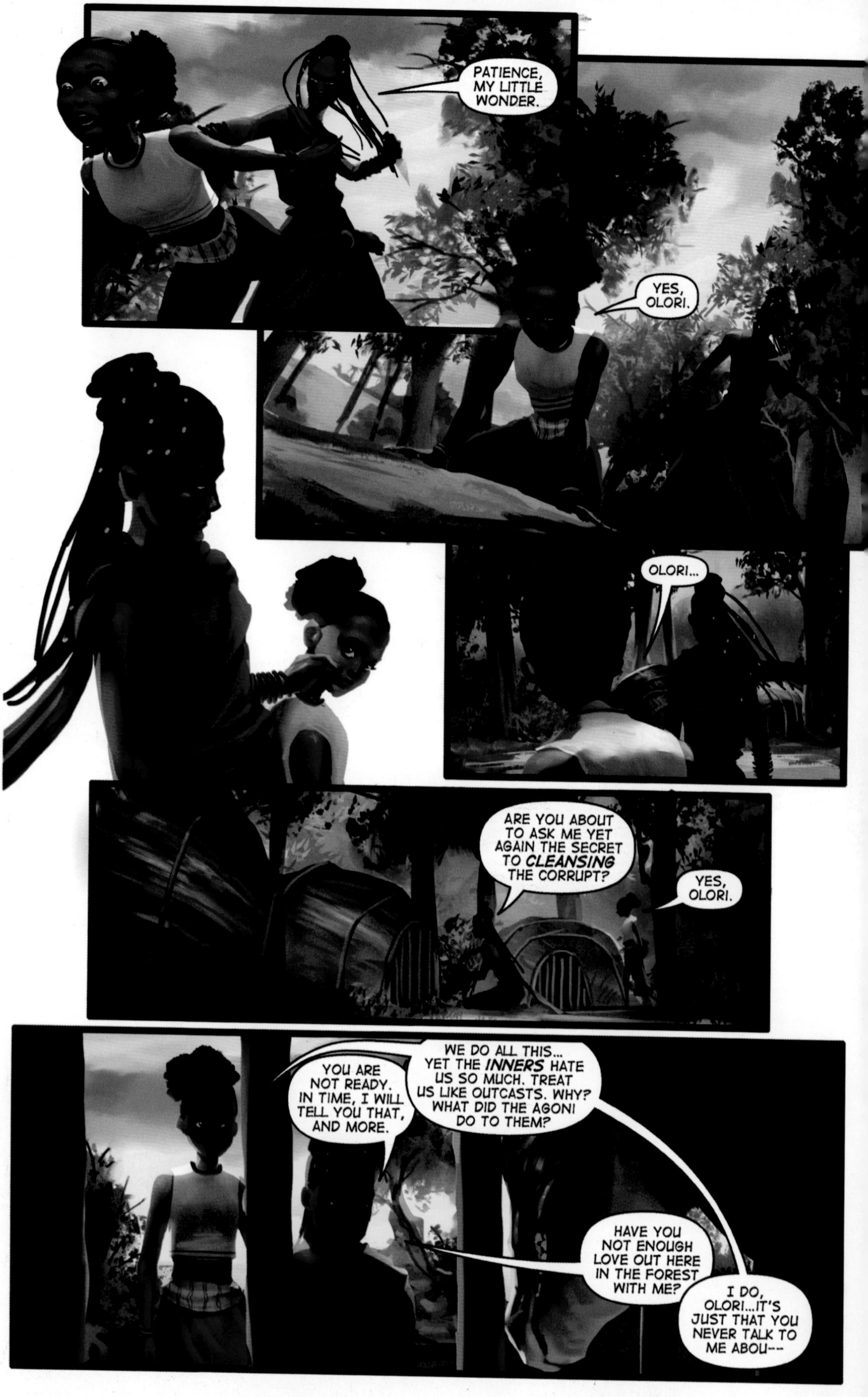
PATIENCE, MY LITTLE WONDER.
YES, OLORI.
OLORI...
ARE YOU ABOUT TO ASK ME YET AGAIN THE SECRET TO *CLEANSING* THE CORRUPT?
YES, OLORI.
WE DO ALL THIS... YET THE *INNERS* HATE US SO MUCH. TREAT US LIKE OUTCASTS. WHY? WHAT DID THE AGONI DO TO THEM?
YOU ARE NOT READY. IN TIME, I WILL TELL YOU THAT, AND MORE.
HAVE YOU NOT ENOUGH LOVE OUT HERE IN THE FOREST WITH ME?
I DO, OLORI...IT'S JUST THAT YOU NEVER TALK TO ME ABOU--

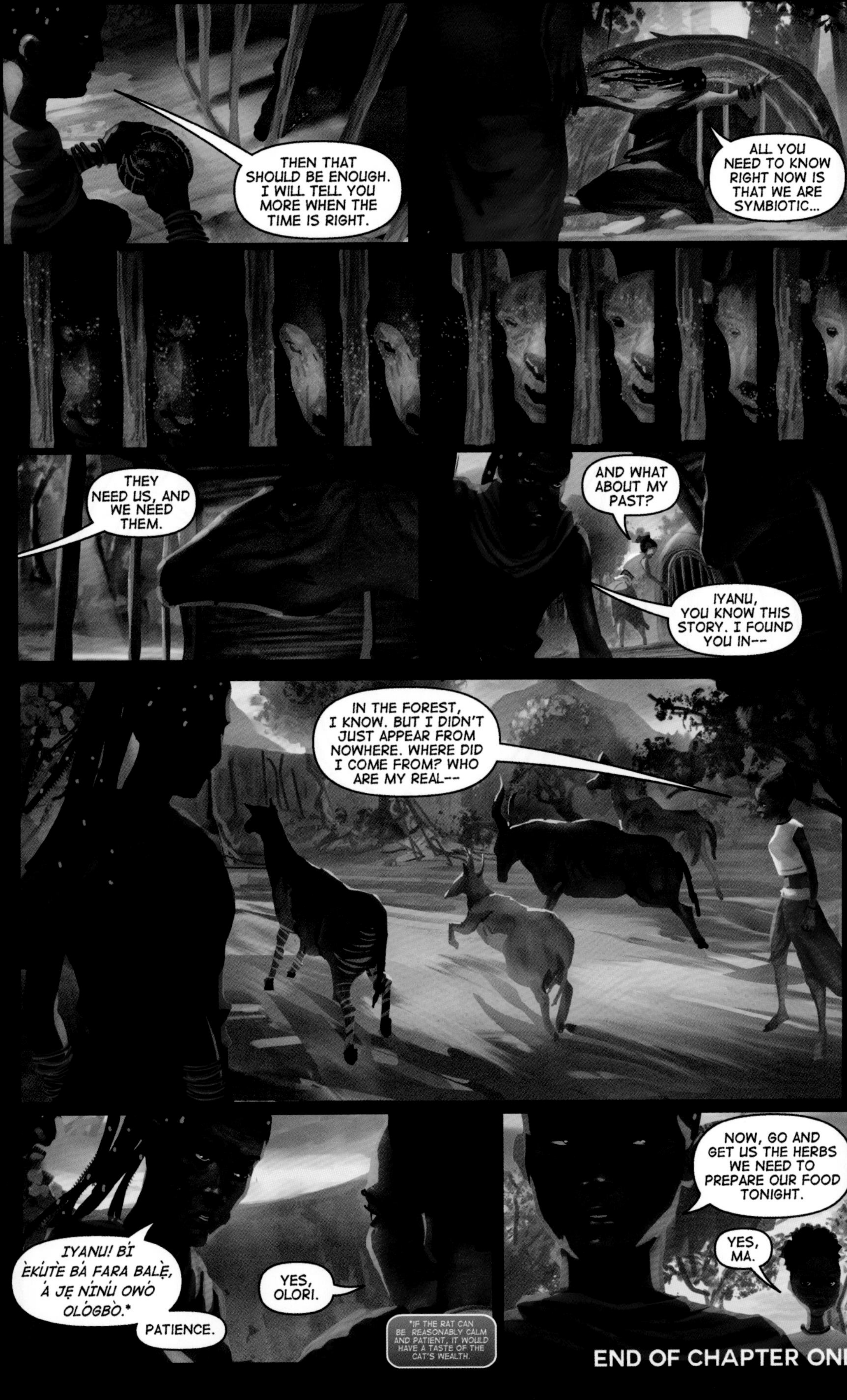
THEN THAT SHOULD BE ENOUGH. I WILL TELL YOU MORE WHEN THE TIME IS RIGHT.
ALL YOU NEED TO KNOW RIGHT NOW IS THAT WE ARE SYMBIOTIC...
THEY NEED US, AND WE NEED THEM.
AND WHAT ABOUT MY PAST?
IYANU, YOU KNOW THIS STORY. I FOUND YOU IN--
IN THE FOREST, I KNOW. BUT I DIDN'T JUST APPEAR FROM NOWHERE. WHERE DID I COME FROM? WHO ARE MY REAL--
IYANU! BÍ ÈKÚTÈ BÁ FARA BALẸ̀, Á JẸ NÍNÚ OWÓ OLÓGBÒ.*
PATIENCE.
YES, OLORI.
*IF THE RAT CAN BE REASONABLY CALM AND PATIENT, IT WOULD HAVE A TASTE OF THE CAT'S WEALTH.
NOW, GO AND GET US THE HERBS WE NEED TO PREPARE OUR FOOD TONIGHT.
YES, MA.
END OF CHAPTER ONE

MAP OF ELU

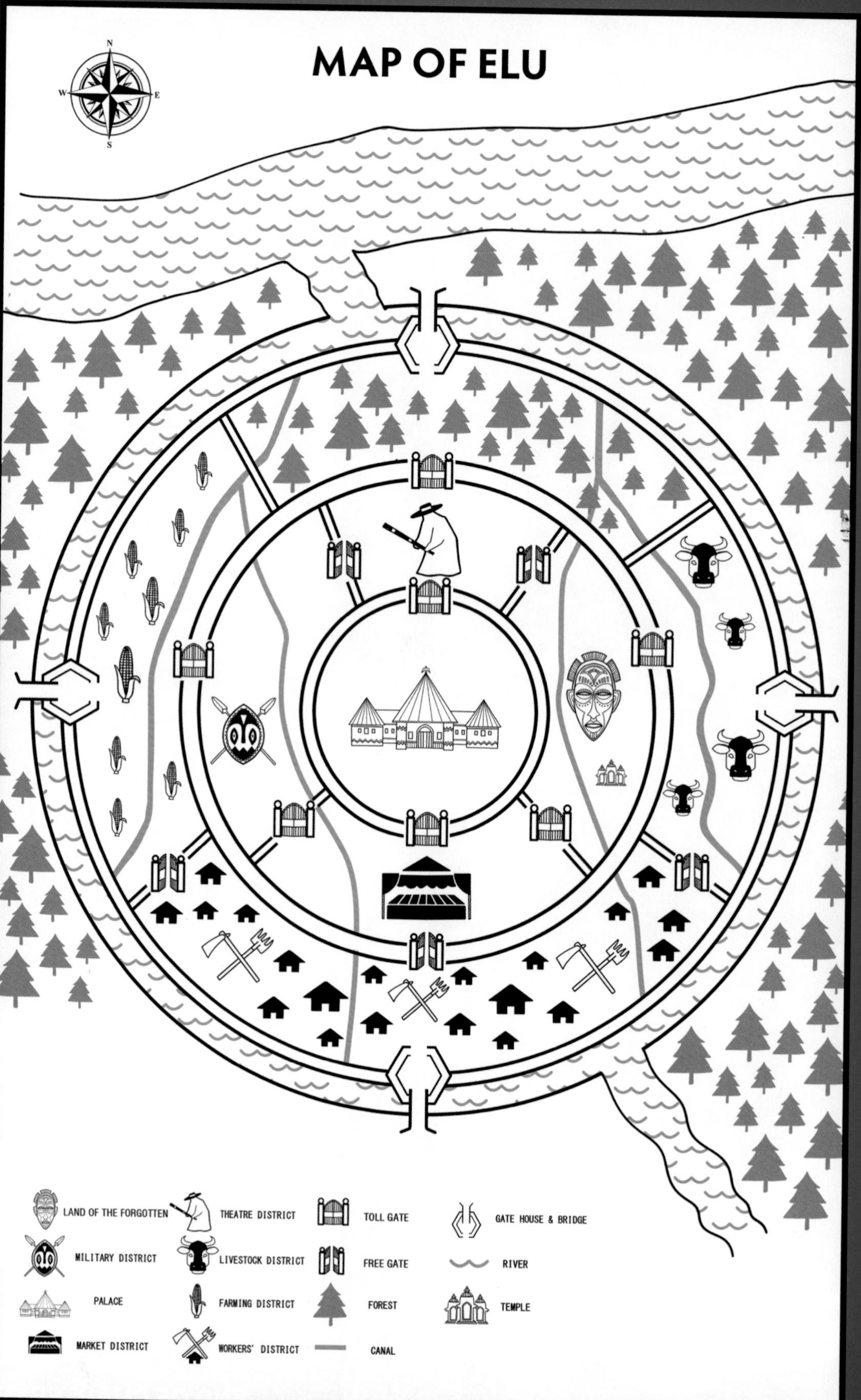
N
W
E
S
LAND OF THE FORGOTTEN
THEATRE DISTRICT
TOLL GATE
GATE HOUSE & BRIDGE
MILITARY DISTRICT
LIVESTOCK DISTRICT
FREE GATE
RIVER
PALACE
FARMING DISTRICT
FOREST
TEMPLE
MARKET DISTRICT
WORKERS' DISTRICT
CANAL

CHAPTER TWO

The City of **Elu**

E lu is the only settlement in all of Yorubaland with walls strong and high enough to consistently keep out the Corrupt. The city is divided into eight separate districts (plus the royal palace at the center of the city). Four of these districts are located within the inner walls—Theater District, Market District, Military District, and the Land of the Forgotten. The other four districts—Workers' District, Farming District, Livestock District, and Forest District—are located within the outer walls.

FUN FACT: The City of Elu is inspired by Benin City (the capital of present-day Edo, Nigeria) and its massive walls, which are said to extend for 16,000 kilometers—four times longer than the Great Wall of China.

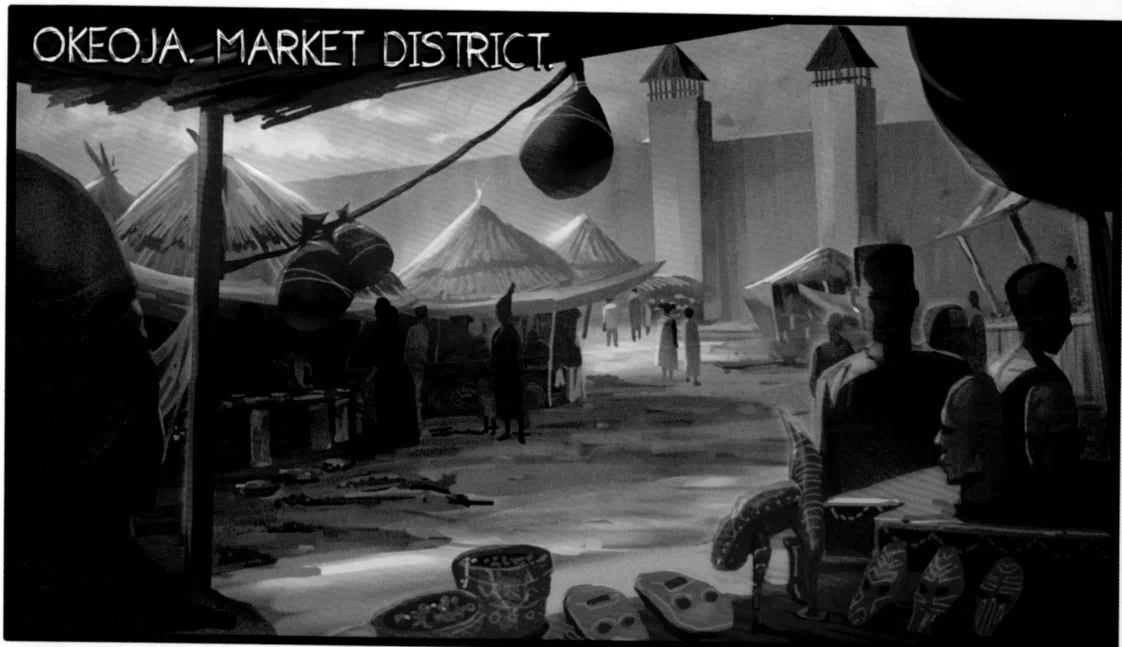
OKEOJA. MARKET DISTRICT.

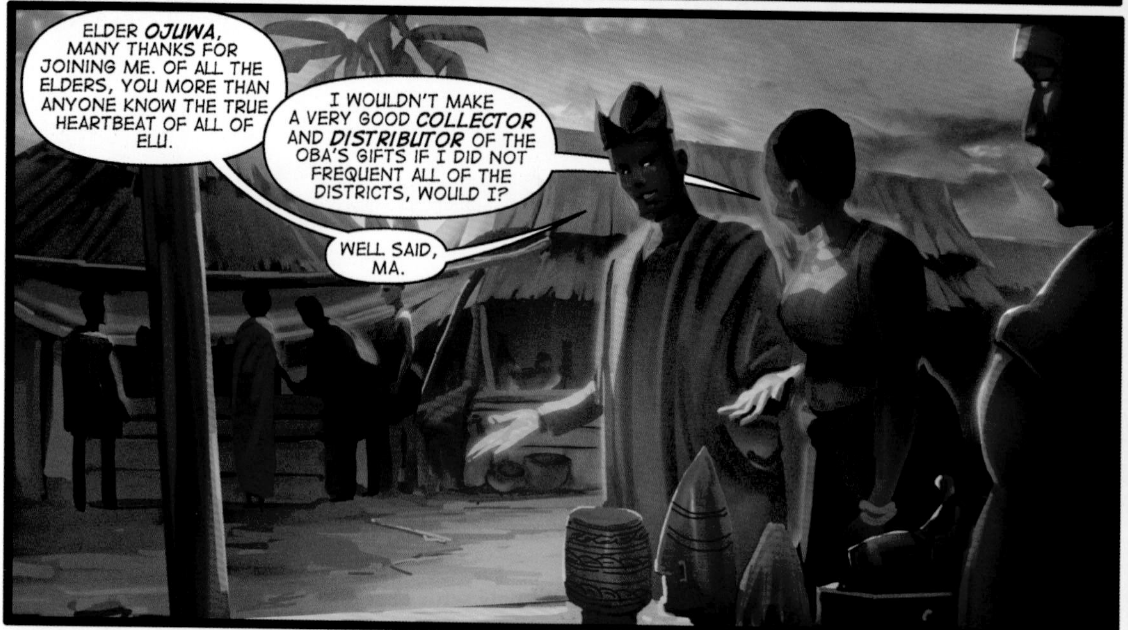
ELDER OJUWA, MANY THANKS FOR JOINING ME. OF ALL THE ELDERS, YOU MORE THAN ANYONE KNOW THE TRUE HEARTBEAT OF ALL OF ELU.
I WOULDN'T MAKE A VERY GOOD COLLECTOR AND DISTRIBUTOR OF THE OBA'S GIFTS IF I DID NOT FREQUENT ALL OF THE DISTRICTS, WOULD I?
WELL SAID, MA.

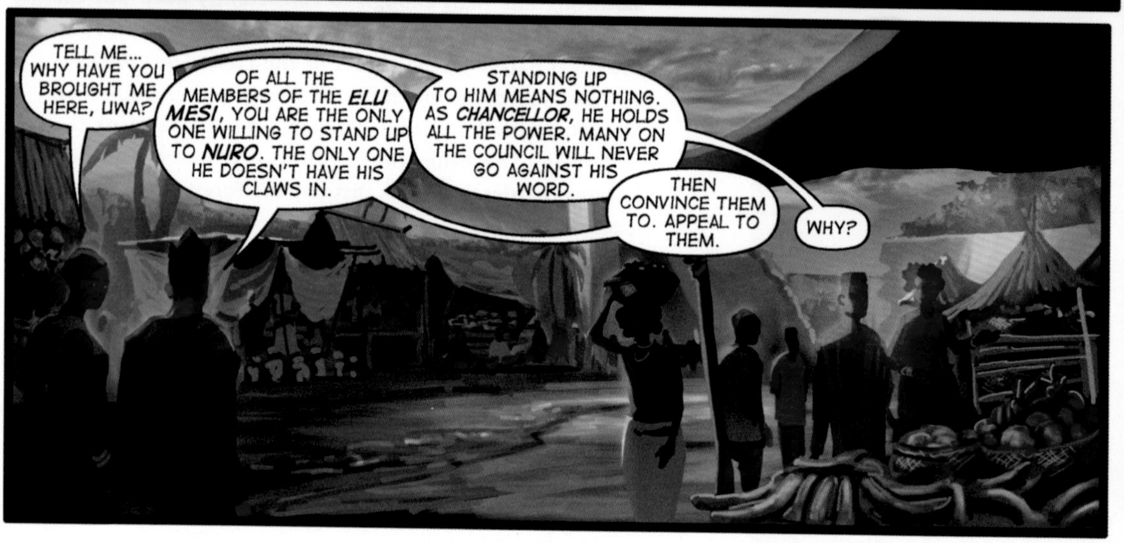
TELL ME... WHY HAVE YOU BROUGHT ME HERE, UWA?
OF ALL THE MEMBERS OF THE ELU MESI, YOU ARE THE ONLY ONE WILLING TO STAND UP TO NURO. THE ONLY ONE HE DOESN'T HAVE HIS CLAWS IN.
STANDING UP TO HIM MEANS NOTHING. AS CHANCELLOR, HE HOLDS ALL THE POWER. MANY ON THE COUNCIL WILL NEVER GO AGAINST HIS WORD.
THEN CONVINCE THEM TO. APPEAL TO THEM.
WHY?

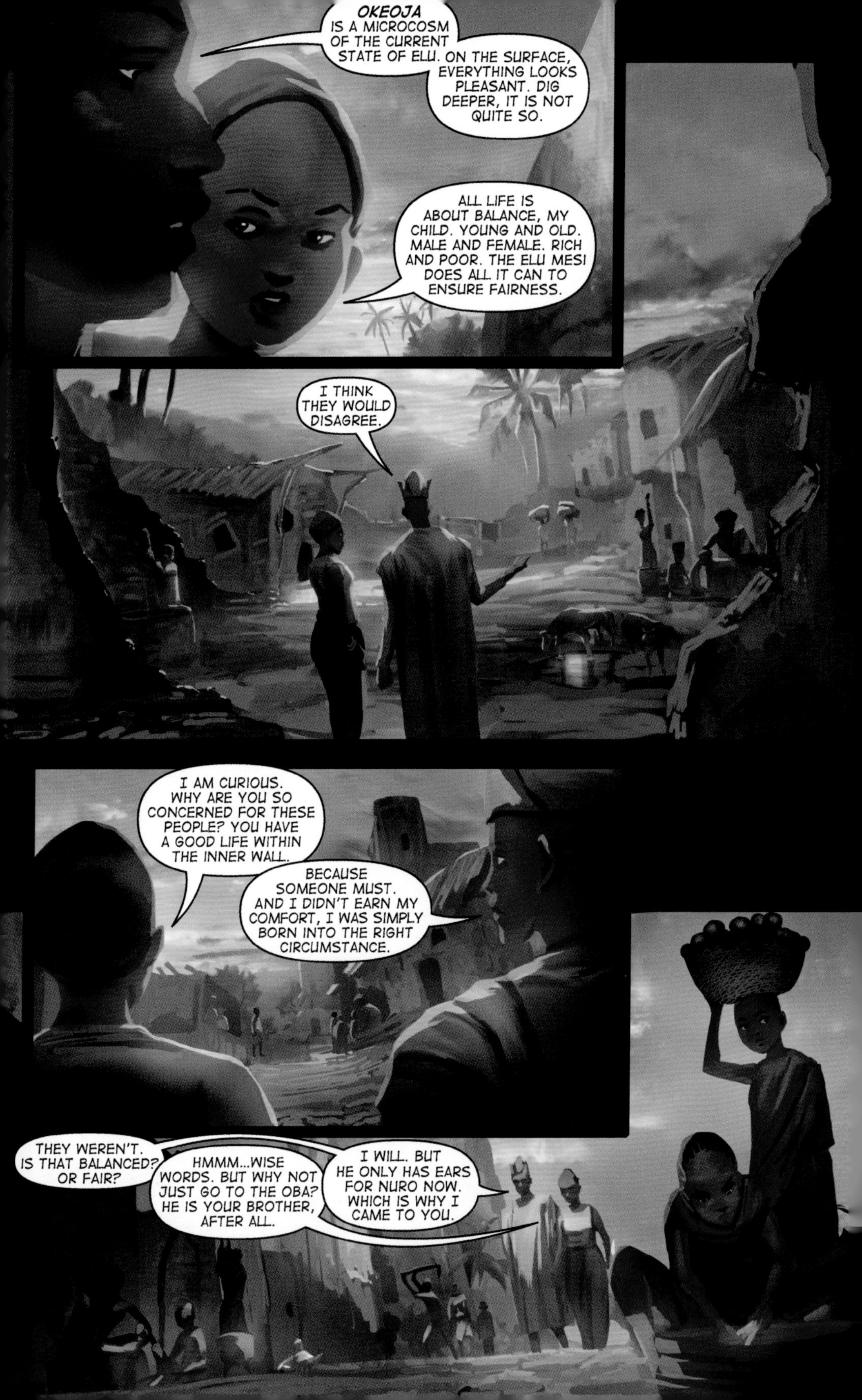
OKEOJA IS A MICROCOSM OF THE CURRENT STATE OF ELU. ON THE SURFACE, EVERYTHING LOOKS PLEASANT. DIG DEEPER, IT IS NOT QUITE SO.
ALL LIFE IS ABOUT BALANCE, MY CHILD. YOUNG AND OLD. MALE AND FEMALE. RICH AND POOR. THE ELU MESI DOES ALL IT CAN TO ENSURE FAIRNESS.
I THINK THEY WOULD DISAGREE.
I AM CURIOUS. WHY ARE YOU SO CONCERNED FOR THESE PEOPLE? YOU HAVE A GOOD LIFE WITHIN THE INNER WALL.
BECAUSE SOMEONE MUST. AND I DIDN'T EARN MY COMFORT, I WAS SIMPLY BORN INTO THE RIGHT CIRCUMSTANCE.
THEY WEREN'T. IS THAT BALANCED? OR FAIR?
HMMM...WISE WORDS. BUT WHY NOT JUST GO TO THE OBA? HE IS YOUR BROTHER, AFTER ALL.
I WILL. BUT HE ONLY HAS EARS FOR NURO NOW. WHICH IS WHY I CAME TO YOU.

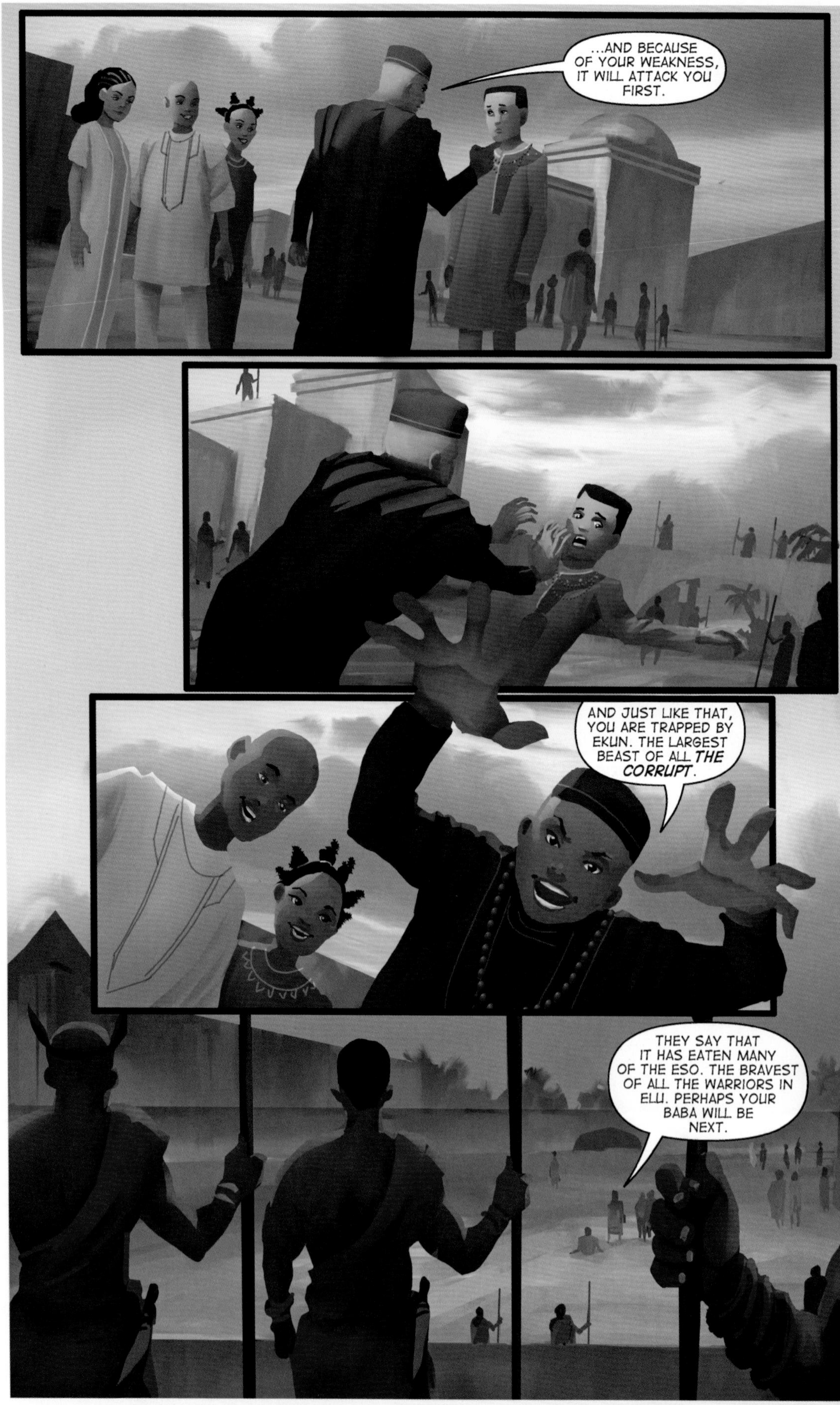
...AND BECAUSE OF YOUR WEAKNESS, IT WILL ATTACK YOU FIRST.
AND JUST LIKE THAT, YOU ARE TRAPPED BY EKUN. THE LARGEST BEAST OF ALL ***THE CORRUPT***.
THEY SAY THAT IT HAS EATEN MANY OF THE ESO. THE BRAVEST OF ALL THE WARRIORS IN ELU. PERHAPS YOUR BABA WILL BE NEXT.

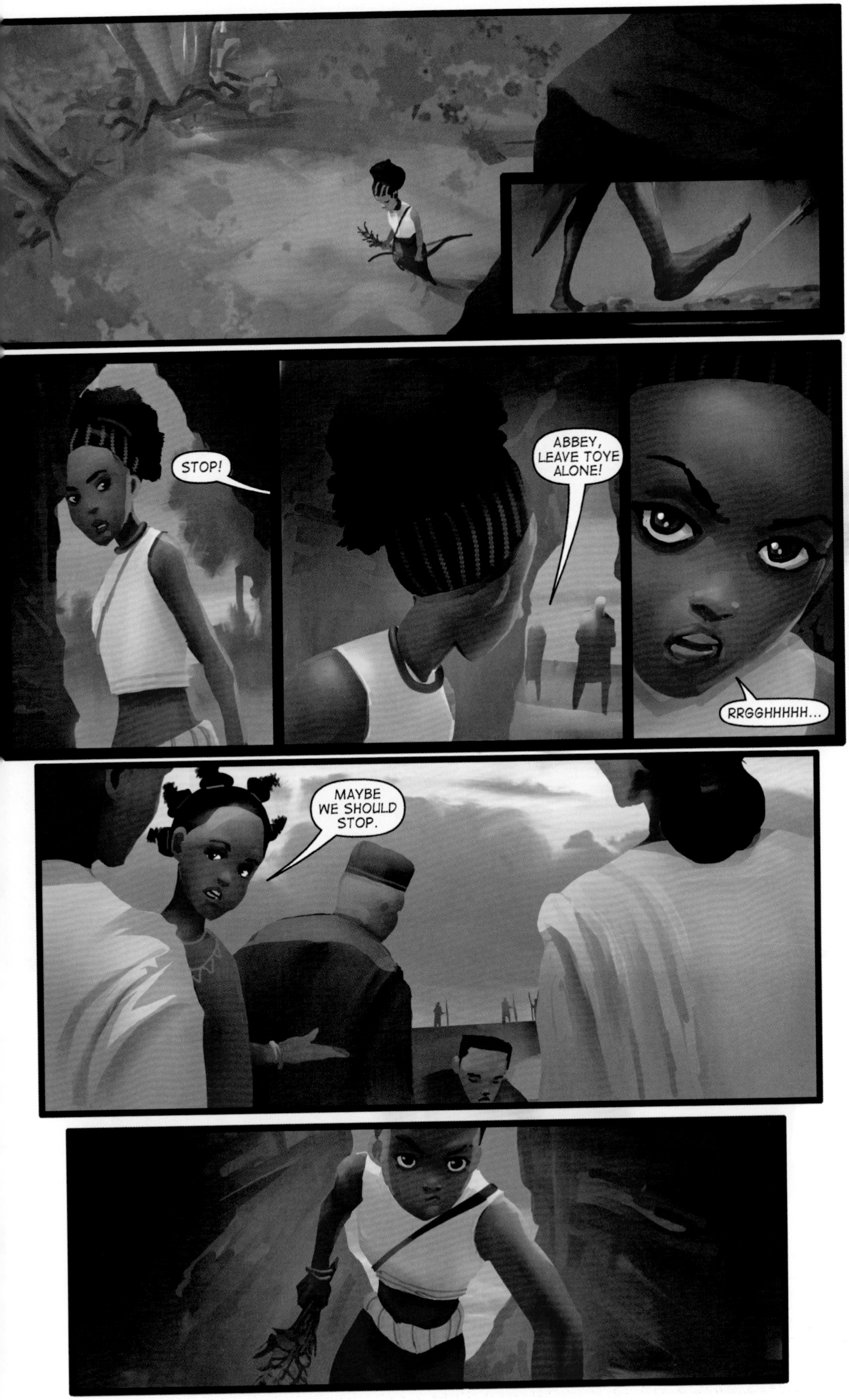
STOP!
ABBEY, LEAVE TOYE ALONE!
RRGGHHHHH...
MAYBE WE SHOULD STOP.

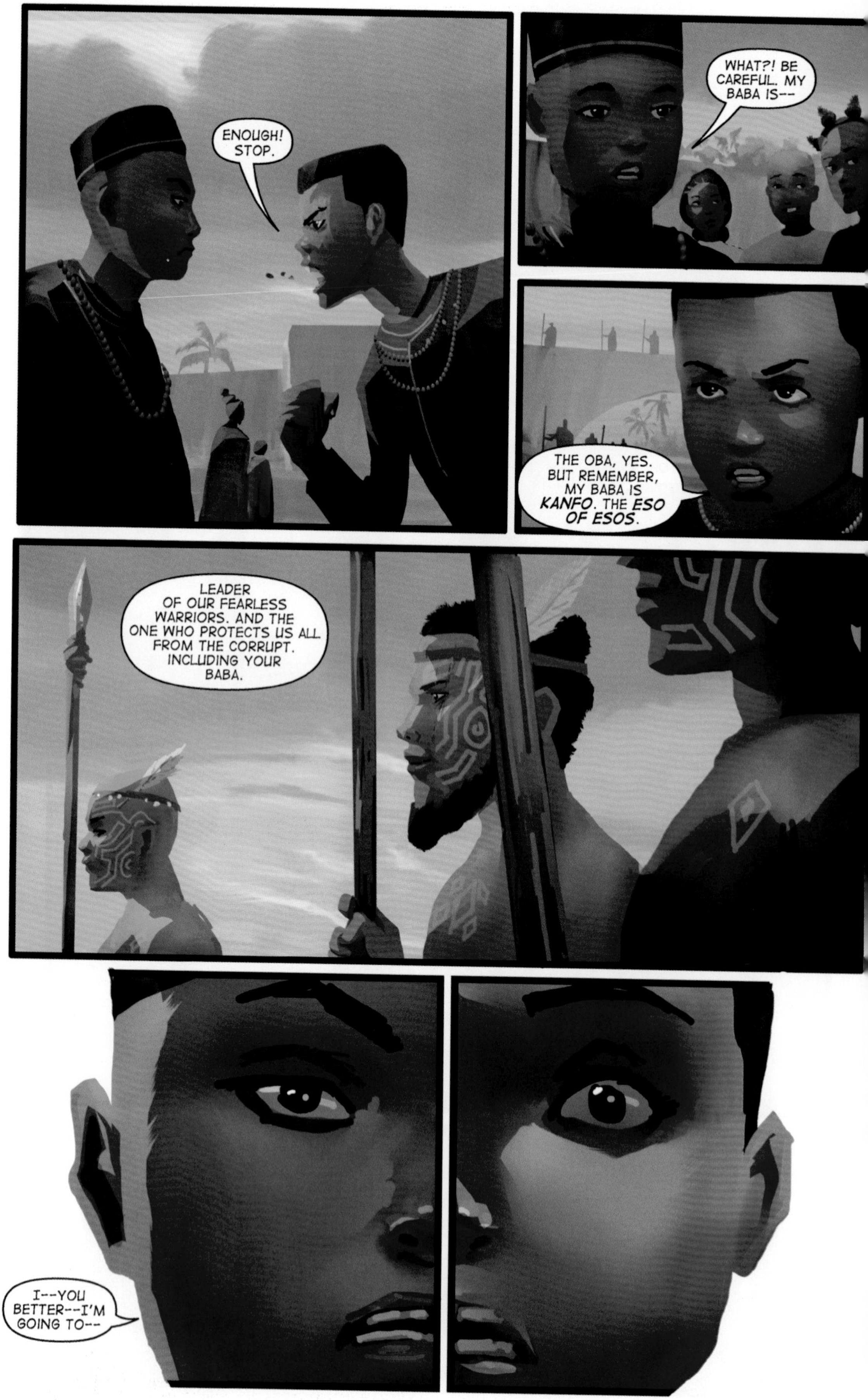
ENOUGH! STOP.
WHAT?! BE CAREFUL. MY BABA IS--
THE OBA, YES. BUT REMEMBER, MY BABA IS *KANFO*. THE *ESO OF ESOS*.
LEADER OF OUR FEARLESS WARRIORS. AND THE ONE WHO PROTECTS US ALL FROM THE CORRUPT. INCLUDING YOUR BABA.
I--YOU BETTER--I'M GOING TO--

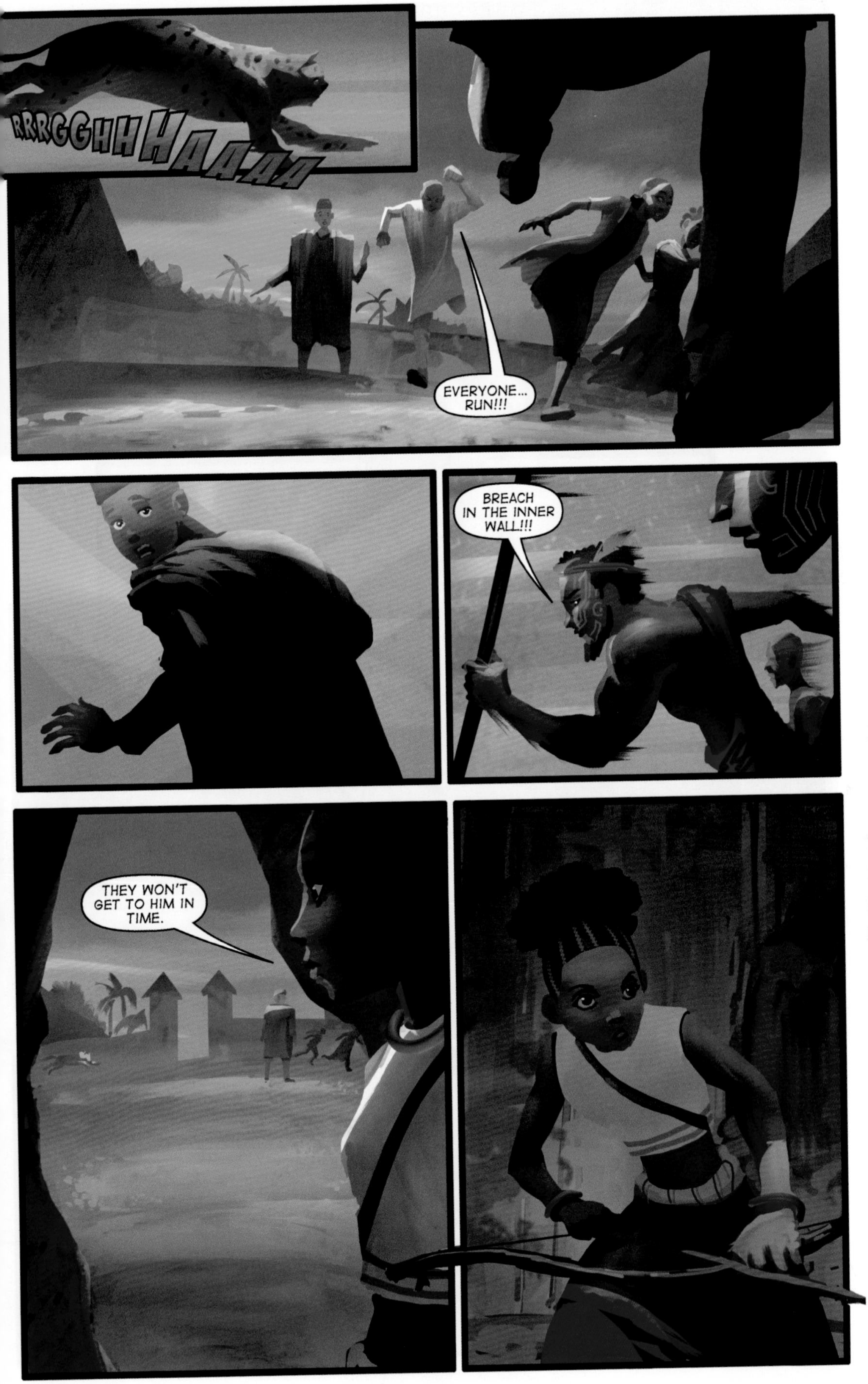
RRRGGHHHAAAAA
EVERYONE... RUN!!!
BREACH IN THE INNER WALL!!!
THEY WON'T GET TO HIM IN TIME.

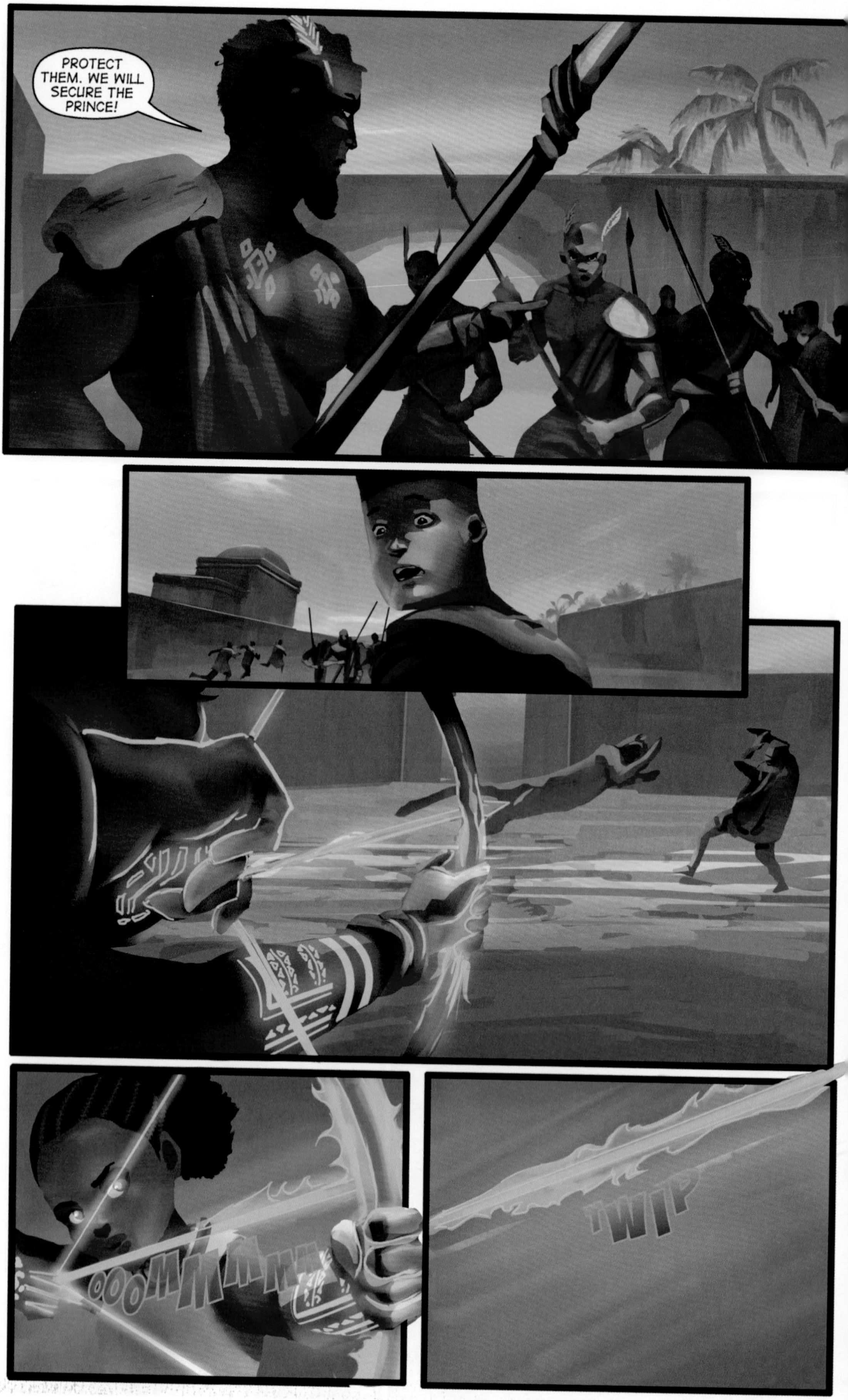
PROTECT THEM. WE WILL SECURE THE PRINCE!
TWIP

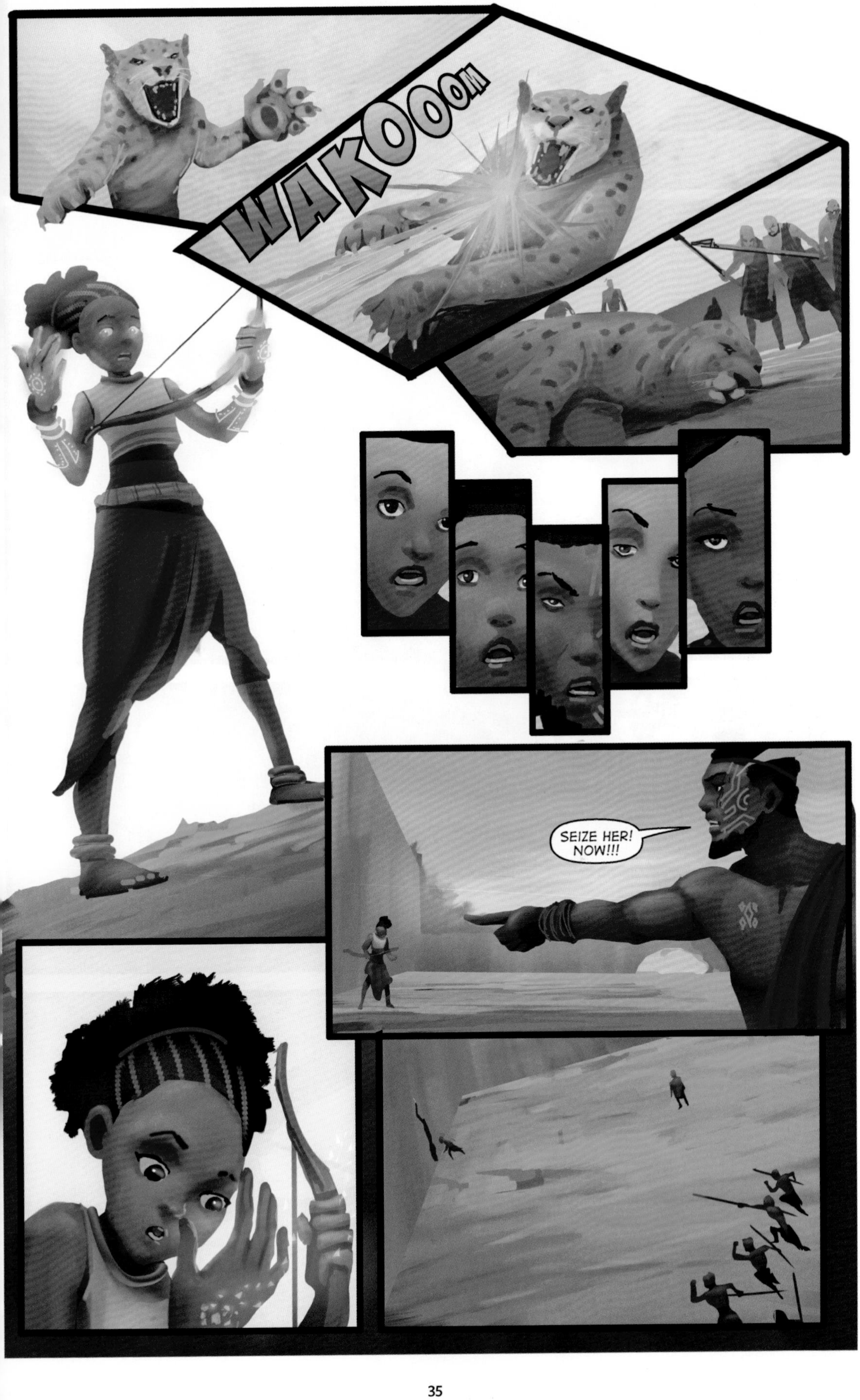
WAKOOOM
SEIZE HER! NOW!!!

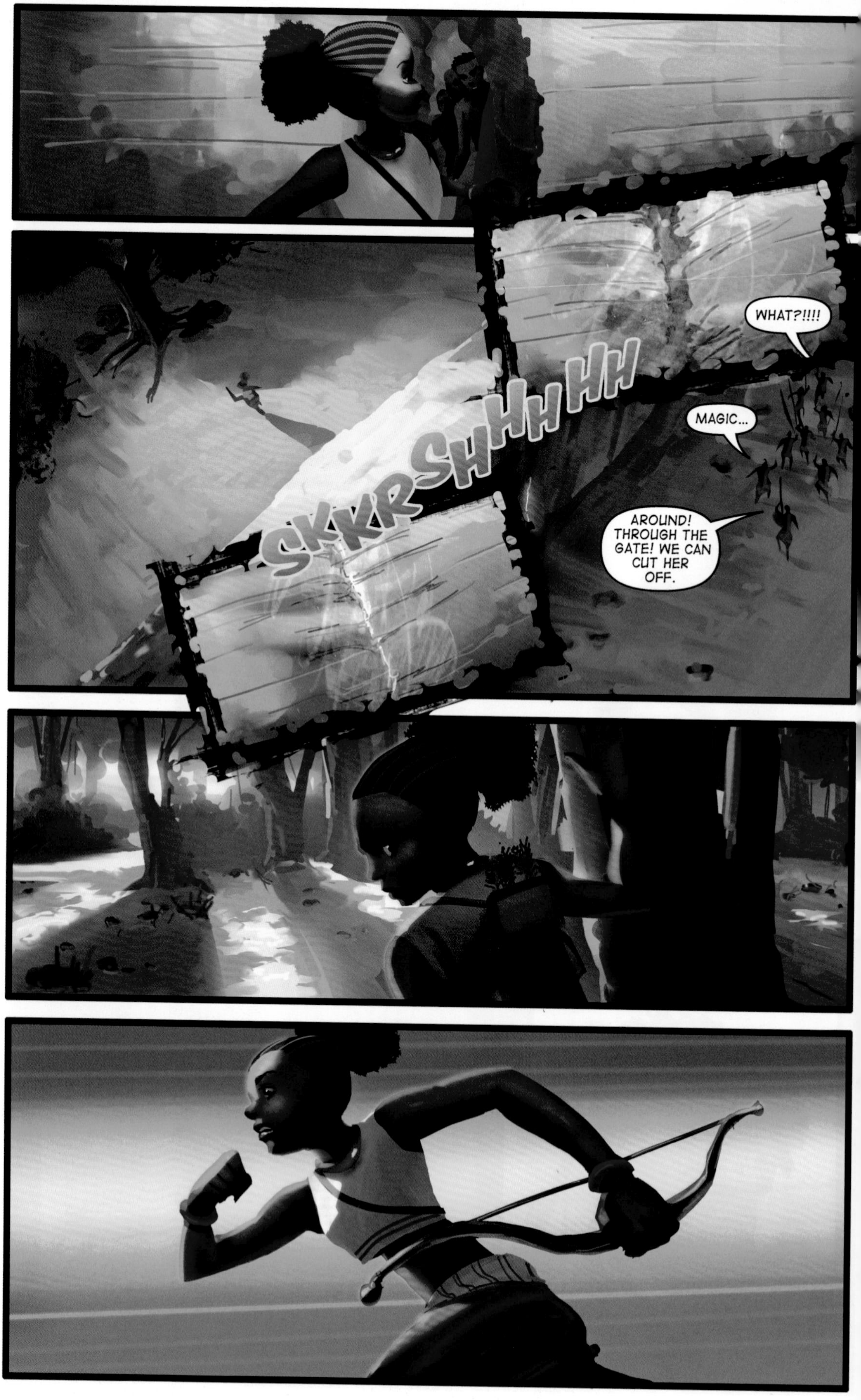
SKKRSHHHHHH
WHAT?!!!!
MAGIC...
AROUND! THROUGH THE GATE! WE CAN CUT HER OFF.

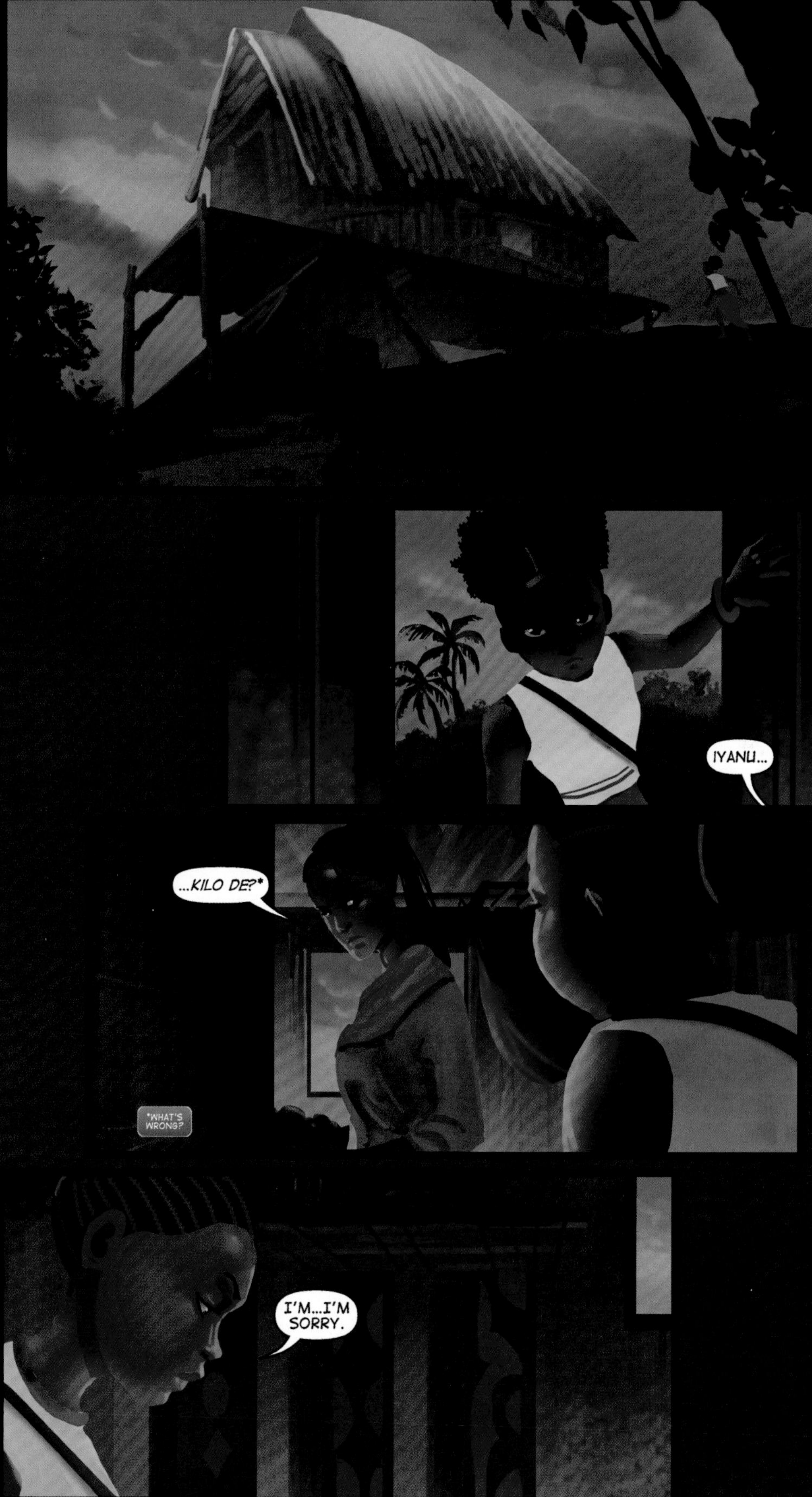
IYANU...
...KILO DE?*
*WHAT'S WRONG?
I'M...I'M SORRY.

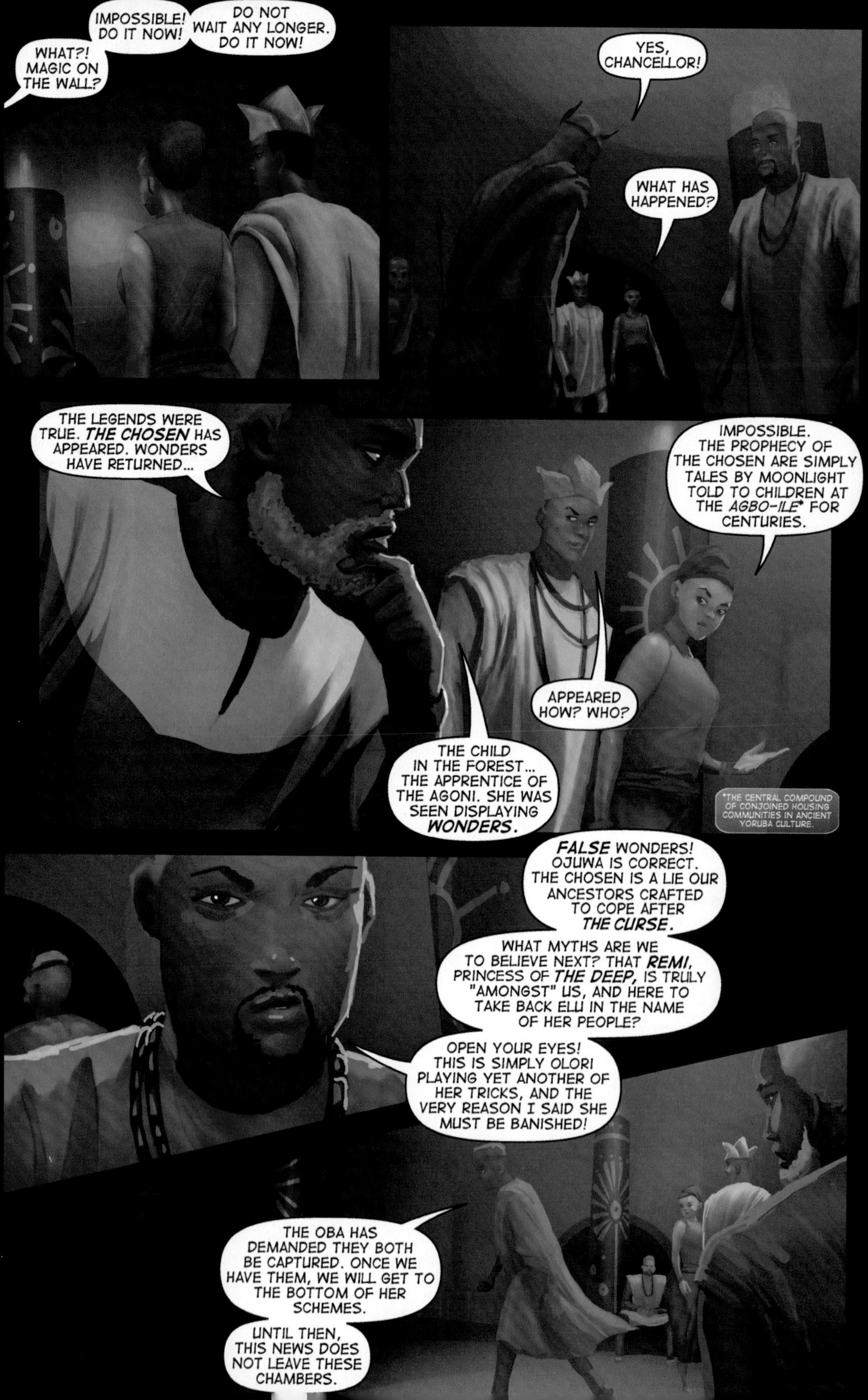
WHAT?! MAGIC ON THE WALL?
IMPOSSIBLE! DO IT NOW!
DO NOT WAIT ANY LONGER. DO IT NOW!
YES, CHANCELLOR!
WHAT HAS HAPPENED?
THE LEGENDS WERE TRUE. THE CHOSEN HAS APPEARED. WONDERS HAVE RETURNED...
IMPOSSIBLE. THE PROPHECY OF THE CHOSEN ARE SIMPLY TALES BY MOONLIGHT TOLD TO CHILDREN AT THE AGBO-ILE* FOR CENTURIES.
APPEARED HOW? WHO?
THE CHILD IN THE FOREST... THE APPRENTICE OF THE AGONI. SHE WAS SEEN DISPLAYING WONDERS.
*THE CENTRAL COMPOUND OF CONJOINED HOUSING COMMUNITIES IN ANCIENT YORUBA CULTURE.
FALSE WONDERS! OJUWA IS CORRECT. THE CHOSEN IS A LIE OUR ANCESTORS CRAFTED TO COPE AFTER THE CURSE.
WHAT MYTHS ARE WE TO BELIEVE NEXT? THAT REMI, PRINCESS OF THE DEEP, IS TRULY "AMONGST" US, AND HERE TO TAKE BACK ELU IN THE NAME OF HER PEOPLE?
OPEN YOUR EYES! THIS IS SIMPLY OLORI PLAYING YET ANOTHER OF HER TRICKS, AND THE VERY REASON I SAID SHE MUST BE BANISHED!
THE OBA HAS DEMANDED THEY BOTH BE CAPTURED. ONCE WE HAVE THEM, WE WILL GET TO THE BOTTOM OF HER SCHEMES.
UNTIL THEN, THIS NEWS DOES NOT LEAVE THESE CHAMBERS.

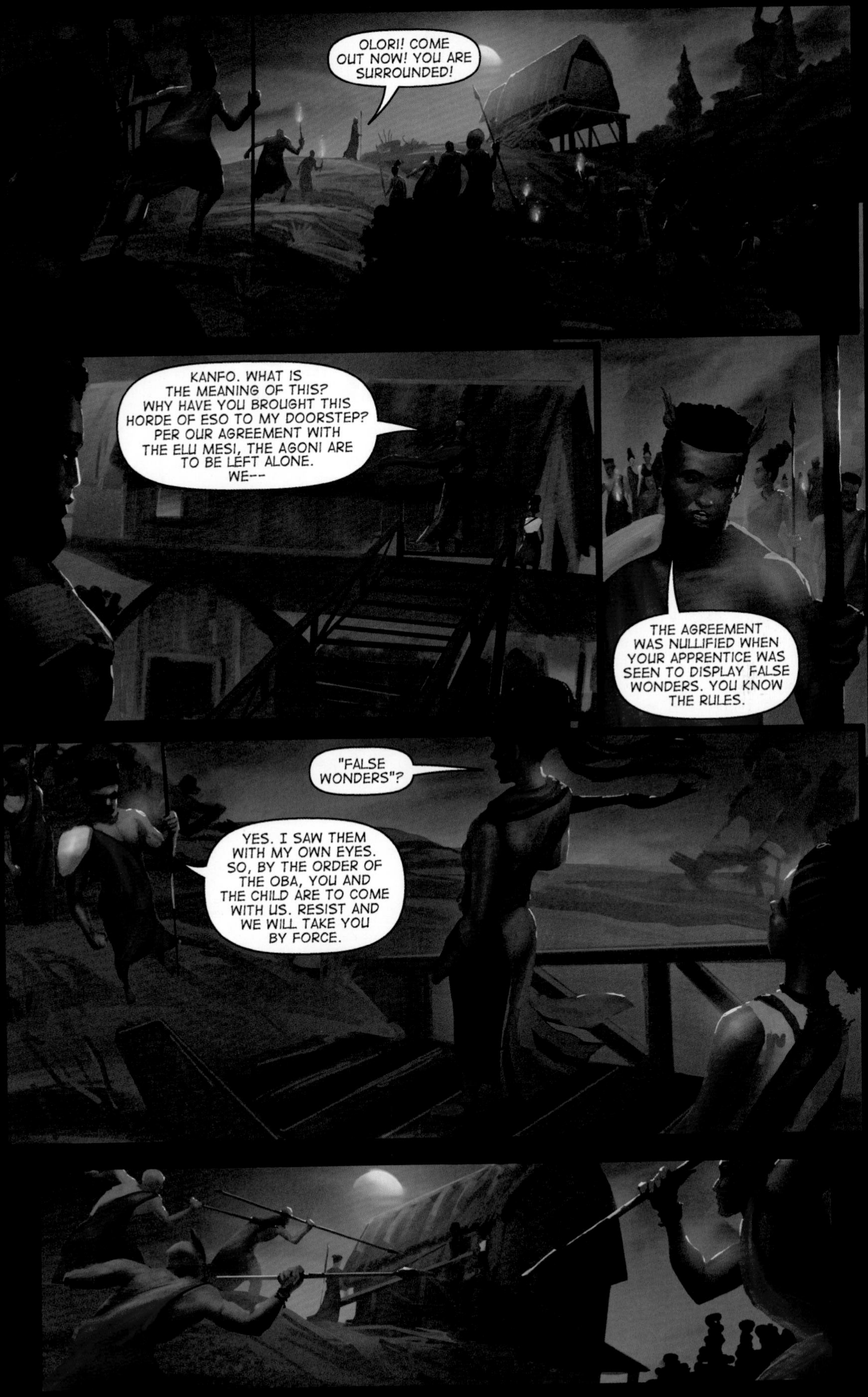
OLORI! COME OUT NOW! YOU ARE SURROUNDED!
KANFO. WHAT IS THE MEANING OF THIS? WHY HAVE YOU BROUGHT THIS HORDE OF ESO TO MY DOORSTEP? PER OUR AGREEMENT WITH THE ELU MESI, THE AGONI ARE TO BE LEFT ALONE. WE--
THE AGREEMENT WAS NULLIFIED WHEN YOUR APPRENTICE WAS SEEN TO DISPLAY FALSE WONDERS. YOU KNOW THE RULES.
"FALSE WONDERS"?
YES. I SAW THEM WITH MY OWN EYES. SO, BY THE ORDER OF THE OBA, YOU AND THE CHILD ARE TO COME WITH US. RESIST AND WE WILL TAKE YOU BY FORCE.

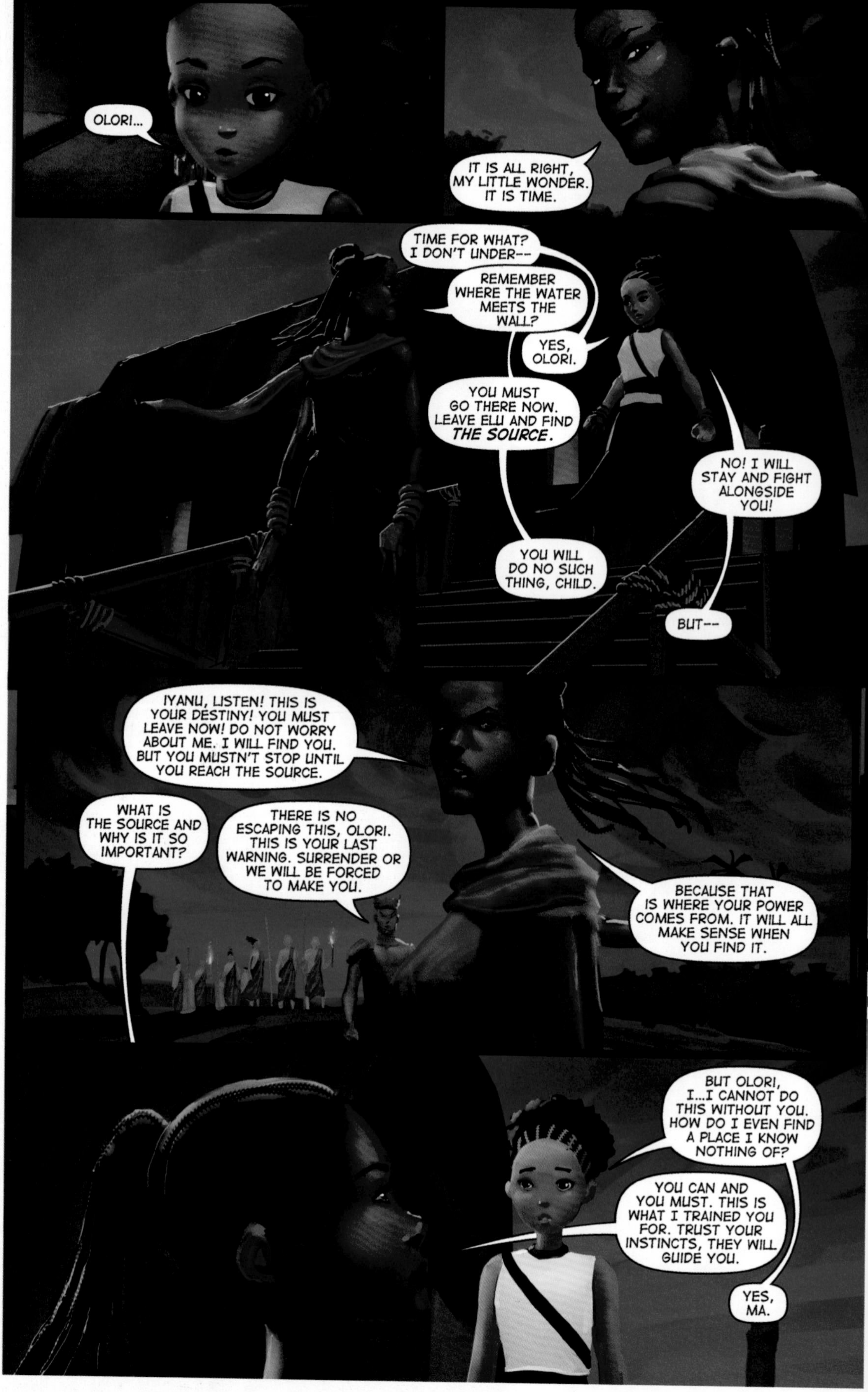

OLORI...
IT IS ALL RIGHT, MY LITTLE WONDER. IT IS TIME.
TIME FOR WHAT? I DON'T UNDER--
REMEMBER WHERE THE WATER MEETS THE WALL?
YES, OLORI.
YOU MUST GO THERE NOW. LEAVE ELU AND FIND THE SOURCE.
NO! I WILL STAY AND FIGHT ALONGSIDE YOU!
YOU WILL DO NO SUCH THING, CHILD.
BUT--
IYANU, LISTEN! THIS IS YOUR DESTINY! YOU MUST LEAVE NOW! DO NOT WORRY ABOUT ME. I WILL FIND YOU. BUT YOU MUSTN'T STOP UNTIL YOU REACH THE SOURCE.
WHAT IS THE SOURCE AND WHY IS IT SO IMPORTANT?
THERE IS NO ESCAPING THIS, OLORI. THIS IS YOUR LAST WARNING. SURRENDER OR WE WILL BE FORCED TO MAKE YOU.
BECAUSE THAT IS WHERE YOUR POWER COMES FROM. IT WILL ALL MAKE SENSE WHEN YOU FIND IT.
BUT OLORI, I...I CANNOT DO THIS WITHOUT YOU. HOW DO I EVEN FIND A PLACE I KNOW NOTHING OF?
YOU CAN AND YOU MUST. THIS IS WHAT I TRAINED YOU FOR. TRUST YOUR INSTINCTS, THEY WILL GUIDE YOU.
YES, MA.

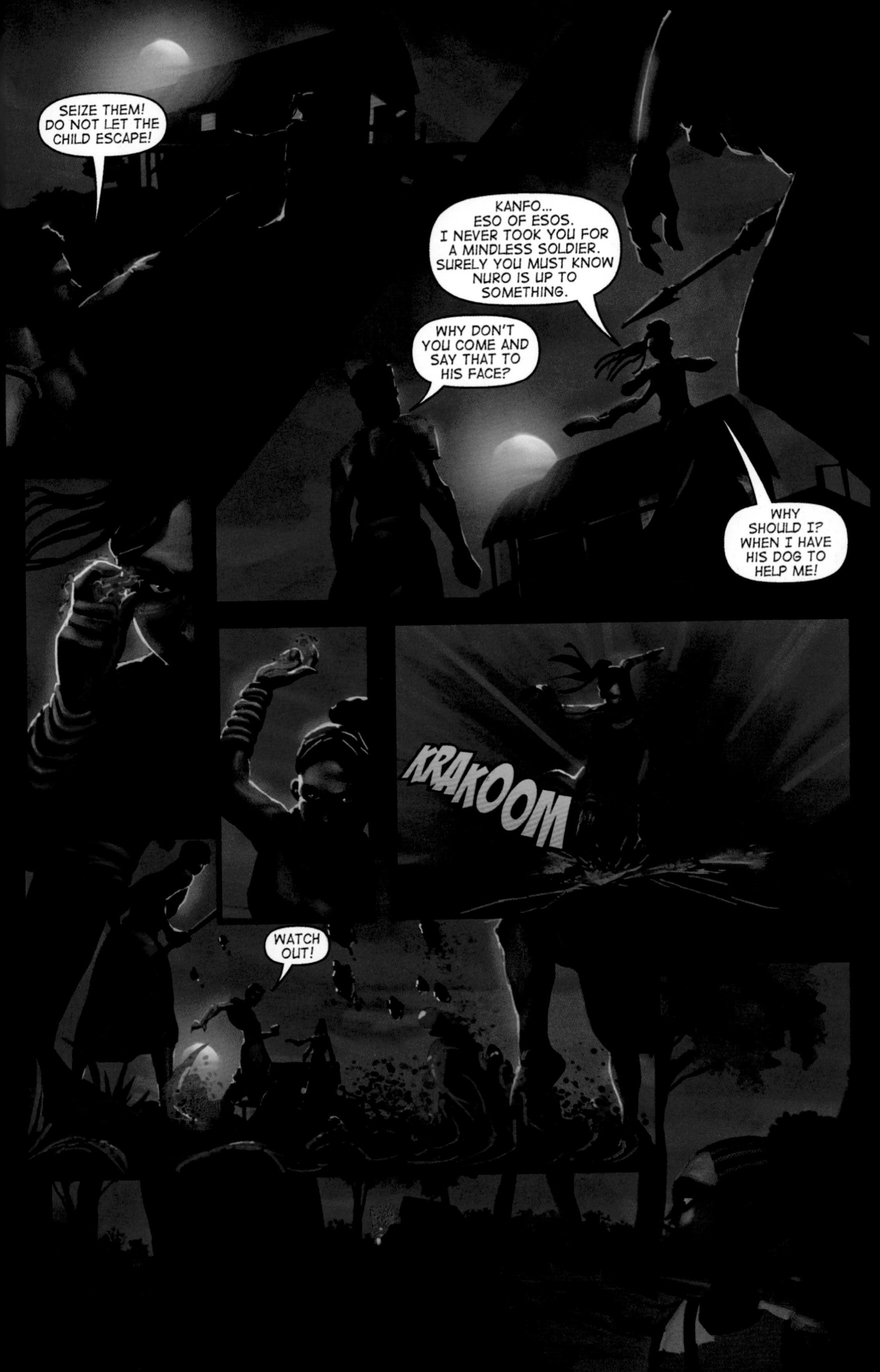
SEIZE THEM! DO NOT LET THE CHILD ESCAPE!
KANFO... ESO OF ESOS. I NEVER TOOK YOU FOR A MINDLESS SOLDIER. SURELY YOU MUST KNOW NURO IS UP TO SOMETHING.
WHY DON'T YOU COME AND SAY THAT TO HIS FACE?
WHY SHOULD I? WHEN I HAVE HIS DOG TO HELP ME!
KRAKOOM
WATCH OUT!

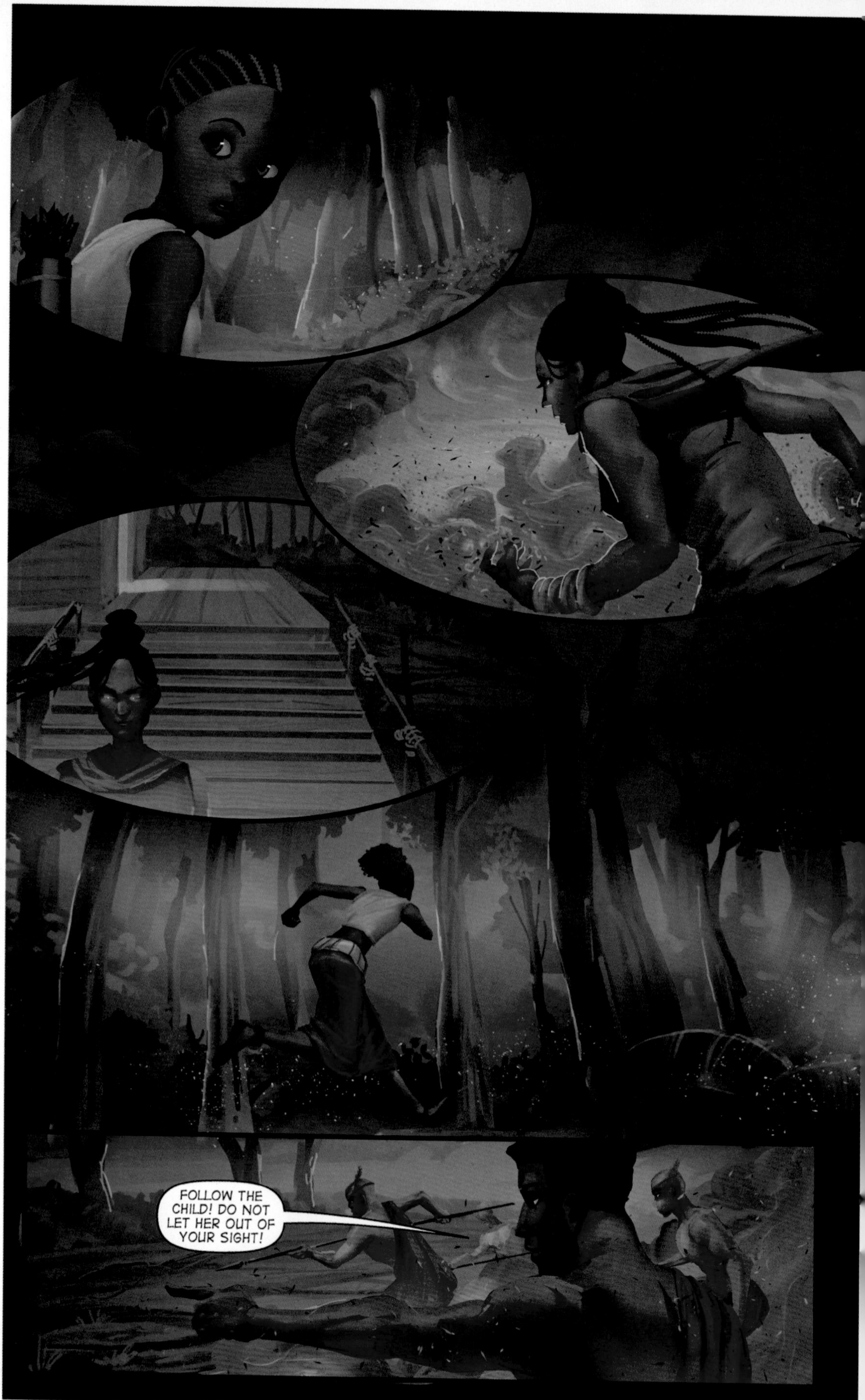
FOLLOW THE CHILD! DO NOT LET HER OUT OF YOUR SIGHT!

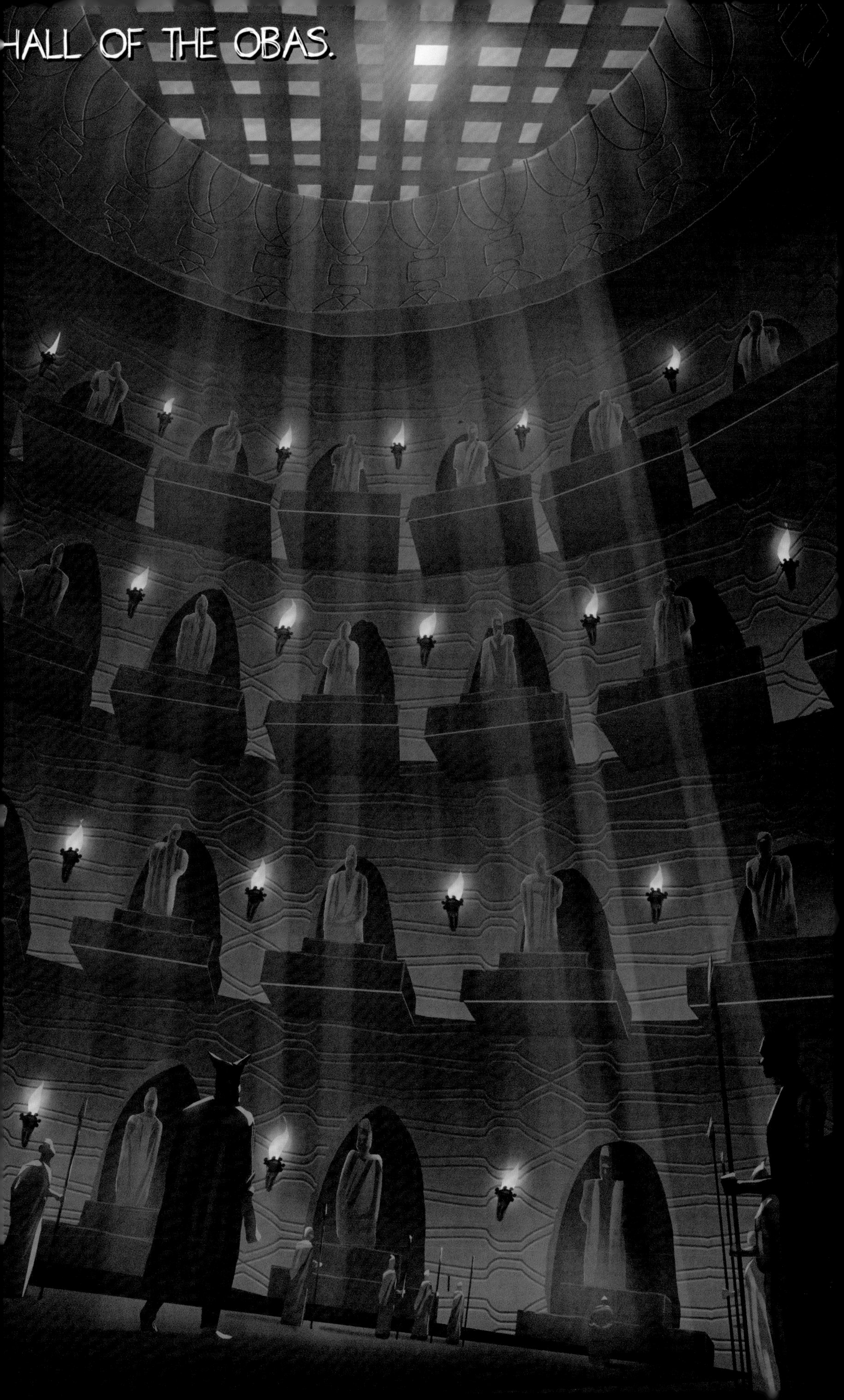
HALL OF THE OBAS.

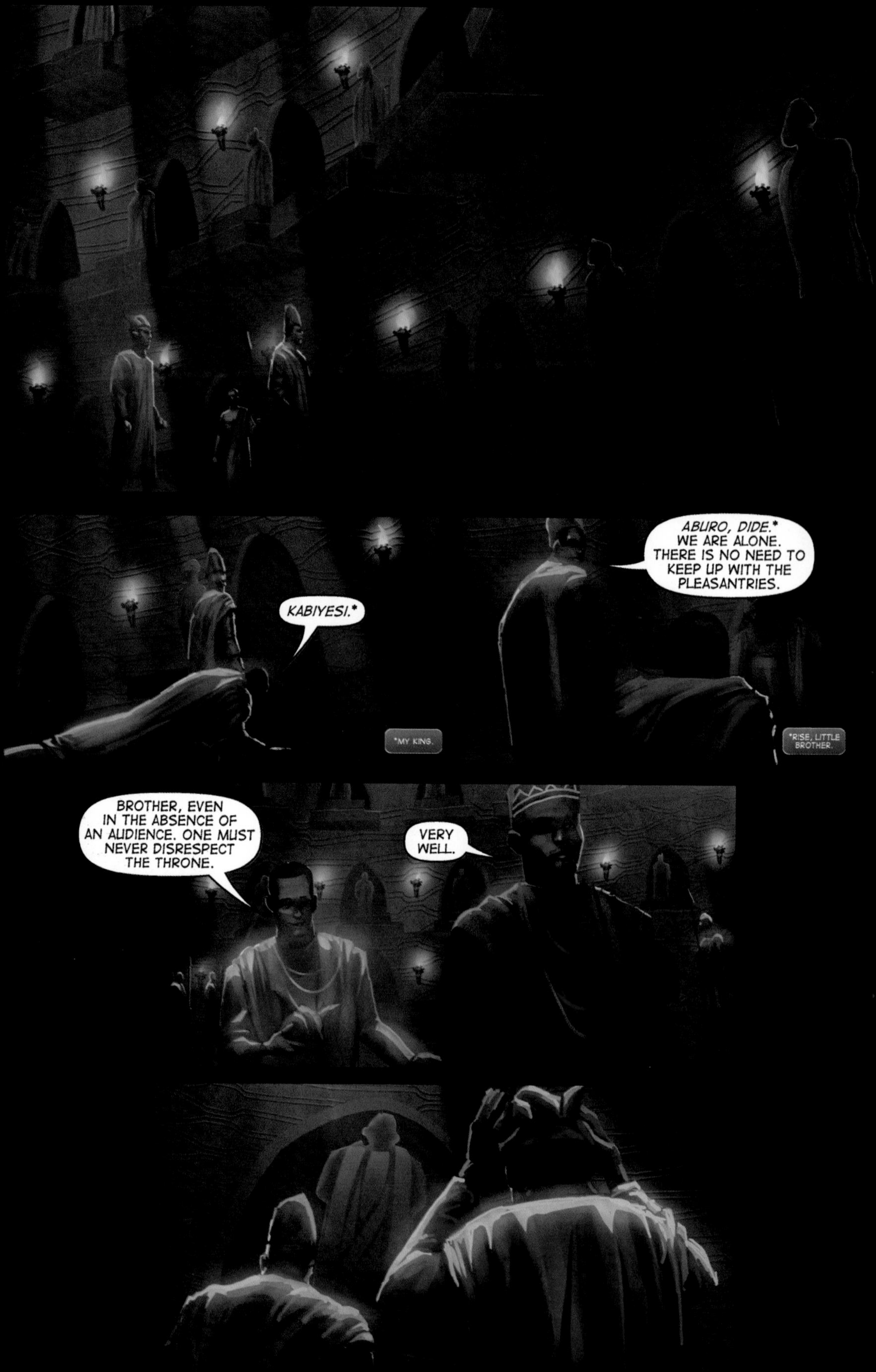
KABIYESI.*
*MY KING.
ABURO, DIDE.* WE ARE ALONE. THERE IS NO NEED TO KEEP UP WITH THE PLEASANTRIES.
*RISE, LITTLE BROTHER.
BROTHER, EVEN IN THE ABSENCE OF AN AUDIENCE. ONE MUST NEVER DISRESPECT THE THRONE.
VERY WELL.

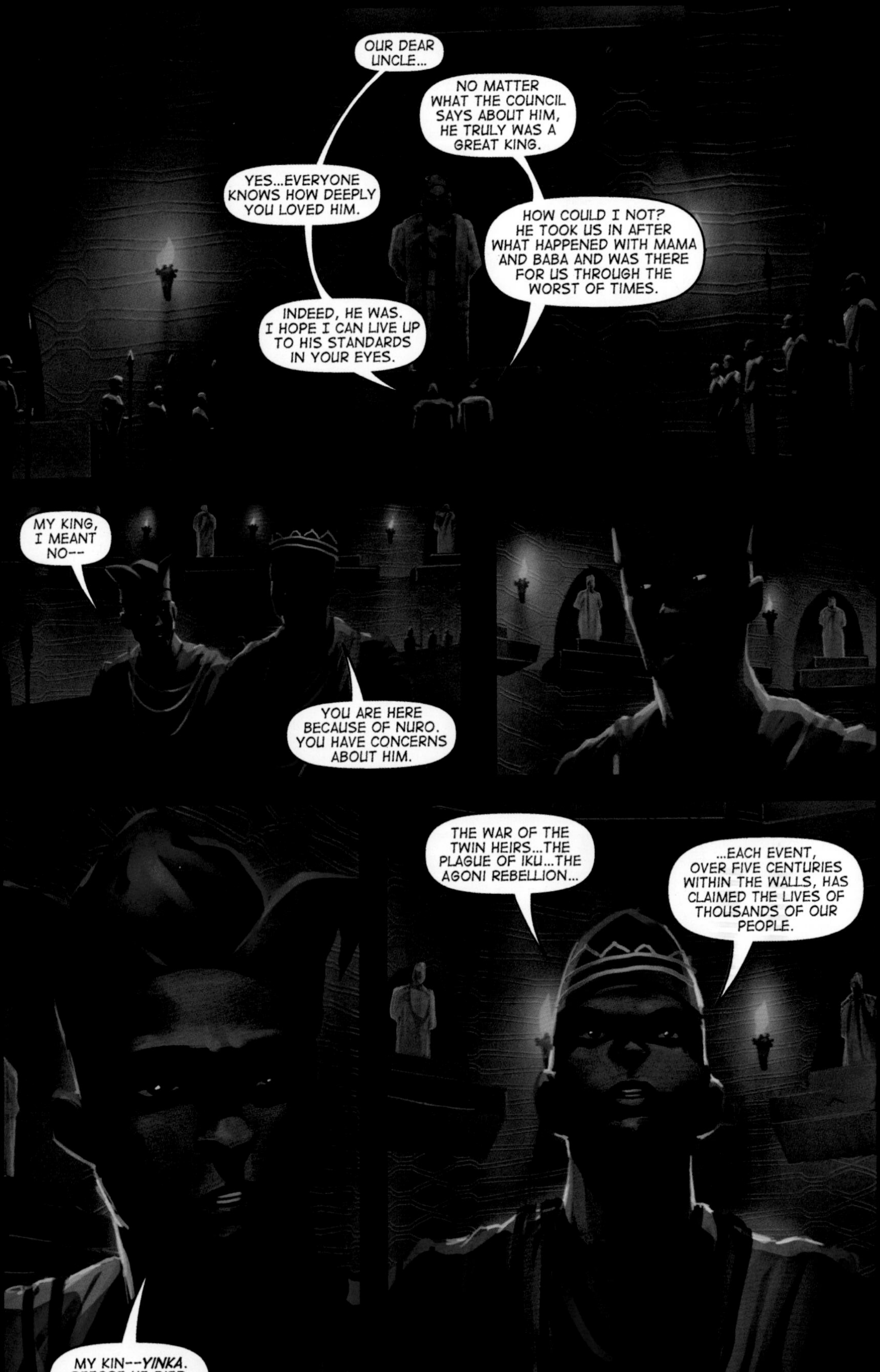
OUR DEAR UNCLE...
NO MATTER WHAT THE COUNCIL SAYS ABOUT HIM, HE TRULY WAS A GREAT KING.
YES...EVERYONE KNOWS HOW DEEPLY YOU LOVED HIM.
HOW COULD I NOT? HE TOOK US IN AFTER WHAT HAPPENED WITH MAMA AND BABA AND WAS THERE FOR US THROUGH THE WORST OF TIMES.
INDEED, HE WAS. I HOPE I CAN LIVE UP TO HIS STANDARDS IN YOUR EYES.
MY KING, I MEANT NO--
YOU ARE HERE BECAUSE OF NURO. YOU HAVE CONCERNS ABOUT HIM.
MY KIN--*YINKA*. BEFORE HE DIED, UNCLE DID WARN US ABOUT--
THE WAR OF THE TWIN HEIRS...THE PLAGUE OF IKU...THE AGONI REBELLION...
...EACH EVENT, OVER FIVE CENTURIES WITHIN THE WALLS, HAS CLAIMED THE LIVES OF THOUSANDS OF OUR PEOPLE.

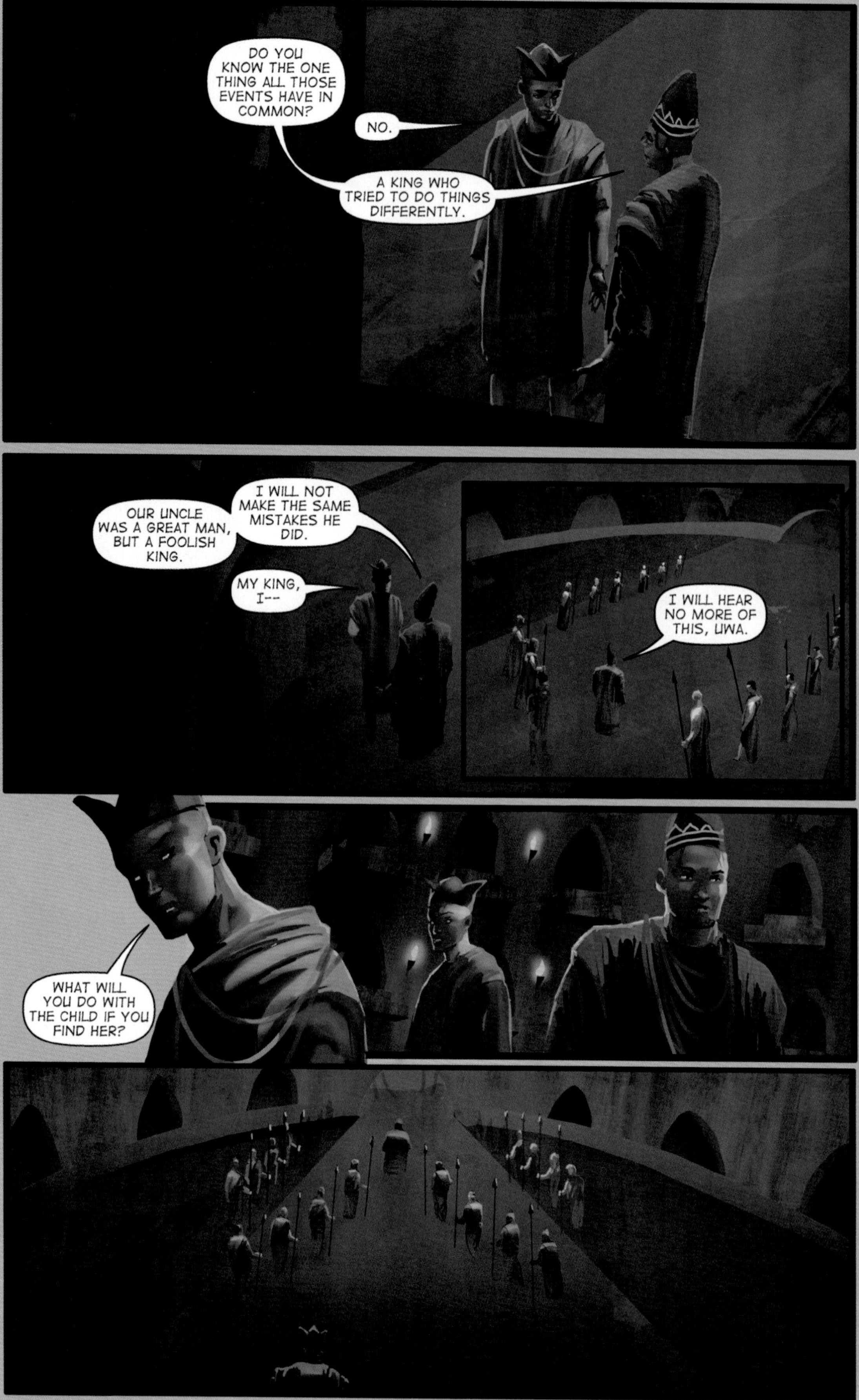
DO YOU KNOW THE ONE THING ALL THOSE EVENTS HAVE IN COMMON?
NO.
A KING WHO TRIED TO DO THINGS DIFFERENTLY.
OUR UNCLE WAS A GREAT MAN, BUT A FOOLISH KING.
I WILL NOT MAKE THE SAME MISTAKES HE DID.
MY KING, I--
I WILL HEAR NO MORE OF THIS, UWA.
WHAT WILL YOU DO WITH THE CHILD IF YOU FIND HER?

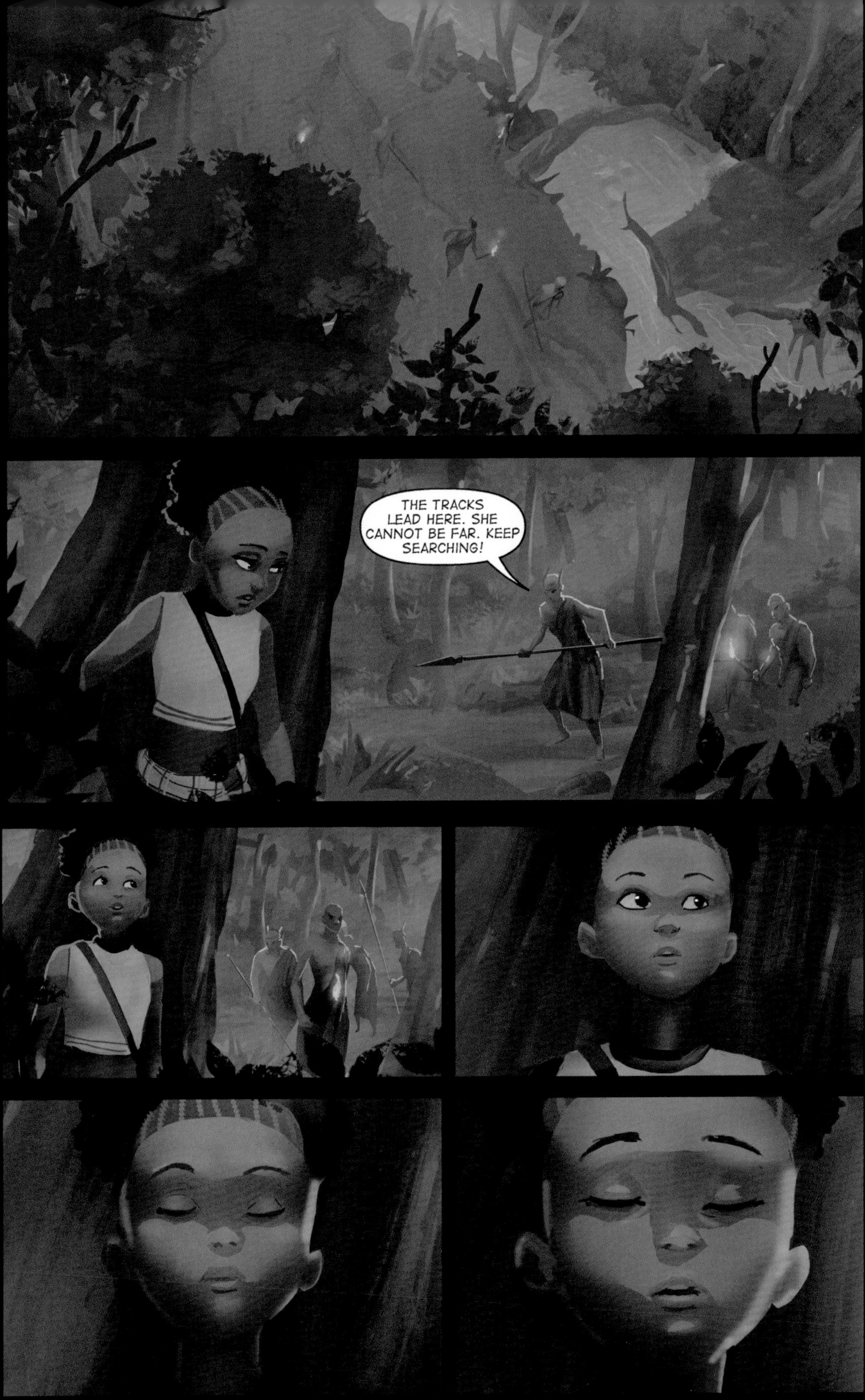
THE TRACKS LEAD HERE. SHE CANNOT BE FAR. KEEP SEARCHING!

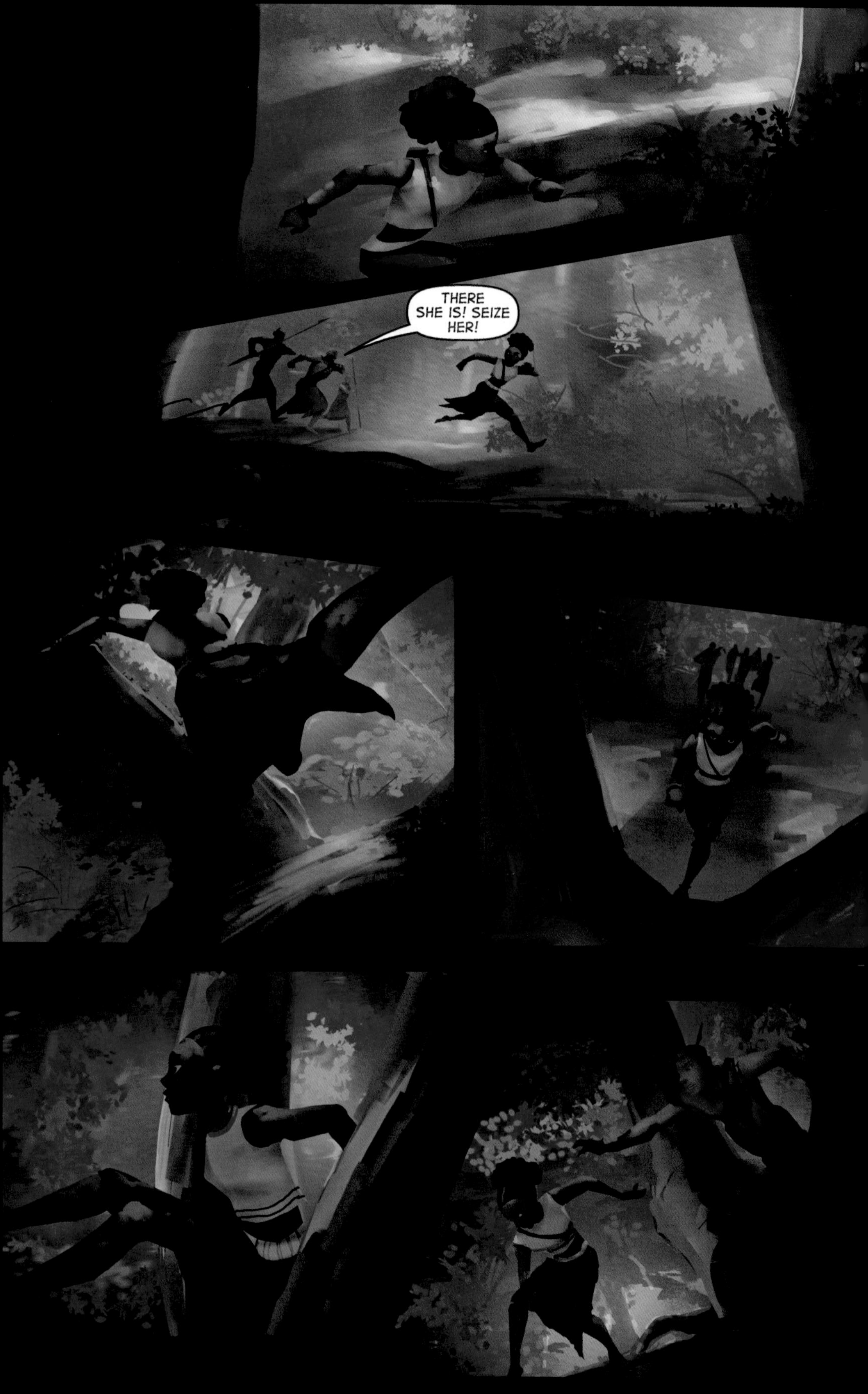
THERE SHE IS! SEIZE HER!

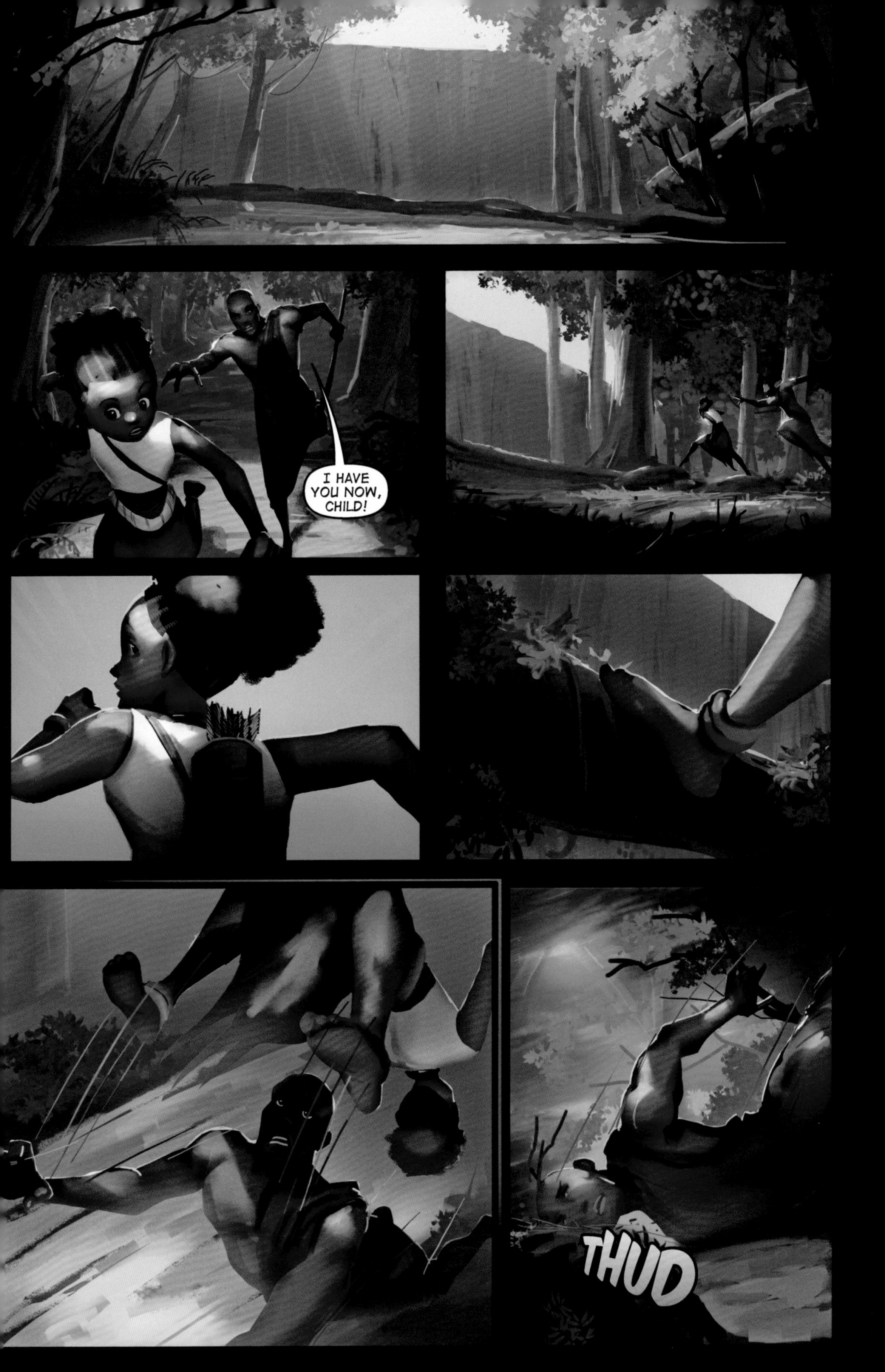
I HAVE YOU NOW, CHILD!
THUD

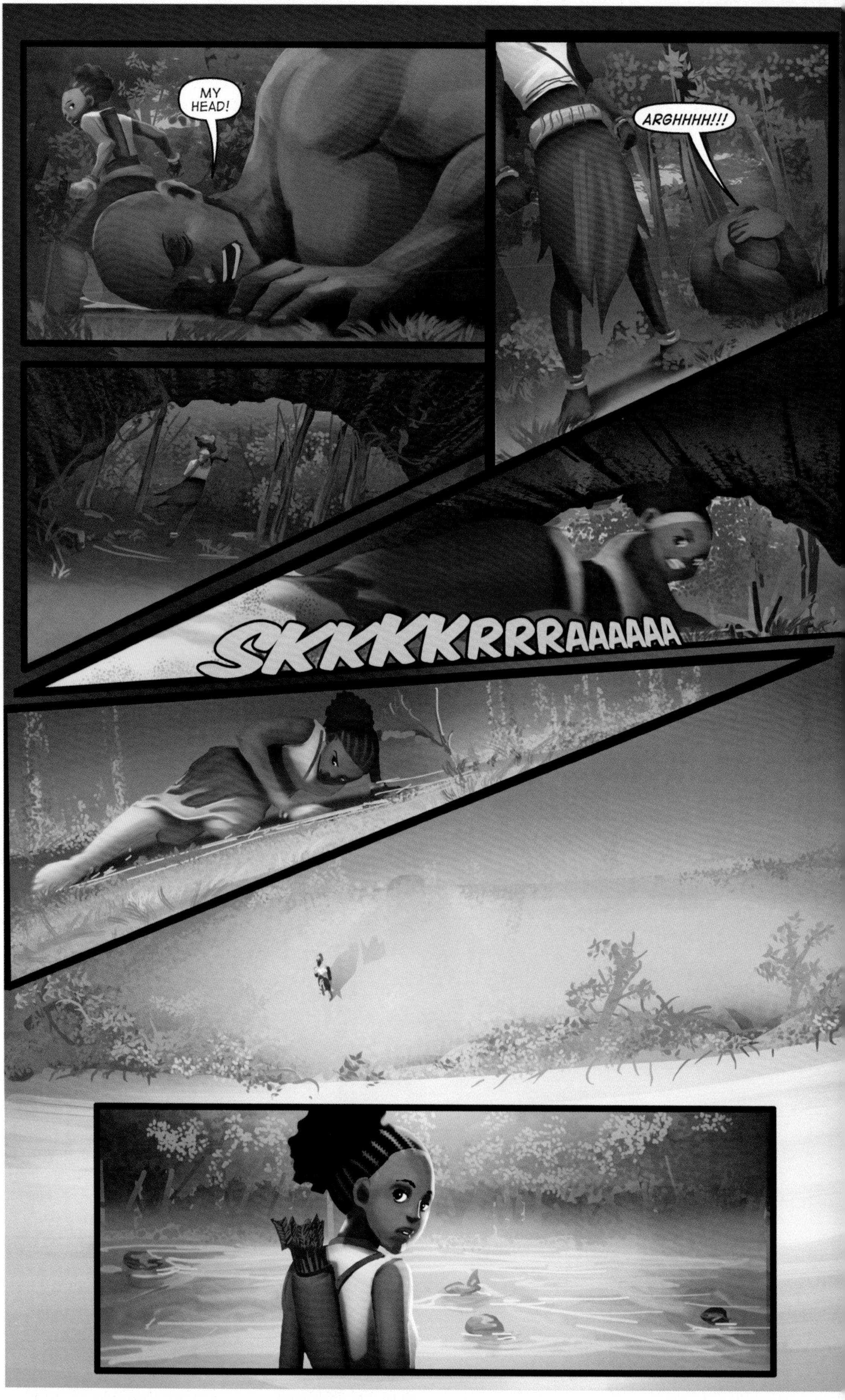
MY HEAD!
ARGHHHH!!!
SKKKKRRRAAAAAA

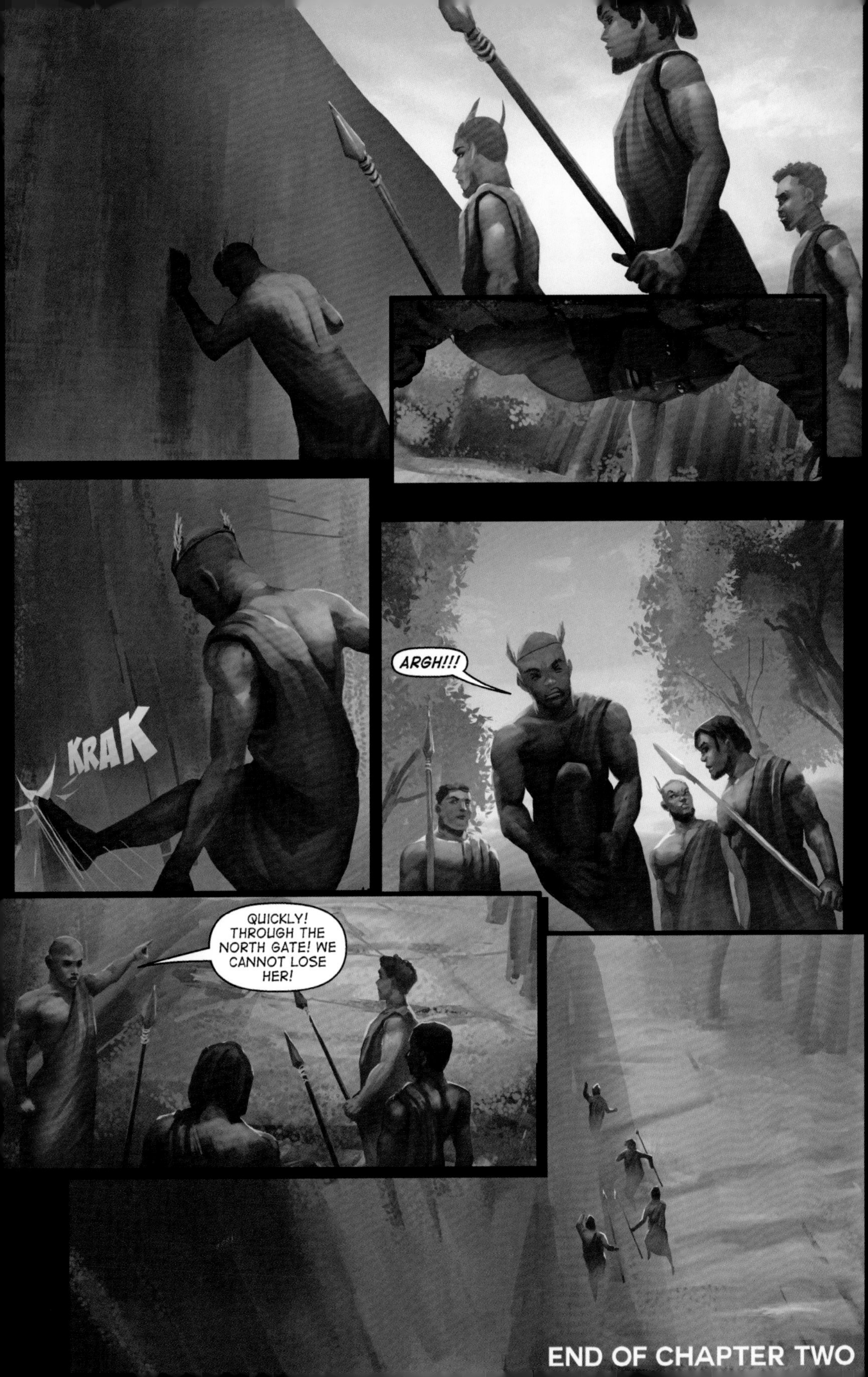
KRAK
ARGH!!!
QUICKLY! THROUGH THE NORTH GATE! WE CANNOT LOSE HER!
END OF CHAPTER TWO

CHAPTER THREE

Yorubaland

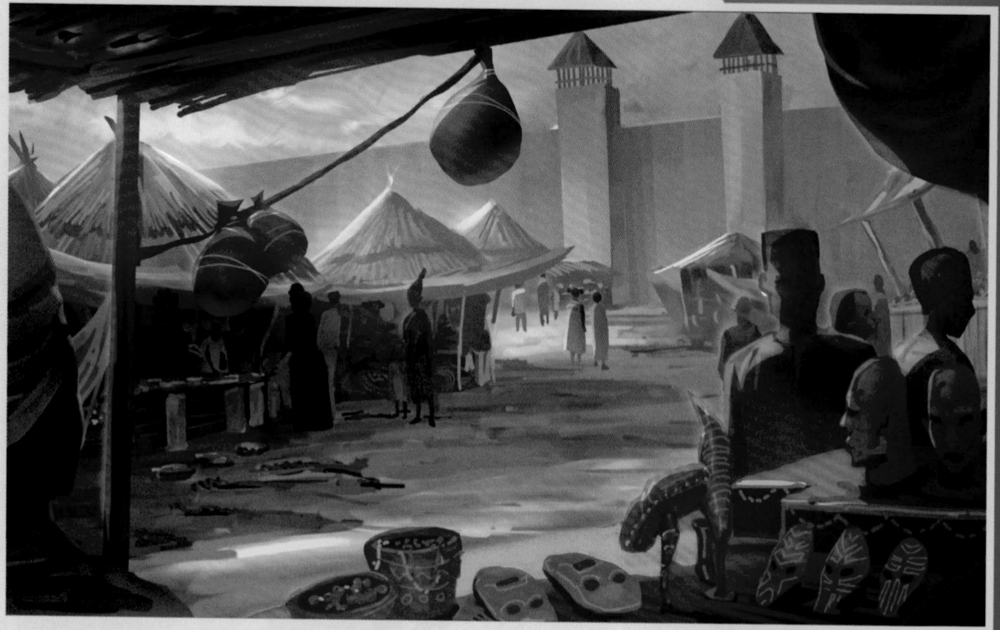

Throughout this story, you will see the term "Yorubaland" used to refer to the region and world our story takes place in. This is very intentional. Though this is a fictional story, it is heavily influenced by the geography, culture (names, locations, costumes, food, humor, and more) and ways of the Yoruba people. It is, however, important to highlight that some liberties have been taken to make this story independent. For example, our version of Yorubaland is different in terms of geography. That being said, we have gone to extreme lengths to keep the overall spirit of the Yoruba people intact, so as not to disrespect the culture in any way.

FUN FACT: The Yoruba people are an African ethnic group that inhabits western Africa, mainly Nigeria and Benin. Youruba also happens to be one of the three major tribes (Hausa and Igno being the other two) in Nigeria.

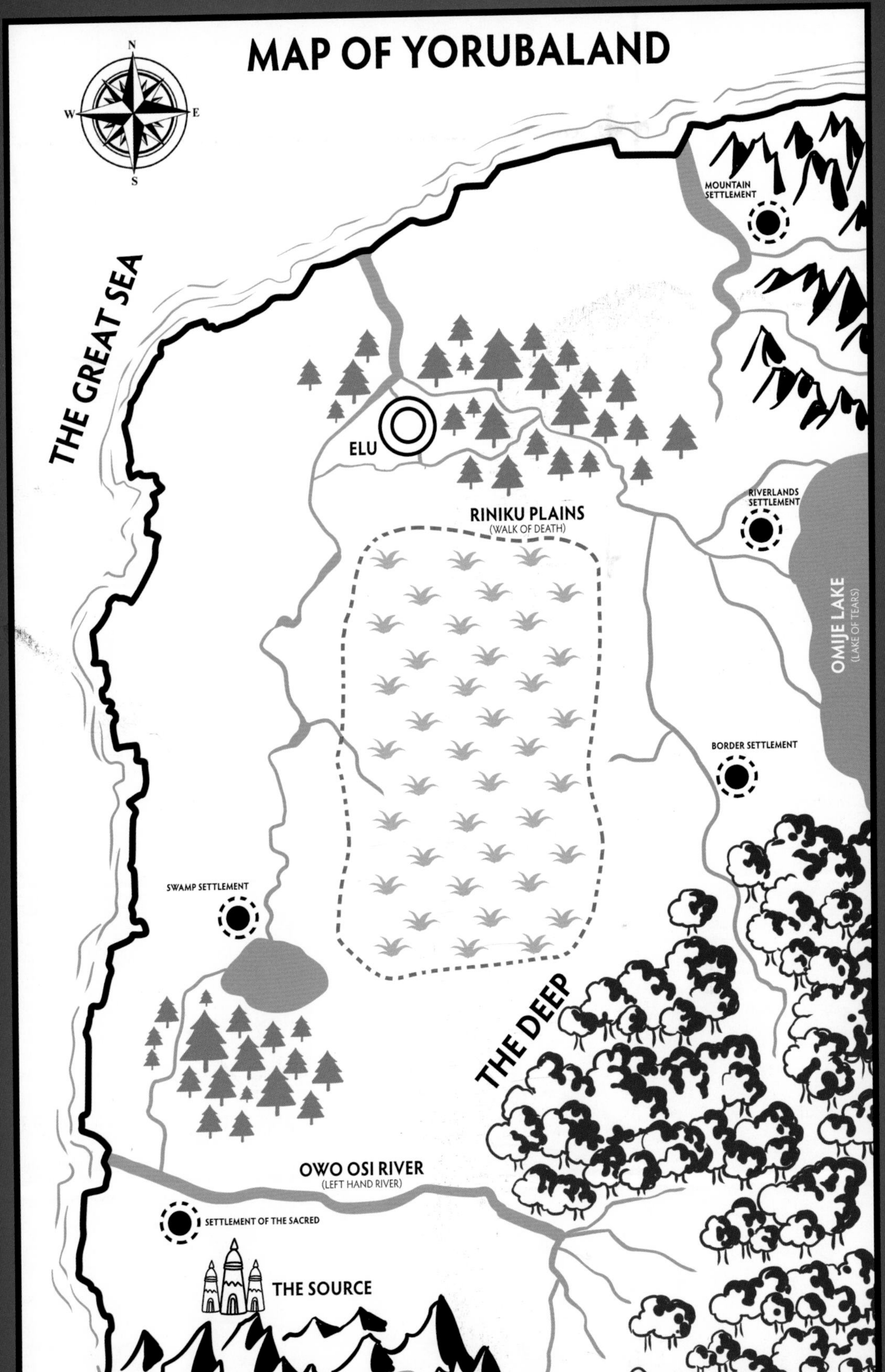

MAP OF YORUBALAND
N
S
E
W
THE GREAT SEA
MOUNTAIN SETTLEMENT
ELU
RINIKU PLAINS
(WALK OF DEATH)
RIVERLANDS SETTLEMENT
OMIJE LAKE
(LAKE OF TEARS)
BORDER SETTLEMENT
SWAMP SETTLEMENT
THE DEEP
OWO OSI RIVER
(LEFT HAND RIVER)
SETTLEMENT OF THE SACRED
THE SOURCE

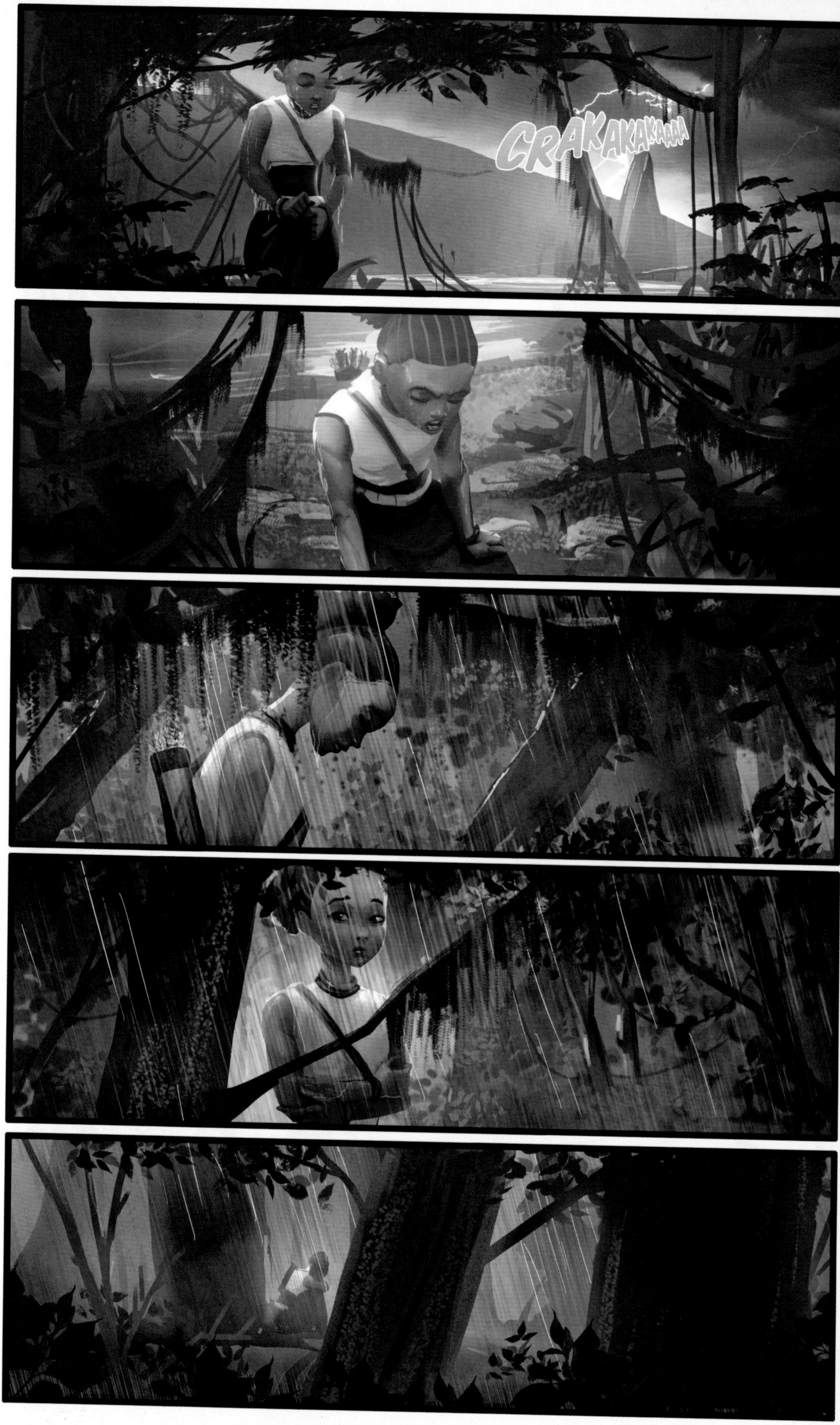
CRAKAKAKAAAA

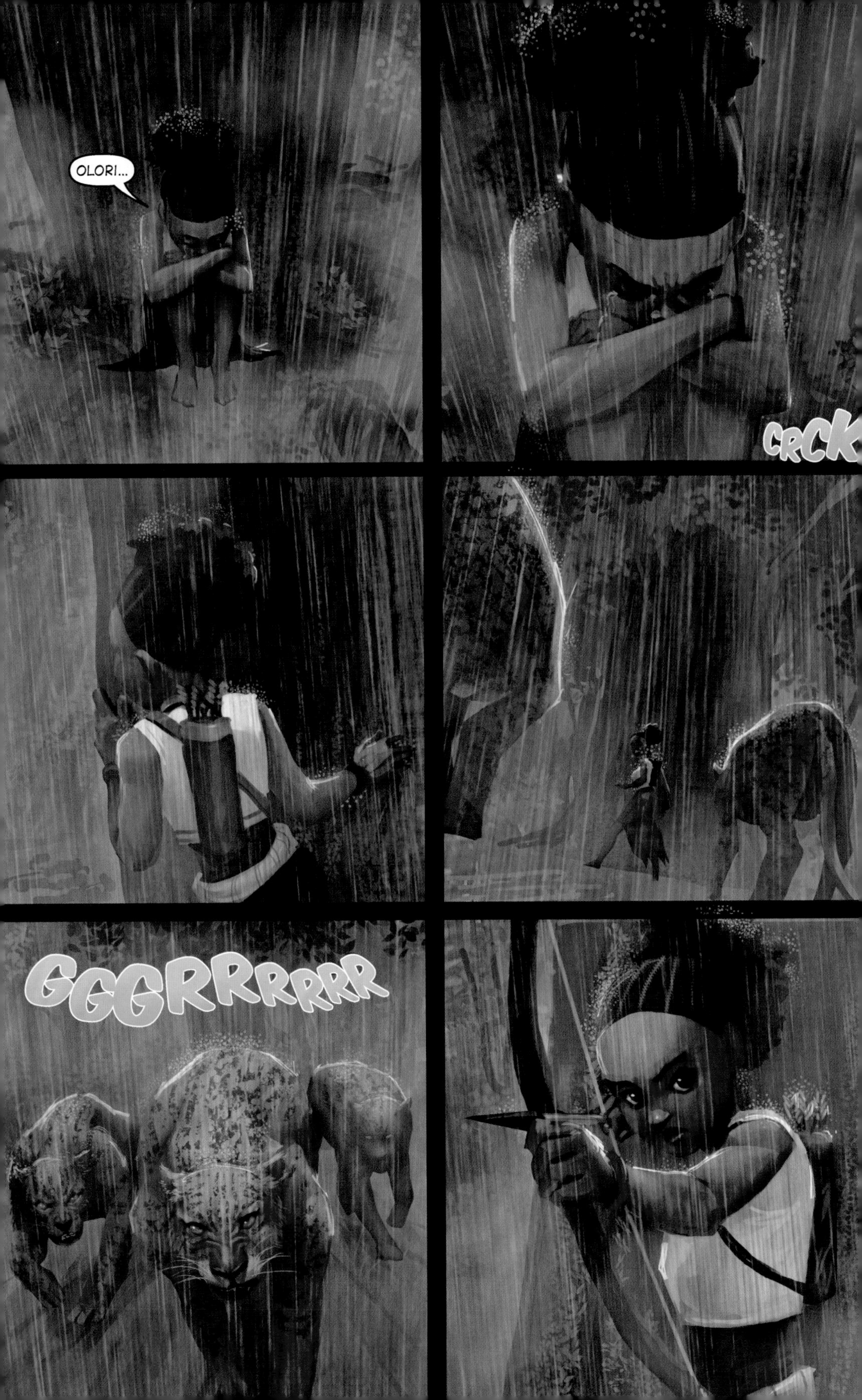
OLORI...
CRCK
GGGRRRRRR

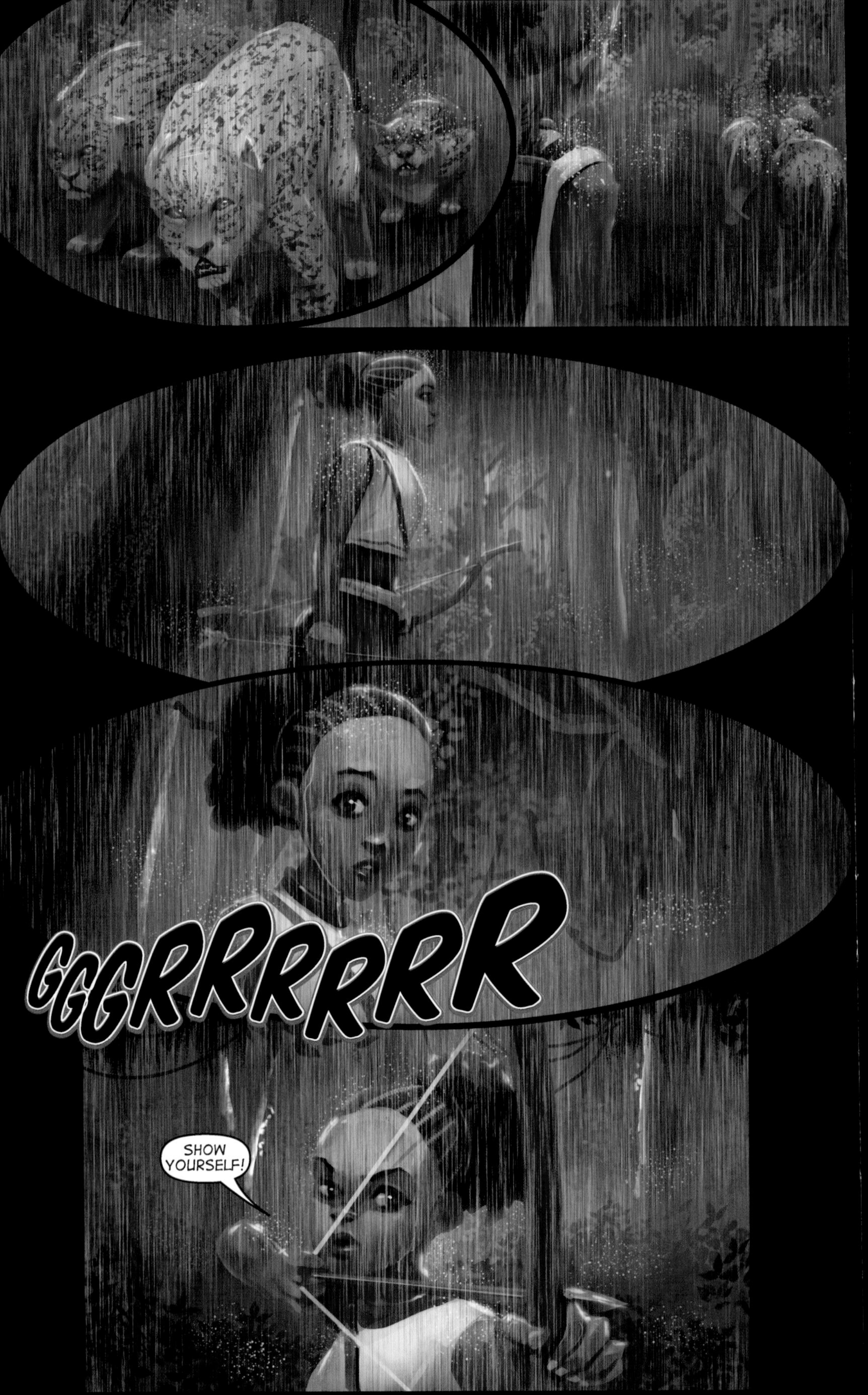
GGGRRRRRR
SHOW YOURSELF!

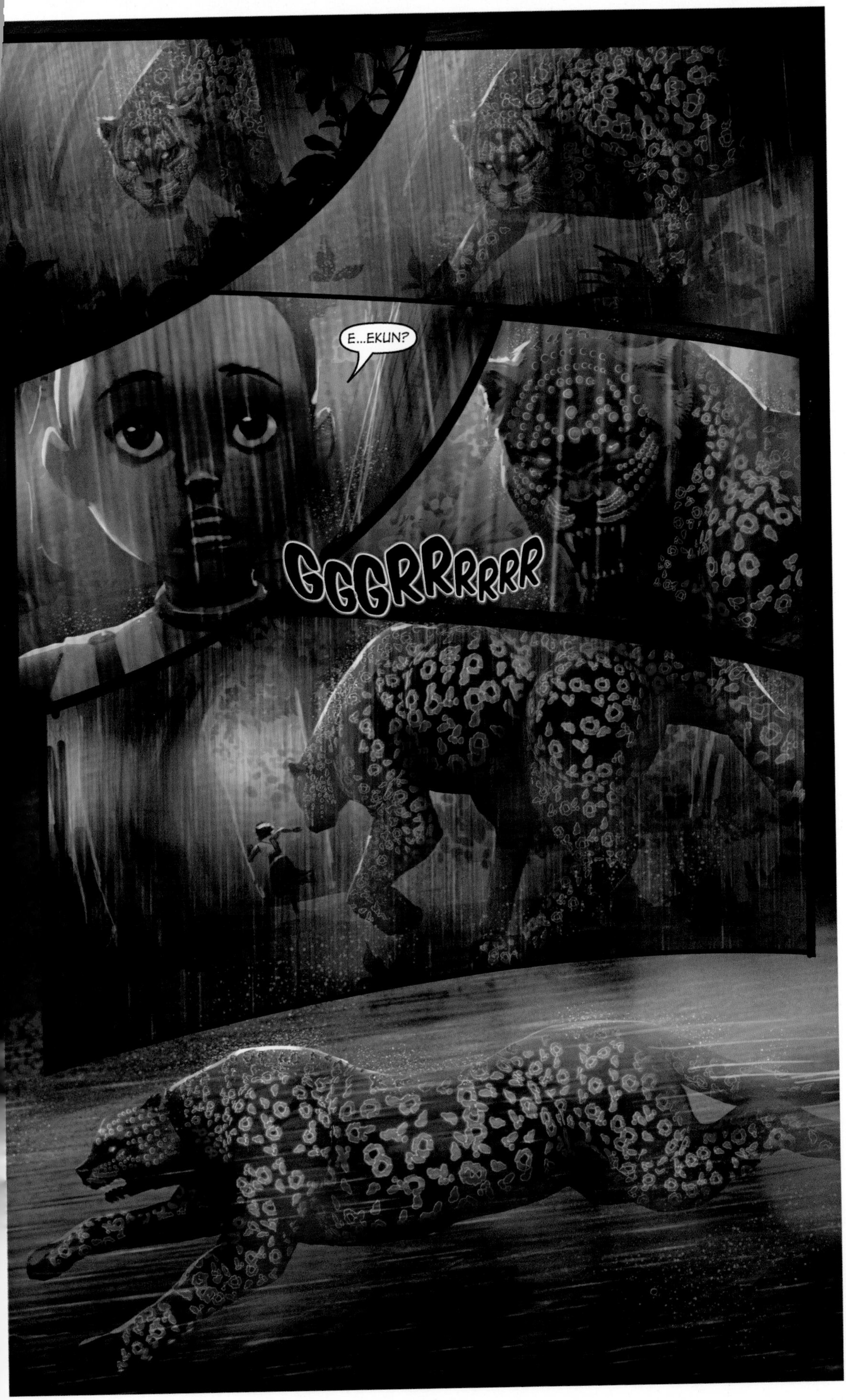
E...EKUN?
GGGRRRRRR

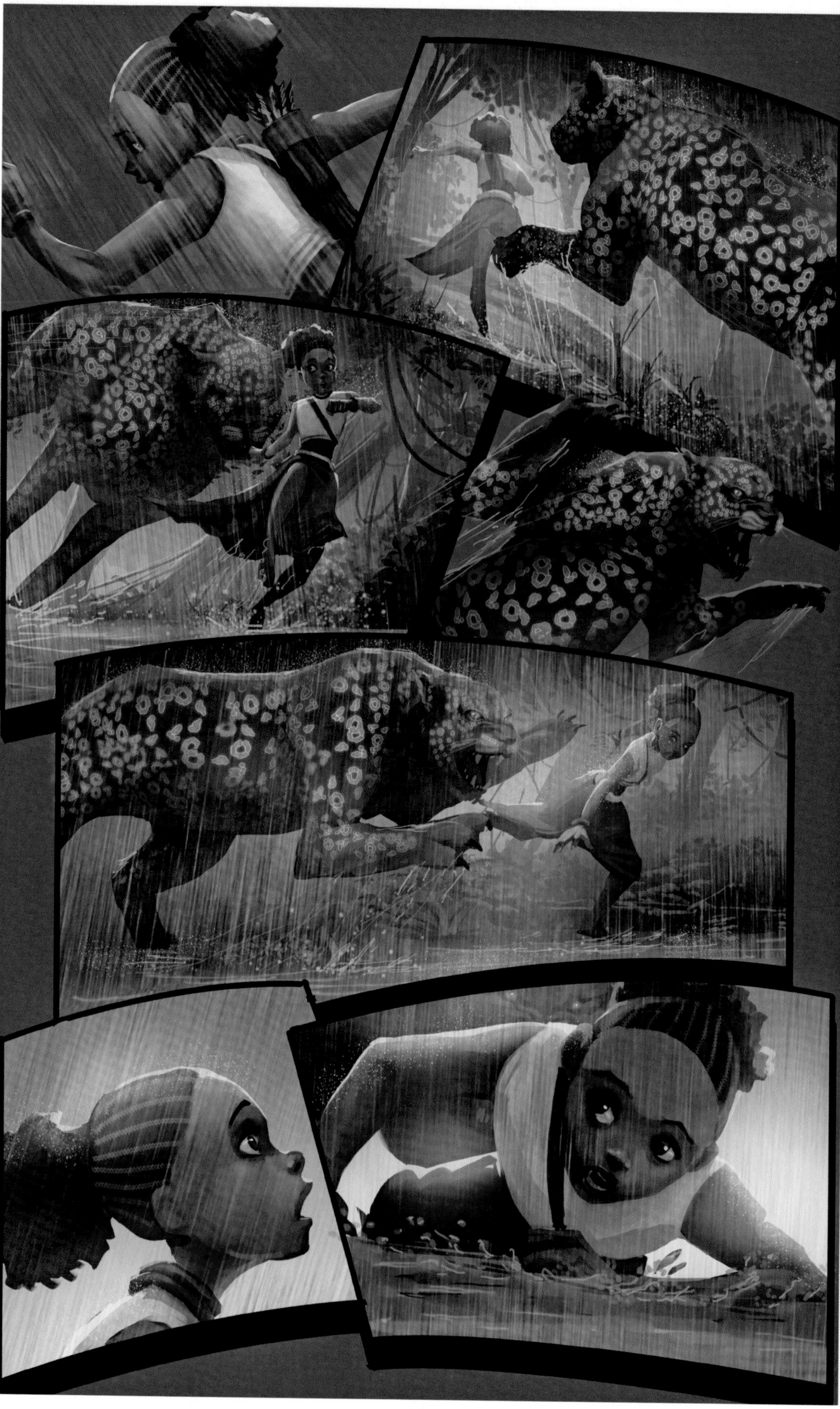

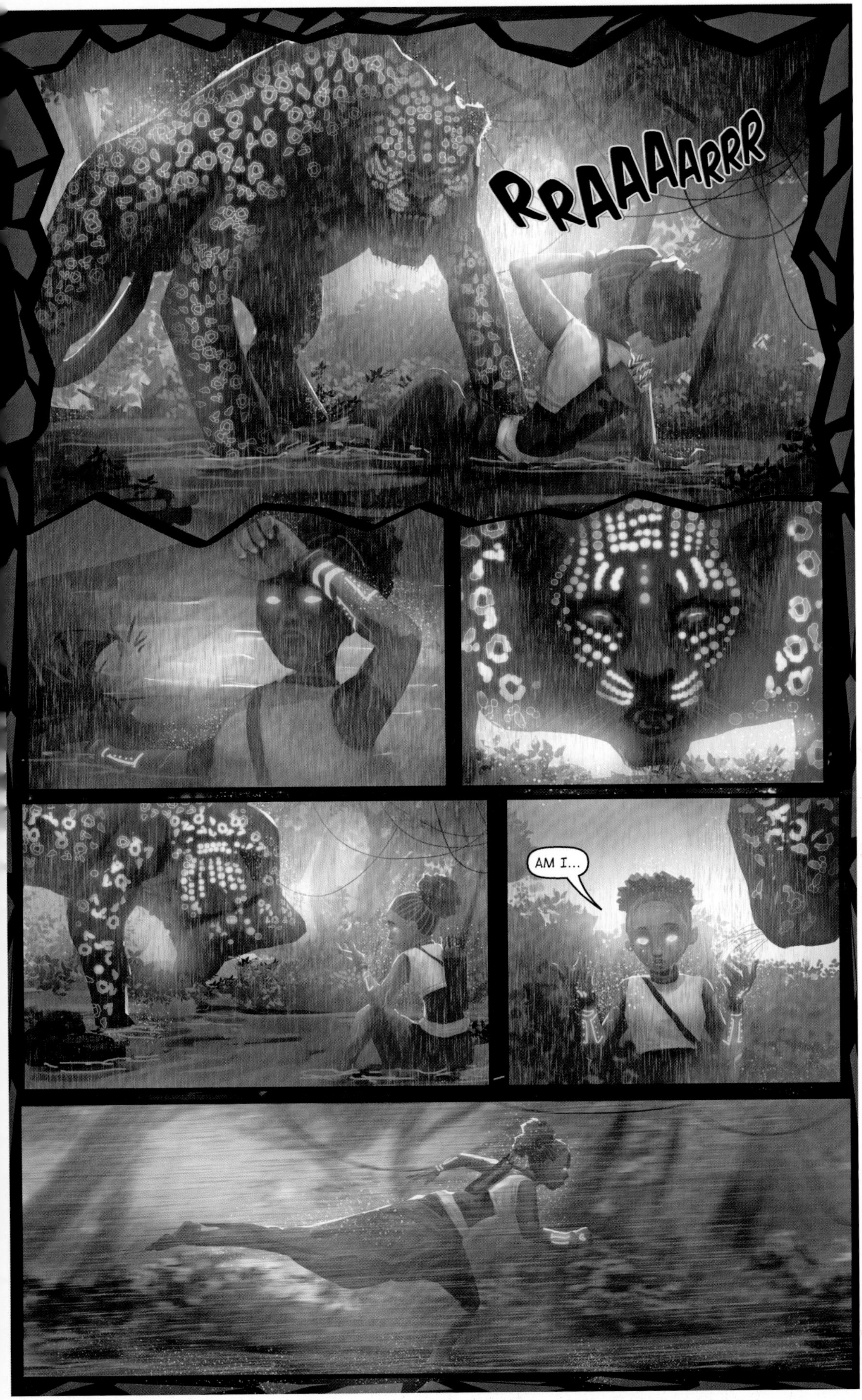
RRAAAARRR
AM I...

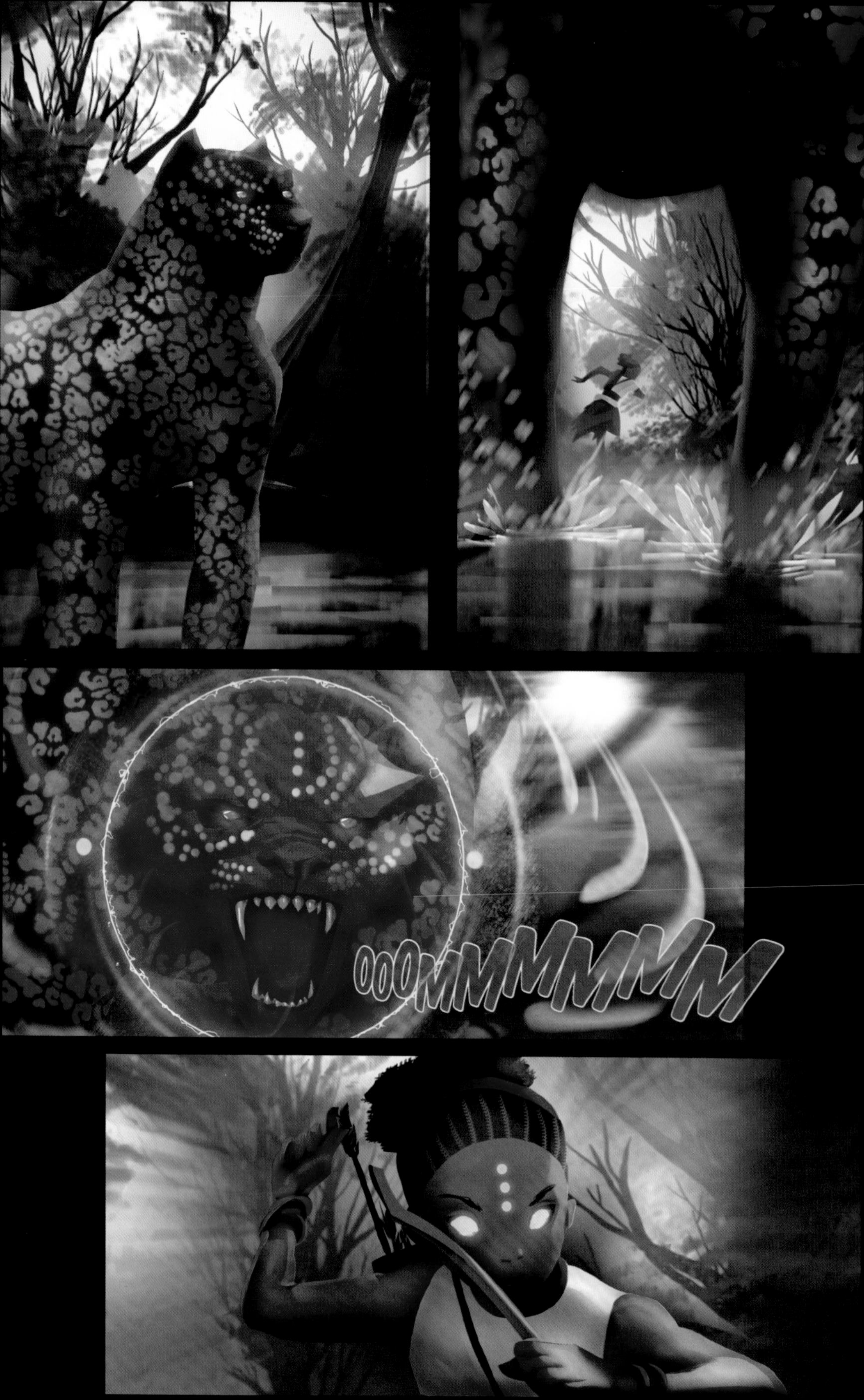
OOOMMMMMMM

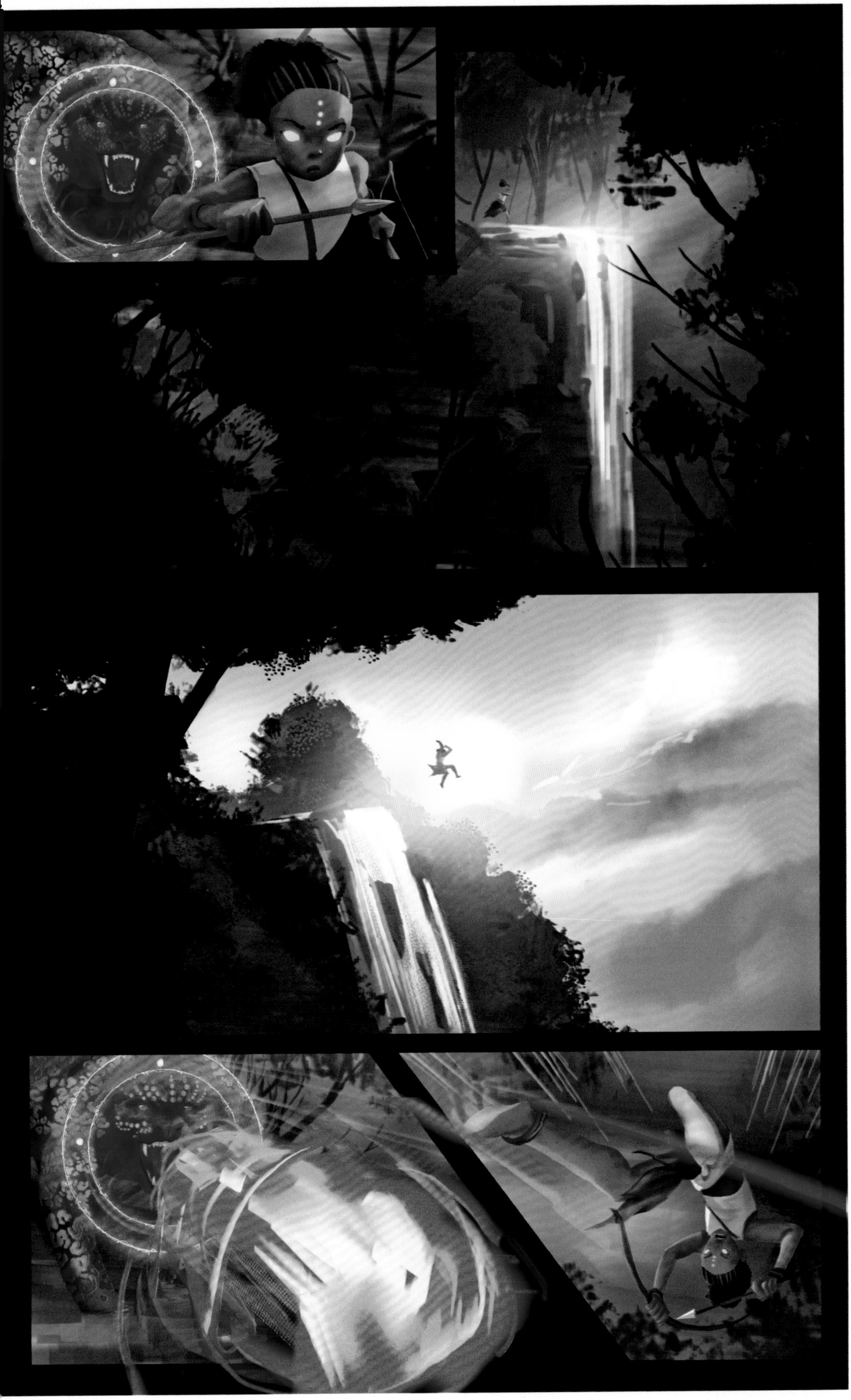

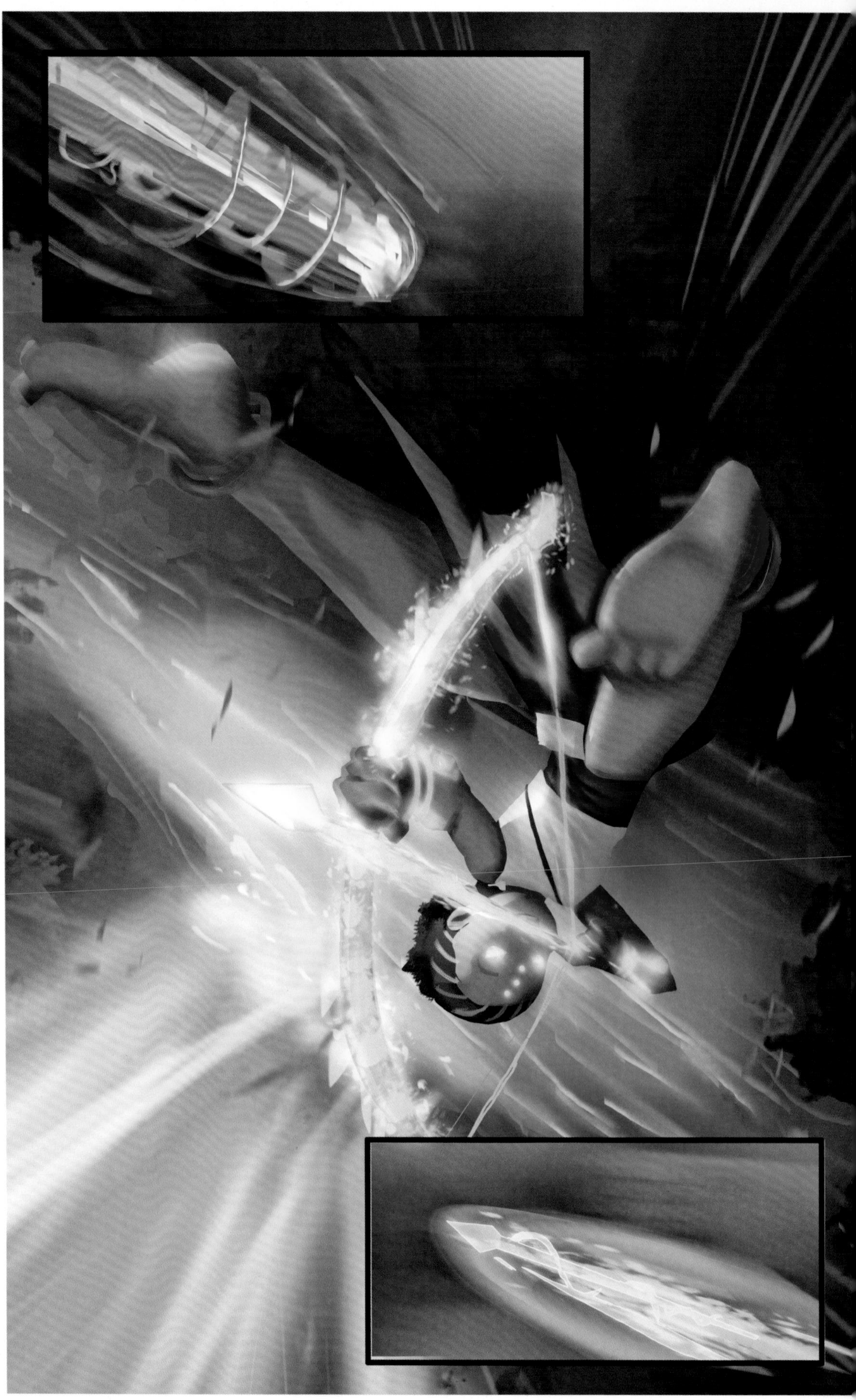

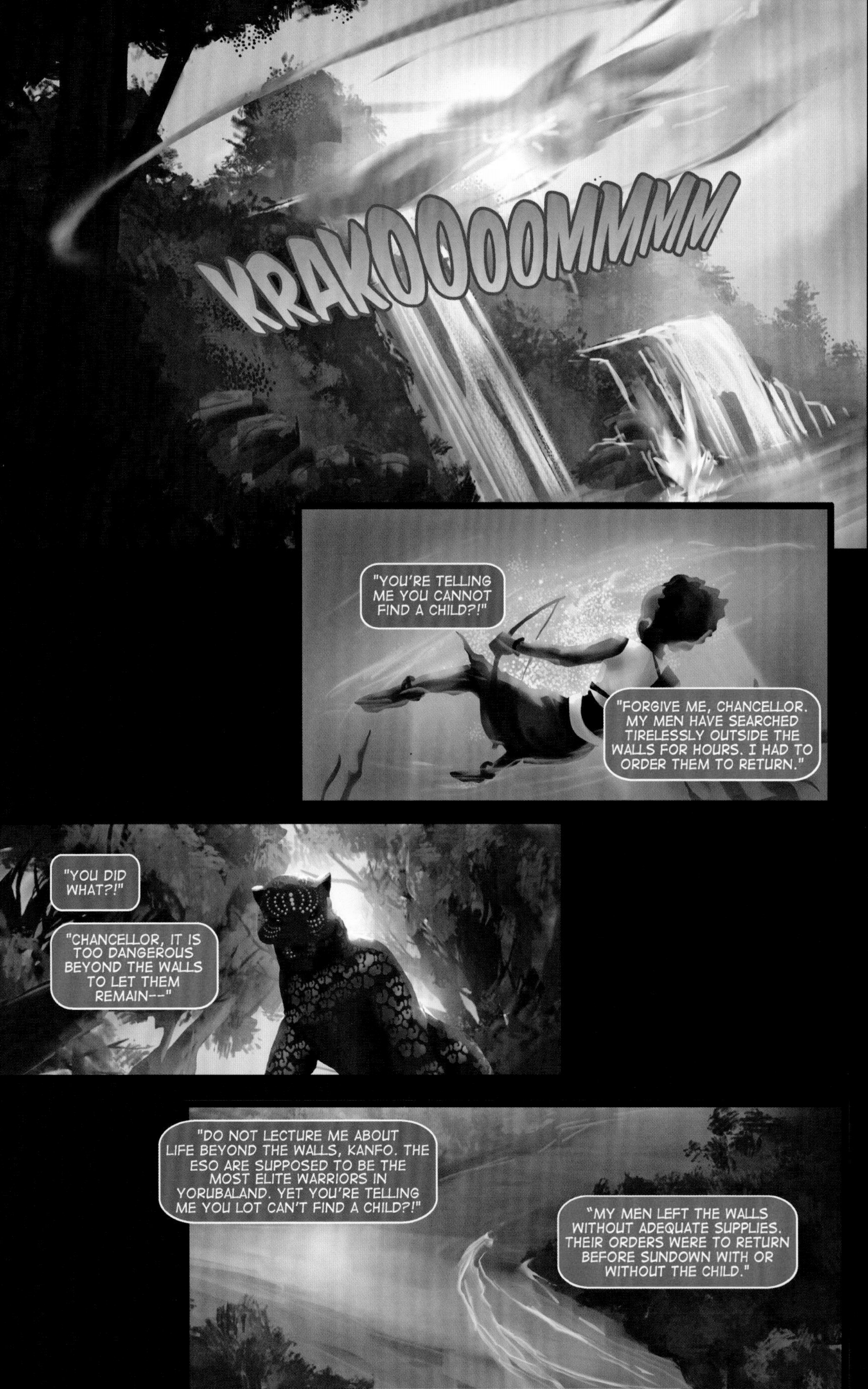
KRAKOOOOMMMM
"YOU'RE TELLING ME YOU CANNOT FIND A CHILD?!"
"FORGIVE ME, CHANCELLOR. MY MEN HAVE SEARCHED TIRELESSLY OUTSIDE THE WALLS FOR HOURS. I HAD TO ORDER THEM TO RETURN."
"YOU DID WHAT?!"
"CHANCELLOR, IT IS TOO DANGEROUS BEYOND THE WALLS TO LET THEM REMAIN--"
"DO NOT LECTURE ME ABOUT LIFE BEYOND THE WALLS, KANFO. THE ESO ARE SUPPOSED TO BE THE MOST ELITE WARRIORS IN YORUBALAND. YET YOU'RE TELLING ME YOU LOT CAN'T FIND A CHILD?!"
"MY MEN LEFT THE WALLS WITHOUT ADEQUATE SUPPLIES. THEIR ORDERS WERE TO RETURN BEFORE SUNDOWN WITH OR WITHOUT THE CHILD."

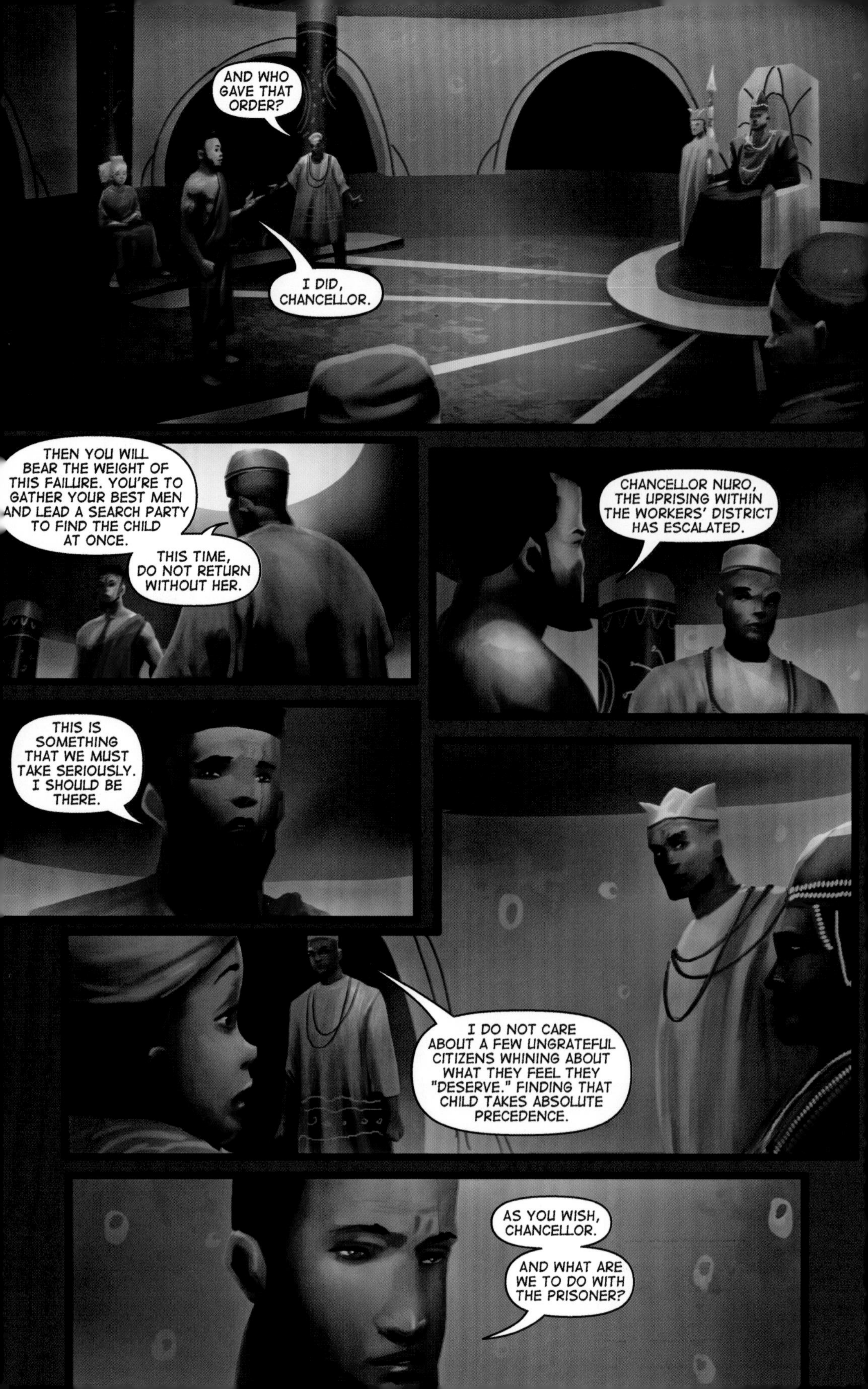
AND WHO GAVE THAT ORDER?
I DID, CHANCELLOR.
THEN YOU WILL BEAR THE WEIGHT OF THIS FAILURE. YOU'RE TO GATHER YOUR BEST MEN AND LEAD A SEARCH PARTY TO FIND THE CHILD AT ONCE.
THIS TIME, DO NOT RETURN WITHOUT HER.
CHANCELLOR NURO, THE UPRISING WITHIN THE WORKERS' DISTRICT HAS ESCALATED.
THIS IS SOMETHING THAT WE MUST TAKE SERIOUSLY. I SHOULD BE THERE.
I DO NOT CARE ABOUT A FEW UNGRATEFUL CITIZENS WHINING ABOUT WHAT THEY FEEL THEY "DESERVE." FINDING THAT CHILD TAKES ABSOLUTE PRECEDENCE.
AS YOU WISH, CHANCELLOR.
AND WHAT ARE WE TO DO WITH THE PRISONER?

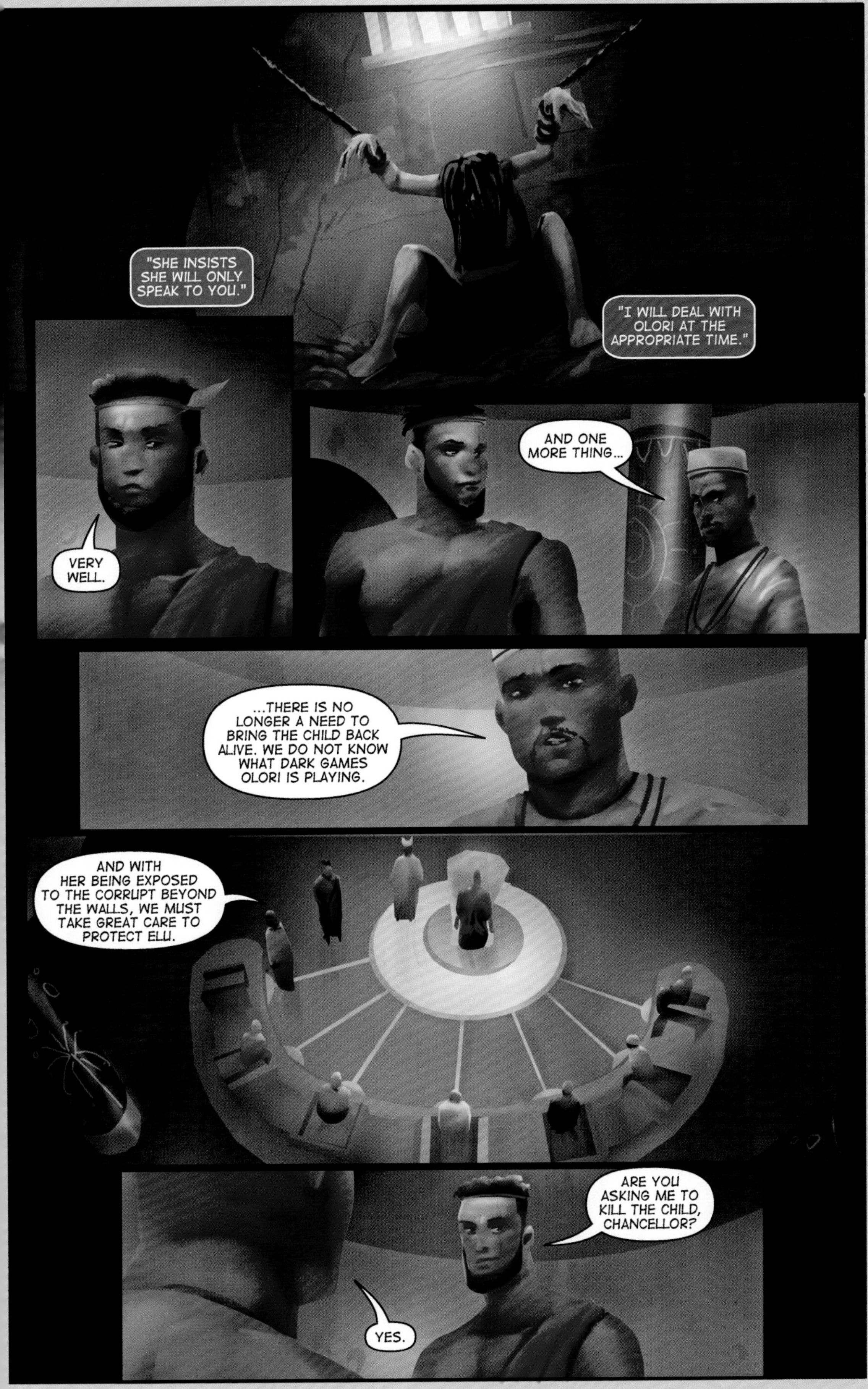
"SHE INSISTS SHE WILL ONLY SPEAK TO YOU."
"I WILL DEAL WITH OLORI AT THE APPROPRIATE TIME."
VERY WELL.
AND ONE MORE THING...
...THERE IS NO LONGER A NEED TO BRING THE CHILD BACK ALIVE. WE DO NOT KNOW WHAT DARK GAMES OLORI IS PLAYING.
AND WITH HER BEING EXPOSED TO THE CORRUPT BEYOND THE WALLS, WE MUST TAKE GREAT CARE TO PROTECT ELU.
ARE YOU ASKING ME TO KILL THE CHILD, CHANCELLOR?
YES.

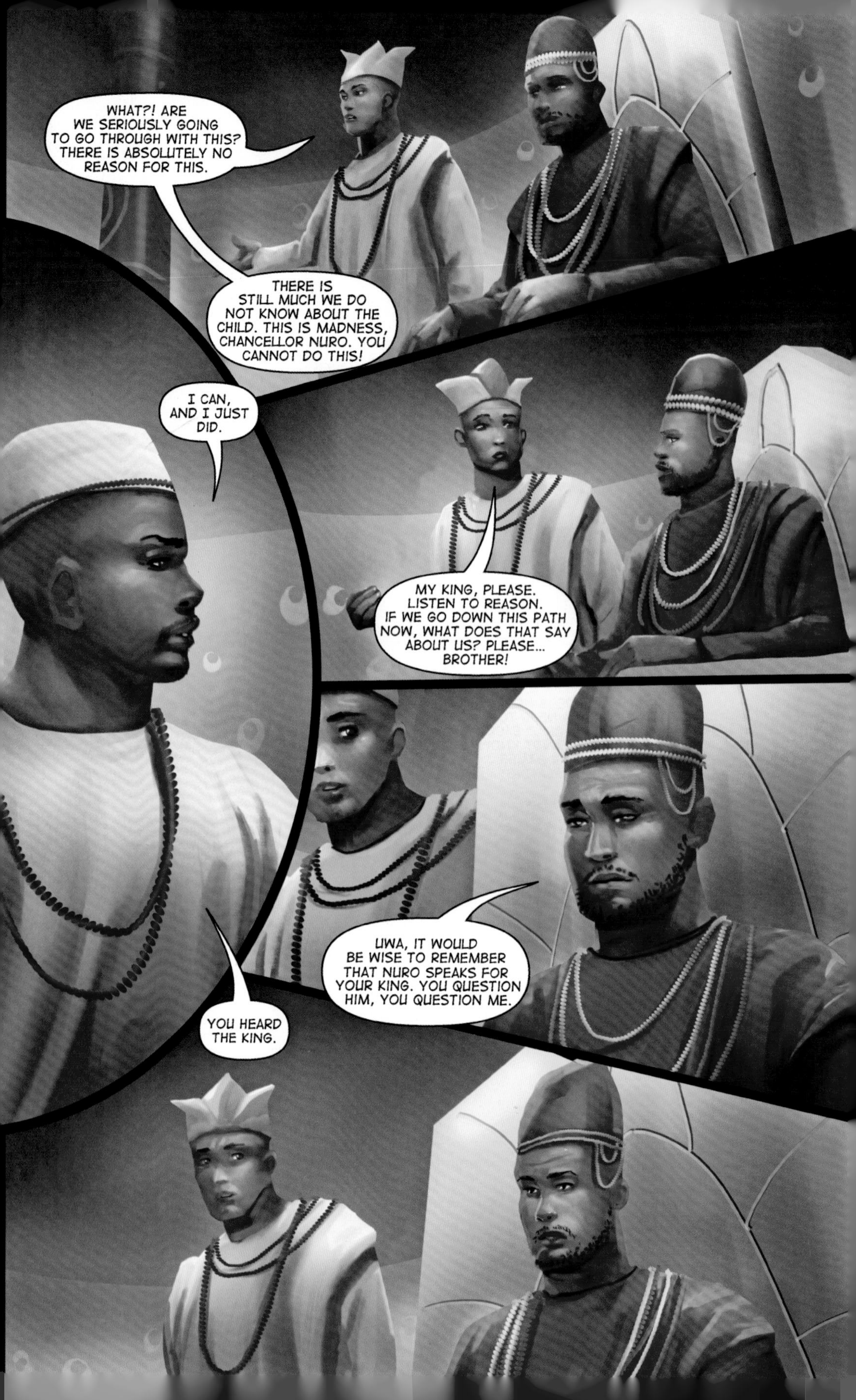
WHAT?! ARE WE SERIOUSLY GOING TO GO THROUGH WITH THIS? THERE IS ABSOLUTELY NO REASON FOR THIS.
THERE IS STILL MUCH WE DO NOT KNOW ABOUT THE CHILD. THIS IS MADNESS, CHANCELLOR NURO. YOU CANNOT DO THIS!
I CAN, AND I JUST DID.
MY KING, PLEASE. LISTEN TO REASON. IF WE GO DOWN THIS PATH NOW, WHAT DOES THAT SAY ABOUT US? PLEASE... BROTHER!
UWA, IT WOULD BE WISE TO REMEMBER THAT NURO SPEAKS FOR YOUR KING. YOU QUESTION HIM, YOU QUESTION ME.
YOU HEARD THE KING.

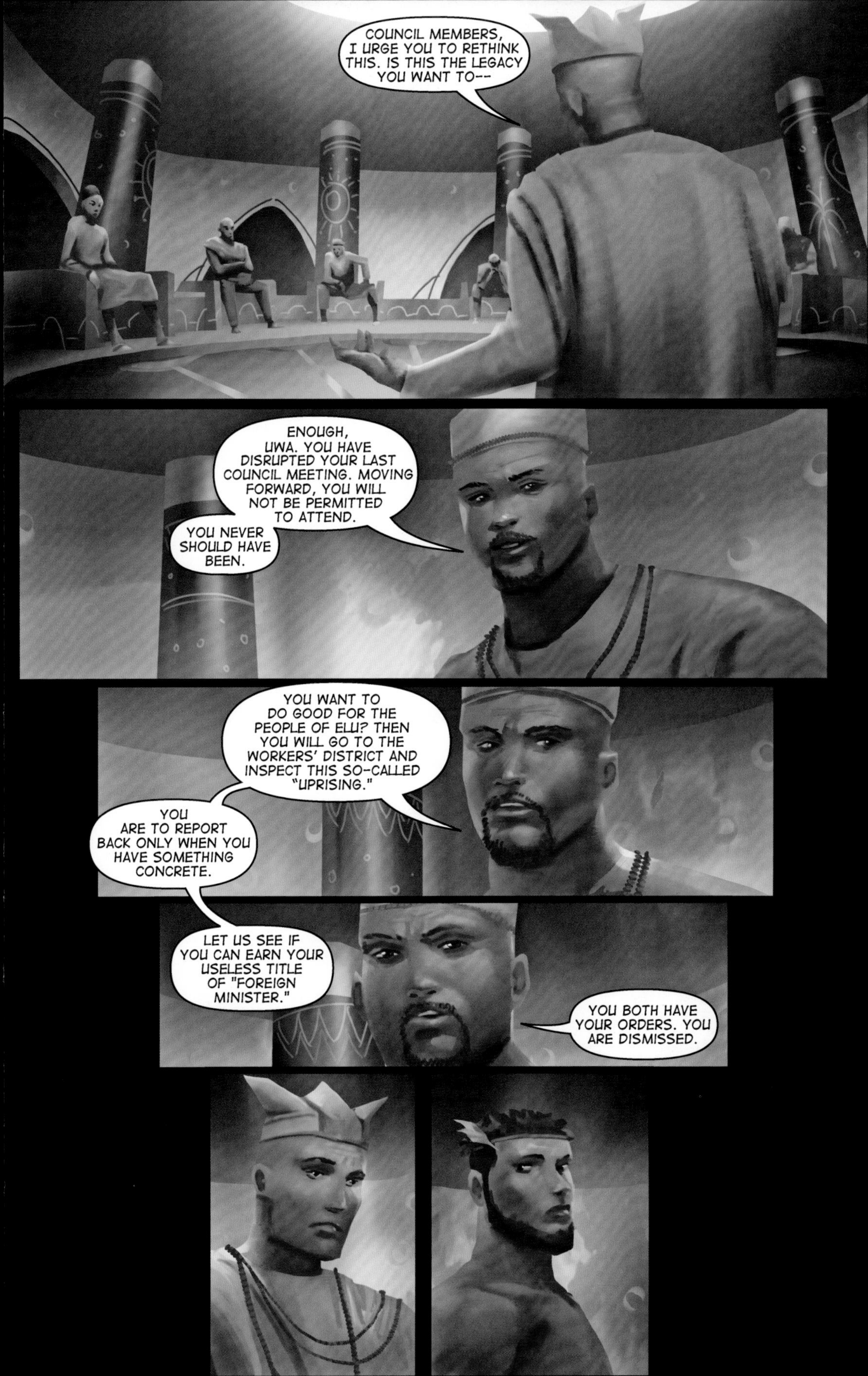
COUNCIL MEMBERS, I URGE YOU TO RETHINK THIS. IS THIS THE LEGACY YOU WANT TO--
ENOUGH, UWA. YOU HAVE DISRUPTED YOUR LAST COUNCIL MEETING. MOVING FORWARD, YOU WILL NOT BE PERMITTED TO ATTEND.
YOU NEVER SHOULD HAVE BEEN.
YOU WANT TO DO GOOD FOR THE PEOPLE OF ELU? THEN YOU WILL GO TO THE WORKERS' DISTRICT AND INSPECT THIS SO-CALLED "UPRISING."
YOU ARE TO REPORT BACK ONLY WHEN YOU HAVE SOMETHING CONCRETE.
LET US SEE IF YOU CAN EARN YOUR USELESS TITLE OF "FOREIGN MINISTER."
YOU BOTH HAVE YOUR ORDERS. YOU ARE DISMISSED.

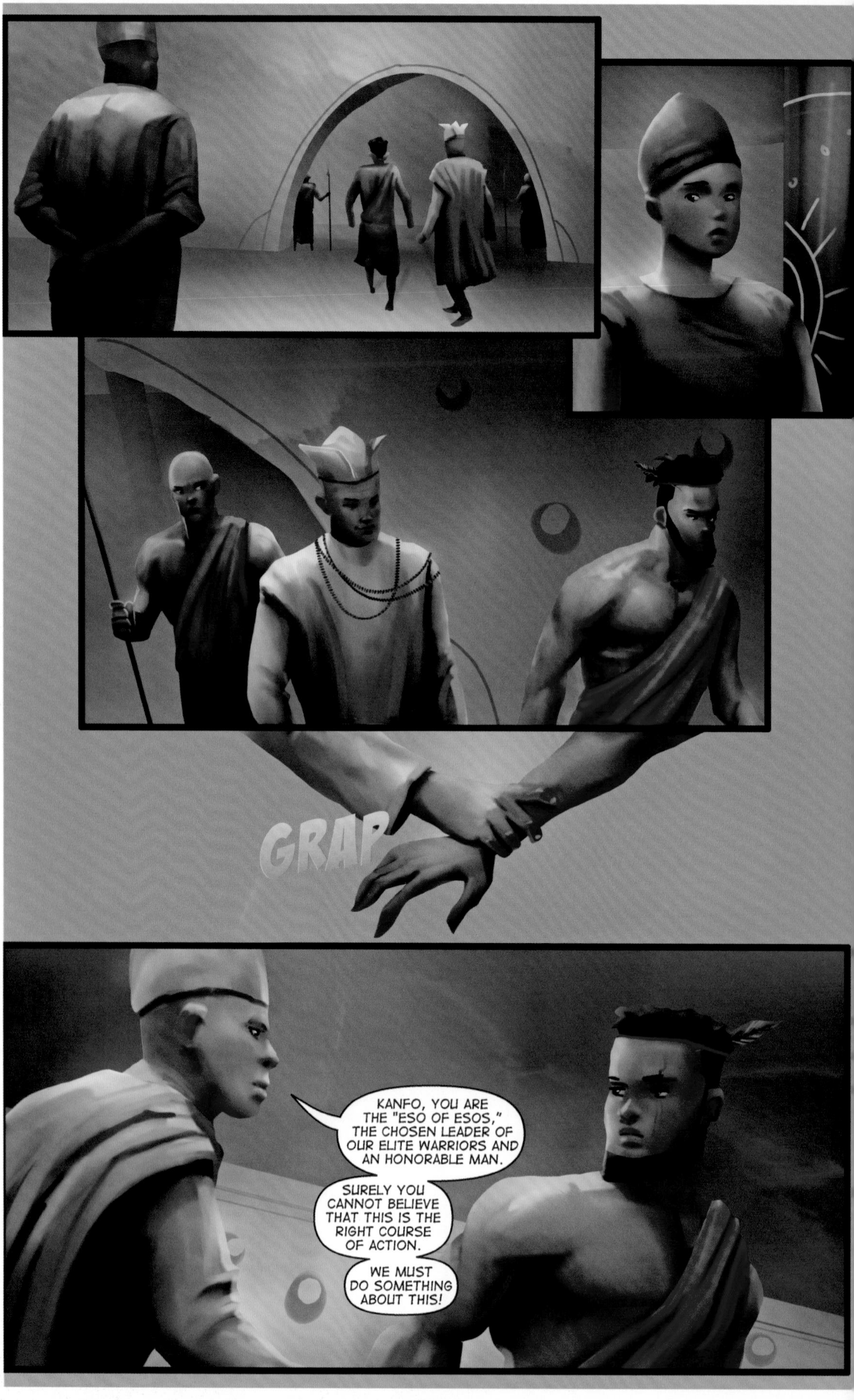
GRAP
KANFO, YOU ARE THE "ESO OF ESOS," THE CHOSEN LEADER OF OUR ELITE WARRIORS AND AN HONORABLE MAN.
SURELY YOU CANNOT BELIEVE THAT THIS IS THE RIGHT COURSE OF ACTION.
WE MUST DO SOMETHING ABOUT THIS!

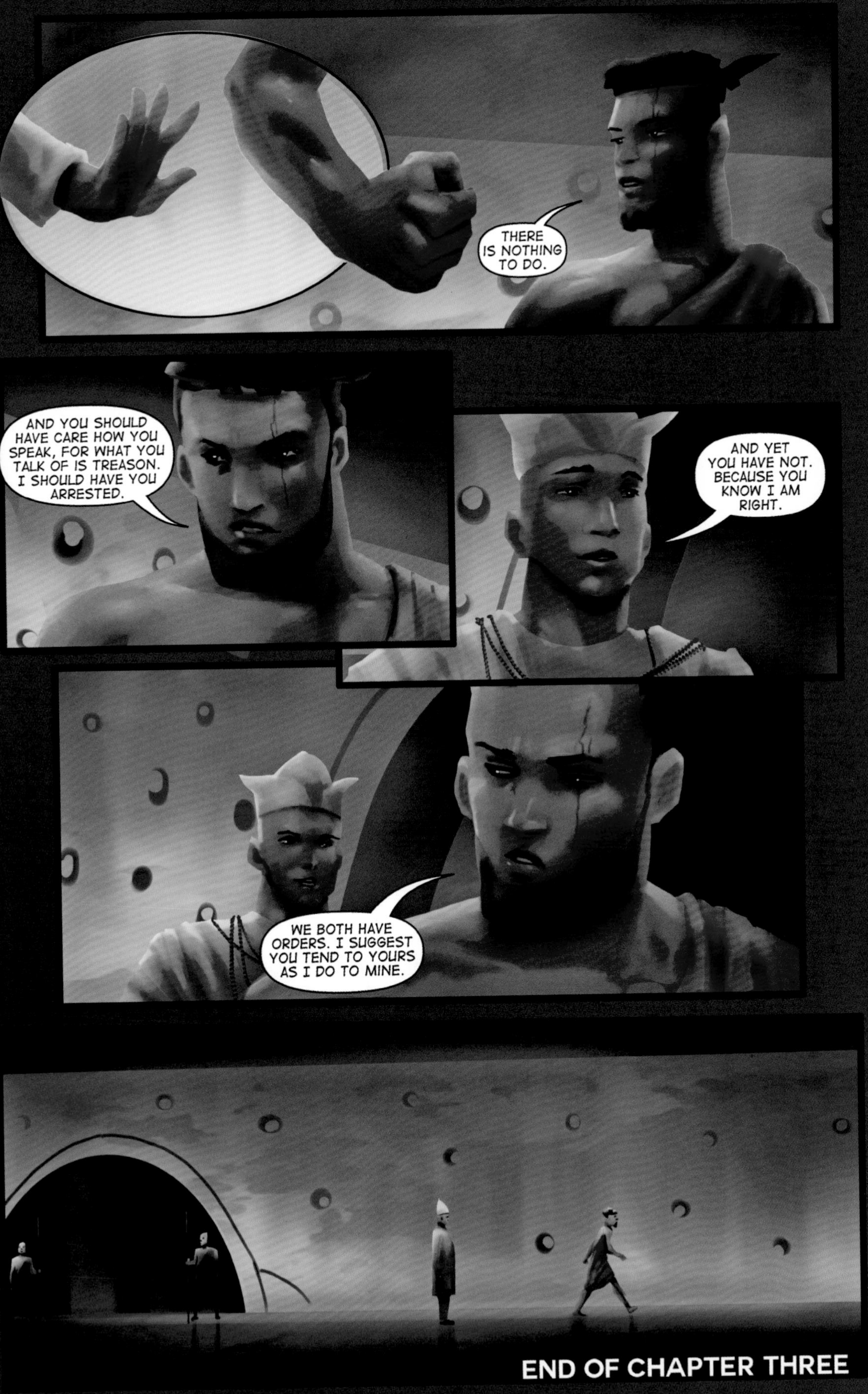
THERE IS NOTHING TO DO.
AND YOU SHOULD HAVE CARE HOW YOU SPEAK, FOR WHAT YOU TALK OF IS TREASON. I SHOULD HAVE YOU ARRESTED.
AND YET YOU HAVE NOT. BECAUSE YOU KNOW I AM RIGHT.
WE BOTH HAVE ORDERS. I SUGGEST YOU TEND TO YOURS AS I DO TO MINE.
END OF CHAPTER THREE

CHAPTER FOUR

The Elu
Mesi
(Council)

The Elu Mesi act as advisors to the Oba (the sitting king of Elu). They are there to keep his power in check. Behind the scenes, they can wield absolute power if an Oba is weak. When an Oba dies, an Aremo (heir) is selected from a pool of princes and princesses of royal lineage by the Elu Mesi. The Elu Mesi meet with the Oba daily in the palace to make all laws and make the highest decisions of government. Such laws and decisions are then announced to the kingdom as the Oba's word.

FUN FACT: The government of Elu takes a lot of inspiration from the structure and government of the ancient Oyo empire (one of the largest Yoruba kingdoms during the 17th and 18th centuries), which was an Elective Monarchy.

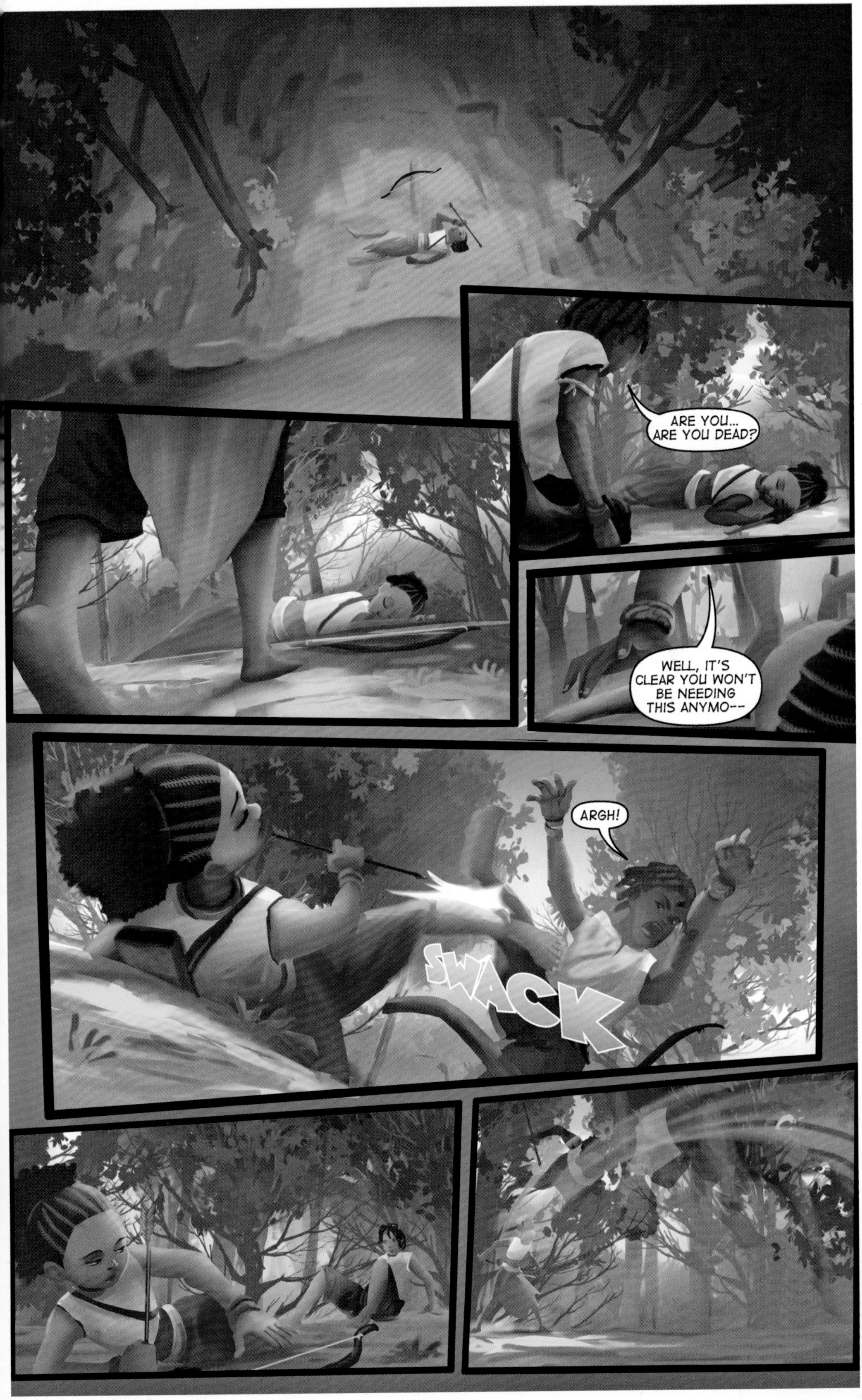
ARE YOU... ARE YOU DEAD?
WELL, IT'S CLEAR YOU WON'T BE NEEDING THIS ANYMO--
ARGH!
SWACK

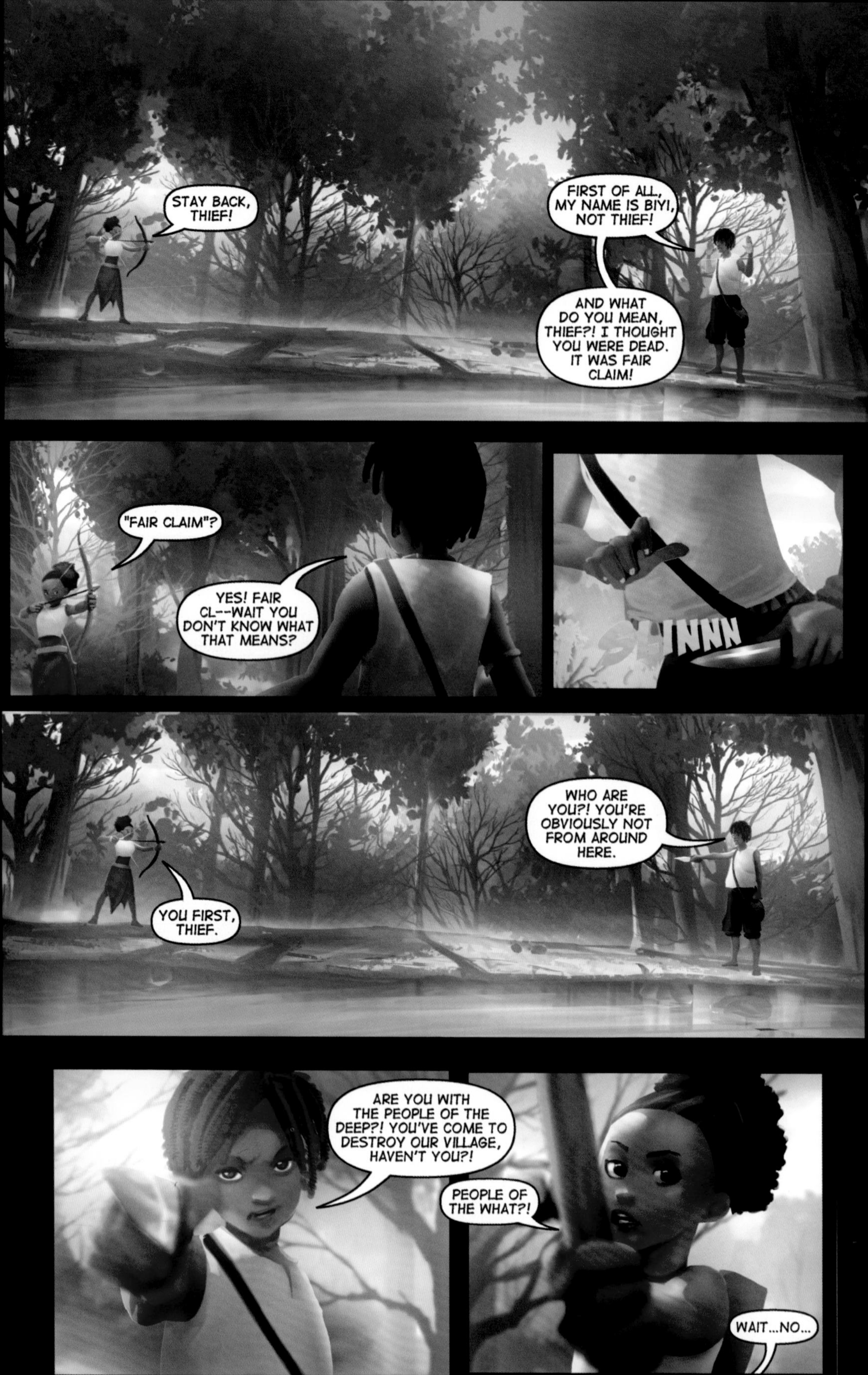
STAY BACK, THIEF!
FIRST OF ALL, MY NAME IS BIYI, NOT THIEF!
AND WHAT DO YOU MEAN, THIEF?! I THOUGHT YOU WERE DEAD. IT WAS FAIR CLAIM!
"FAIR CLAIM"?
YES! FAIR CL--WAIT YOU DON'T KNOW WHAT THAT MEANS?
SHINNN
WHO ARE YOU?! YOU'RE OBVIOUSLY NOT FROM AROUND HERE.
YOU FIRST, THIEF.
ARE YOU WITH THE PEOPLE OF THE DEEP?! YOU'VE COME TO DESTROY OUR VILLAGE, HAVEN'T YOU?!
PEOPLE OF THE WHAT?!
WAIT...NO...

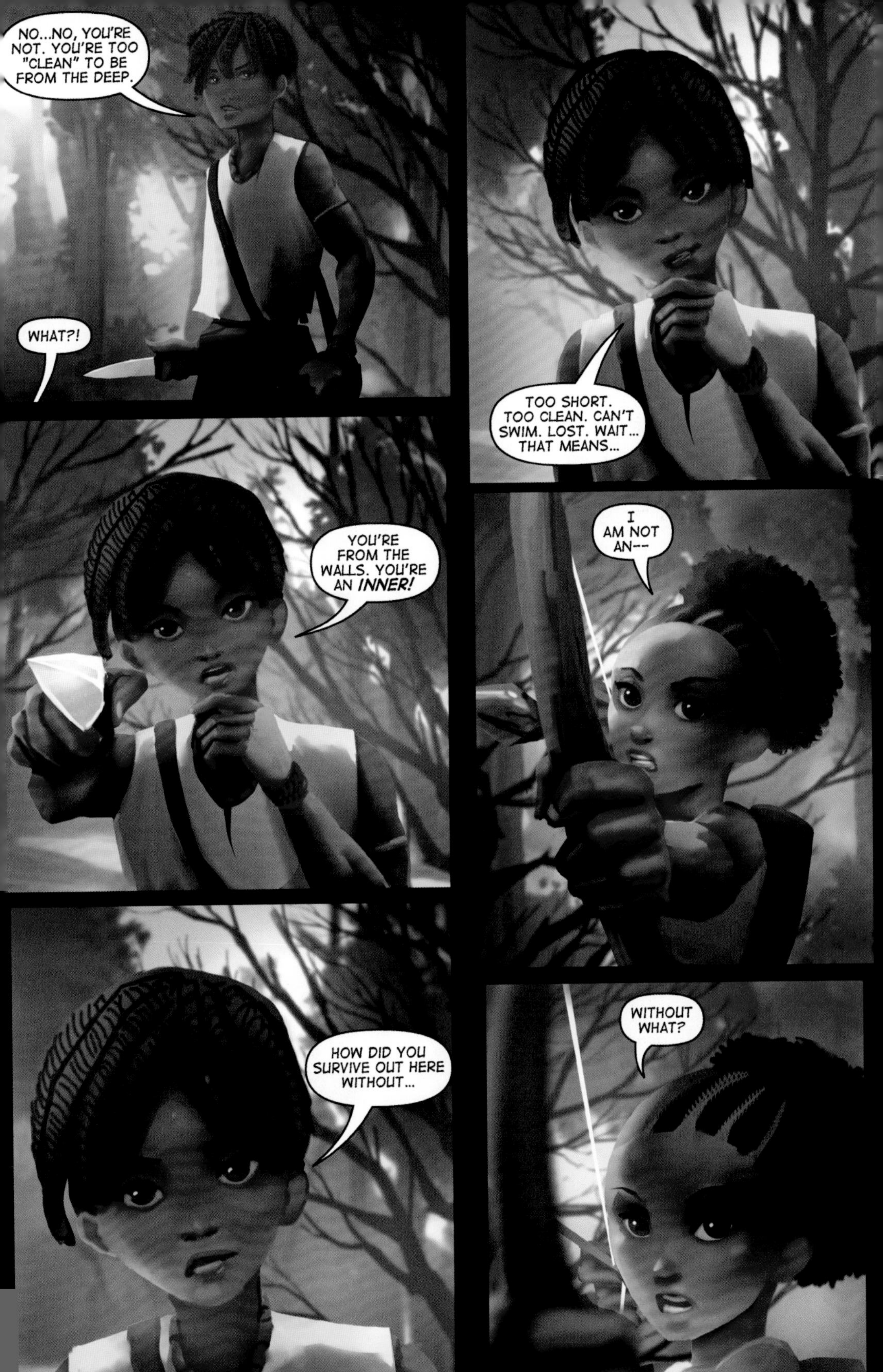
NO...NO, YOU'RE NOT. YOU'RE TOO "CLEAN" TO BE FROM THE DEEP.
WHAT?!
TOO SHORT. TOO CLEAN. CAN'T SWIM. LOST. WAIT... THAT MEANS...
YOU'RE FROM THE WALLS. YOU'RE AN *INNER!*
I AM NOT AN--
HOW DID YOU SURVIVE OUT HERE WITHOUT...
WITHOUT WHAT?

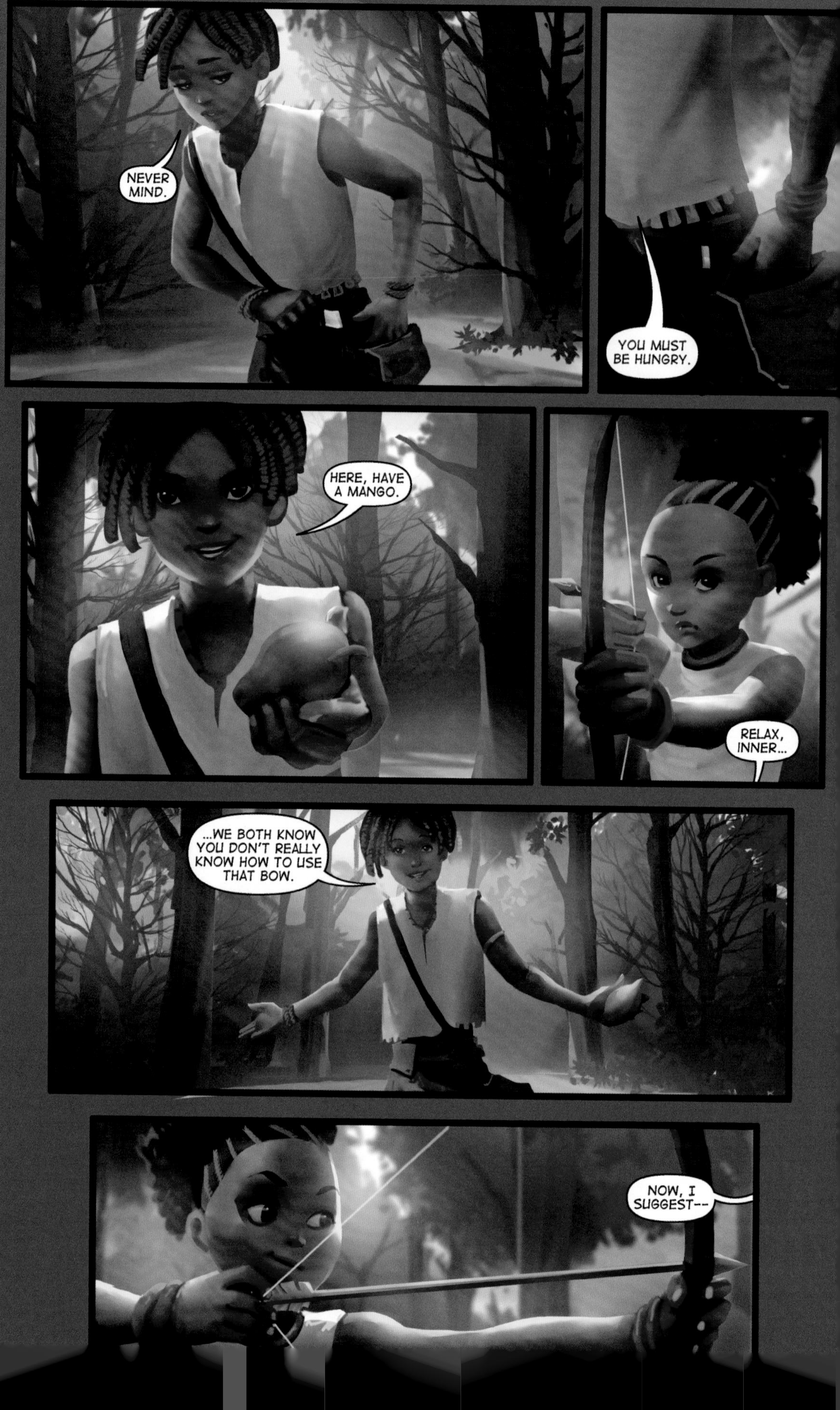
NEVER MIND.
YOU MUST BE HUNGRY.
HERE, HAVE A MANGO.
RELAX, INNER...
...WE BOTH KNOW YOU DON'T REALLY KNOW HOW TO USE THAT BOW.
NOW, I SUGGEST--

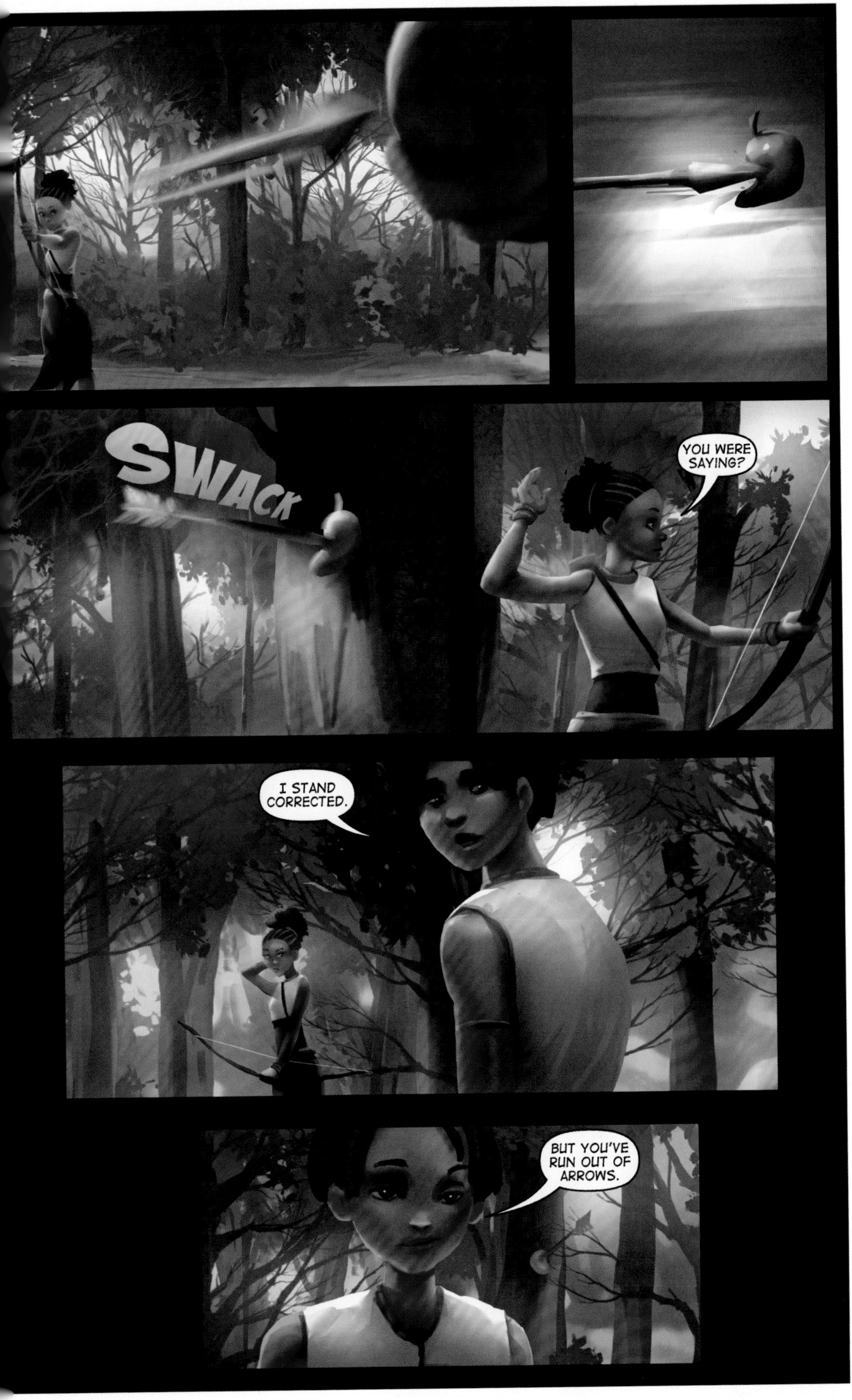
SWACK
YOU WERE SAYING?
I STAND CORRECTED.
BUT YOU'VE RUN OUT OF ARROWS.

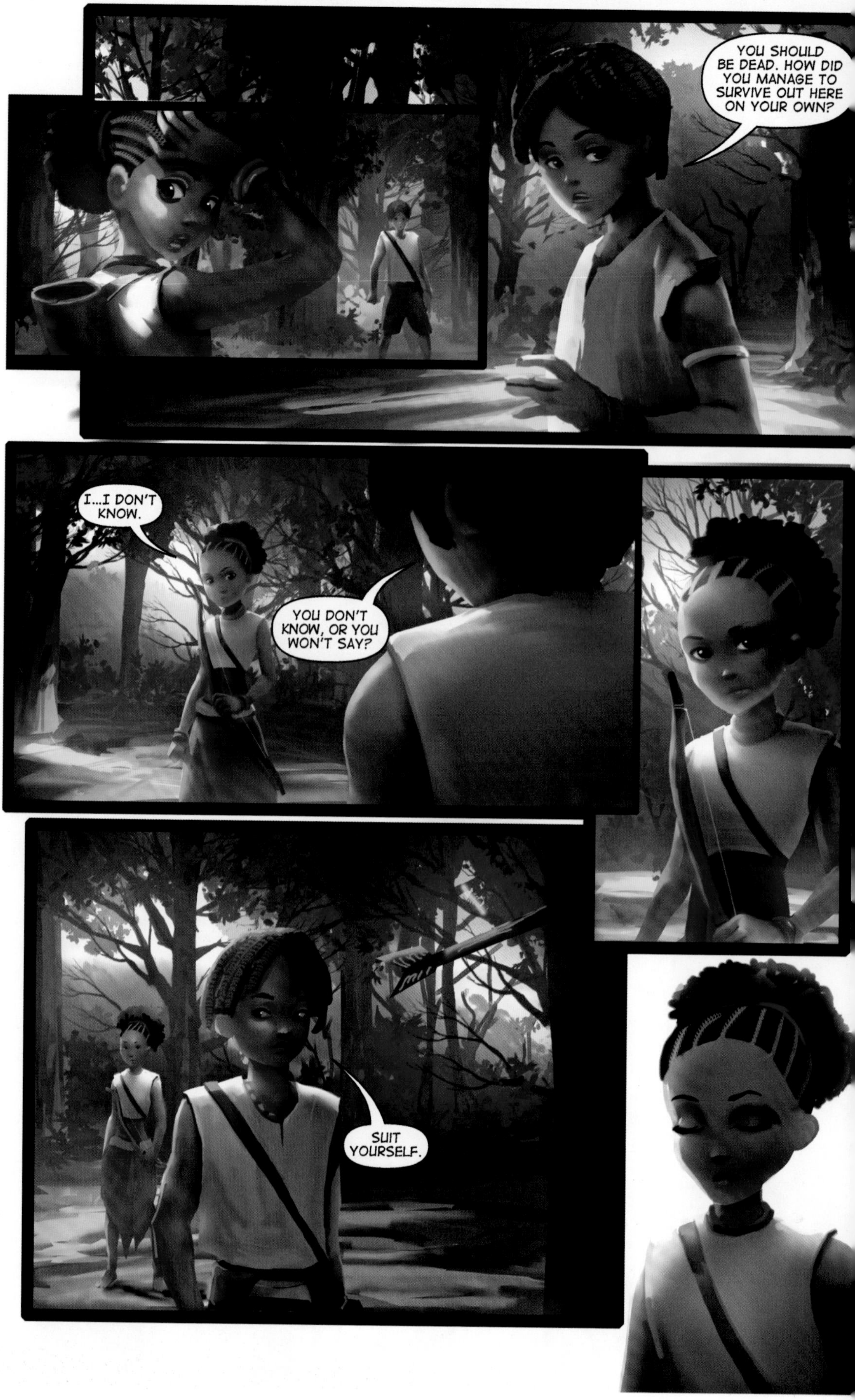
YOU SHOULD BE DEAD. HOW DID YOU MANAGE TO SURVIVE OUT HERE ON YOUR OWN?
I...I DON'T KNOW.
YOU DON'T KNOW, OR YOU WON'T SAY?
SUIT YOURSELF.

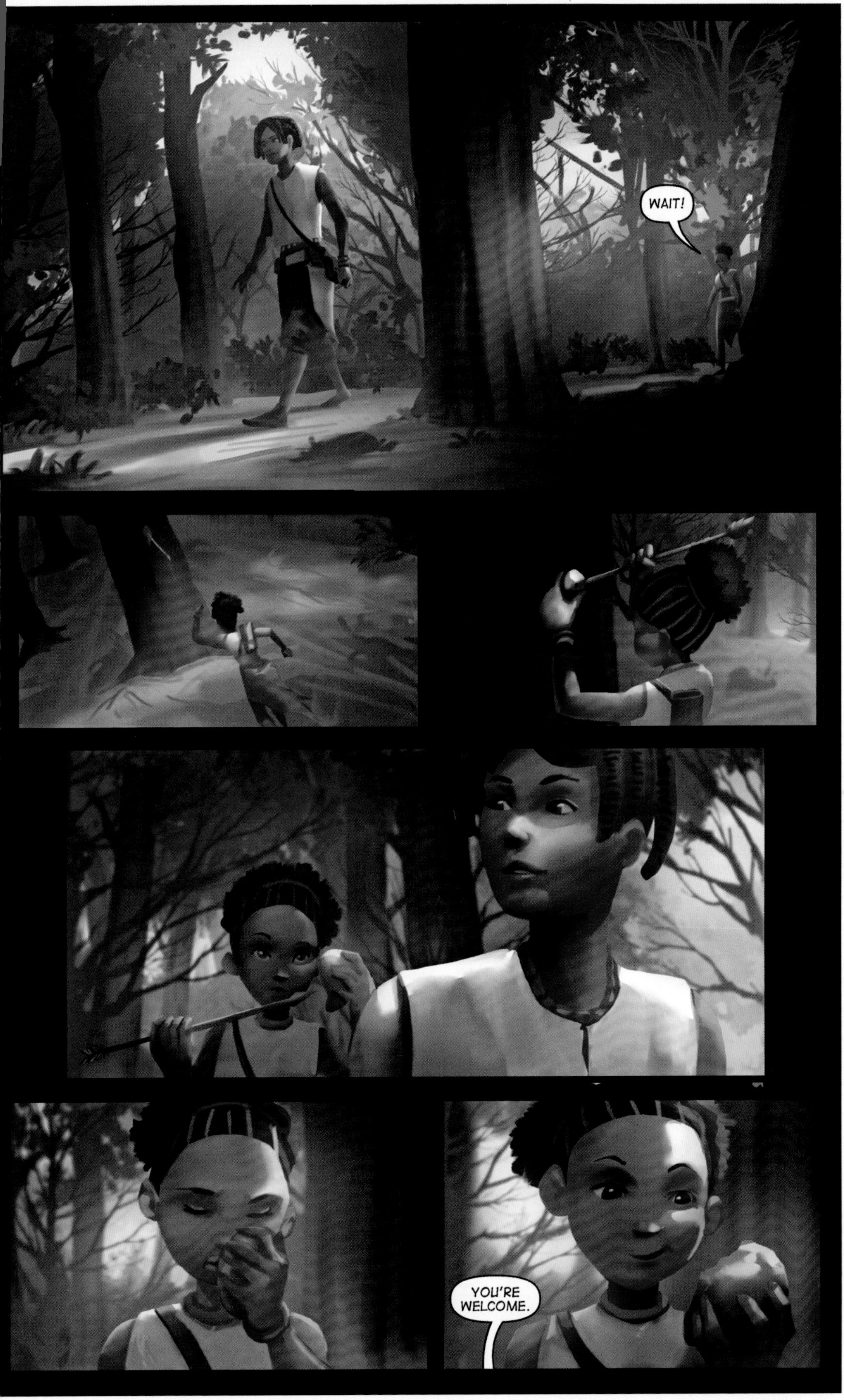
WAIT!
YOU'RE WELCOME.

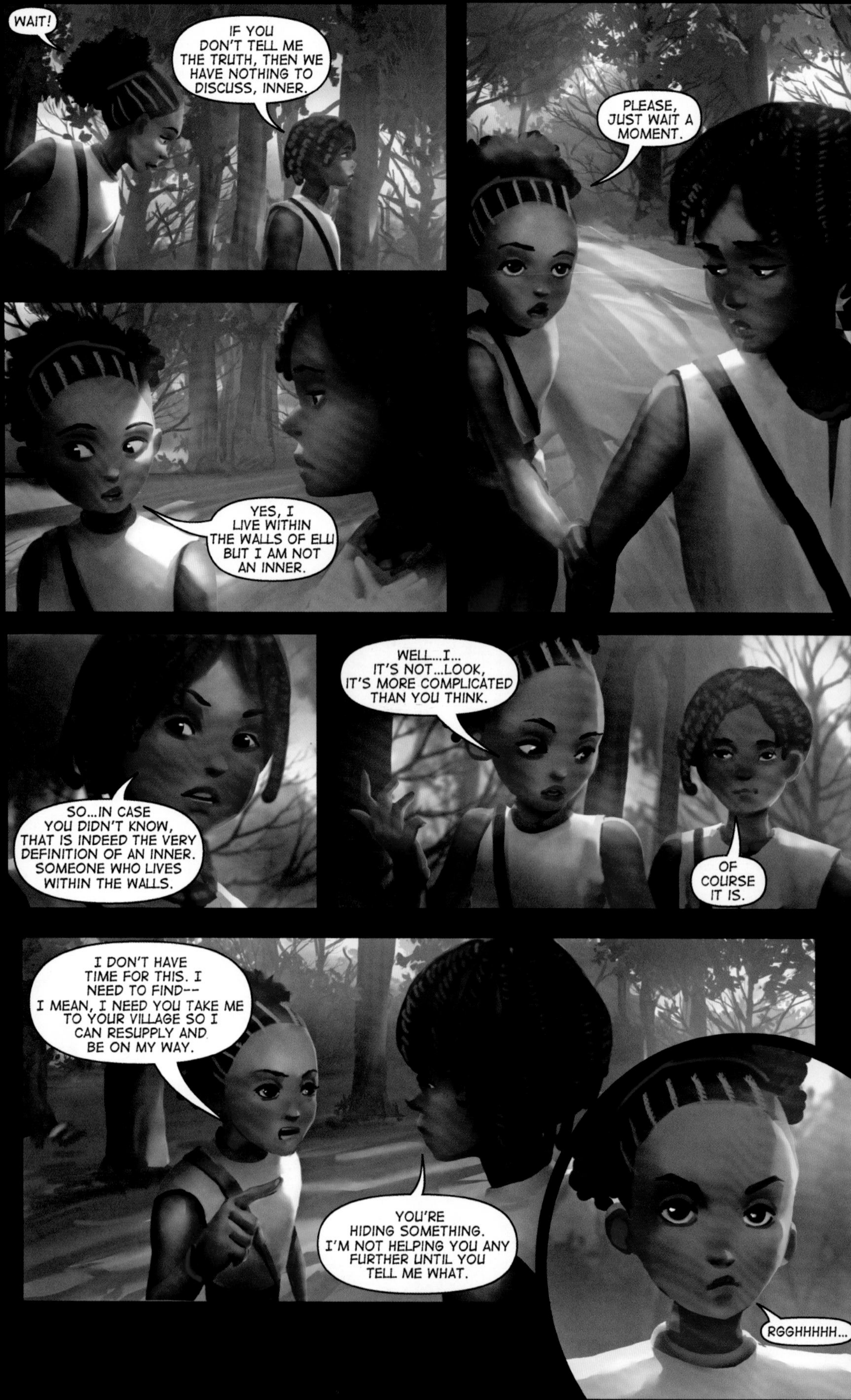
WAIT!
IF YOU DON'T TELL ME THE TRUTH, THEN WE HAVE NOTHING TO DISCUSS, INNER.
PLEASE, JUST WAIT A MOMENT.
YES, I LIVE WITHIN THE WALLS OF ELU BUT I AM NOT AN INNER.
SO...IN CASE YOU DIDN'T KNOW, THAT IS INDEED THE VERY DEFINITION OF AN INNER. SOMEONE WHO LIVES WITHIN THE WALLS.
WELL...I... IT'S NOT...LOOK, IT'S MORE COMPLICATED THAN YOU THINK.
OF COURSE IT IS.
I DON'T HAVE TIME FOR THIS. I NEED TO FIND-- I MEAN, I NEED YOU TAKE ME TO YOUR VILLAGE SO I CAN RESUPPLY AND BE ON MY WAY.
YOU'RE HIDING SOMETHING. I'M NOT HELPING YOU ANY FURTHER UNTIL YOU TELL ME WHAT.
RGGHHHHH...

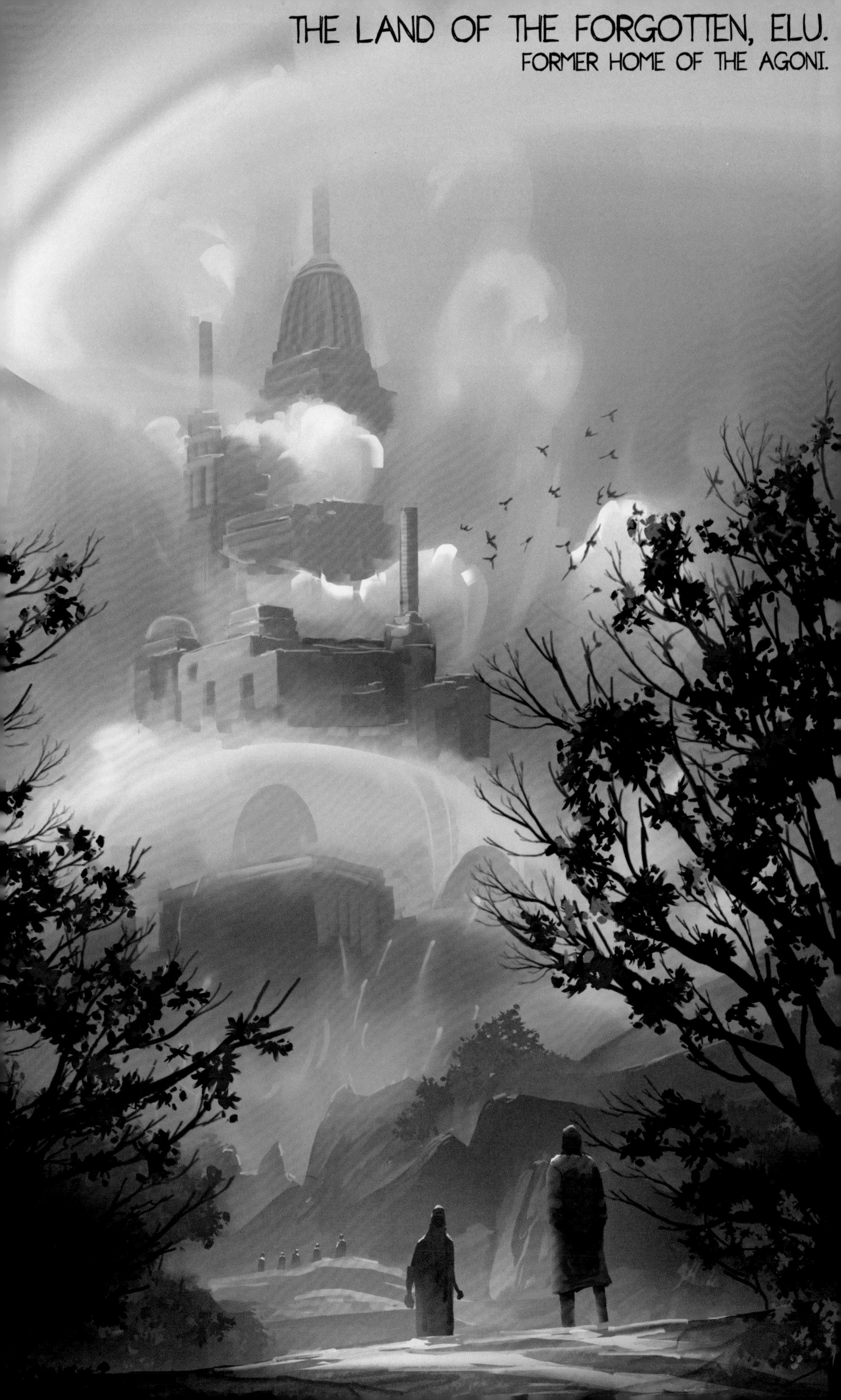
THE LAND OF THE FORGOTTEN, ELU.
FORMER HOME OF THE AGONI.

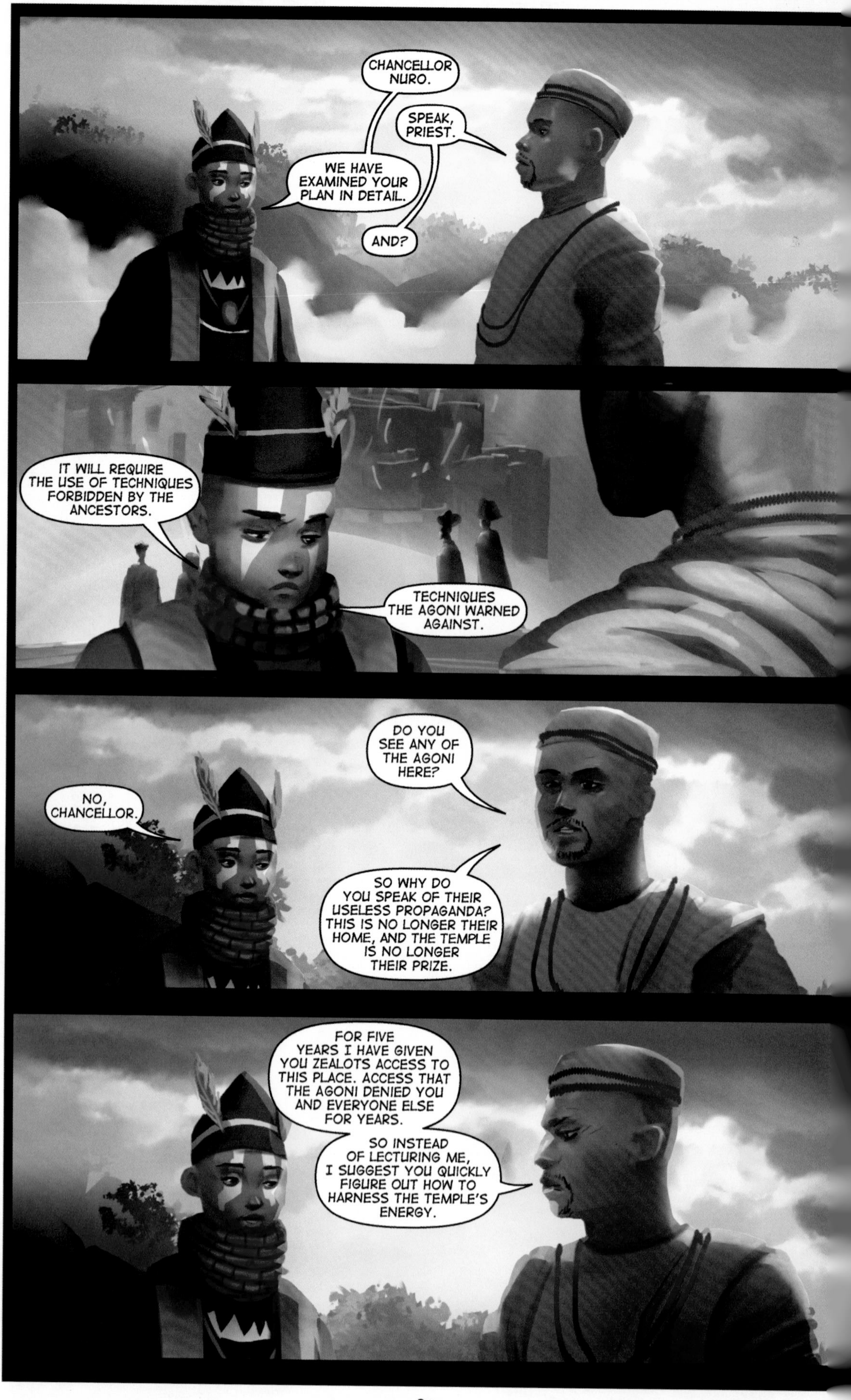
CHANCELLOR NURO.
WE HAVE EXAMINED YOUR PLAN IN DETAIL.
SPEAK, PRIEST.
AND?
IT WILL REQUIRE THE USE OF TECHNIQUES FORBIDDEN BY THE ANCESTORS.
TECHNIQUES THE AGONI WARNED AGAINST.
DO YOU SEE ANY OF THE AGONI HERE?
NO, CHANCELLOR.
SO WHY DO YOU SPEAK OF THEIR USELESS PROPAGANDA? THIS IS NO LONGER THEIR HOME, AND THE TEMPLE IS NO LONGER THEIR PRIZE.
FOR FIVE YEARS I HAVE GIVEN YOU ZEALOTS ACCESS TO THIS PLACE. ACCESS THAT THE AGONI DENIED YOU AND EVERYONE ELSE FOR YEARS.
SO INSTEAD OF LECTURING ME, I SUGGEST YOU QUICKLY FIGURE OUT HOW TO HARNESS THE TEMPLE'S ENERGY.

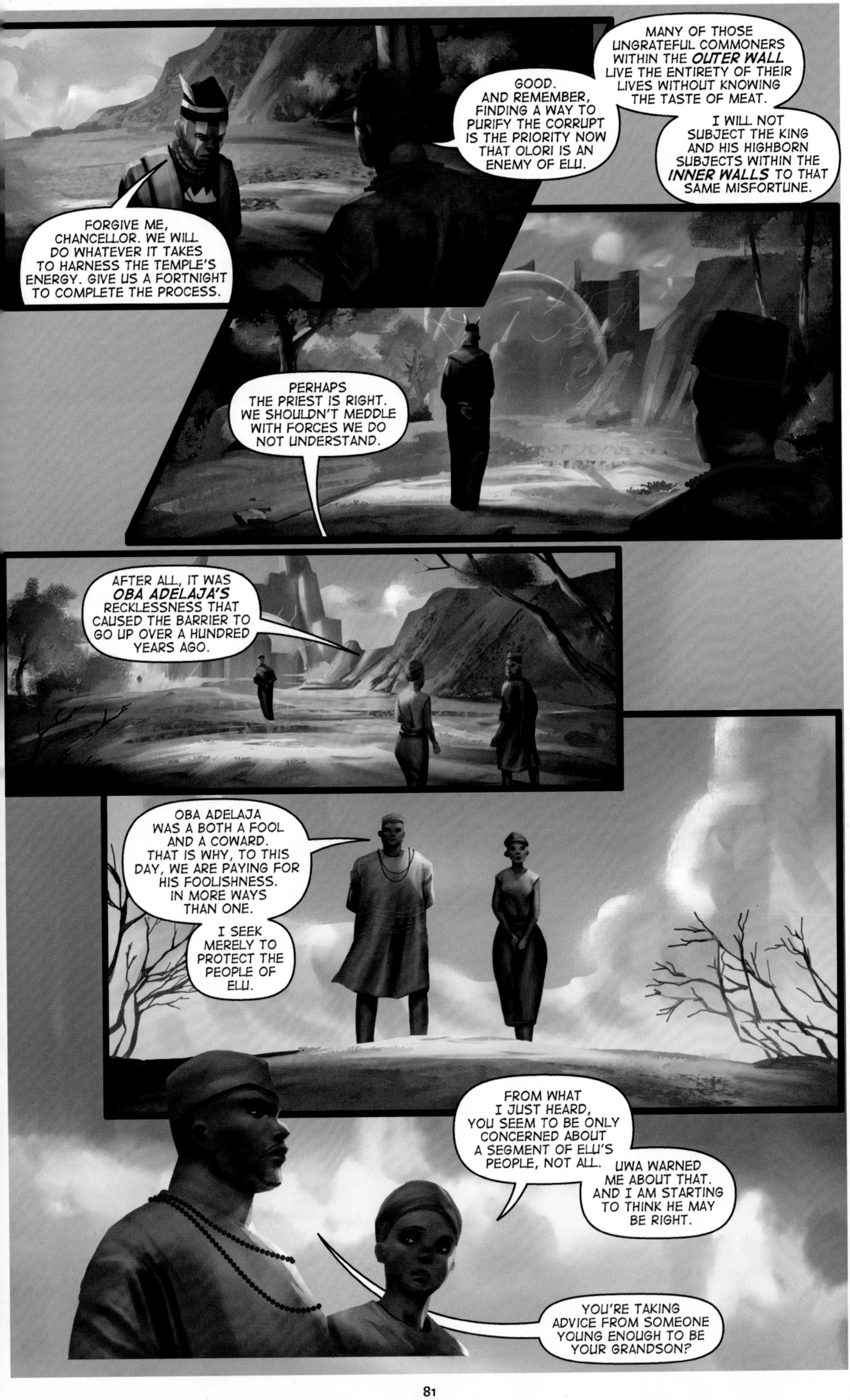
FORGIVE ME, CHANCELLOR. WE WILL DO WHATEVER IT TAKES TO HARNESS THE TEMPLE'S ENERGY. GIVE US A FORTNIGHT TO COMPLETE THE PROCESS.
GOOD. AND REMEMBER, FINDING A WAY TO PURIFY THE CORRUPT IS THE PRIORITY NOW THAT OLORI IS AN ENEMY OF ELU.
MANY OF THOSE UNGRATEFUL COMMONERS WITHIN THE OUTER WALL LIVE THE ENTIRETY OF THEIR LIVES WITHOUT KNOWING THE TASTE OF MEAT.
I WILL NOT SUBJECT THE KING AND HIS HIGHBORN SUBJECTS WITHIN THE INNER WALLS TO THAT SAME MISFORTUNE.
PERHAPS THE PRIEST IS RIGHT. WE SHOULDN'T MEDDLE WITH FORCES WE DO NOT UNDERSTAND.
AFTER ALL, IT WAS OBA ADELAJA'S RECKLESSNESS THAT CAUSED THE BARRIER TO GO UP OVER A HUNDRED YEARS AGO.
OBA ADELAJA WAS A BOTH A FOOL AND A COWARD. THAT IS WHY, TO THIS DAY, WE ARE PAYING FOR HIS FOOLISHNESS. IN MORE WAYS THAN ONE.
I SEEK MERELY TO PROTECT THE PEOPLE OF ELU.
FROM WHAT I JUST HEARD, YOU SEEM TO BE ONLY CONCERNED ABOUT A SEGMENT OF ELU'S PEOPLE, NOT ALL.
UWA WARNED ME ABOUT THAT. AND I AM STARTING TO THINK HE MAY BE RIGHT.
YOU'RE TAKING ADVICE FROM SOMEONE YOUNG ENOUGH TO BE YOUR GRANDSON?

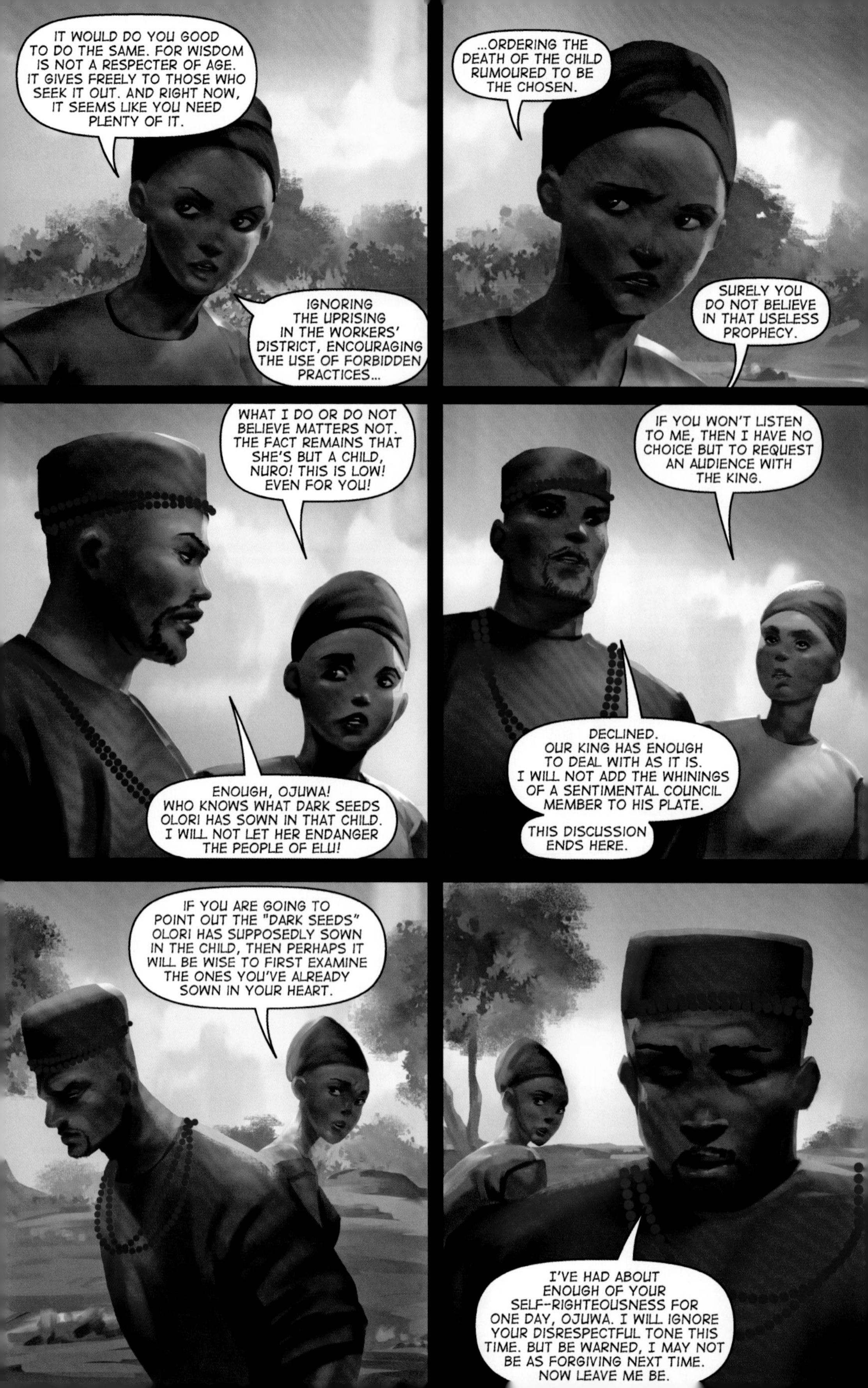
IT WOULD DO YOU GOOD TO DO THE SAME. FOR WISDOM IS NOT A RESPECTER OF AGE. IT GIVES FREELY TO THOSE WHO SEEK IT OUT. AND RIGHT NOW, IT SEEMS LIKE YOU NEED PLENTY OF IT.
IGNORING THE UPRISING IN THE WORKERS' DISTRICT, ENCOURAGING THE USE OF FORBIDDEN PRACTICES...
...ORDERING THE DEATH OF THE CHILD RUMOURED TO BE THE CHOSEN.
SURELY YOU DO NOT BELIEVE IN THAT USELESS PROPHECY.
WHAT I DO OR DO NOT BELIEVE MATTERS NOT. THE FACT REMAINS THAT SHE'S BUT A CHILD, NURO! THIS IS LOW! EVEN FOR YOU!
ENOUGH, OJUWA! WHO KNOWS WHAT DARK SEEDS OLORI HAS SOWN IN THAT CHILD. I WILL NOT LET HER ENDANGER THE PEOPLE OF ELU!
IF YOU WON'T LISTEN TO ME, THEN I HAVE NO CHOICE BUT TO REQUEST AN AUDIENCE WITH THE KING.
DECLINED. OUR KING HAS ENOUGH TO DEAL WITH AS IT IS. I WILL NOT ADD THE WHININGS OF A SENTIMENTAL COUNCIL MEMBER TO HIS PLATE.
THIS DISCUSSION ENDS HERE.
IF YOU ARE GOING TO POINT OUT THE "DARK SEEDS" OLORI HAS SUPPOSEDLY SOWN IN THE CHILD, THEN PERHAPS IT WILL BE WISE TO FIRST EXAMINE THE ONES YOU'VE ALREADY SOWN IN YOUR HEART.
I'VE HAD ABOUT ENOUGH OF YOUR SELF-RIGHTEOUSNESS FOR ONE DAY, OJUWA. I WILL IGNORE YOUR DISRESPECTFUL TONE THIS TIME. BUT BE WARNED, I MAY NOT BE AS FORGIVING NEXT TIME. NOW LEAVE ME BE.

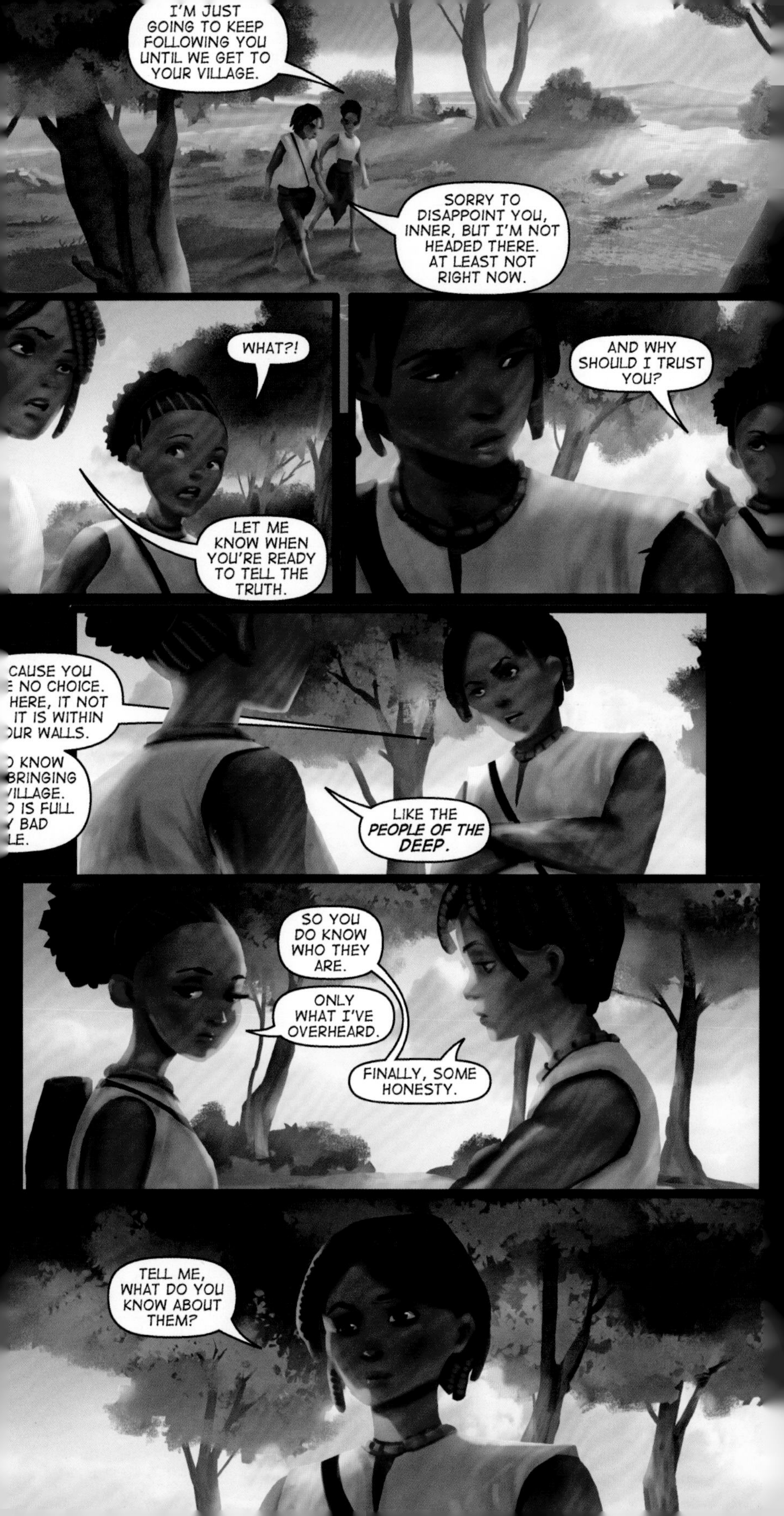
I'M JUST GOING TO KEEP FOLLOWING YOU UNTIL WE GET TO YOUR VILLAGE.
SORRY TO DISAPPOINT YOU, INNER, BUT I'M NOT HEADED THERE. AT LEAST NOT RIGHT NOW.
WHAT?!
LET ME KNOW WHEN YOU'RE READY TO TELL THE TRUTH.
AND WHY SHOULD I TRUST YOU?
CAUSE YOU E NO CHOICE. HERE, IT NOT IT IS WITHIN OUR WALLS.
O KNOW BRINGING VILLAGE. O IS FULL Y BAD LE.
LIKE THE *PEOPLE OF THE DEEP*.
SO YOU DO KNOW WHO THEY ARE.
ONLY WHAT I'VE OVERHEARD.
FINALLY, SOME HONESTY.
TELL ME, WHAT DO YOU KNOW ABOUT THEM?

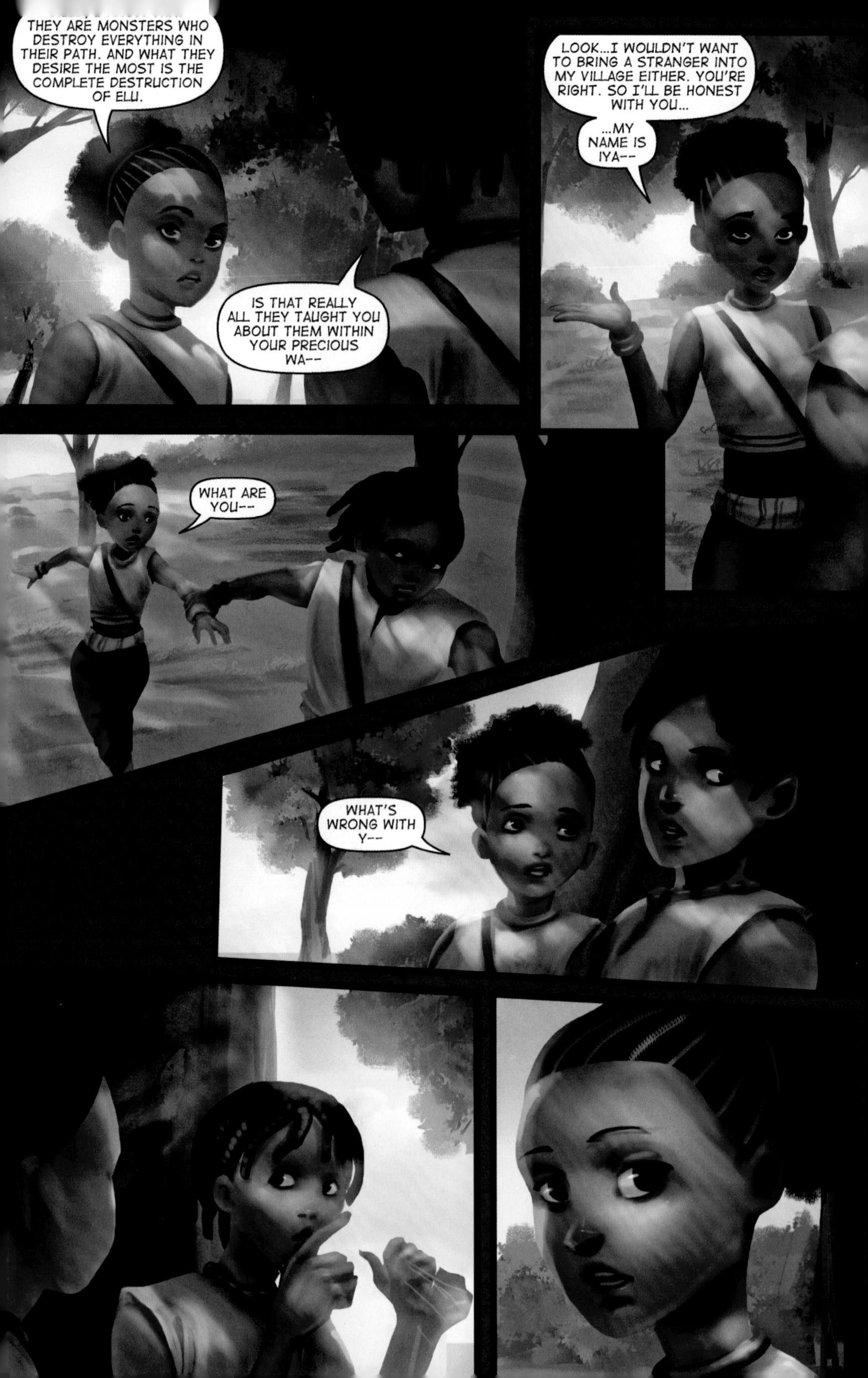
THEY ARE MONSTERS WHO DESTROY EVERYTHING IN THEIR PATH. AND WHAT THEY DESIRE THE MOST IS THE COMPLETE DESTRUCTION OF ELU.
IS THAT REALLY ALL THEY TAUGHT YOU ABOUT THEM WITHIN YOUR PRECIOUS WA--
LOOK...I WOULDN'T WANT TO BRING A STRANGER INTO MY VILLAGE EITHER. YOU'RE RIGHT. SO I'LL BE HONEST WITH YOU...
...MY NAME IS IYA--
WHAT ARE YOU--
WHAT'S WRONG WITH Y--

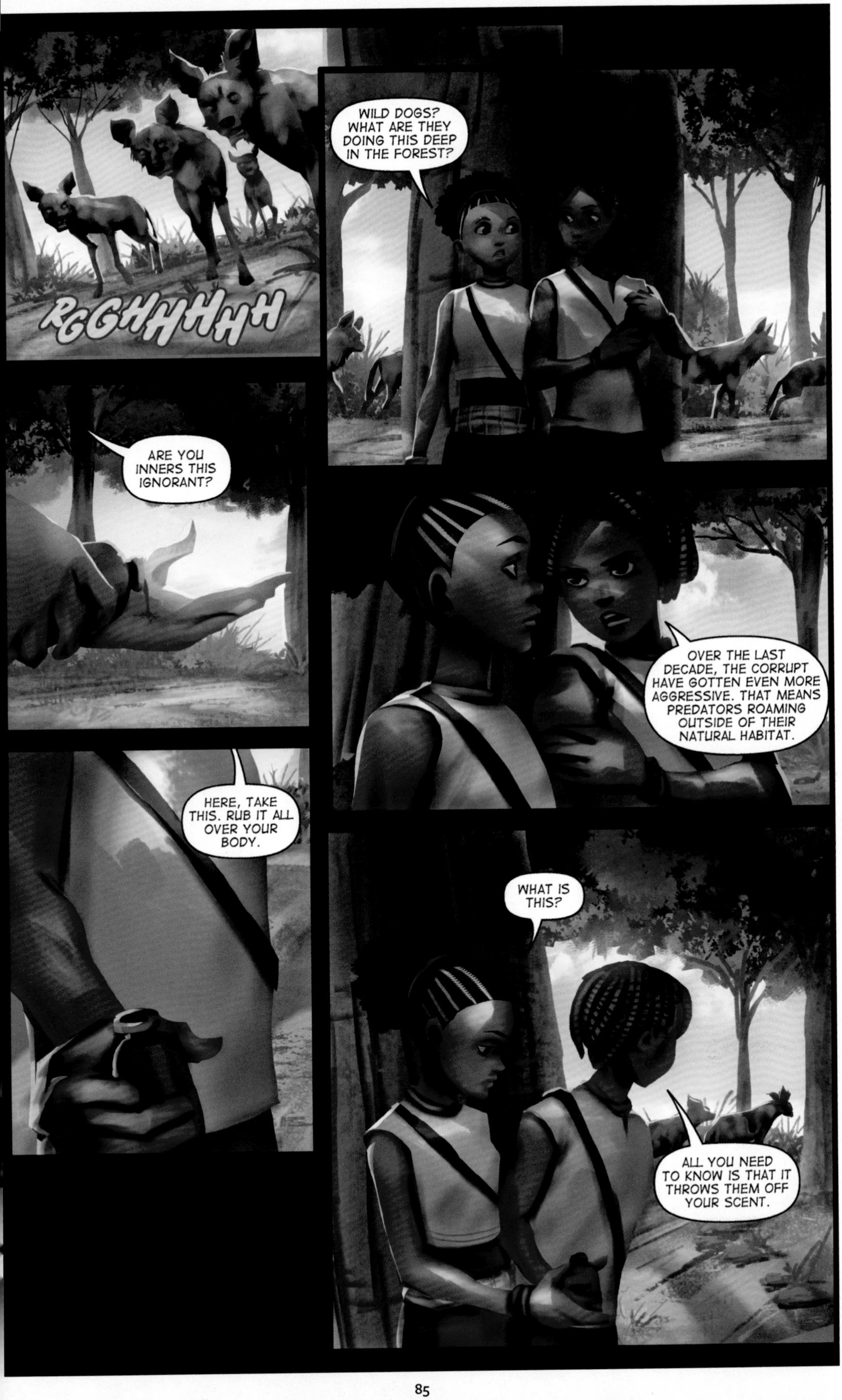
RGGHHHHHH
WILD DOGS? WHAT ARE THEY DOING THIS DEEP IN THE FOREST?
ARE YOU INNERS THIS IGNORANT?
OVER THE LAST DECADE, THE CORRUPT HAVE GOTTEN EVEN MORE AGGRESSIVE. THAT MEANS PREDATORS ROAMING OUTSIDE OF THEIR NATURAL HABITAT.
HERE, TAKE THIS. RUB IT ALL OVER YOUR BODY.
WHAT IS THIS?
ALL YOU NEED TO KNOW IS THAT IT THROWS THEM OFF YOUR SCENT.

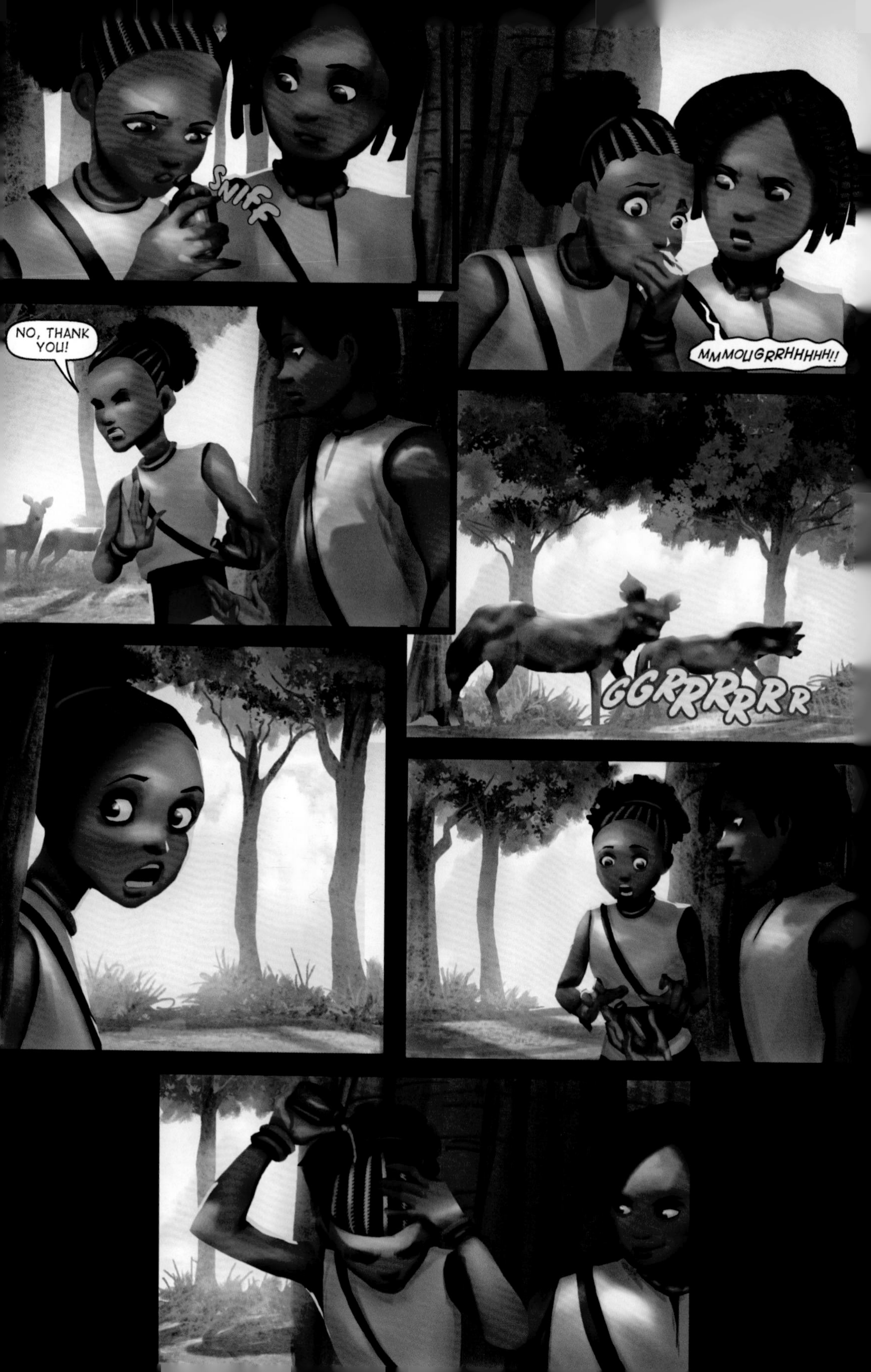

SNIFF
MMMOUGRRHHHHH!!
NO, THANK YOU!
GGRRRRRRR

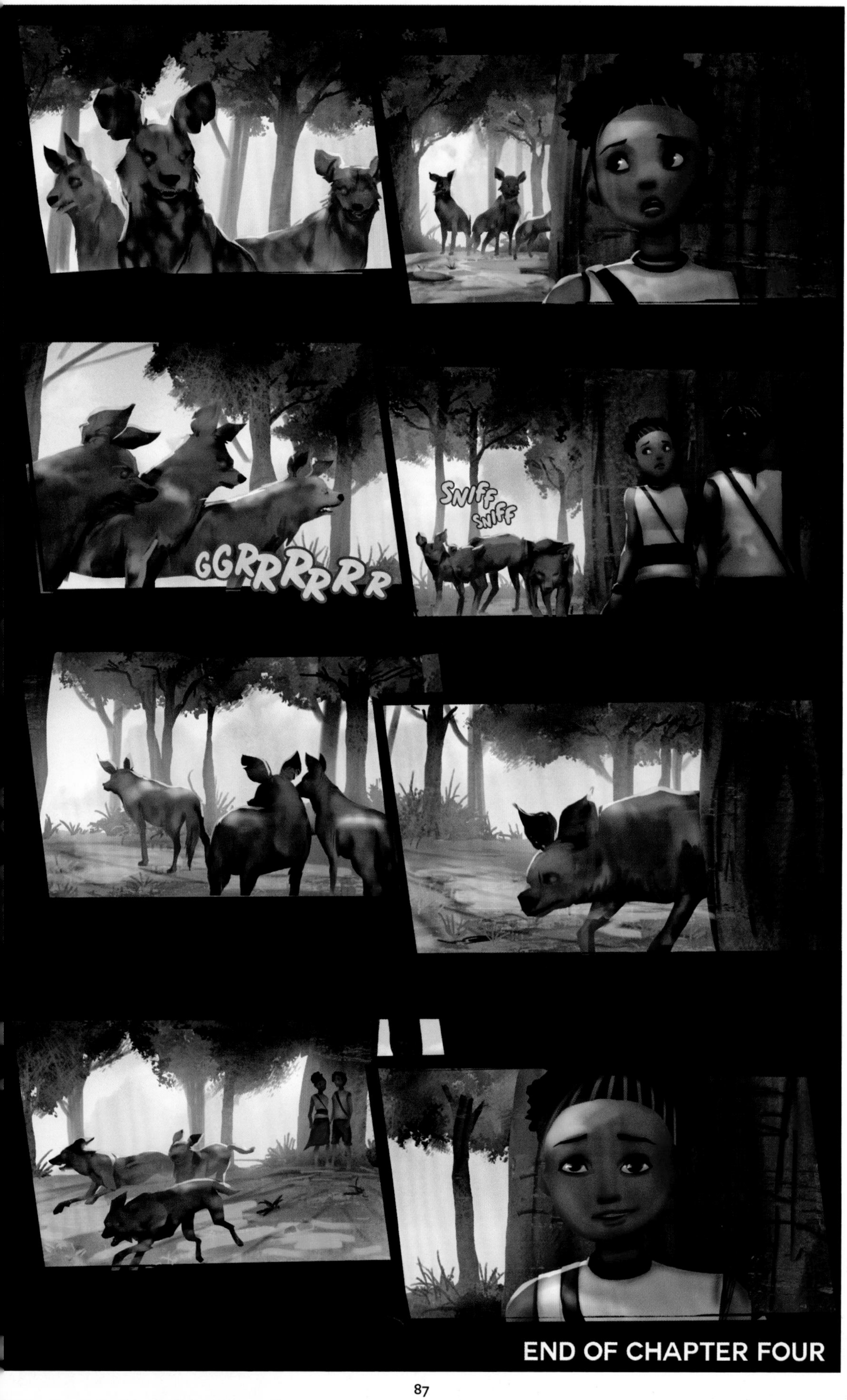
GGRRRRRR
SNIFF
SNIFF
END OF CHAPTER FOUR

CHAPTER FIVE

The Corrupt

After the Curse of the Fallen One, all animals have become exponentially more aggressive. They now seek to kill humans at all costs. Aside from the obvious dangers of attacks from these animals (especially predators), the Curse also rendered their meat inedible for humans. Eating meat from the Curse is basically a death sentence. This makes the rare "purified" livestock (thanks to the help of the Agoni) a luxury only a few can afford.

FUN FACT: The one exception to the Curse is fully aquatic animals (e.g. fish). It is said that they are immune to the Curse because they are not required to breathe the contaminated air other land-dwelling animals do.

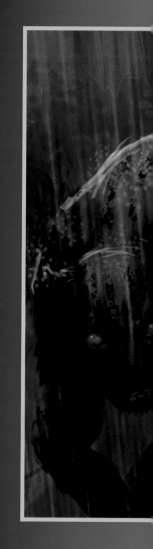

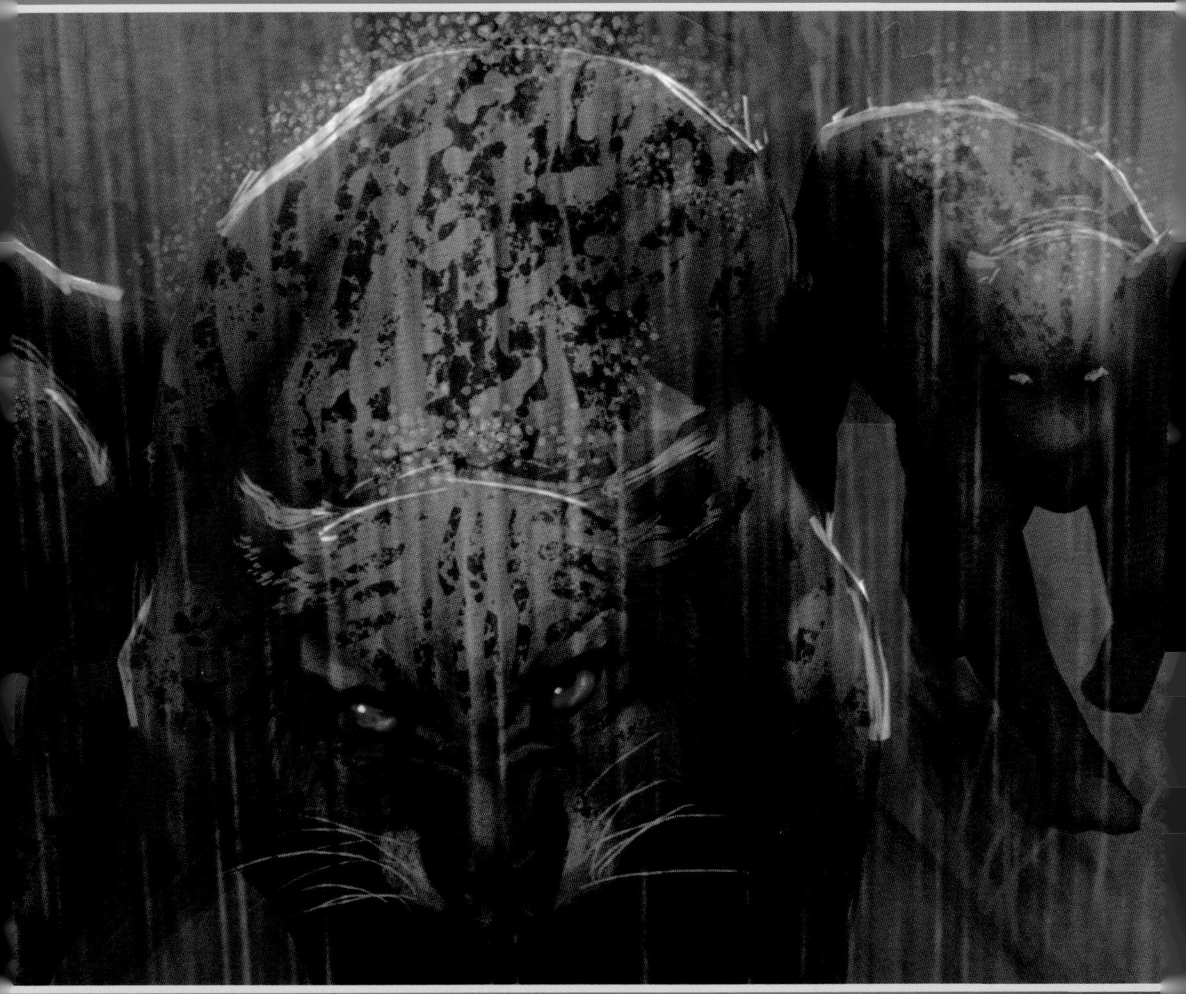

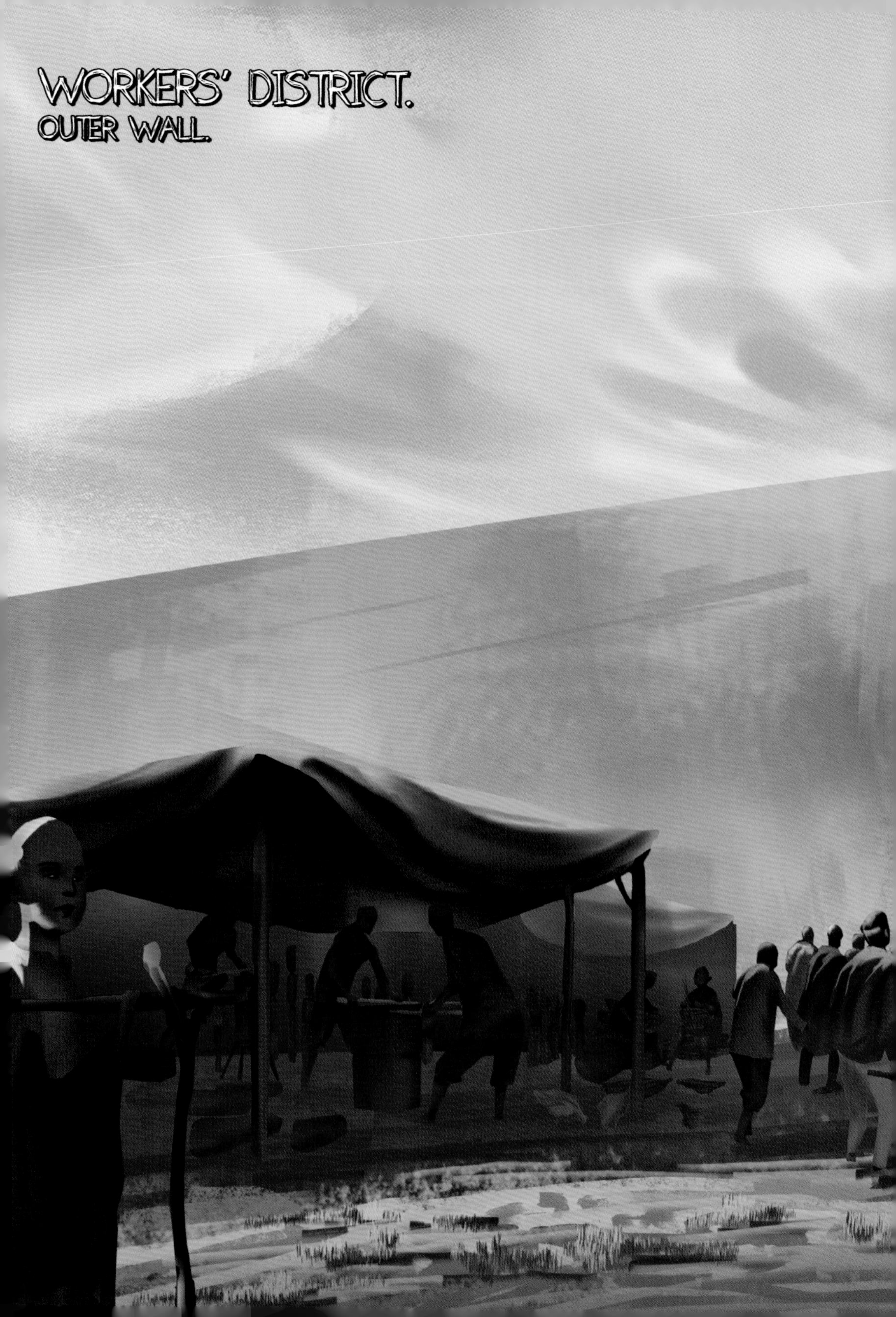
WORKERS' DISTRICT.
OUTER WALL.

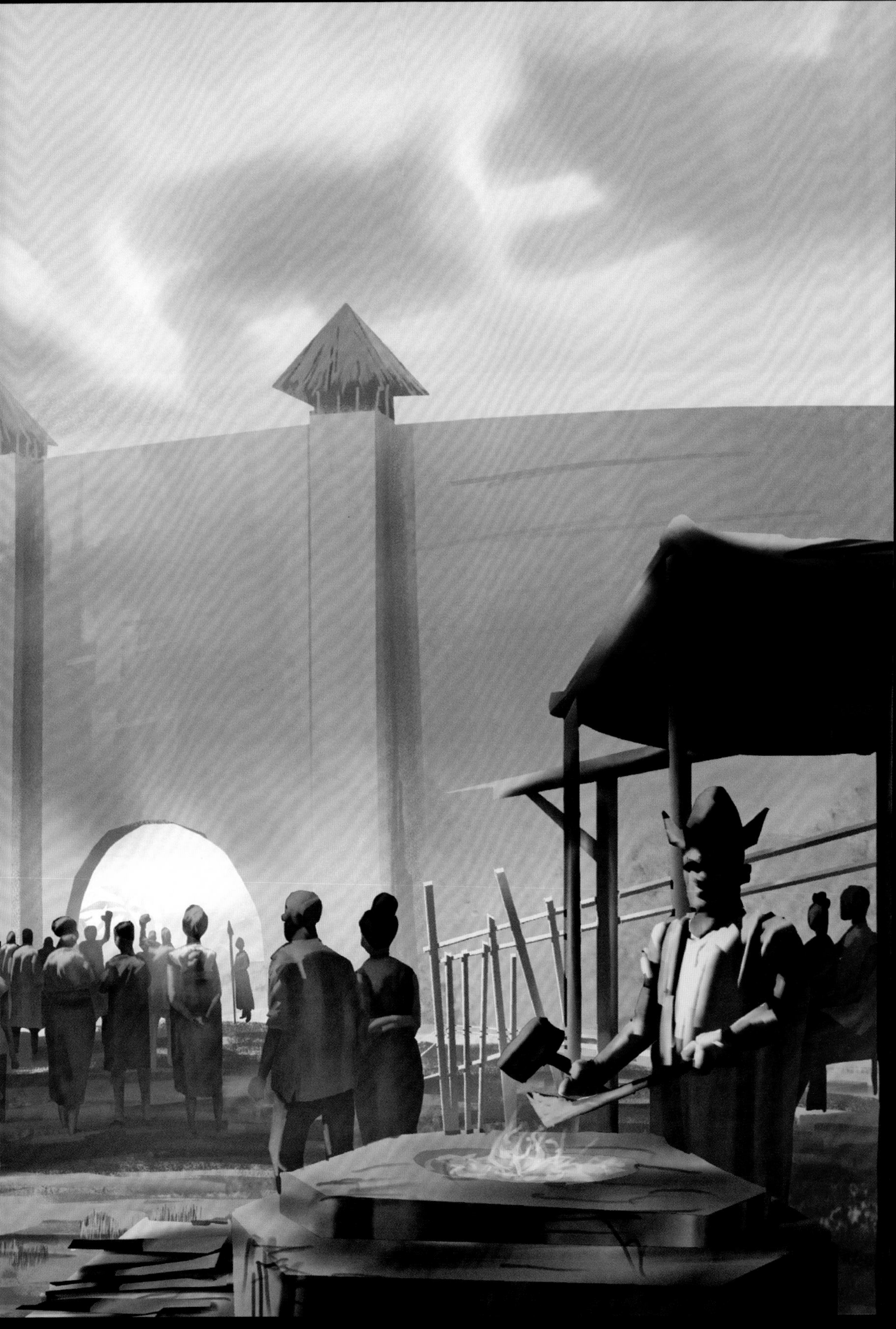

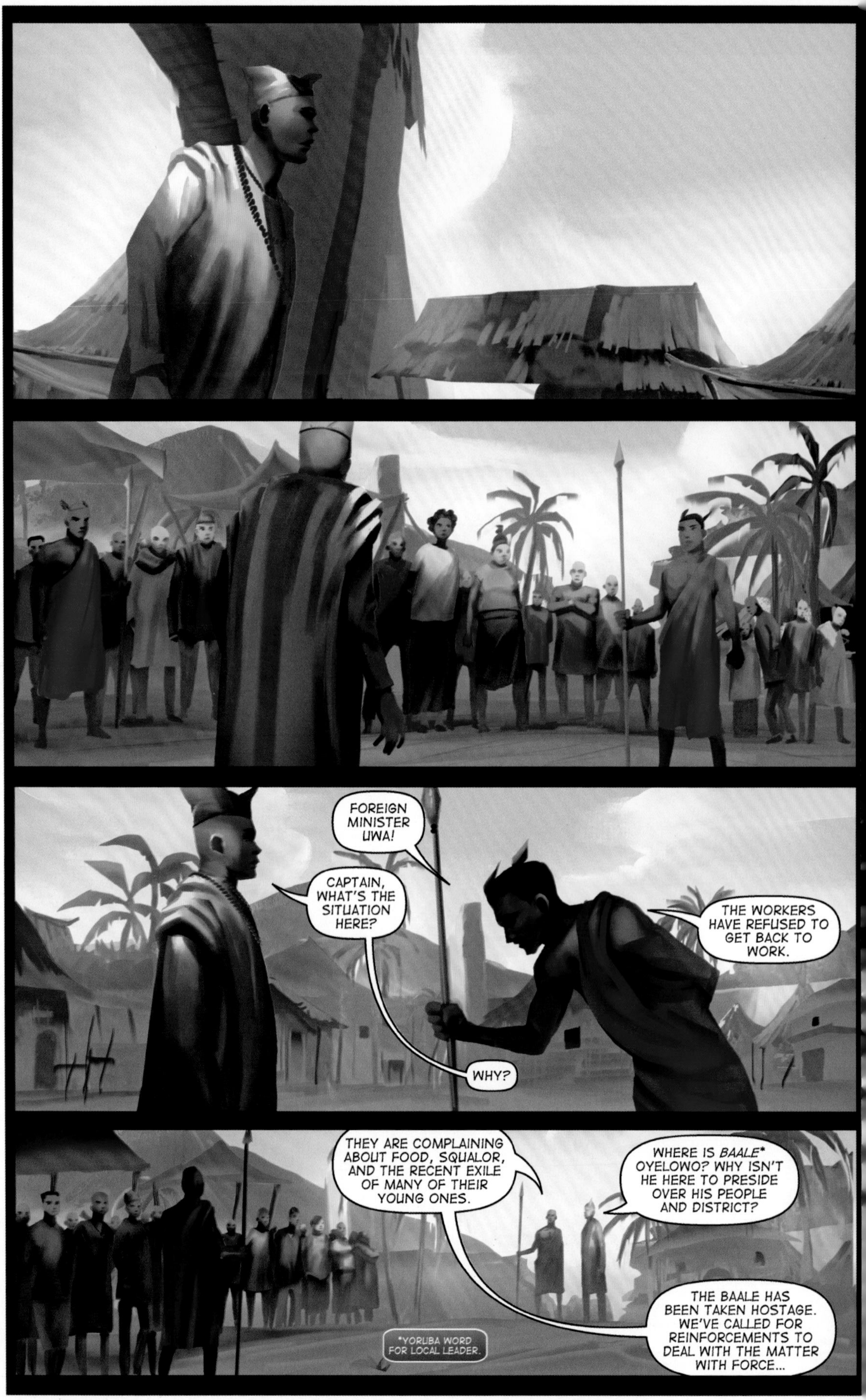
FOREIGN MINISTER UWA!
CAPTAIN, WHAT'S THE SITUATION HERE?
THE WORKERS HAVE REFUSED TO GET BACK TO WORK.
WHY?
THEY ARE COMPLAINING ABOUT FOOD, SQUALOR, AND THE RECENT EXILE OF MANY OF THEIR YOUNG ONES.
WHERE IS *BAALE** OYELOWO? WHY ISN'T HE HERE TO PRESIDE OVER HIS PEOPLE AND DISTRICT?
THE BAALE HAS BEEN TAKEN HOSTAGE. WE'VE CALLED FOR REINFORCEMENTS TO DEAL WITH THE MATTER WITH FORCE...
*YORUBA WORD FOR LOCAL LEADER.

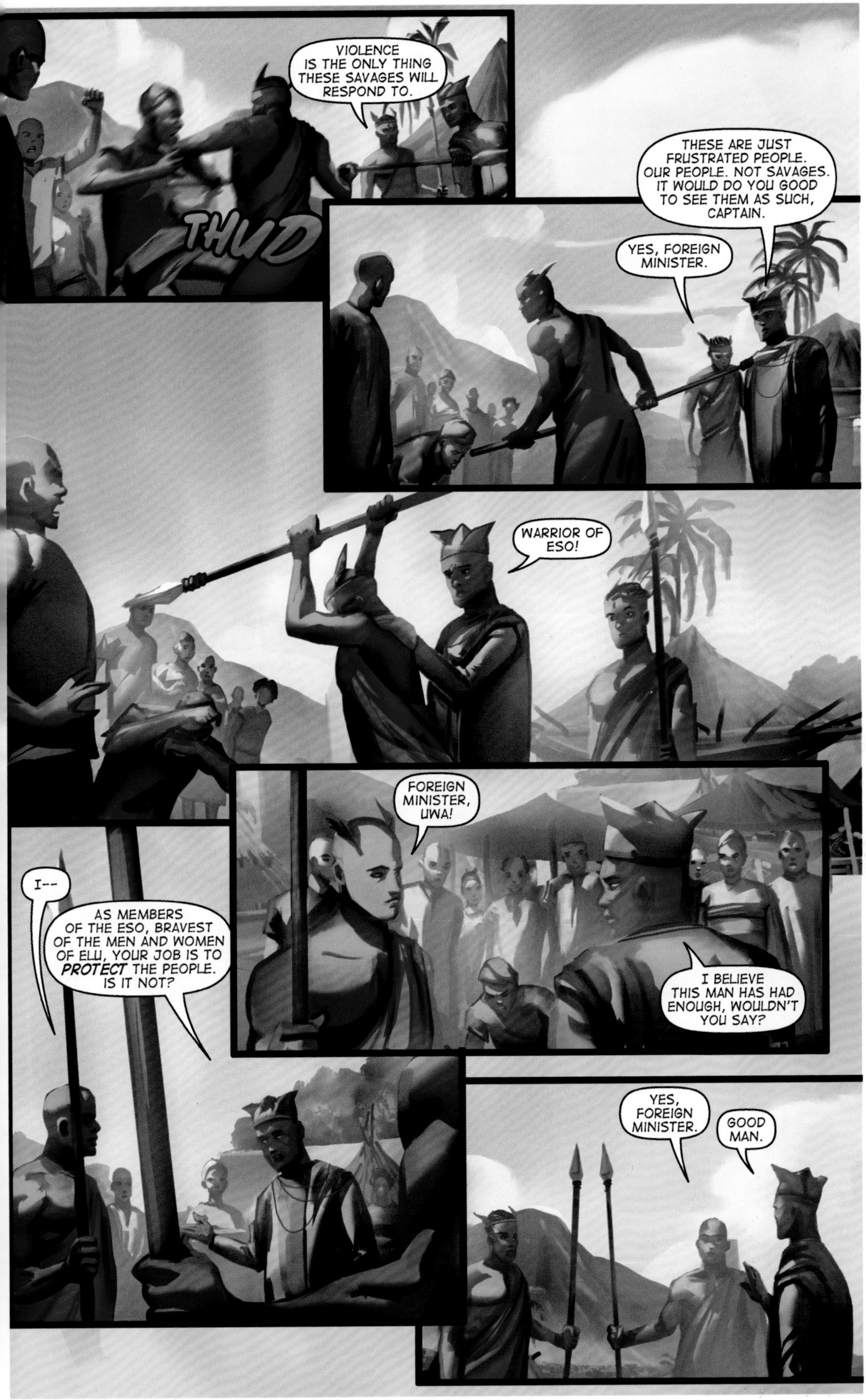
VIOLENCE IS THE ONLY THING THESE SAVAGES WILL RESPOND TO.
THUD
THESE ARE JUST FRUSTRATED PEOPLE. OUR PEOPLE. NOT SAVAGES. IT WOULD DO YOU GOOD TO SEE THEM AS SUCH, CAPTAIN.
YES, FOREIGN MINISTER.
WARRIOR OF ESO!
FOREIGN MINISTER, UWA!
I BELIEVE THIS MAN HAS HAD ENOUGH, WOULDN'T YOU SAY?
I--
AS MEMBERS OF THE ESO, BRAVEST OF THE MEN AND WOMEN OF ELU, YOUR JOB IS TO PROTECT THE PEOPLE. IS IT NOT?
YES, FOREIGN MINISTER.
GOOD MAN.

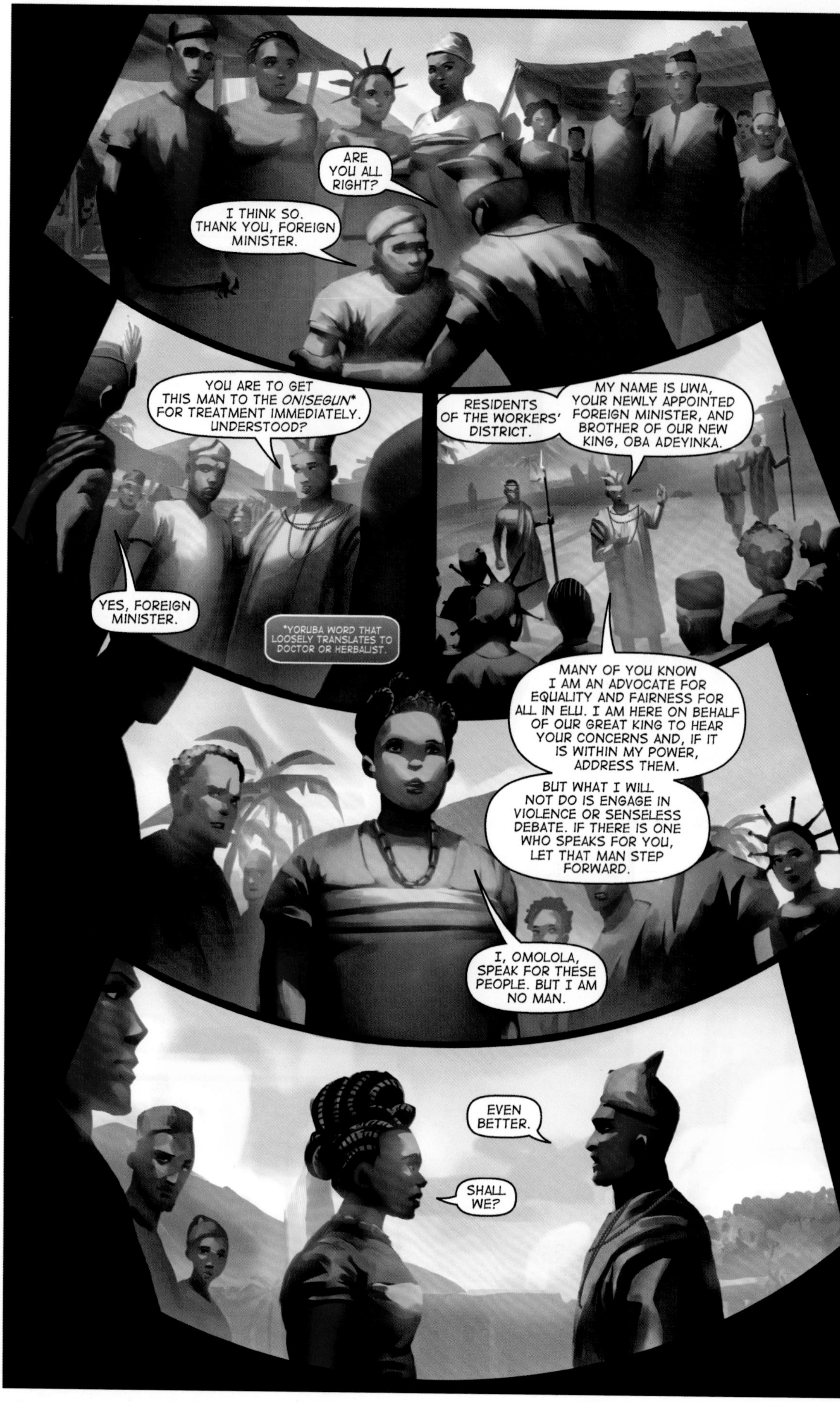
ARE YOU ALL RIGHT?
I THINK SO. THANK YOU, FOREIGN MINISTER.
YOU ARE TO GET THIS MAN TO THE ONISEGUN* FOR TREATMENT IMMEDIATELY. UNDERSTOOD?
YES, FOREIGN MINISTER.
*YORUBA WORD THAT LOOSELY TRANSLATES TO DOCTOR OR HERBALIST.
RESIDENTS OF THE WORKERS' DISTRICT.
MY NAME IS UWA, YOUR NEWLY APPOINTED FOREIGN MINISTER, AND BROTHER OF OUR NEW KING, OBA ADEYINKA.
MANY OF YOU KNOW I AM AN ADVOCATE FOR EQUALITY AND FAIRNESS FOR ALL IN ELU. I AM HERE ON BEHALF OF OUR GREAT KING TO HEAR YOUR CONCERNS AND, IF IT IS WITHIN MY POWER, ADDRESS THEM.
BUT WHAT I WILL NOT DO IS ENGAGE IN VIOLENCE OR SENSELESS DEBATE. IF THERE IS ONE WHO SPEAKS FOR YOU, LET THAT MAN STEP FORWARD.
I, OMOLOLA, SPEAK FOR THESE PEOPLE. BUT I AM NO MAN.
EVEN BETTER.
SHALL WE?

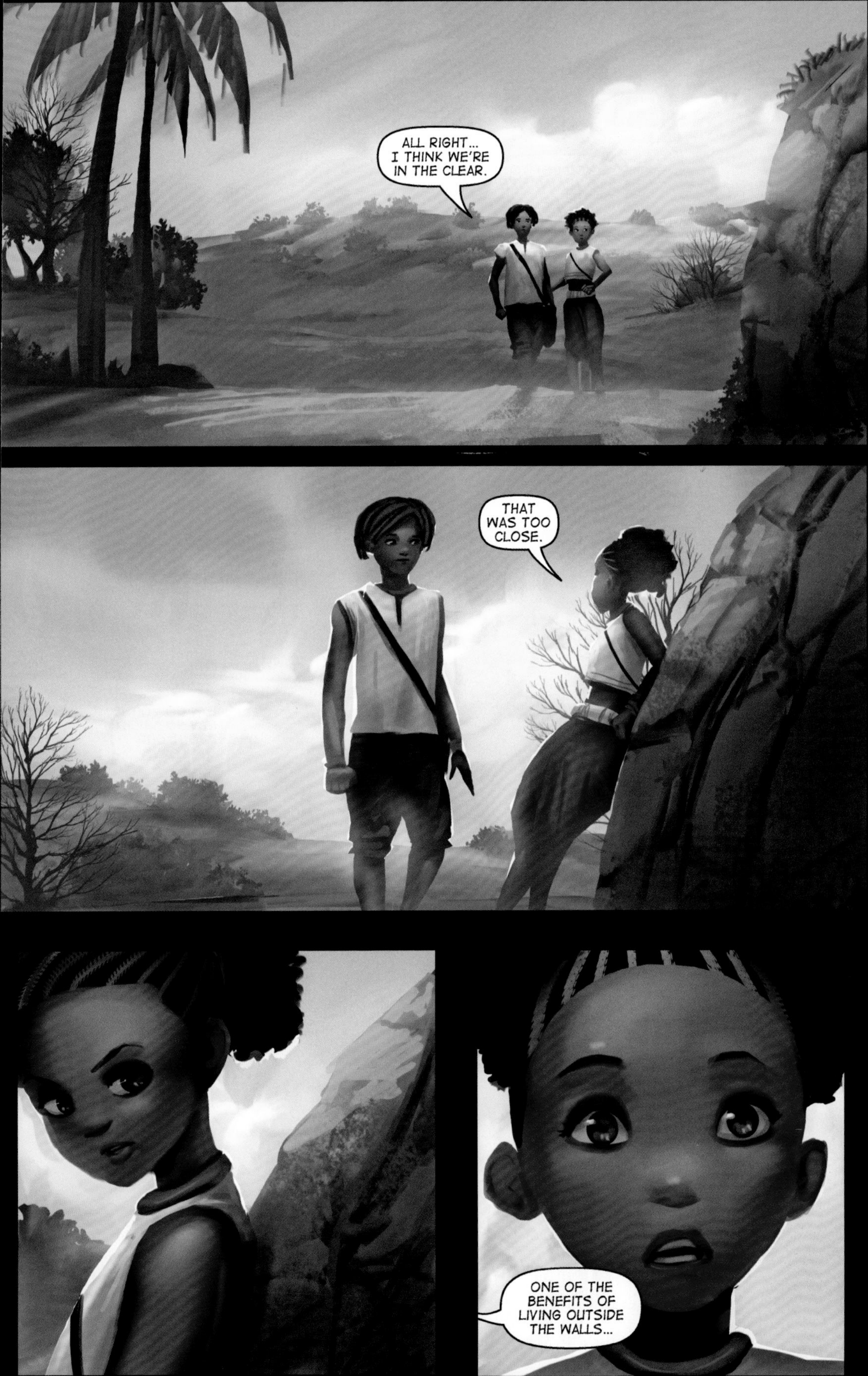
ALL RIGHT... I THINK WE'RE IN THE CLEAR.
THAT WAS TOO CLOSE.
ONE OF THE BENEFITS OF LIVING OUTSIDE THE WALLS...

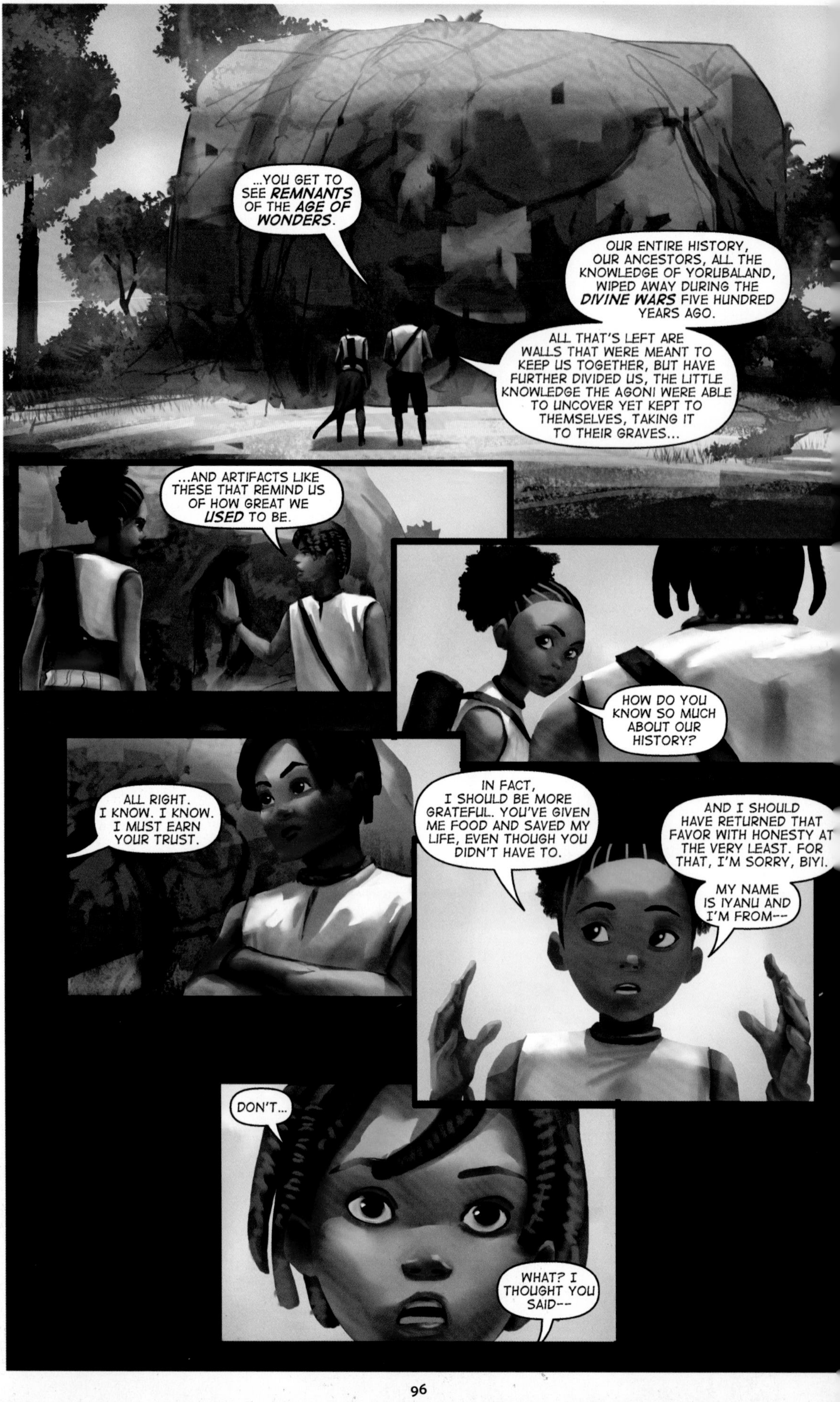
...YOU GET TO SEE REMNANTS OF THE AGE OF WONDERS.
OUR ENTIRE HISTORY, OUR ANCESTORS, ALL THE KNOWLEDGE OF YORUBALAND, WIPED AWAY DURING THE DIVINE WARS FIVE HUNDRED YEARS AGO.
ALL THAT'S LEFT ARE WALLS THAT WERE MEANT TO KEEP US TOGETHER, BUT HAVE FURTHER DIVIDED US, THE LITTLE KNOWLEDGE THE AGONI WERE ABLE TO UNCOVER YET KEPT TO THEMSELVES, TAKING IT TO THEIR GRAVES...
...AND ARTIFACTS LIKE THESE THAT REMIND US OF HOW GREAT WE USED TO BE.
HOW DO YOU KNOW SO MUCH ABOUT OUR HISTORY?
ALL RIGHT. I KNOW. I KNOW. I MUST EARN YOUR TRUST.
IN FACT, I SHOULD BE MORE GRATEFUL. YOU'VE GIVEN ME FOOD AND SAVED MY LIFE, EVEN THOUGH YOU DIDN'T HAVE TO.
AND I SHOULD HAVE RETURNED THAT FAVOR WITH HONESTY AT THE VERY LEAST. FOR THAT, I'M SORRY, BIYI.
MY NAME IS IYANU AND I'M FROM--
DON'T...
WHAT? I THOUGHT YOU SAID--

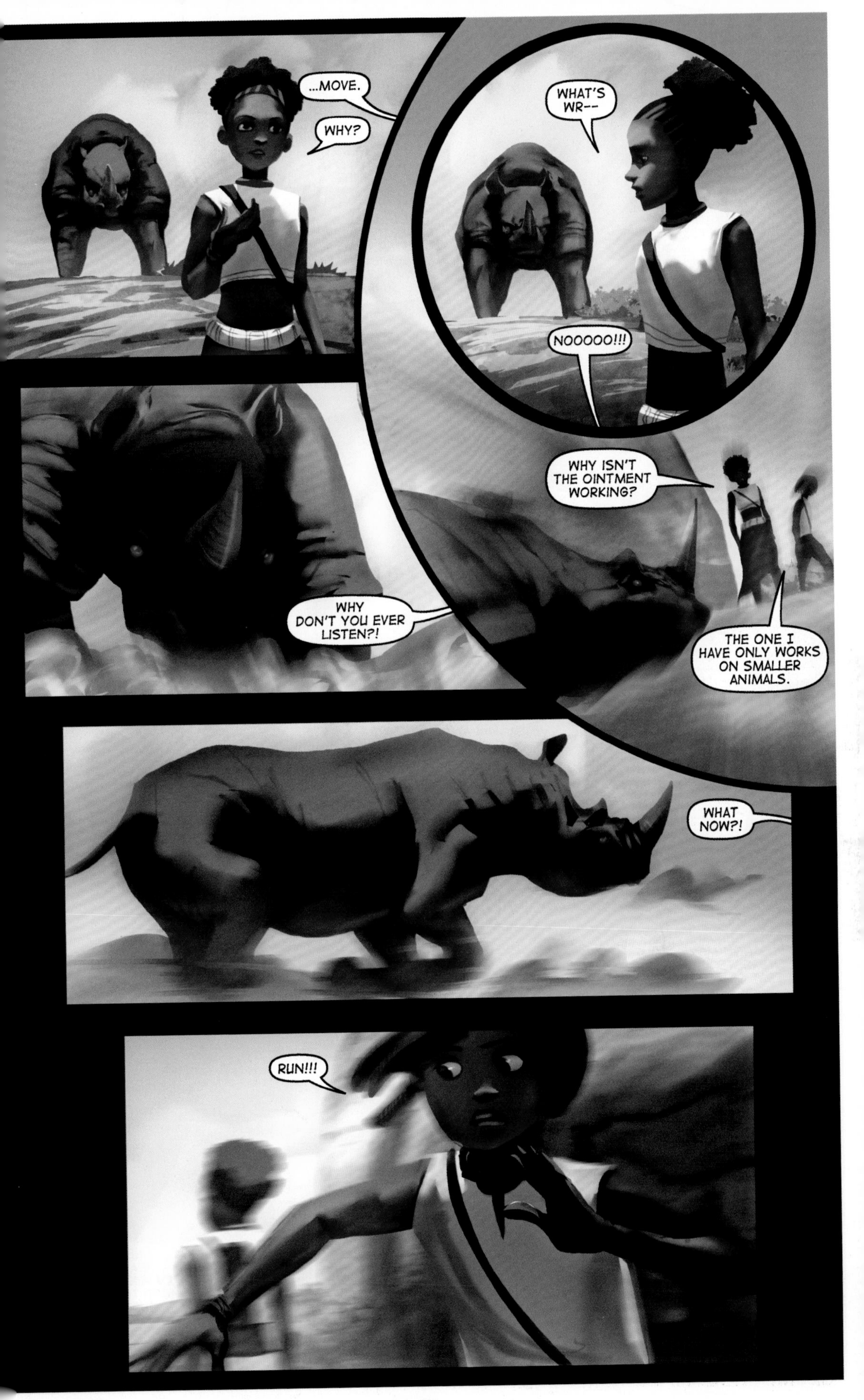

...MOVE.
WHY?
WHAT'S WR--
NOOOOO!!!
WHY DON'T YOU EVER LISTEN?!
WHY ISN'T THE OINTMENT WORKING?
THE ONE I HAVE ONLY WORKS ON SMALLER ANIMALS.
WHAT NOW?!
RUN!!!

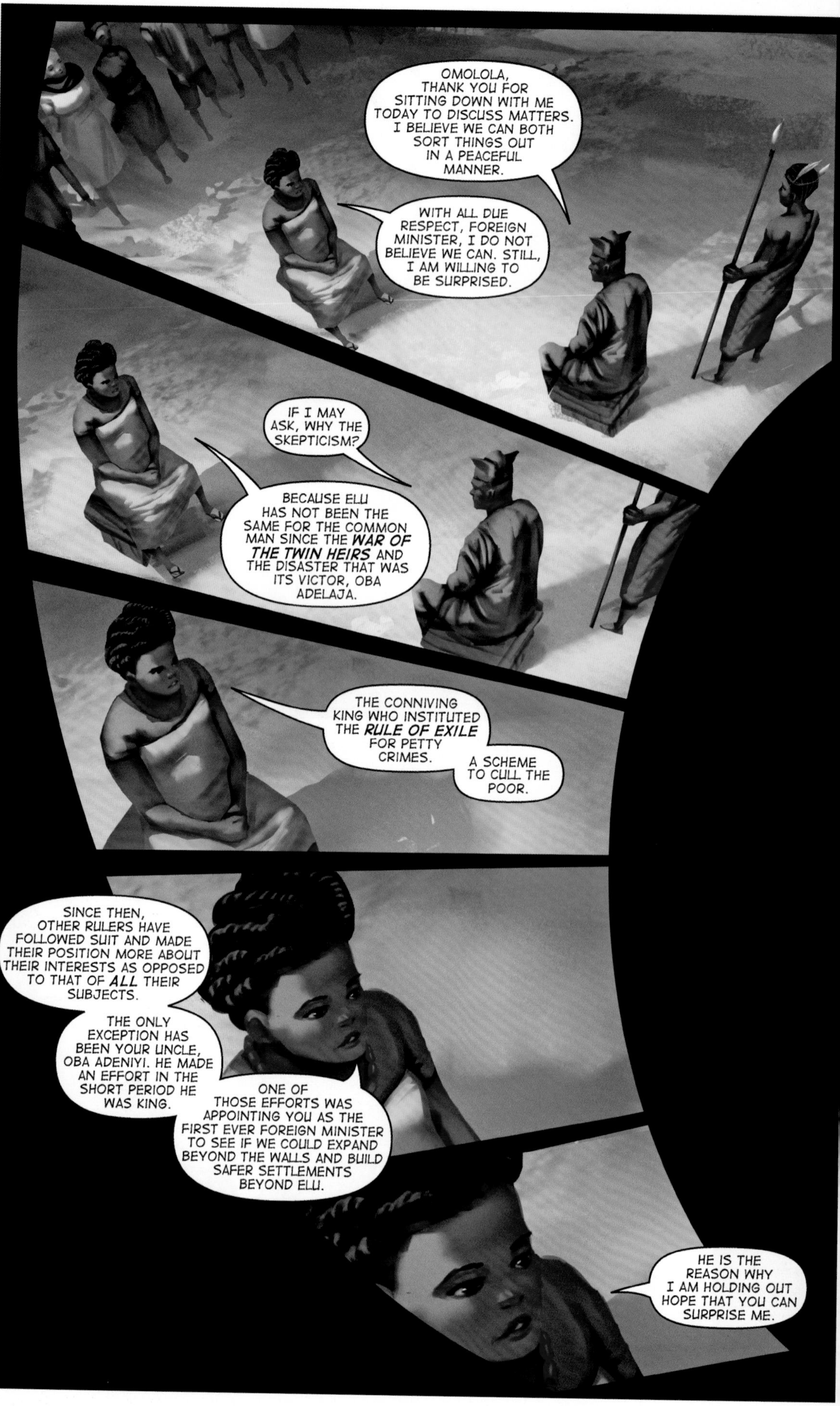
OMOLOLA, THANK YOU FOR SITTING DOWN WITH ME TODAY TO DISCUSS MATTERS. I BELIEVE WE CAN BOTH SORT THINGS OUT IN A PEACEFUL MANNER.
WITH ALL DUE RESPECT, FOREIGN MINISTER, I DO NOT BELIEVE WE CAN. STILL, I AM WILLING TO BE SURPRISED.
IF I MAY ASK, WHY THE SKEPTICISM?
BECAUSE ELU HAS NOT BEEN THE SAME FOR THE COMMON MAN SINCE THE ***WAR OF THE TWIN HEIRS*** AND THE DISASTER THAT WAS ITS VICTOR, OBA ADELAJA.
THE CONNIVING KING WHO INSTITUTED THE ***RULE OF EXILE*** FOR PETTY CRIMES.
A SCHEME TO CULL THE POOR.
SINCE THEN, OTHER RULERS HAVE FOLLOWED SUIT AND MADE THEIR POSITION MORE ABOUT THEIR INTERESTS AS OPPOSED TO THAT OF ***ALL*** THEIR SUBJECTS.
THE ONLY EXCEPTION HAS BEEN YOUR UNCLE, OBA ADENIYI. HE MADE AN EFFORT IN THE SHORT PERIOD HE WAS KING.
ONE OF THOSE EFFORTS WAS APPOINTING YOU AS THE FIRST EVER FOREIGN MINISTER TO SEE IF WE COULD EXPAND BEYOND THE WALLS AND BUILD SAFER SETTLEMENTS BEYOND ELU.
HE IS THE REASON WHY I AM HOLDING OUT HOPE THAT YOU CAN SURPRISE ME.

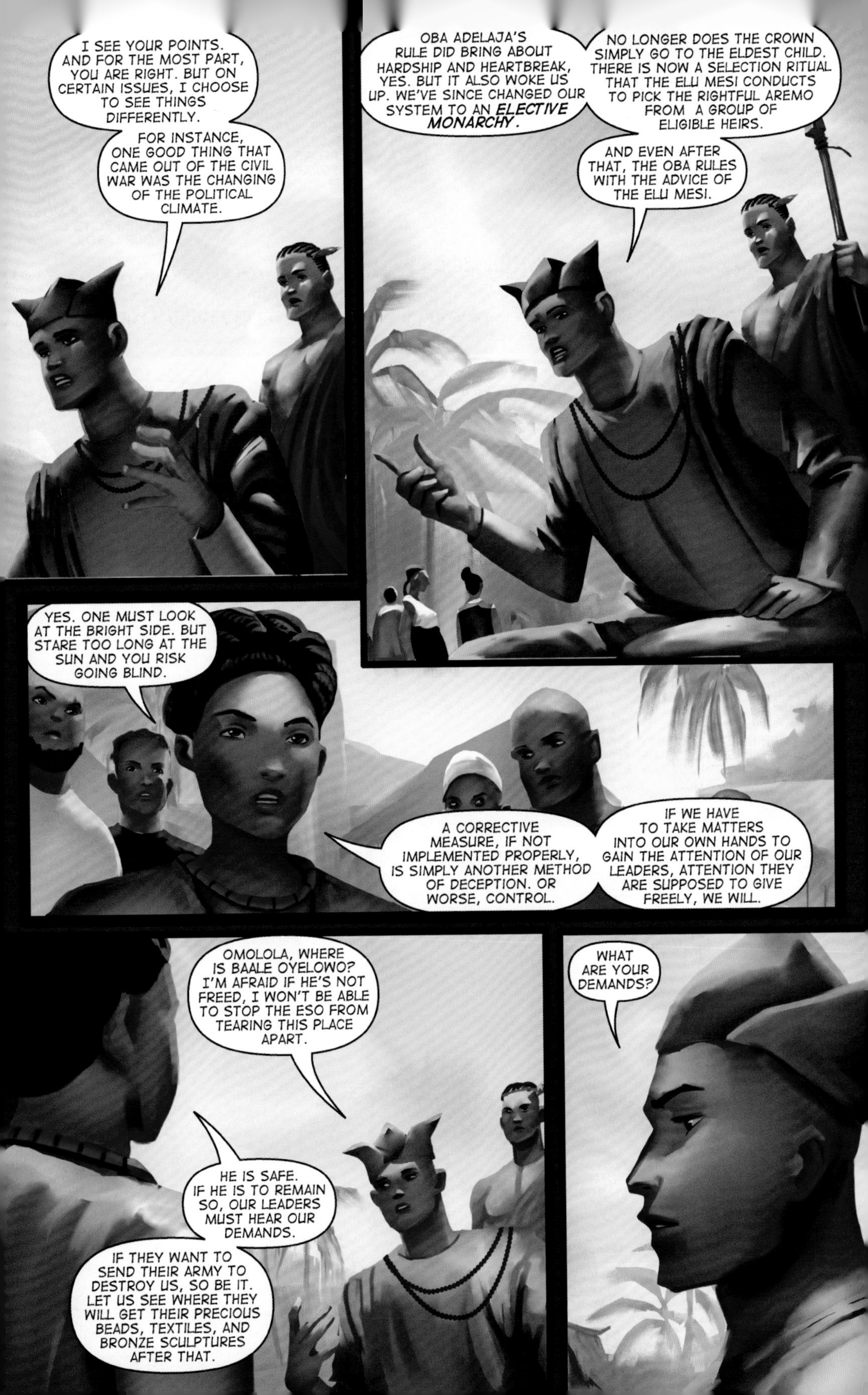
I SEE YOUR POINTS. AND FOR THE MOST PART, YOU ARE RIGHT. BUT ON CERTAIN ISSUES, I CHOOSE TO SEE THINGS DIFFERENTLY.
FOR INSTANCE, ONE GOOD THING THAT CAME OUT OF THE CIVIL WAR WAS THE CHANGING OF THE POLITICAL CLIMATE.
OBA ADELAJA'S RULE DID BRING ABOUT HARDSHIP AND HEARTBREAK, YES. BUT IT ALSO WOKE US UP. WE'VE SINCE CHANGED OUR SYSTEM TO AN *ELECTIVE MONARCHY*.
NO LONGER DOES THE CROWN SIMPLY GO TO THE ELDEST CHILD. THERE IS NOW A SELECTION RITUAL THAT THE ELU MESI CONDUCTS TO PICK THE RIGHTFUL AREMO FROM A GROUP OF ELIGIBLE HEIRS.
AND EVEN AFTER THAT, THE OBA RULES WITH THE ADVICE OF THE ELU MESI.
YES. ONE MUST LOOK AT THE BRIGHT SIDE. BUT STARE TOO LONG AT THE SUN AND YOU RISK GOING BLIND.
A CORRECTIVE MEASURE, IF NOT IMPLEMENTED PROPERLY, IS SIMPLY ANOTHER METHOD OF DECEPTION. OR WORSE, CONTROL.
IF WE HAVE TO TAKE MATTERS INTO OUR OWN HANDS TO GAIN THE ATTENTION OF OUR LEADERS, ATTENTION THEY ARE SUPPOSED TO GIVE FREELY, WE WILL.
OMOLOLA, WHERE IS BAALE OYELOWO? I'M AFRAID IF HE'S NOT FREED, I WON'T BE ABLE TO STOP THE ESO FROM TEARING THIS PLACE APART.
HE IS SAFE. IF HE IS TO REMAIN SO, OUR LEADERS MUST HEAR OUR DEMANDS.
IF THEY WANT TO SEND THEIR ARMY TO DESTROY US, SO BE IT. LET US SEE WHERE THEY WILL GET THEIR PRECIOUS BEADS, TEXTILES, AND BRONZE SCULPTURES AFTER THAT.
WHAT ARE YOUR DEMANDS?

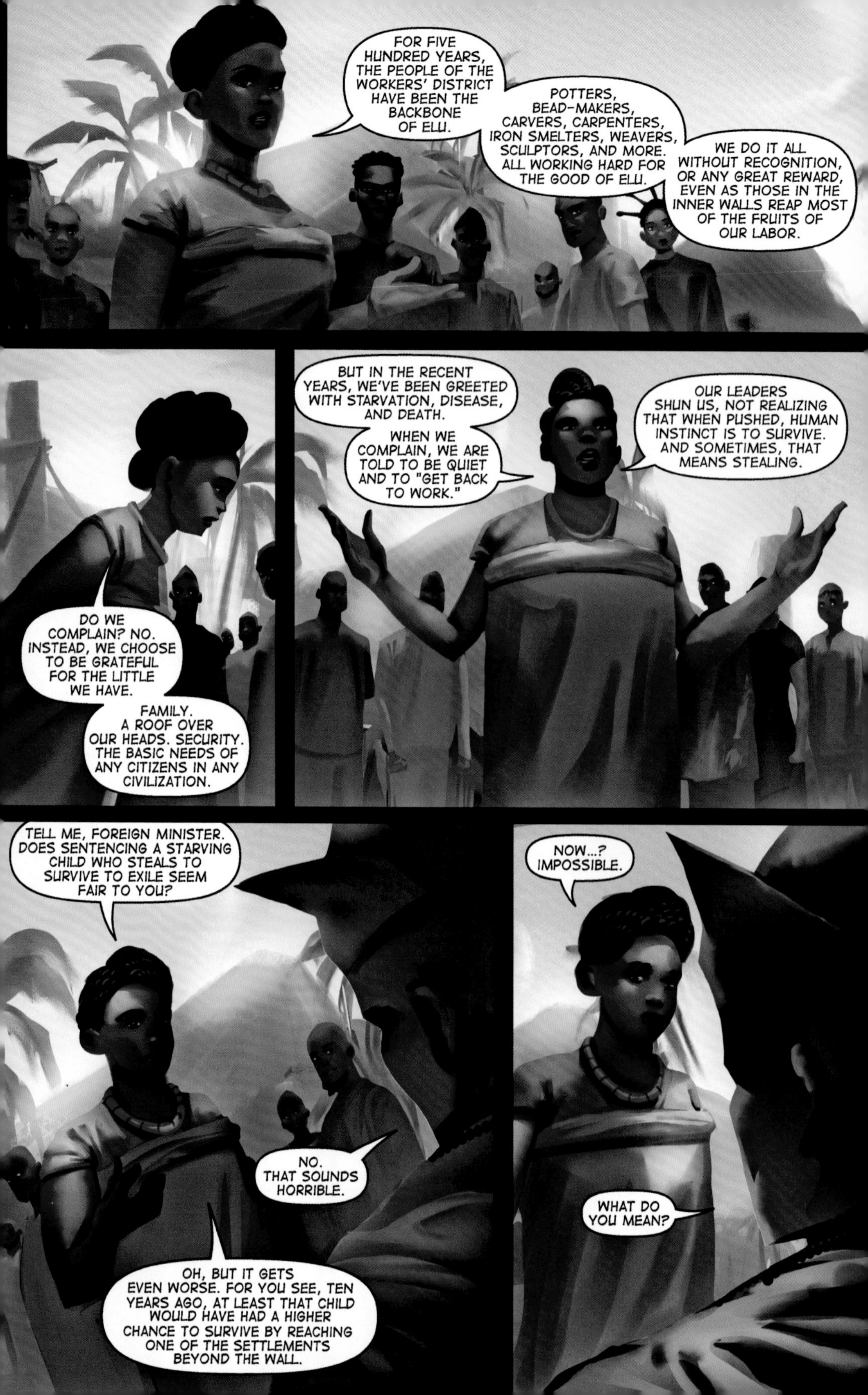
FOR FIVE HUNDRED YEARS, THE PEOPLE OF THE WORKERS' DISTRICT HAVE BEEN THE BACKBONE OF ELU.
POTTERS, BEAD-MAKERS, CARVERS, CARPENTERS, IRON SMELTERS, WEAVERS, SCULPTORS, AND MORE. ALL WORKING HARD FOR THE GOOD OF ELU.
WE DO IT ALL WITHOUT RECOGNITION, OR ANY GREAT REWARD, EVEN AS THOSE IN THE INNER WALLS REAP MOST OF THE FRUITS OF OUR LABOR.
DO WE COMPLAIN? NO. INSTEAD, WE CHOOSE TO BE GRATEFUL FOR THE LITTLE WE HAVE.
FAMILY. A ROOF OVER OUR HEADS. SECURITY. THE BASIC NEEDS OF ANY CITIZENS IN ANY CIVILIZATION.
BUT IN THE RECENT YEARS, WE'VE BEEN GREETED WITH STARVATION, DISEASE, AND DEATH.
WHEN WE COMPLAIN, WE ARE TOLD TO BE QUIET AND TO "GET BACK TO WORK."
OUR LEADERS SHUN US, NOT REALIZING THAT WHEN PUSHED, HUMAN INSTINCT IS TO SURVIVE. AND SOMETIMES, THAT MEANS STEALING.
TELL ME, FOREIGN MINISTER. DOES SENTENCING A STARVING CHILD WHO STEALS TO SURVIVE TO EXILE SEEM FAIR TO YOU?
NO. THAT SOUNDS HORRIBLE.
OH, BUT IT GETS EVEN WORSE. FOR YOU SEE, TEN YEARS AGO, AT LEAST THAT CHILD WOULD HAVE HAD A HIGHER CHANCE TO SURVIVE BY REACHING ONE OF THE SETTLEMENTS BEYOND THE WALL.
NOW...? IMPOSSIBLE.
WHAT DO YOU MEAN?

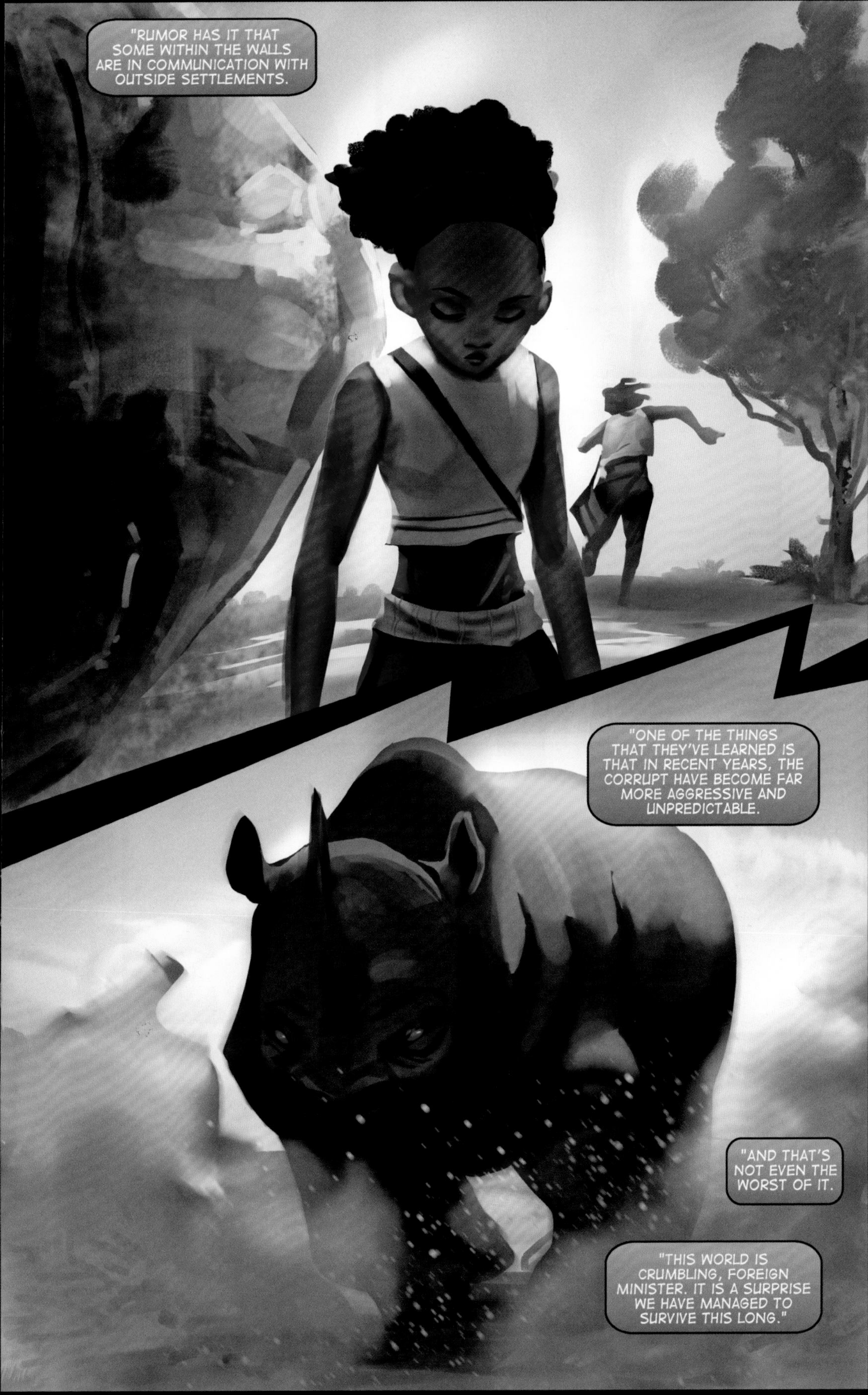
"RUMOR HAS IT THAT SOME WITHIN THE WALLS ARE IN COMMUNICATION WITH OUTSIDE SETTLEMENTS.
"ONE OF THE THINGS THAT THEY'VE LEARNED IS THAT IN RECENT YEARS, THE CORRUPT HAVE BECOME FAR MORE AGGRESSIVE AND UNPREDICTABLE.
"AND THAT'S NOT EVEN THE WORST OF IT.
"THIS WORLD IS CRUMBLING, FOREIGN MINISTER. IT IS A SURPRISE WE HAVE MANAGED TO SURVIVE THIS LONG."

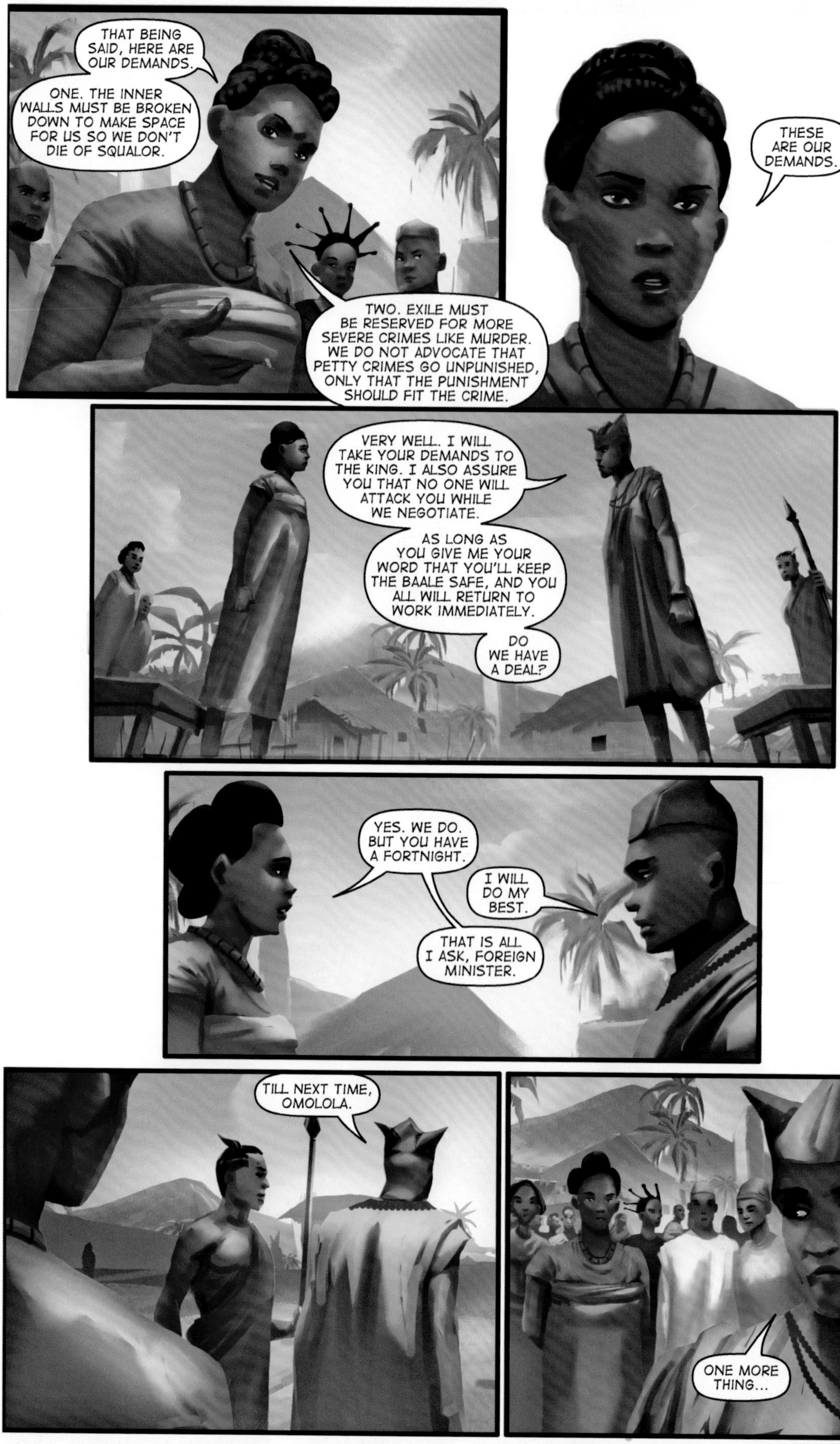
THAT BEING SAID, HERE ARE OUR DEMANDS.
ONE. THE INNER WALLS MUST BE BROKEN DOWN TO MAKE SPACE FOR US SO WE DON'T DIE OF SQUALOR.
THESE ARE OUR DEMANDS.
TWO. EXILE MUST BE RESERVED FOR MORE SEVERE CRIMES LIKE MURDER. WE DO NOT ADVOCATE THAT PETTY CRIMES GO UNPUNISHED, ONLY THAT THE PUNISHMENT SHOULD FIT THE CRIME.
VERY WELL. I WILL TAKE YOUR DEMANDS TO THE KING. I ALSO ASSURE YOU THAT NO ONE WILL ATTACK YOU WHILE WE NEGOTIATE.
AS LONG AS YOU GIVE ME YOUR WORD THAT YOU'LL KEEP THE BAALE SAFE, AND YOU ALL WILL RETURN TO WORK IMMEDIATELY.
DO WE HAVE A DEAL?
YES. WE DO. BUT YOU HAVE A FORTNIGHT.
I WILL DO MY BEST.
THAT IS ALL I ASK, FOREIGN MINISTER.
TILL NEXT TIME, OMOLOLA.
ONE MORE THING...

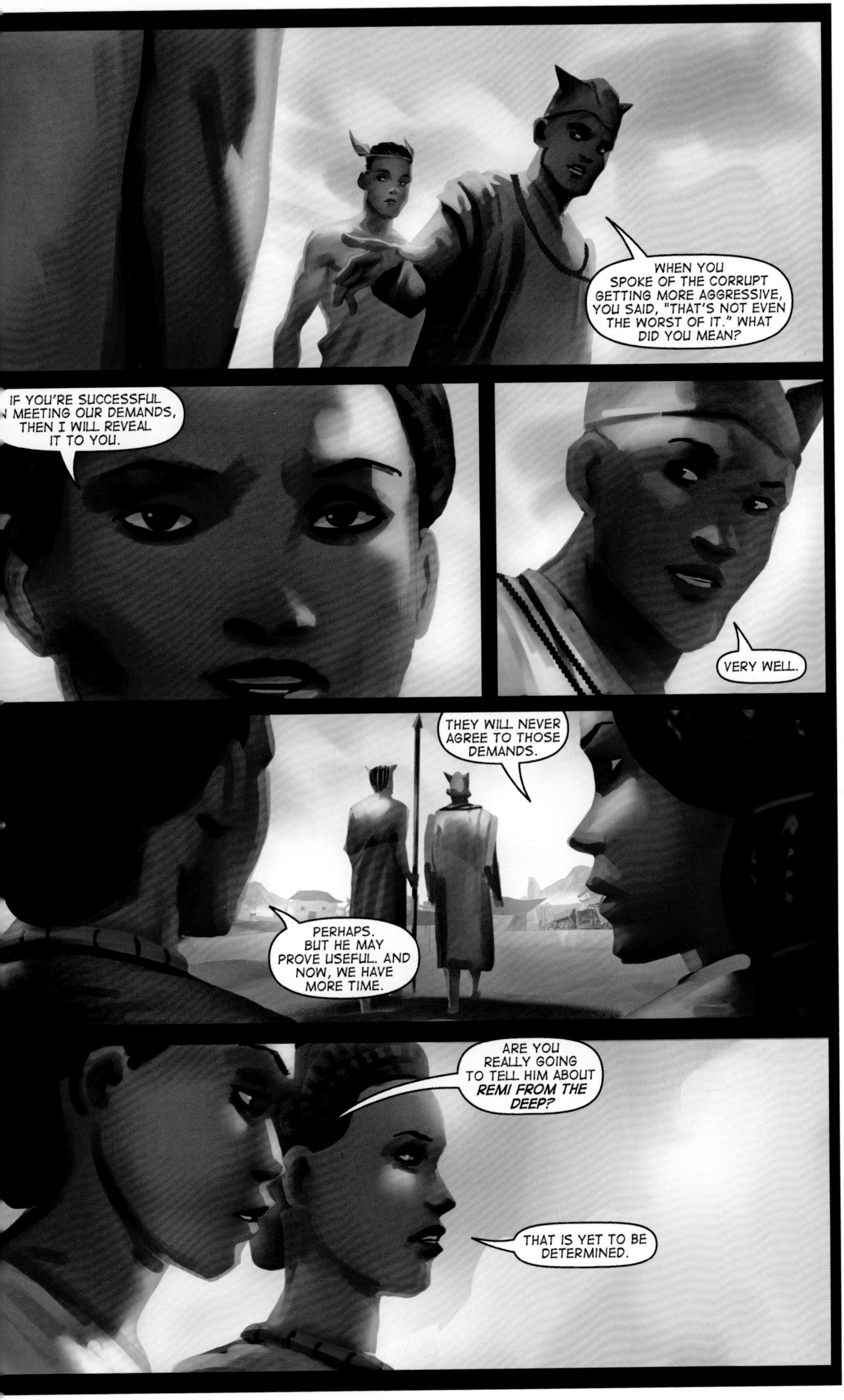
WHEN YOU SPOKE OF THE CORRUPT GETTING MORE AGGRESSIVE, YOU SAID, "THAT'S NOT EVEN THE WORST OF IT." WHAT DID YOU MEAN?
IF YOU'RE SUCCESSFUL N MEETING OUR DEMANDS, THEN I WILL REVEAL IT TO YOU.
VERY WELL.
THEY WILL NEVER AGREE TO THOSE DEMANDS.
PERHAPS. BUT HE MAY PROVE USEFUL. AND NOW, WE HAVE MORE TIME.
ARE YOU REALLY GOING TO TELL HIM ABOUT *REMI FROM THE DEEP?*
THAT IS YET TO BE DETERMINED.

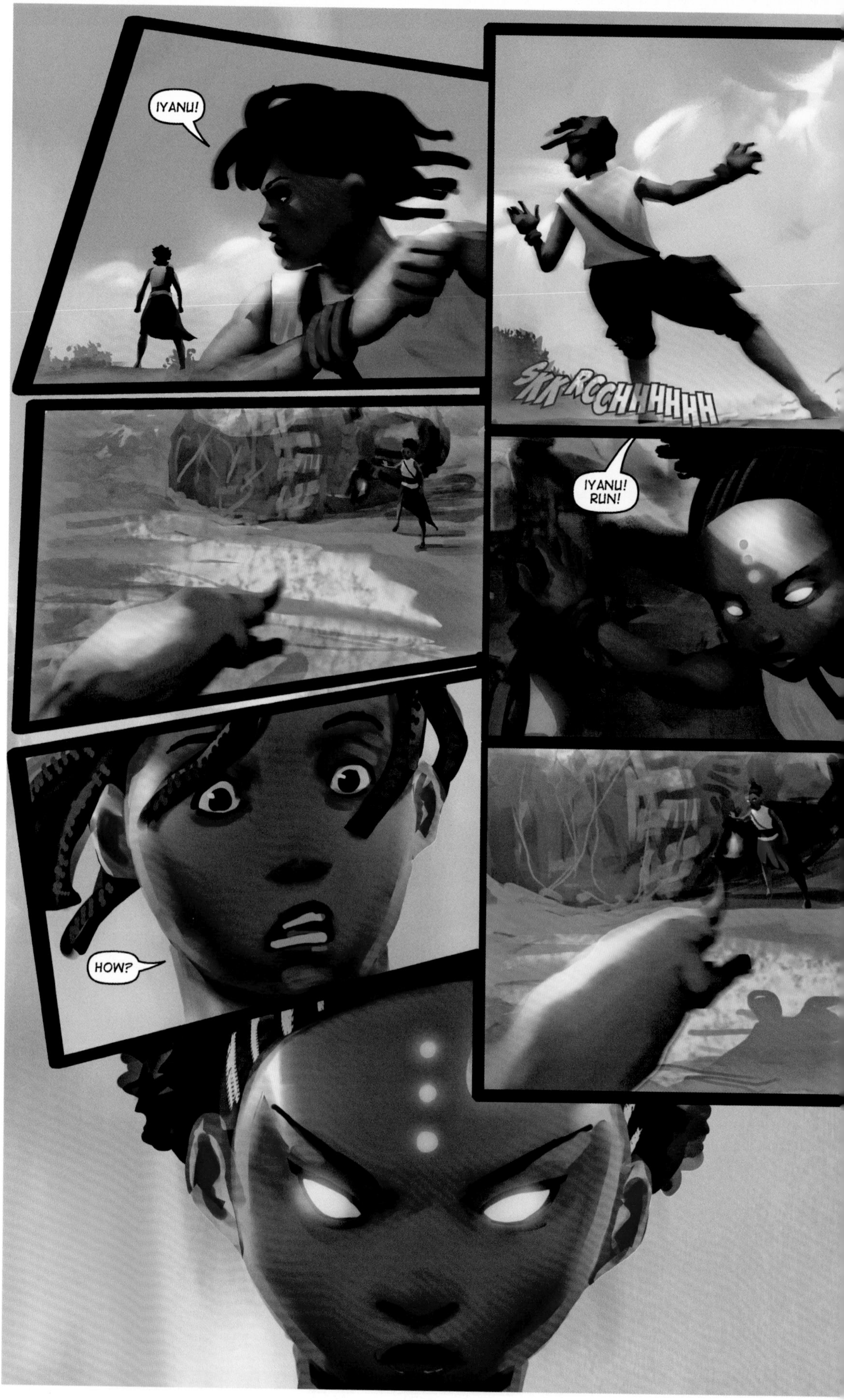

IYANU!
SKKRCCHHHHHH
IYANU! RUN!
HOW?

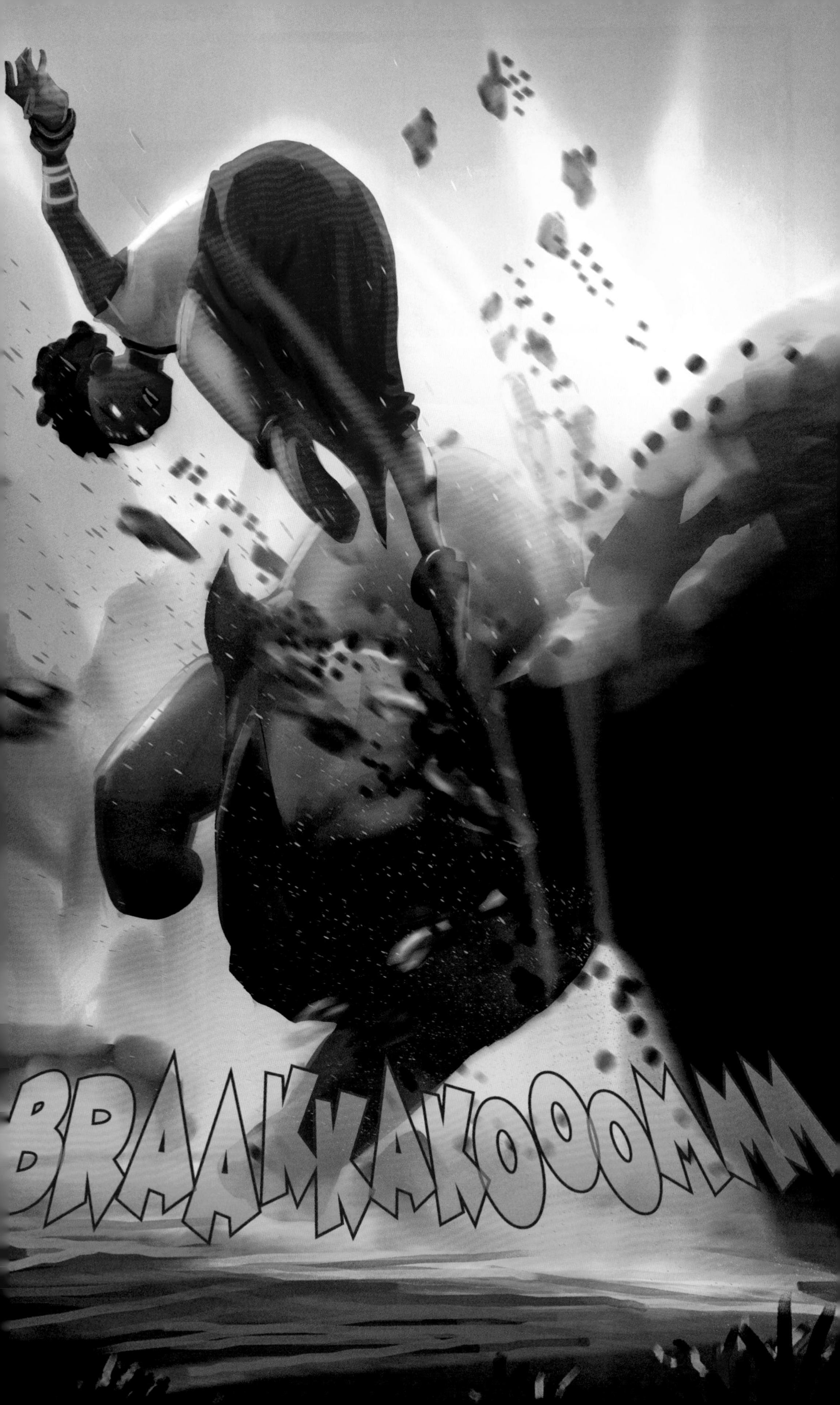
BRAAKAKOOOMM

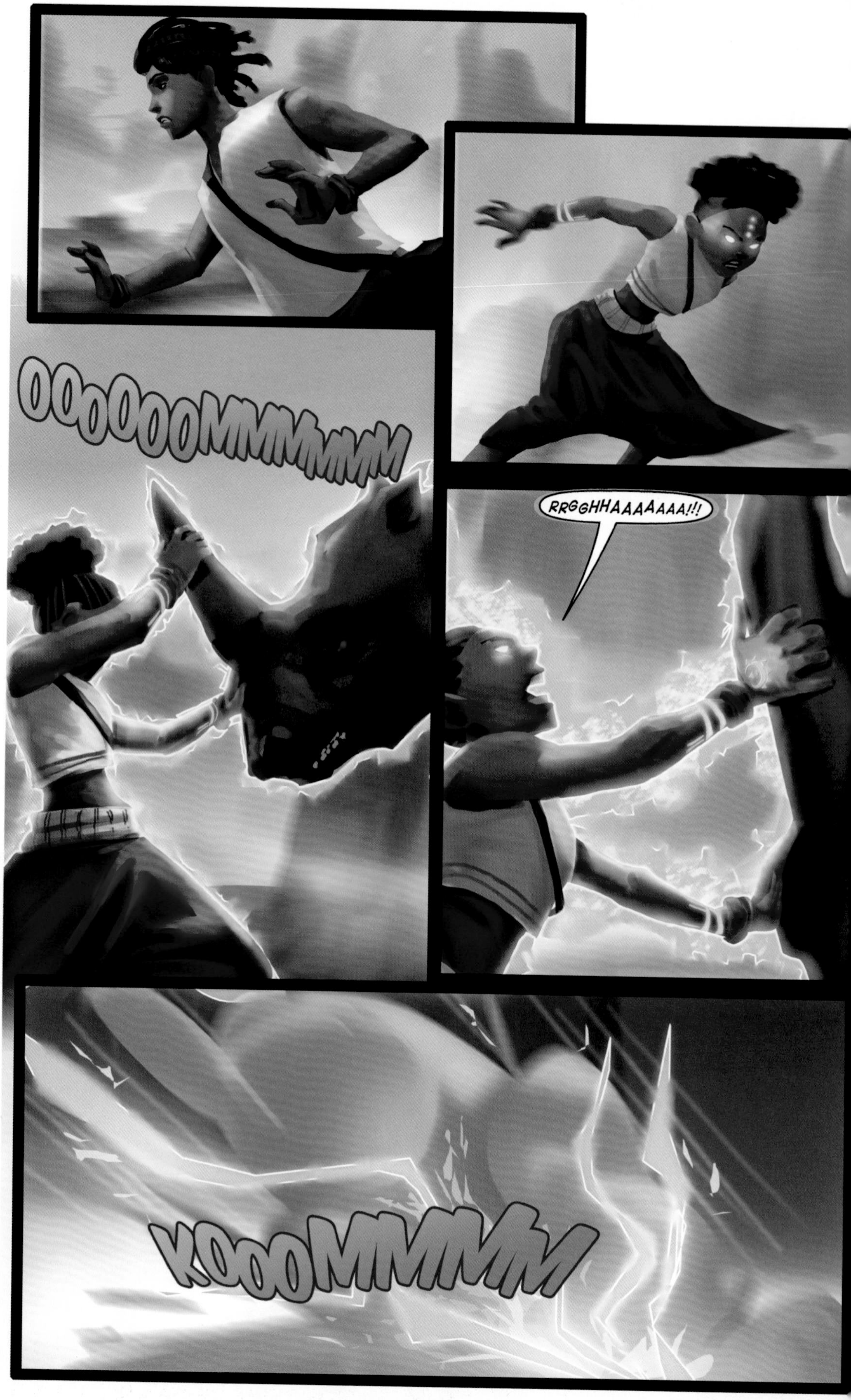
OOOOOOMMMMMMM
RRGGHHAAAAAAA!!!
KOOOMMMM

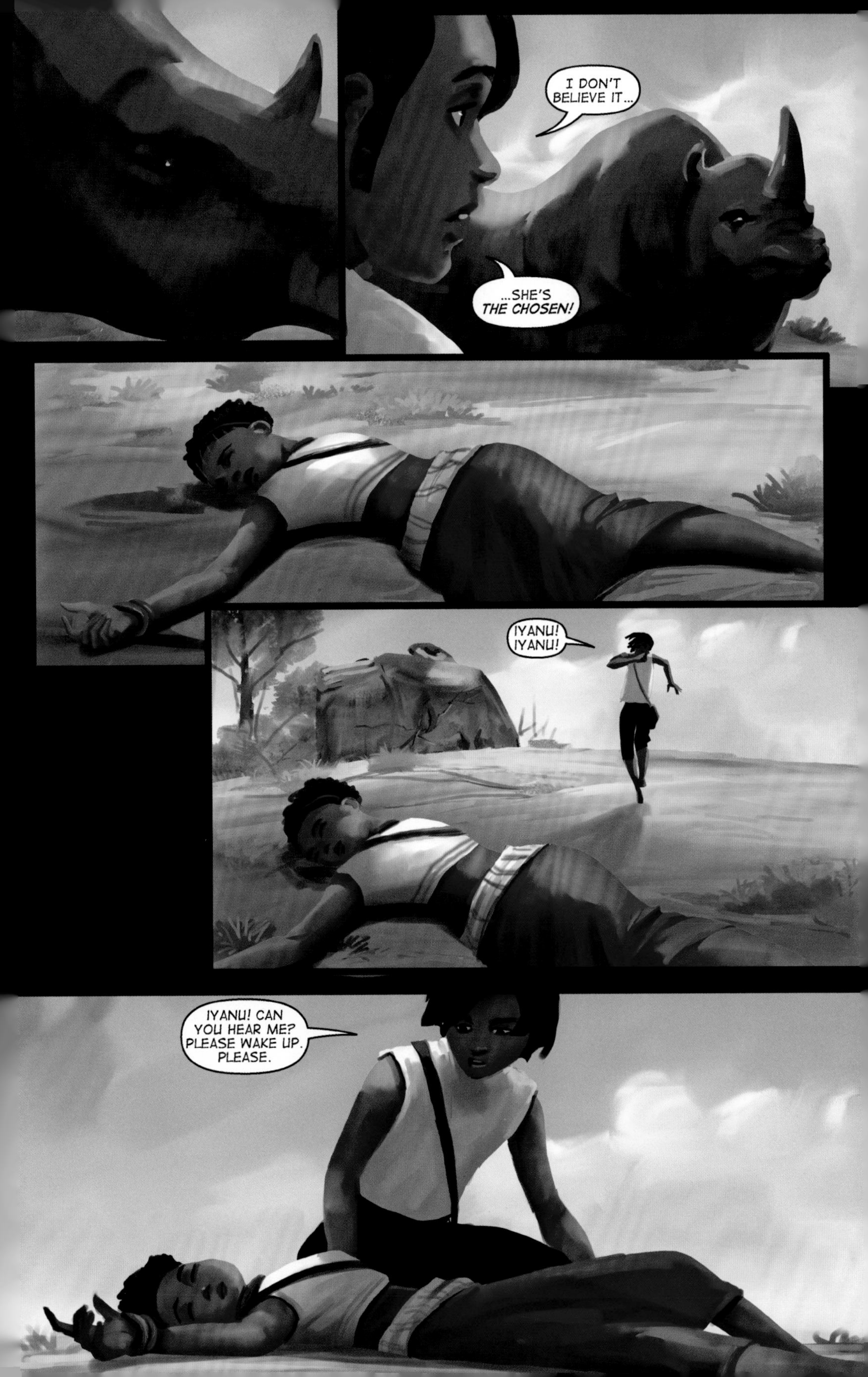
I DON'T BELIEVE IT...
...SHE'S *THE CHOSEN!*
IYANU! IYANU!
IYANU! CAN YOU HEAR ME? PLEASE WAKE UP. PLEASE.

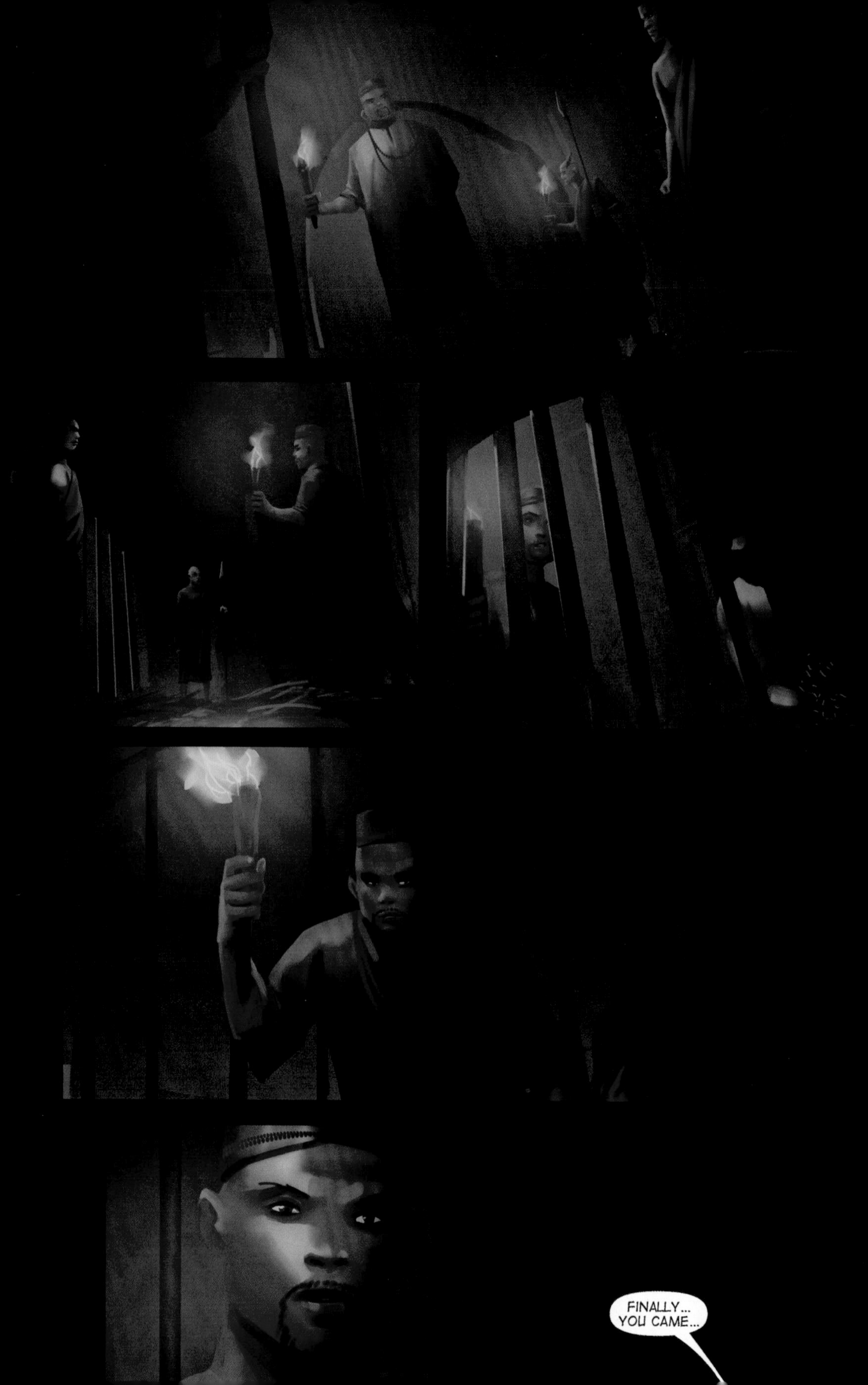
FINALLY... YOU CAME...

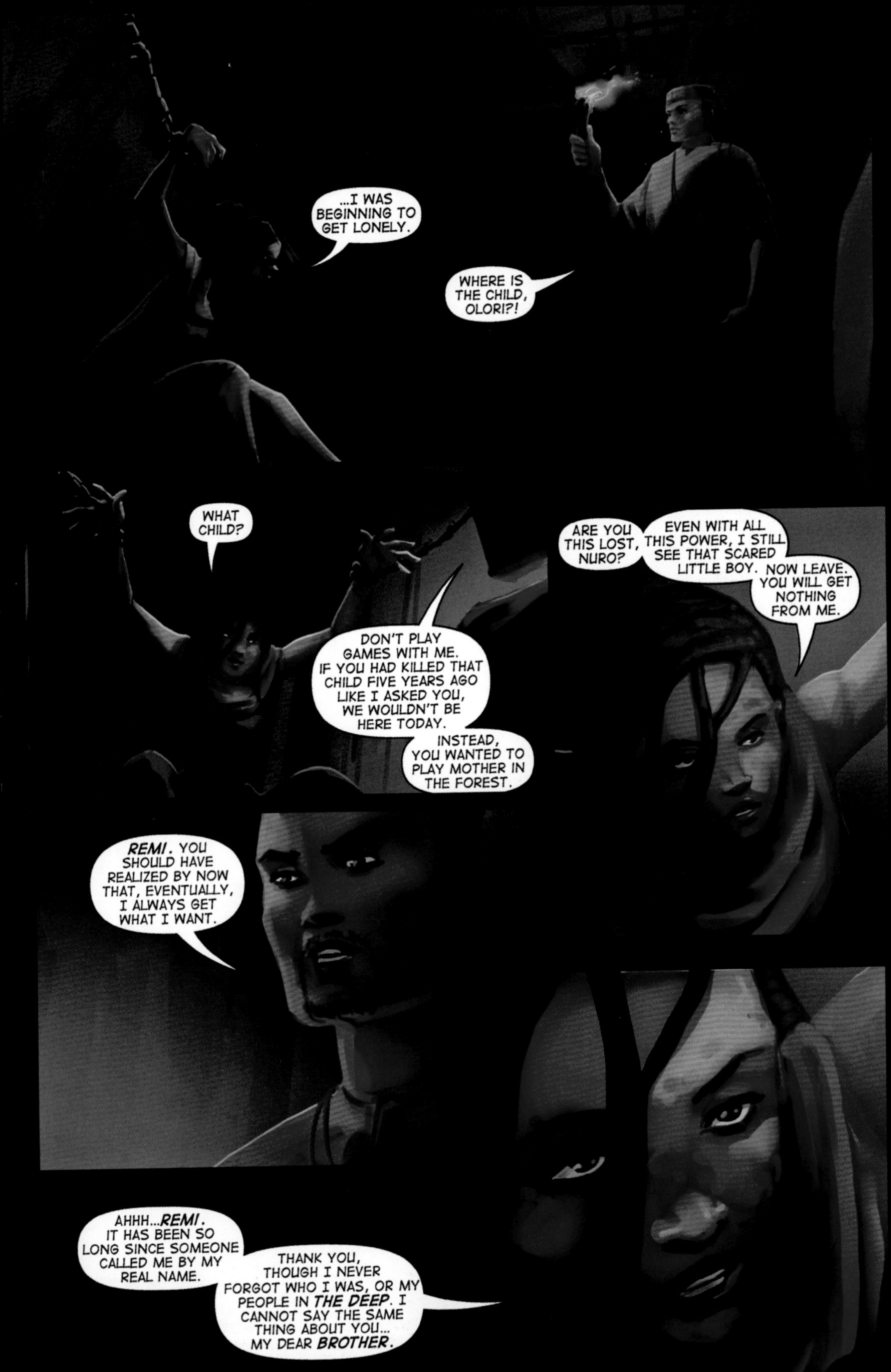

...I WAS BEGINNING TO GET LONELY.
WHERE IS THE CHILD, OLORI?!
WHAT CHILD?
DON'T PLAY GAMES WITH ME. IF YOU HAD KILLED THAT CHILD FIVE YEARS AGO LIKE I ASKED YOU, WE WOULDN'T BE HERE TODAY.
INSTEAD, YOU WANTED TO PLAY MOTHER IN THE FOREST.
ARE YOU THIS LOST, NURO?
EVEN WITH ALL THIS POWER, I STILL SEE THAT SCARED LITTLE BOY.
NOW LEAVE. YOU WILL GET NOTHING FROM ME.
REMI. YOU SHOULD HAVE REALIZED BY NOW THAT, EVENTUALLY, I ALWAYS GET WHAT I WANT.
AHHH...REMI. IT HAS BEEN SO LONG SINCE SOMEONE CALLED ME BY MY REAL NAME.
THANK YOU, THOUGH I NEVER FORGOT WHO I WAS, OR MY PEOPLE IN THE DEEP. I CANNOT SAY THE SAME THING ABOUT YOU... MY DEAR BROTHER.

TO BE CONTINUED...

IYANU™

CHILD OF WONDER

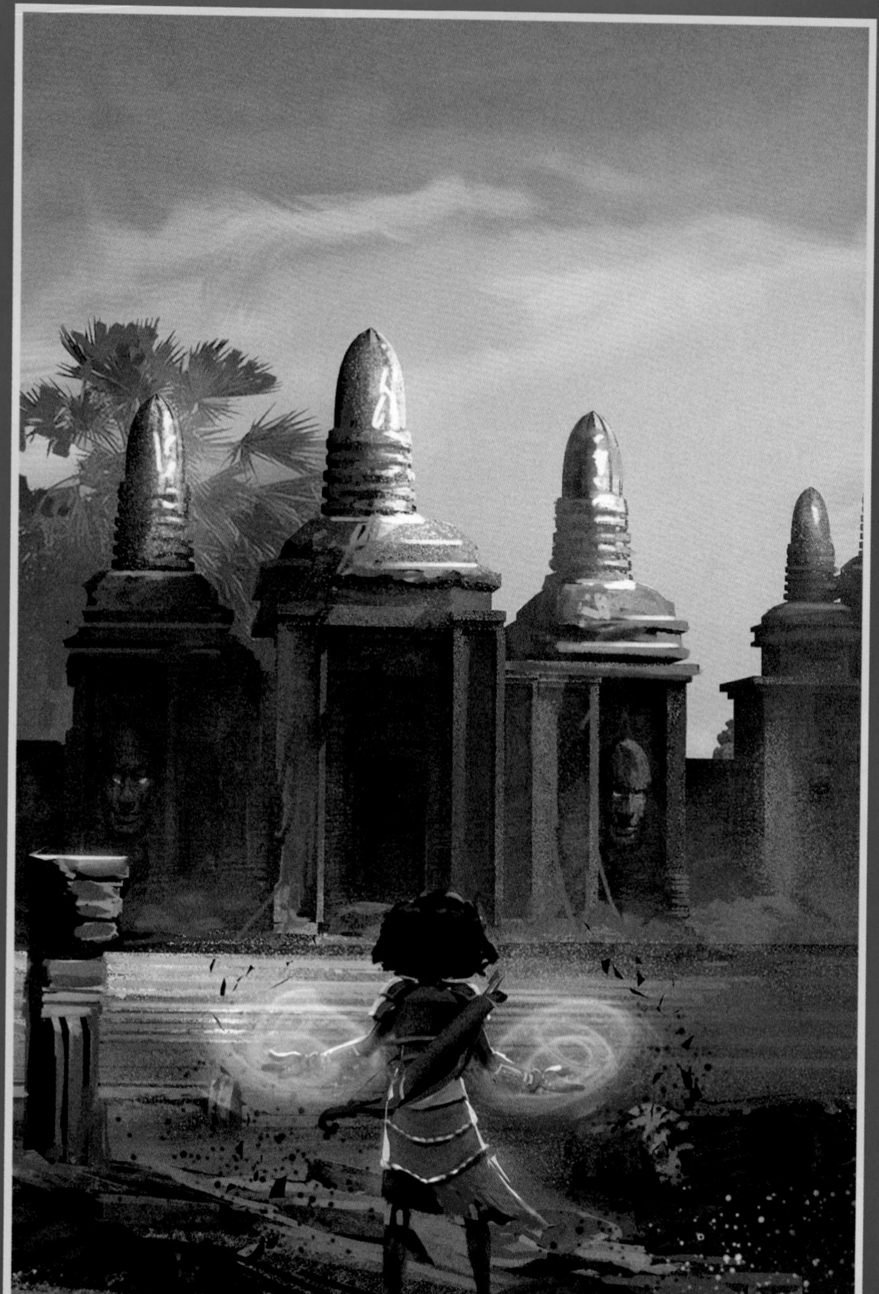

To be continued in *Iyanu: Child of Wonder* Volume 2—
from Roye Okupe, Godwin Akpan, and Spoof Animation!

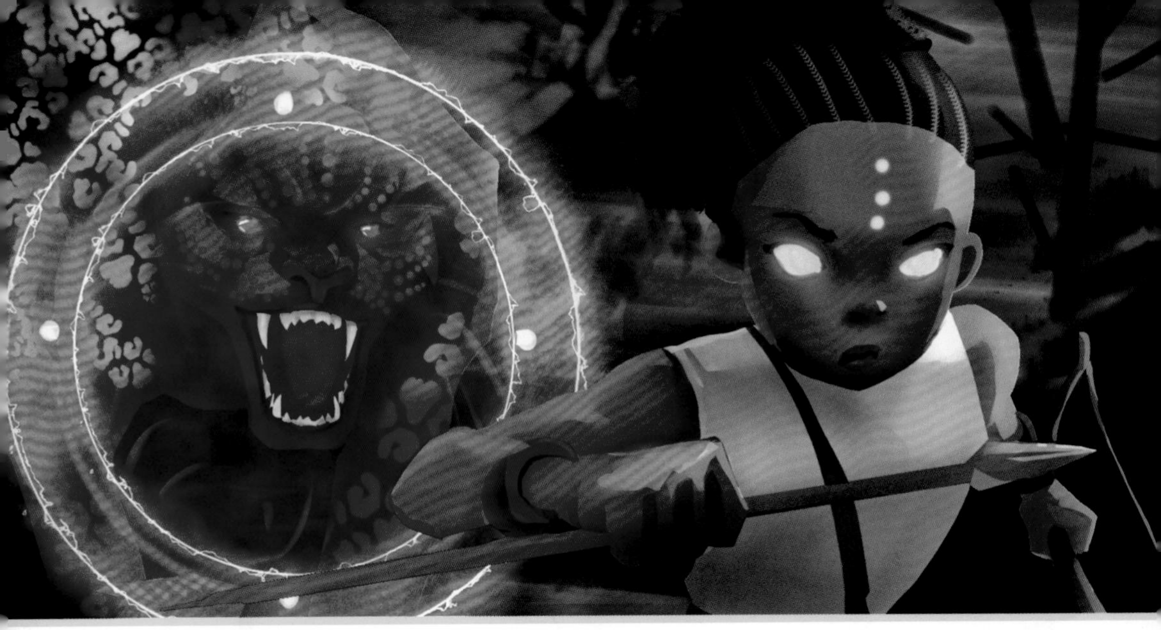

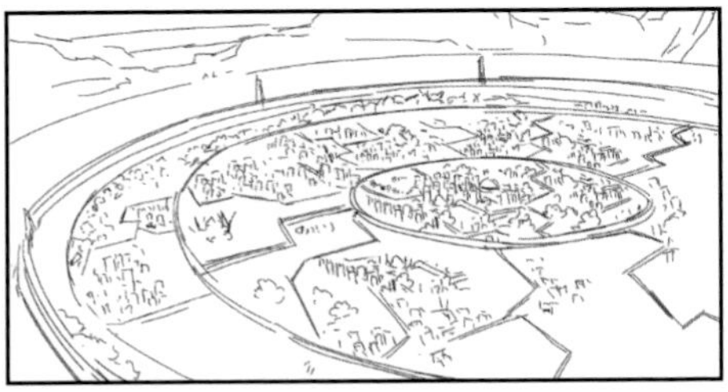

Creator's Corner with Roye Okupe

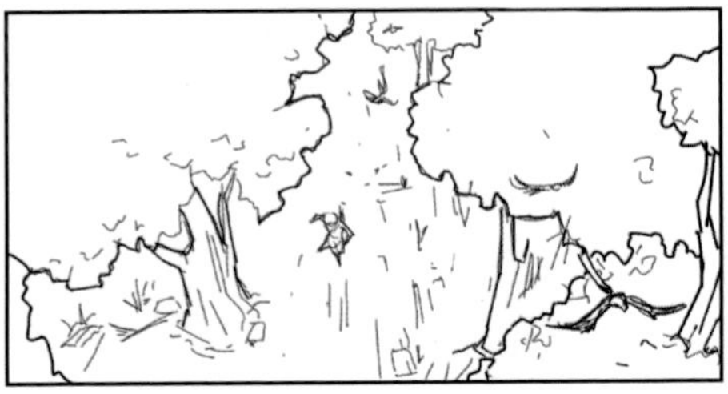

All sketches and concept art by Godwin Akpan

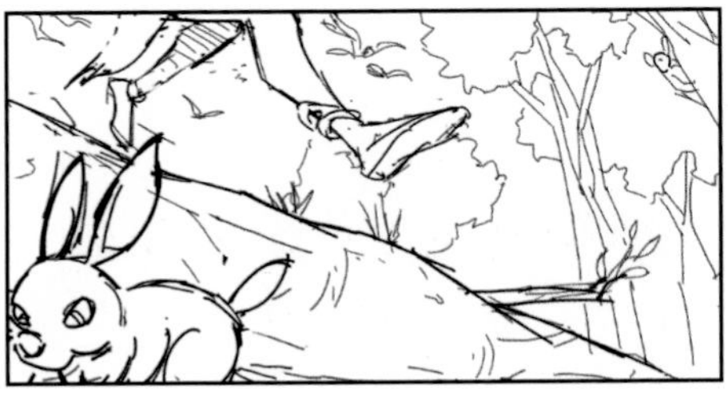

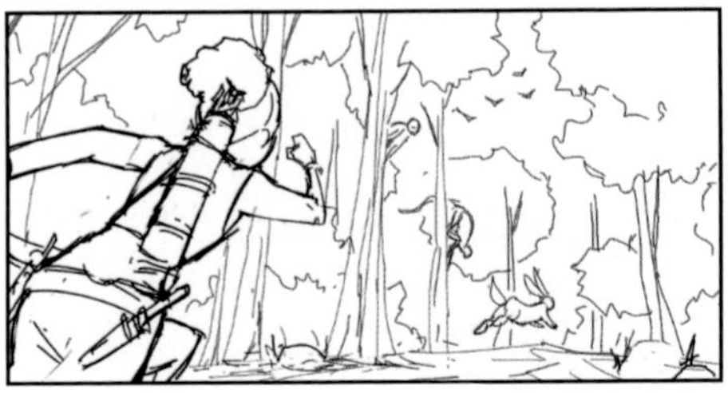

HEY, GUYS! ROYE here! Hope you've enjoyed *Iyanu* Volume 1. I thought it'd be a cool idea if I added, as a bonus, some more backstory to peel back the layers of this beautiful, massive world and geek out with you a bit about it. For the next few pages, I'll be giving some behind-the-scenes backstory about key characters, locations, and events pertaining to the world of Iyanu in chronological order. In order to do that, I've used the **conclusion** of the main event, the **Divine Wars**, as an anchor point to measure time. So **BDW** stands for "Before the Divine Wars," while **ADW** stands for "After the Divine Wars."

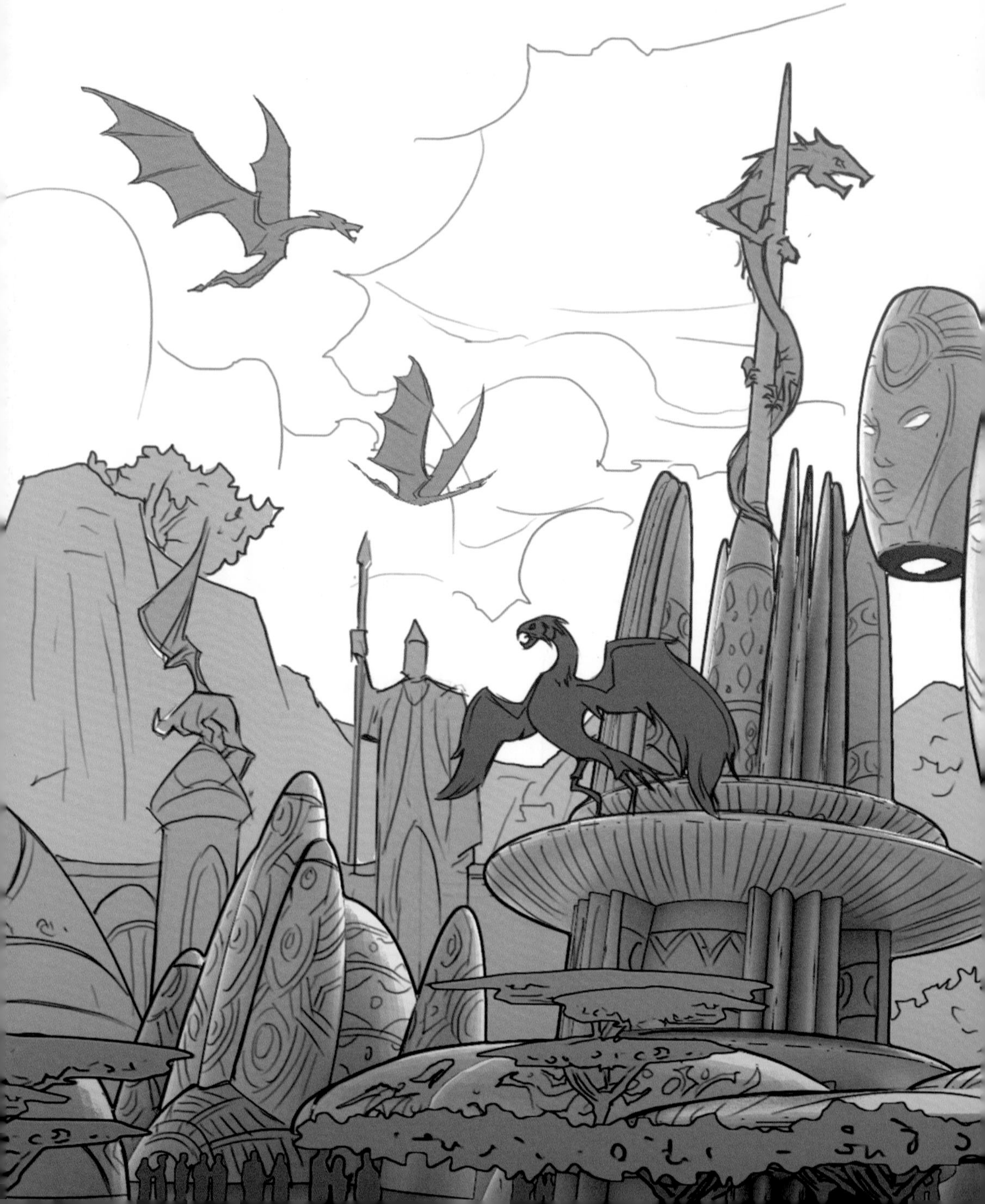

The Age of Wonders

(1,000-0 BDW)

THE MYTH OF this world begins with the **Divine Ones**, mighty guardians (sometimes referred to as Angels) sent to Yorubaland by **Akoda Aye** (the **Creator**) thousands of years ago. Lead by the **First Father**, king of the Divine Ones, their role on earth was to act as advocates, comforters, intercessors, and spiritual guides for humanity. For a thousand years, mankind, guided by the Divine Ones, flourished and lived in an unprecedented era of peace and prosperity. An era now known as the Age of Wonders! An era filled with spiritual, physical, structural, and technological marvels.

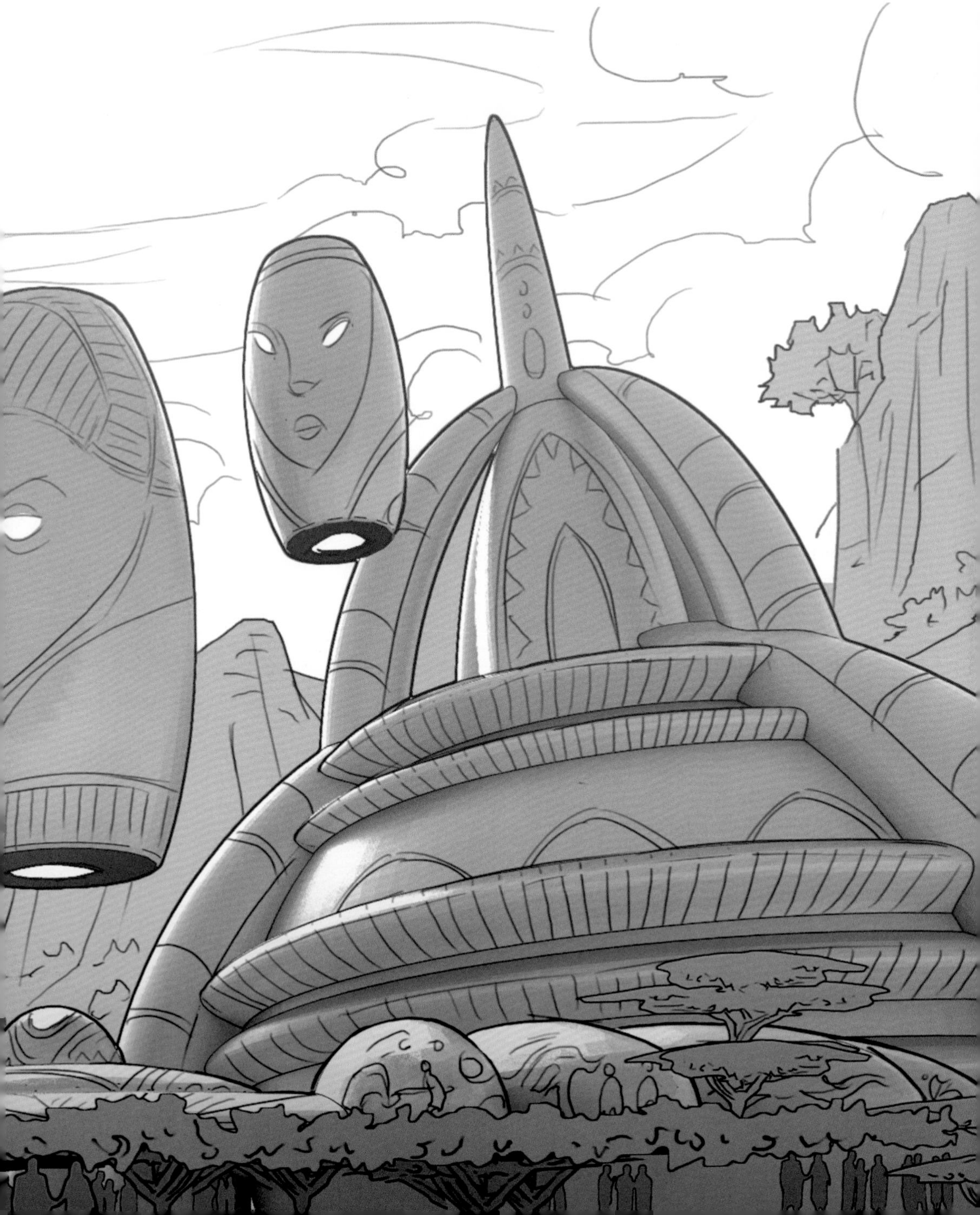

The Divine Wars
(10-0 BDW)

UNFORTUNATELY, PEACE AND PROSPERITY would one day come to an end. One of the sons of the First Father, who would later go on to be known as the **Fallen One**, decided to take a different path. After being seduced by forbidden dark magic, the Fallen One felt that the "inferior humans" should instead worship the Divine Ones. He would then go on to turn a third of the Divine Ones to his cause, splitting them into two camps: Those who relied upon pure divine power (the Armies of Light) given by the Creator and those who were seduced by dark magic (the Armies of Darkness). And thus began the Divine Wars.

The End of the Divine Wars
(0 BDW)

AFTER A DECADE of countless battles, the Divine Wars ended with the Fallen One and his camp defeated. But there were massive casualties on both sides. Sensing his imminent defeat, the Fallen would go on to commit two acts of vengeance towards humanity before he was put in an eternal prison:

The Curse

THE FALLEN ONE cursed the entirety of Yorubaland, turning all the animals against humanity. The animals they were created to have dominion over would now have dominion over them (the **Corrupt**).

The Destruction

KNOWING THAT a people cannot properly progress without knowing where they come from, the Fallen One would also go on to destroy buildings, records, structures, and every form of historical artifact of the people of Yorubaland and the Divine Ones, leaving only the **City of Elu** as the last standing walled city in Yorubaland.

This action would have a ripple effect on the following centuries, as culture became knowledge, knowledge became history, and history became mythology for all in Yorubaland.

ARCHITECTURAL BLUEPRINT

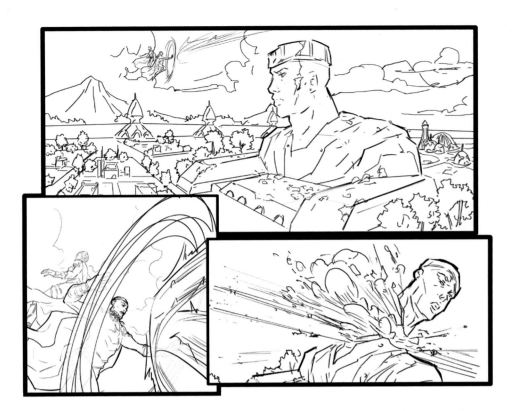

A New Yorubaland
(0 - 10 ADW)

AFTER THE DUST of the Divine Wars settled, the rest of the people of Yorubaland, the last hope of a once great civilization, rallied behind the massive **Walls of Elu** to protect themselves from the Corrupt. With the Divine Ones no longer around to guide them and with most people blaming their former deities for the war and destruction in Elu, most sought to veer far away from the history they shared with their former guardians. One of the first ways they would do this was by choosing their first ever human king: **Oba Ade**.

It is important to note that not all people turned their backs on the Divine Ones. In fact, a group of female-only priestesses, the **Agoni**, gathered together all the remnants they could find of the glory days and sought to preserve what knowledge they could through the centuries.

The Time of Peace
(10 - 399 ADW)

THOUGH THERE WAS the minor squabble here and there, the years from 10 to 399 ADW were a time of peace, harmony, and growth for the people of Yorubaland. While few were exiled due to extremely violent crimes and some willingly decided to explore life beyond the walls (a very dangerous decision because of the Corrupt), most of the people of Yorubaland lived within the walls of Elu.

This period was also filled with a massive growth in population. A blessing that would quickly turn into a curse as overpopulation quickly became a huge concern for the people of Elu towards the end of the era as the darker side of humanity slowly began to creep in.

UNIQUE COMBINATIONS.

The War of Twin Princes
(399 ADW)

IT IS FUNNY how one mistake or one moment of weakness by a ruler can set off a chain reaction of bad events that ripple centuries into the future of civilization. For the people of Elu, that ruler was **Oba Deji** (short for **Adedeji**). His mistake? Not naming an heir before he died.

Oba Deji had twin boys—**Prince Adelaja (Laja)** and **Prince Adebowale (Debo)**. He hesitated to name an heir, then he suddenly died of a mysterious illness. Both sons equally (and some thought, rightfully) believed they deserved the throne, and neither was willing to concede it. This split Elu in two, with powerful families choosing to side with whom they thought they could get the most from.

Up until this point in time, the system of monarchy had worked flawlessly through one single family—the royal bloodline of Oba Ade, the first king of Elu. Each successor was chosen simply because he (or she) was the eldest child. But because Oba Adedeji had twins and failed to name an heir before he died, it was unclear who the rightful **Aremo** was. It is also important to note that the Agoni stayed far away from this conflict. In general, they do not interfere with the politics of Elu.

The Exile of Prince Debo
(400 ADW)

AFTER ABOUT A YEAR OF CIVIL WAR, Prince Laja would emerge victorious after his brother Prince Debo surrendered. But the damage had already been done on both sides. So furious about the war, Prince Adelaja, for his first act as King of Elu, exiled his twin brother and his allies. Thousands of people and their families were displaced overnight. Some say Prince Laja did this to kill two birds with one stone. First, exiling his own brother would send a strong message to anyone who would dare challenge him. Second, banishing a hundred thousand people would do wonders for the population problem.

For Prince Debo and his followers, this was a death sentence. Their exile came right before the people of Elu learned how to make boats to sail the many channels of rivers outside the city in greater Yorubaland. In essence, their only hope was to travel hundreds of miles southwest to a place called the **Deep**. A region of extremely dense forests that were rumored to have an aura of magic around them that kept most of the Corrupt at bay. But in the absence of boats, Prince Debo and his people would have to walk across the **Riniku Plains**, the shortest distance between Elu and the Deep. This is a trek that very few, if any, dare to make, for the Riniku Plains is a vast savanna/grassland filled with hundreds of the Corrupt, apex predators included.

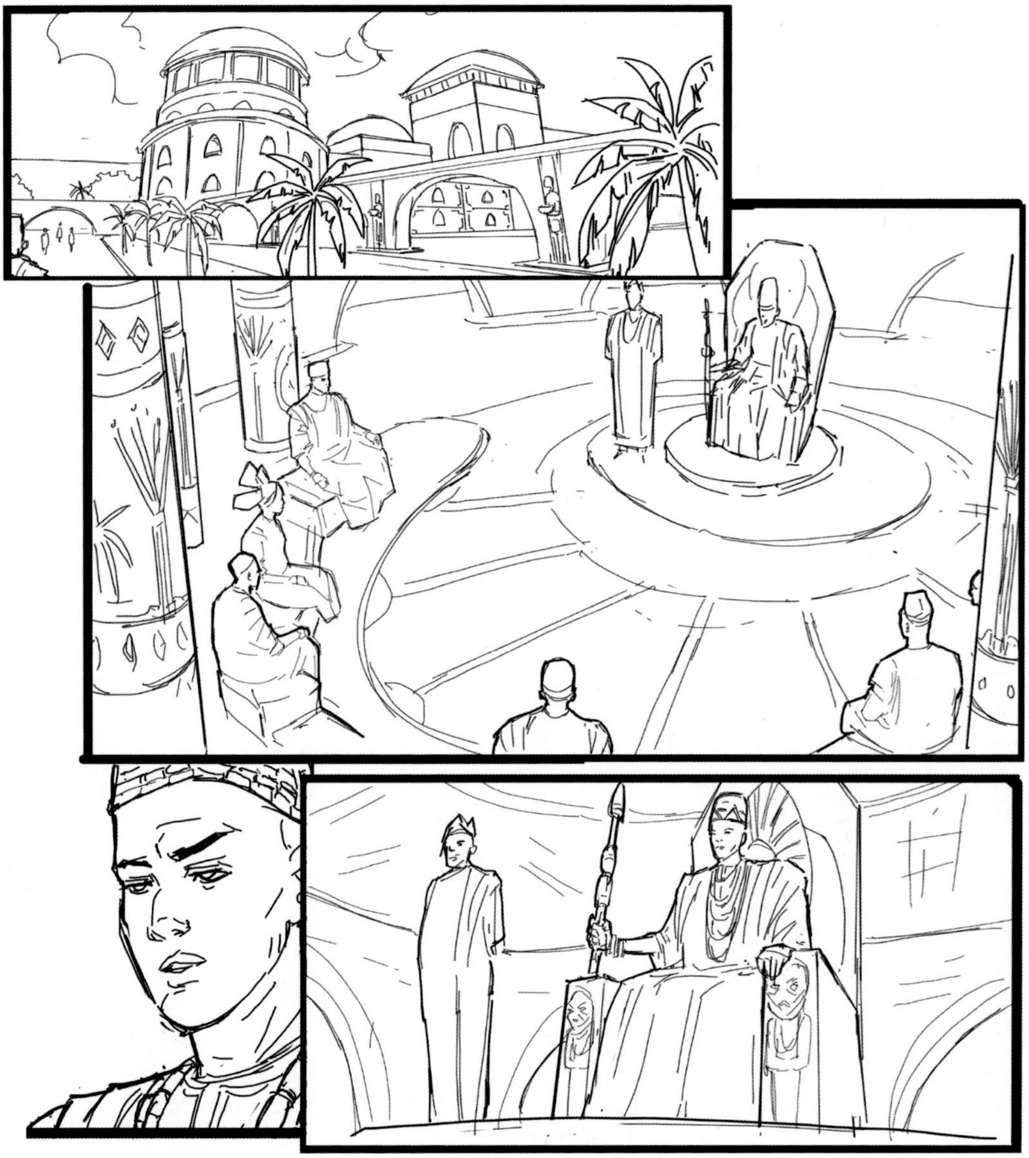

The Selective Monarchy

(405 - 525 ADW)

AFTER THE TERRIBLE TRAGEDY that was Oba Deji, the Elu Mesi and the Agoni would come together (a rare occurrence) to change Elu's system of leadership to a **Selective Monarchy**. Granting the Elu Mesi and the Agoni power to select (via a selection ritual) from a group of heirs (people with royal bloodline) the next king, as opposed to age just being the deciding factor.

Prince Adesoji, who would later become Oba Adesoji, was the first king selected by the Elu Mesi in a ritual that has lasted over one hundred years—up to present-day (525 ADW) king Oba Adeyinka.

It is also important to note that before this, the Elu Mesi were simply just advisors to the current Oba.

Conclusion

Now that you're all caught up with the history of Yorubaland, I can't wait for you to see what's in store for *Iyanu: Child of Wonder* Volume 2. Stay tuned!

–ROYE OKUPE, APRIL 2021

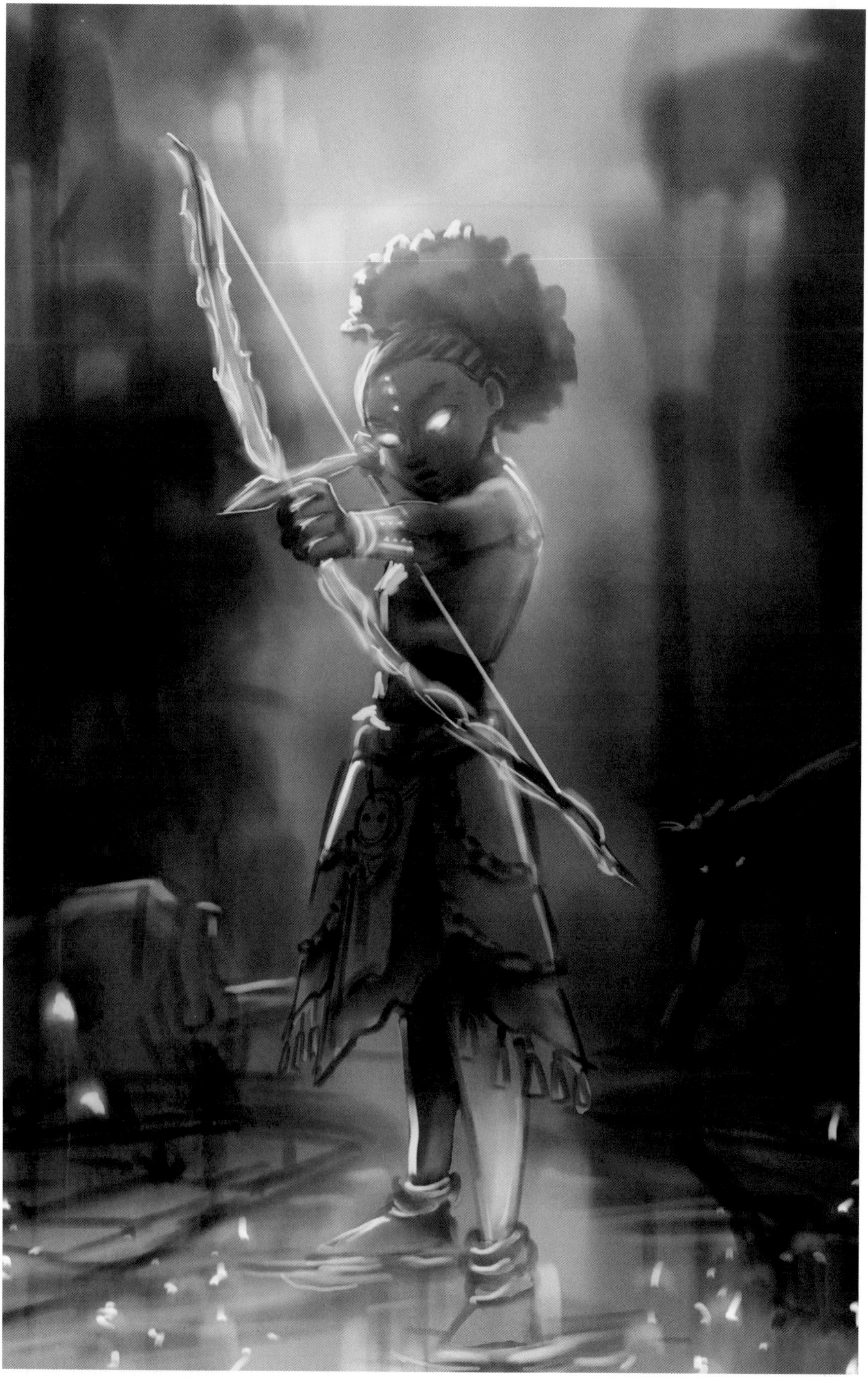

MALIKA
Warrior Queen
VOLUME ONE
ROYE OKUPE
WITH CHIMA KALU
AND RAPHAEL KAZEEM

Dark Horse Books and YouNeek Studios are proud to present a shared universe of fantasy and superhero stories inspired by African history, culture, and mythology—created by the best Nigerian comics talent!

Malika: Warrior Queen Volume 1

(pronounced: "Ma-Lie-Kah")

Written by Roye Okupe.
Illustrated by Chima Kalu.
Colors by Raphael Kazeem.
Letters by Spoof Animation.

Begins the tale of the exploits of queen and military commander Malika, who struggles to keep the peace in her ever-expanding empire, Azzaz.

SEPT. 2021 TRADE PAPERBACK 336 PAGES
$24.99 US $33.99 CA • 9781506723082

Malika: Warrior Queen Volume 2

Written by Roye Okupe.
Illustrated by Sunkanmi Akinboye.
Colors by Etubi Onucheyo and Toyin Ajetunmobi.
Letters by Spoof Animation.

DEC. 2021 TRADE PAPERBACK 280 PAGES
$24.99 US $33.99 CA • 9781506723075

Iyanu: Child of Wonder Volume 1

(pronounced: "Ee-Yah-Nu")

Written by Roye Okupe.
Illustrated by Godwin Akpan.
Letters by Spoof Animation.

A teenage orphan with no recollection of her past discovers that she has abilities that rival the ancient deities told of in folklore. These abilities are the key to bringing back an "age of wonders," to save a world on the brink of destruction!

SEPT. 2021 TRADE PAPERBACK 112 PAGES
$19.99 US $25.99 CA • 9781506723044

WindMaker Volume 1

Written by Roye Okupe.
Illustrated by Sunkanmi Akinboye and Toyin Ajetunmobi.
Letters by Spoof Animation.

The West African nation of Atala is thrust into an era of unrest and dysfunction after their beloved president turns vicious dictator.

APRIL 2022 TRADE PAPERBACK 144 PAGES
$19.99 US $25.99 CA • 9781506723112

E.X.O.: The Legend of Wale Williams Volume 1

Written by Roye Okupe.
Illustrated by Sunkanmi Akinboye.
Colors by Raphael Kazeem.
Letters by Spoof Animation.

The oldest son of a world-renowned scientist, Wale Williams—aka tech-savvy superhero EXO—tries to save Lagoon City from a deadly group of extremists. But before this "pending" superhero can do any good for his city, there is one person he must save first—himself!

OCT. 2021 TRADE PAPERBACK 280 PAGES
$24.99 US $33.99 CA • 9781506723020

E.X.O.: The Legend of Wale Williams Volume 2

Written by Roye Okupe.
Illustrated by Sunkanmi Akinboye.
Colors by Etubi Onucheyo and Tarella Pablo.
Letters by Spoof Animation.

FEB. 2022 TRADE PAPERBACK 280 PAGES
$24.99 US $33.99 CA • 9781506723037

ROYE OKUPE with GODWIN AKPAN
IYANU
CHILD OF WONDER
VOLUME ONE

E.X.O.
THE LEGEND OF WALE WILLIAMS
VOLUME ONE
ROYE OKUPE • SUNKANMI AKINBOYE • RAPHAEL KAZEEM

DARK HORSE BOOKS · YOUNEEK STUDIOS

DARKHORSE.COM

Press Inquiries:
pr@darkhorse.com

Sales Inquiries:
tradesales@darkhorse.com